To Be A Queen
(The Lady of the Mercians)

Annie Whitehead

Acknowledgements

No matter how extensive my research, and despite my long-held passion for this period of history, there remained inevitable gaps in my knowledge and I am grateful to those who were kind enough to answer my questions and/or direct me to the appropriate source material. All of those whom I consulted met my enquiries with kindness, patience and encouragement and I wish to thank the following people:

Simon Keynes, for helping me to interpret the charters and Debby Banham for answering my questions about health and diet in the Anglo-Saxon period; Kevin Leahy, for his insights into the workings of mills and Stephen Pollington for advice about metalworking and the siting of forges. Morgan Jones kindly corrected my Welsh grammar. My thanks also go to my son, Adam, for all his technical assistance.

My largest debt of gratitude is owed to Ann Williams, who not only helped me with source material and period detail but made herself available as a sounding board throughout the whole writing process. It was Ann who, as my tutor and lecturer when I was an undergraduate, inspired my love and interest in the period known as the Dark Ages.

The House of Wessex

{King Athelred d.871}
Alfred, his brother, king of Wessex
Ewith, Alfred's wife, a Mercian princess
Æthelflæd, their daughter
Edward, their son
Athelstan, Edward's son
Thelwold, Athelred's son

The Mercians

Burgred, king, married to Alfred of Wessex's sister
Beornoth, his kinsman
Brihtsige, Beornoth's son
Ceolwulf, rival king of Mercia
Wulf of the tribe Gaini, brother of Ewith, Alfred's wife
Ethelred of the tribe Hwicce

Glossary

Atheling: a potential heir to the throne, almost always of royal blood.

Ealdorman: equivalent to the mediaeval earl; the highest ranking nobleman.

Fyrd: Anglo-Saxon fighting force.

Hide: a unit of land, varying in acreage

Hundred: an administrative area approximately of 100 hides, a sub-division of a shire.

Moot: meeting

Thegn: a landholder and fighting-man; also the title of those with specific duties on the royal estates.

Scop: poet.

Witan: the king's council, made up of ealdormen, bishops and leading thegns.

Witanagemot: the meeting of the witan.

At the end of the ninth century, England was not one nation, but several. The old kingdoms of Northumbria in the northeast and East Anglia in the southeast had been overrun by Viking invaders. They had come to fight, and then to stay, occupying a vast swathe of England that was to become known as the 'Danelaw'. Two Anglo-Saxon kingdoms remained independent ~ Wessex in the southwest, and Mercia in the midlands. In Wessex, the West Saxon king who would come to be known as Alfred the Great, was nominally in alliance with Mercia, having given his sister as bride to the Mercian king Burgred. He then sent his eldest child, a daughter, to be fostered at the Mercian court.

Part I – Mæden (Girl)

AD874

Gloucester, Mercia

In her dreams, the much talked-of Vikings appeared as monsters. They were twice as tall as a grown man, their heads were made of metal and green flames burned in the eye sockets. Venomous serpents coiled around the axe blades, where blood congealed and then dripped in sticky blobs to the ground. No-one ever told her whether these vile fiends came by foot, but at night behind her shut eyelids, they rode dragons whose black, pointed teeth parted in a terrifying smile as the creatures belched flames that curled out to caress the edges of thatched, vulnerable roofs. Then kiss would turn to bite and the burning wood would spread as fire consumed whole villages. The people did not scream, but ran from their houses, arms out in supplication, wide-eyed faces atop bodies that looked like the spit-turned meat served at feasts. Charred, walking lumps lunged towards her, bare-bone fingers reaching out to her, clawing, snatching.

She sat up in bed and gasped. "I am the daughter of a king."

The serving-woman was standing by the linen chest. She held a half-folded kirtle in mid-air. "Yes you are, my proud chick. And so you will fare well." She lowered the dress and flipped it over her forearm to fold it once more before placing it into a smaller travel chest and tucking a bunch of dried herbs between the top two layers of material.

The little girl watched her. The woman had misunderstood. There had been no pride behind her words; it only felt that if she reminded herself often enough who she was, then she would no longer be afraid. The woman continued with her packing, moving back and forth across the candlelight, casting fluid shadows on the wall as she emptied all the jewel boxes and hid the contents between piles of sheets. The little girl pulled the blankets up around her shoulders and slid back down again, lying with her nose just poking out beyond the covers. Soon, Brada would finish her chores and settle down in the bed next to her charge and then it would really be bedtime and the snoring woman's presence would act as sentinel, keeping nightmare demons away. And yet…

Æthelflæd sat up. "Brada, why are you putting all my belongings into cart boxes?"

She found her aunt, the queen, in the hall. She was pulling all the tableware from the trestles and throwing the metal plate into large brown sacks.

Raising her voice above the rhythmic clang and thud, the girl said, "Why are we leaving?"

Her aunt span round and put the candlesticks back down on the table, where they wobbled back and forth and clattered down, rolling across the table and clanking on the floor. Crouching down, she hugged the child to her, squeezed tight, let go and stood up. She retrieved the candlesticks and, as she continued to reduce her life into sacks, chests and saddlebags, she spoke all in a rush, as if there was not time to tell a whole tale.

The child stood politely and listened, as she had been taught to do, but she barely understood one word in three. Her bare feet were beginning to soak up the chill from the floor, and she curled her toes against the under-draught, trying to slide her right foot away from the gap between the boards. She concentrated, trying to focus and hold on to the parts of her aunt's diatribe that she could comprehend.

12

"So now the Vikings are at Repton and soon will overrun us. The whoreson Ceolwulf came to terms with them and your uncle is king no more. He has had the king-helm knocked from his head and we must flee."

The little girl nodded. Repton was to the north, and the only north she knew was the wood beyond another of her aunt's houses, where she had played last summer, running through the delicate flowers on the woodland floor. So the Vikings were on their way and would trample through the bluebell wood. Uncle Burgred had been hit on the head and his crown had fallen onto the floor, and 'Ceolwulf' was a rude word.

With a whirl of sleeves, her aunt flung the remaining gold plate into the largest wooden chest and raised her arms. "This is what it has come to. My brother wed me to Burgred so that the fellowship between the two kingdoms would hold fast. Where is my brother Alfred now; where are the men at arms?

Æthelflæd had been asked a question, so she should answer. "They must be busy stopping them from squashing the bluebells."

"What?" The queen looked as if she were cross, but her mouth snapped shut and she knelt down, clasping the child by the shoulders. "What can I tell a five-year-old who will grow up to forget that I ever lived?" She sighed and glanced down at the floor before looking up to meet her niece's barely blinking gaze. "Your father, my brother, sent me to Mercia as a bride. Then he sent you, his eldest, his firstling, for me to foster. You have been as my own child and I have loved you dearly. But you must hold that love safe in your heart as you go now, home to Wessex, free from harm."

The girl gasped as her aunt's hug squeezed the breath from her. She smelled the queen's delicate rosewater perfume and then she took a deep breath, aware now that this would be the last time and she must savour the feel of the soft cheek against her own. "My father is a king."

"Yes, Sweeting, as was mine. May your standing in this world hold fast. Whatever your fate, always keep a sad heart hidden and show gladness to the world, even when you feel only sorrow." She released her ward and stood up, smoothing her skirts.

"One day I will be a queen like you."

"Not in Wessex, for they do not call any king's wife by that name. But you are a daughter of kings and your best hope lies there, not with Burgred and me over the sea. It breaks my heart to leave you, but you must understand." The queen peered at her, lines furrowing her forehead. "Do you?"

The girl nodded. She understood. The Viking monsters had killed all the flowers, her aunt was sending her away, and she would never be a queen.

AD878

Chippenham, Wiltshire, Wessex

Only at night now did she hear the screams. Behind eyelids held tight shut she saw the death-bringers, spitting their heathen Viking oaths and screaming their curses as the swords wrought in hell's furnace came crashing down, cleaving skulls and spilling brains onto the bloody ground. She had seen her brother and cousin wielding their wooden practice swords and heard the older thegns telling the boys how to make the most effective cuts and slashes; down through the top of the head, sideways into the shoulder or neck, upwards into the leg unprotected by a shield held too high. But what of those who had no shields, no blades, of wood or iron? The old hag down by the water told tales every day of the wounds inflicted on helpless women and children. The crone told the women by the river about other hurts done to the mothers and older girls but while the women crossed themselves and shuddered, Æthelflæd did not understand. In her dreams all she could think of to do was to throw whatever she was holding in order to frighten them away. The menacing horde came closer, reaching horned hands out to her, but always she awoke before they touched her.

This evening she had stayed up for the celebration of Twelfth Night. Her tummy was taut, overstuffed with boiled mutton, roast beef, and bread made from finely sifted wheat that was softer to chew and did not stick so much in the teeth. She had been permitted to drink wine instead of buttermilk and at very nearly nine years old, she felt most grown-up. Bowls of hazelnuts, overflowing at the start of the meal, now held a small remainder, tempting the younger children who began to throw them into each others' mouths. Her parents had been in unusually high spirits. Alfred, her father, was wearing a splendid red silk tunic and his beard, as always, was neatly trimmed. Her mother was dressed in her favourite blue kirtle, and had fixed a big garnet at her neck, and she looked to her daughter every inch the Mercian princess, daughter of the chief of the Gaini folk. Sometimes, her mother smiled. Not a teeth-baring, blithe grin, but her lips lifted enough to suggest a promise that tonight there would not be an incident; no muffled sobs and muttered oaths when the children were thought to be sleeping. Uncle Wulf of the Gaini was telling his usual awful jokes. Her father was laughing; a rare sight. She watched, amazed, as his jaw moved like a rusty hinge recently greased. Even the sombre-faced lord of Somerset managed to break a smile through his usually tight jowls. His hearth-friend and fighting companion, the lord of Wiltshire, was sitting beside him, an indulgent grin softening the skin around his eyes into creases. She liked it when these two men sat together; Somerset, dark-featured, with close-cropped hair and square jowls, and Wiltshire, with bristly grey-tipped hair, pale eyebrows and blond moustache. So dissimilar yet nearly always seen side by side, these two men of her father's inner chamber always made her think of salt and black pepper. The only others present were men of the hall, Alfred's close deputies. The fighting-men of the fyrd, having served their days in the army shadowing the enemy along the border, sometimes as hawk, sometimes as hare, had been sent home to their families. The company around Alfred's hearth this special evening was family, friend; familiar. Æthelflæd yawned, the wine in her belly seeming to exert an unnatural pull on her eyelids and jaw. Uncle Wulf spotted her and beckoned her to him. "Come, Little Teasel, sit on my lap and I will tell you some new tales."

She lay with her head on his huge chest, listening to his voice rumbling up from deep within him, as he told his wild stories of wood-sprites, beautiful women who were really witches, and of a pet elf whom he sent into battle to remove Viking belts, so that the invaders' breeches fell down when they raised their sword arms. She giggled and ran her fingers rhythmically through his soft beard as he talked, delighting, as always, in the silky feel of the long hair that grew from such initially sharp bristles. They played out their ritual; he, like a hound being scratched, paused every now and again to direct her hand to another tangle in need of freeing. At least once, she knew, he would tell his audience that she could tame a wolf's fur with her diligent combing. Afterwards, happy and sleepy, she settled down on her bed feeling safe and snug.

But the nightmare came again. The bony fingers of the marauders reached across the remnants of yet another burning village, stretching towards her, always closer. She sat up in her bed, eyes staring until darkness melted a little and allowed her vision to detect recognisable shapes, familiar outlines bringing awareness of reality. Sweat cooling rapidly on her brow, she left the ladies' sleeping bower and sought safety by the great hearth in the main hall. Among the jumble of bodies there, she saw the bright blond hair of her brother, its wild spikes sticking up like scythed wheat stalks above the edge of his blanket. He opened one eye, the movement flowing on until his brow rose up, questioning.

"I was cold. It's begun to snow."

Edward smiled, the expression on his face a cross between a tease and affectionate indulgence. He reached out in a stretch, nudging the person next to him, showing his sister that even though he would only be eight next birthday, he was sleeping with the older youths. And here, amongst the warmth of sleeping warriors and burly servants, she smiled too, for the nightmare was left behind in the dark and seemed silly and impotent in the fire light. She snuggled down, butting her head against the soft belly of a hound, lulled by the thrum of the beast's gently wagging tail.

A scream from outside perforated the silence within. She held her breath but did not open her eyes. It had not been the high-pitched shriek of a woman being goosed by a drunken reveller, but the last gasp of a fighting man caught in mortal combat. More shouts and bangs mingled with the scrapes and clattering inside as the slumbering hall awoke and came to. Æthelflæd opened her eyes, but the nightmare vision did not fade. Her father, Uncle Wulf, Somerset and Wiltshire were on their feet, swords in their hands. A guard, sweating and bloody, crashed into the hall. "Vikings!"

Gwynedd, North Wales

He put his hand to his brow against the early morning sun as he looked out across the valley. Nothing moved below except the river; from here, no more than a shimmering suggestion of flowing water. White sheep-shapes lay in motionless groups as the beasts rested until daybreak proper. Remains of the blue dawn light washed across the vista, blotches of mist lingering over the vale bottom and clinging to the sides of the steeper rise beyond, where grazing-land gave way to the less benign slopes of Snowdonia. Ethelred of the Hwicce continued to scan the horizon. He knew they were out there somewhere, up beyond the tree line on the far side of the valley, watching him. Dark Welsh eyes staring, unseen, at the Mercian force raised against them.

Wulf of the Gaini came to stand beside him. "See them?"

"No."

The older man scratched his chin through his beard. "But they're there?"

Ethelred lowered his hand and turned back towards the camp. "They're there."

Wulf followed, taking two strides for one of Ethelred's until he drew level. "We need to draw them out of hiding. As in the hunt, we must send the beaters to lure them into our nets. We cannot play this game of 'hide go seek' for much longer." He and Ethelred nodded to Lord Beornoth and Sigulf of Shrewsbury who were sitting on a bench outside Ethelred's tent.

Beornoth slapped the billowing tent wall flapping at his back. "Damn wind. It goes right through me."

Wulf laughed, leaned back and prodded his own sturdy belly. "You should put some more meat on your middle. I always find that the wind takes its time getting from one side of me to the other."

Beornoth expelled a snort. "I would rather pray than eat, for as you know, I..."

Wulf took a step forward and feigned a headache, clutching both temples and rolling his eyeballs upwards. "I beg you, spare me the tale of how it should be you sitting where King Ceolwulf sits. I have it word for word already, so often have you clacked it to me." He leaned over and thumped Beornoth on the shoulder.

Beornoth snorted again and sat up straight, straining for dignity beneath Wulf's heavy paw and loud laugh. "It is a tale worth telling. All men know that King Burgred was my kinsman, and that when he fled overseas the kingship became mine by rights."

Wulf's features opened up again as he laughed. "Fight him for it, will you, little friend? Brain him with your bible? Oh, that's it, stand up to your full height, all five feet naught with your hat on."

Sigulf of Shrewsbury put out a hand and with a gentle exertion on his arm, persuaded Beornoth to sit down again. As Wulf squatted down to rub his hands by the campfire, Sigulf watched while Beornoth settled down again, like a hen returning to the nest, and then spoke to Wulf. "You are right, though, about these slippery Welsh. We must find a way to make them stand and fight. My men are nearing the end of their owed fighting days and they will wish to be home for harvest."

Wulf stood up again, took out his hand-sæx and polished it with the hem of his tunic. He breathed on it, rubbed once more and inspected the blade, turning it first one way then the other. He pointed with it as he spoke. "They draw us into their woodland where we cannot see them, then they strike. We need to fight on open ground. But how to find a way? How do we become the hawk and flush the hare from its hiding-hole?"

Ethelred continued to stare out across the valley. How to tempt them out indeed? *Or perhaps we should learn to fight their way?* He sighed and turned to face Wulf. "We should not even be here." What was King Ceolwulf thinking of, dragging his men into a futile war with the Welsh while, at home, the heathens plagued Mercia still with their murderous rampages? Ever since Repton, they had overrun the ancient kingdom going to and from their spats with Wessex. And always Ceolwulf was happy to let them, whilst he rode off in the other direction in search of glory, commanding his noblemen to follow him. Twelve months. A whole year had passed since Ceolwulf formally ceded the whole of eastern Mercia to Guthrum the Dane. Ethelred ground his heel into the dirt. "We should not be here," he said again.

Wulf slapped the knife blade on his thigh. "As always, your words fly like arrows straight to the mark. We should be at home, shoving those Vikings out of Mercia."

Beornoth batted the tent canvas again.

Sigulf said, "Now that Alfred of Wessex has beaten Guthrum, you mean?"

Ethelred nodded. For days now the camp had been twitching with the news and Ethelred could only pray that it was true. For if Alfred and Lord Somerset had truly come out of hiding from the Somerset marshes, and defeated Guthrum and his Vikings, then some of the hope that had faded in western Mercia when they heard about the raid at Chippenham on Twelfth Night would be renewed. It was not ideal; Guthrum had, reportedly, undergone Christian baptism but Alfred had apparently given him leave to return to East Anglia, there to live under Danish law. Alfred's victory might not have been complete, but at least he had taken the trouble to pick up his sword and wave it at the Vikings. The English would never be free of the invaders as long as one kingdom put up a fight and another rolled over like a tame hound. "Yes," he said, in answer to Sigulf's question, "We should follow Alfred's lead." He stood up and swung his right arm in a circle, loosening his sword-arm shoulder. "If Ceolwulf had not let the Vikings in and made them so welcome in Mercia, they would not have had the gall to attack Chippenham."

Wulf's shoulders slumped. He ran his hand down his beard, smoothing it and squeezing it into a point. "It was a grim night, my friend. I was drunk. No shame in that, for it was Twelfth Night and we were all merry. And who would start a fight at such a time of year? But fight they did, in winter when we were weak and without the fyrdsmen. I gathered up my little niece and nephew and I ran with them. I do not know who took my sister's other children, but I took Little Teasel and young Edward west into Somerset and when they were safe, I came home to Mercia, thinking to find a free land where men were willing to hold fast against the foe." Wulf lowered his gaze. "And yet I found in Ceolwulf a king who deemed the Vikings less of a bane than the West Saxons, so much so that he had given over half his kingdom to them without raising so much as a fist against them." He came to stand next to Ethelred. "I know that you feel as I do. So why are we here, my friend? I have heard that even while we stand here baiting the Welsh, Guthrum churns Mercia to barren mud on his way through to East Anglia. We should be at home. Why do we follow blindly where Ceolwulf leads?"

Beornoth slapped at the tent wall again, using both hands this time, and Ethelred put a hand to Wulf's elbow, steering him around to the other side of the fire and beyond Beornoth's hearing. "There are too many foes; we must deal with them one at a time. We cannot beat them all, so for now, we must do his bidding."

Wulf looked around and lowered his voice to just above a whisper. "Ever since you were a small child you have been fearless, but this? You mean one day to fight both King Ceolwulf and the Vikings?"

Ethelred shrugged. "Hit one, and the other will bleed. Ceolwulf only wears the king-helm because Guthrum's Vikings hold it on his head."

Wulf scratched his beard and stroked it smooth once more. "The hunter welcomes a fight that is not fair, but not when he is weaker than the beast he hunts. Could we truly beat them both?"

Ethelred kicked at the fire, allowing sparks to rest on the boot of his toe before shaking them off. Now they had come to the nub of it. Alfred had succeeded in pushing the Vikings out of Wessex. Somehow he must be persuaded to help Mercia push them further. "Wessex is strong now and fighting back. But Alfred's peace has come at a cost. This is not the end; the Vikings will come again and Alfred will need help. A fellowship with him is the only way that Mercia can breathe freely. "

Wulf ran his hand through his hair. "Much good that did Burgred, wed to Alfred's sister but left with no help against Ceolwulf's treachery. Still, old Beornoth will be glad to have his king-helm at last.

"No," said Ethelred. "The two houses have been fighting for too long and have opened up a gap that let the heathen in. Besides, you said it yourself; Beornoth is not a fighter. Look at him."

Beornoth had given up wrestling with the tent and now sat with his eyes closed, his hand held in supplication and his lips moving.

Ethelred said, "He does not understand that God gives strength to the sword arm as well as to the hands that pray."

Wulf nodded and conceded the point. "But whoever would lead us, even with Ceolwulf out of the way, there are many who would not welcome such talk. Burgred's kin might not have the balls to fight for their rights, but they will never forgive Alfred for not coming to help Burgred. I have oft heard it said that Ceolwulf sups with the Vikings in order that he can keep the West Saxons out of Mercia. My sister is wed to Wessex and even she hates the West Saxons. And you forget one thing. I know Alfred; my sister's husband is a proud man who feels let down by all the wrangling in Mercia."

"It is the only way."

"Foe hard by!"

The cry alerted the guards and a young thegn ran over to the cluster of tents. "My lords, the Welsh; they have come round behind us."

The lords and thegns armed themselves, reaching out in the scrabble to pick up their shields, quickly identifying their own by the individual decoration. Ethelred ducked inside his tent and reached for his helm and mail coat. Outside, the Mercians had gathered, a straggle of men caught napping. Ethelred looked about as hastily buckled sword belts, spears held aloft and shields joining the wall gradually smoothed the ragged ranks, an unseen broom sweeping the untidy men into a neat line. He frowned. They must never be found wanting again. Why had Ceolwulf not posted more guards? It was his damn battle, after all. To the rear of the shield wall, Ceolwulf stood, languidly raising his arms to allow his servants to slip his mail coat on. Well, let him tarry; the men of Mercia would not.

As Ethelred ran down the slope with his men, he felt the air temperature around his face drop as he descended into a pocket of mist. Certain that this straggle of Welshmen represented naught but a diversion, he glanced often at the thick cluster of trees to his right. Surely that was where the danger lurked?

Wulf, leading the men of the Gaini, came to trot beside him. He was smiling. "It might be that God will give us an answer this day. Kings have been known to fall on the field."

Ethelred said nothing. The God he knew was usually

more perverse.

Wulf reached across and, without breaking stride, nudged Ethelred in the ribs. "You did not ask me why I named her so."

"Who?"

"Alfred's firstling, Little Teasel."

Ethelred, having all but forgotten the mention of Alfred's children, ignored him but Wulf persisted.

"Do you not wonder why I call her 'Little Teasel'?"

Ethelred wanted to concentrate on the scene before him. He tried to count the enemy in view, to assess what proportion they represented of those still hidden. He turned his head. Why did the man's jaw not ache from holding up such a huge, smug smile? His old friend was pleased with himself, so Ethelred bestowed a verbal pat on the head. "So, tell me then, if you must, why do you call her so?"

"Think of a Teasel, and what it does."

Small and prickly. Oh, he must be pleased with that one. But the joke had needed only an acknowledgement, bringing one moment of levity before the next moment where death might be lurking and when Ethelred glanced again at Wulf, he now saw only the stern features of a seasoned warrior, shield up, sword ready, soul prepared.

Ahead by some lengths, the Welsh runners cleared the edge of the trees and veered sharply right at the other side of the wood. The Englishmen giving chase took the more direct line of pursuit, through the trees. *Fools.* Knowing that he would not be heard, Ethelred forbore to shout a warning. Instead, he spread his arms wide and waved up and down, directing those behind him to slow their pace. The ambush among the trees began, played out in bold, unreserved noise for the unwilling listeners. Ethelred caught Wulf's attention. He pointed at the men of the Gaini, drawing a circle in the air and then he waved his arm towards the edge of the copse. Wulf nodded and followed the exact path taken by the Welsh decoys, while Ethelred stepped back before turning sharp right into the covert.

He stepped into hell. Dying sons screamed for their mothers. The distinct odour of freshly spilled blood and opened entrails filled the air so viciously that it was hard to breathe. The men who had followed the Welsh runners had been led into a clearing where they had been assaulted from all sides. Ethelred knew that beyond him, and beyond all help, Mercian fyrdsmen lay dead and dying, pierced by arrows, punctured by spears, mangled, torn, defeated. But Ethelred could not see them, for having pulled up short before he entered the woods, he had come up behind the ambushers, who now stood between him and their victims and swerved to face him and his men. He only caught glimpses of moving iron, an arm hacking up and down, a sniper's arrow sneaking at speed through the trees. More and more Mercians gathered behind him as the men from the old tribes of the Magonsæte and the Cilternsæte followed his route. Sigulf of Shrewsbury brought his Wreocensæte and came to stand alongside Ethelred. Ceolwulf arrived with his contingent, the king's thegns, and shouldered his way through the ranks. Ethelred nodded at him. "Now, it is a fair fight." More of the Welsh gradually turned their attention from their sitting targets, realising that another force was at their backs. Ethelred's men tried to edge out beyond their leader into the clearing in order to form their traditional shield wall. Amongst the trees they would not be able freely to swing their axes, but Ethelred nevertheless laid a hand on his neighbour's shoulder and said, "No. No wall. Spread out and do not let them get behind us. We will draw the net around them and see how they like it." God gave them a blissful respite of a moment's silence before the Welsh hurtled towards them. Ethelred was aware of fighting to his right and left, the sparking clash of metal meeting its own kind, the guttural exhalations as men suffered bruises and wounds. A reassuring singing past his ears told him that the bowmen snipers were behind them, aiming at and picking off any open targets. But he could not turn his head, for in front of him his immediate foe, a black-haired man, was snarling at him as he raised an axe. Sigulf of Shrewsbury stepped forward but the Welshman had already begun to swing his axe down. Ethelred shoved Sigulf hard and his friend stumbled to the left, clear of the deathly arc. Ethelred lifted his shield and raised his sword, slashing to cut across the Welshman's neck, but his adversary dodged the blow and brought the axe whirling back towards Ethelred. It smashed against Ethelred's left arm, rendering him numb from elbow to shoulder. But Ethelred lifted his sword once more and the blade sliced through the Welshman's arm, the flesh yielding until the iron edge made contact with and shattered the bone beneath.

Sigulf gasped his thanks. "I owe you my life."

"I might yet have need of it." Pushing the falling man away with his shield, Ethelred yelled out, "Push on. Do not let them through," and leaped forward to meet the next attacker. His numbed arm was beginning to tingle back to life and only then did he realise that the flesh was rent, blood oozing from the wound. Deflecting a spear thrust with his shield, he cut at the man's unprotected belly, withdrew his blade and lunged again, this time hacking behind his foe's leg to bring him to the ground. The man screamed and folded into the ground. A Welsh spear hurtled towards Ethelred's right side and he jumped to the left, hacking at another adversary in whose path he now found himself. A gap appeared in front of him and he used the moment to turn and assess the formation of the men behind him. Where was Ceolwulf? Fallen, perhaps, as Wulf had predicted. Ethelred wiped sweat from his eyes. More likely his king was skulking behind the men of Mercia, who fought in his name out of duty, not love. He pressed on, but fewer Welshmen came forward and those who did found that they faced at least two Mercians each. Harsh clanging of metal against metal, dull thuds of spear points on shields, the screams of the dying and the grunted exertions of the living; every battle was different but the sound was always the same and Ethelred listened for the moment when it began to tail off, the changes in battle noise that heralded the beginning of the end. As the ground before him cleared, he saw the Teulu, the noble fighting force who protected the king of Gwynedd. Ethelred's king was behind him, possibly dead, maybe alive. It was impossible to know, so he readied himself to push forward without him, to finish the fight. He gulped some air into his mouth, though it burned his dry throat, and raised his weapons once more. Then he heard it, the change in pitch of the battle music. Some of the Welsh were already turning away from the Mercians and Ethelred knew it was because they now had another enemy at their backs. Shouts from beyond the clearing told him that Wulf had circled round and brought his Gaini up close behind the Welsh. Pairs of men continued to fight, but the whirling intensity began to ease, as more and more of those in the centre of the clearing became aware that the Mercians now had the Welsh surrounded. From the closely packed group of the Teulu, an authoritative shout rose up. The protective cordon opened up and Ethelred saw King Rhodri of Gwynedd step forward. The action was simple but clear; the Welshman merely raised his right hand and dropped his sword to the ground.

There was nothing more to be said. All parties had been in this situation before. The Mercians knew that Rhodri would now select noble men who would be surrendered as hostages, a guarantee of peace. Ethelred stood, waiting for his ragged breathing to even into a regular rhythm. He eyed the group of Welshmen. Many times it had been said that all Welsh looked alike, how their heads were wider and their faces more rounded than the narrower Saxon features, but the resemblance between Rhodri and the youth at his side was so remarkable that it caught Ethelred staring. The dark eyes of that race were the usual brown, but both men had lashes which curled up long and thick. Both matched Ethelred for height, but were broader across the shoulder. Ethelred touched his own beard as he considered the shaven chins of the two Welshmen, both with indents at the centre. Above their foreheads, both men had fringes that at once flopped down, but grew up again, as if they had been licked by a cow. They were more than compatriots; these men were kin. His guess was that he was looking at King Rhodri's eldest son.

The long moment of near silence continued, all men breathing hard, swords half raised, bow strings taut and shaking from held tension. Ceolwulf, smiling indolently to see the work done on his behalf, came forward.

Rhodri finished his consultation and turned to bow his head at the victors. "Chi piau'r dydd," he said. "The day is yours." He turned to beckon his selected hostages to come forward.

The left corner of Ceolwulf's mouth lifted into a sneer. "No, that will not end it." He unsheathed his sæx and flung it at the Welsh king's back.

Ethelred rolled his gaze heavenward. What kind of treacherous madness was this? Not enough that his men won a battle for him, but the arrogant fool must be named personal victor. He gripped his sword hilt.

The young man who had stood beside Rhodri let out a howl. His face crumpled with the grief that would leave everlasting creases on his features. He hurled himself at Ceolwulf, but a quick-thinking thegn pulled the Mercian king away so that the grief-stricken young man managed only to cast a glancing blow to Ceolwulf's shoulder. The rest of the Teulu began their revenge attacks and Ethelred found himself assaulted by so many at once that he had to throw down his shield and fight with sword in one hand and sæx in the other. Stabbing and slashing, he fought blindly, lashing out at every fleet-footed target, responding to every thrust and blow. The Welsh fought with agonised blood-feud anger; those who had laid down their weapons in a gesture of trust snatched them up again and lunged forward, but their numbers were too small now. Battling for space to stand and command, Ethelred pushed a young Welshman away from him with the flat of his sword and shouted to his fyrdsmen. "Enough! Their king is dead. That is enough." *His father is dead. And that is too much.*

Wulf came to stand beside him and his words came back to Ethelred. Aye, a king had, after all, died this day. The wrong king.

Ethelred lowered his weapons and stood aside to let the Welsh leaders through.

Rhodri's eldest son stopped in front of him. "Anarawd ydw i. I am Anarawd." He pointed to the edge of the trees where Ceolwulf was sitting having his wounds dressed. "That man killed a king, my father. But he is nothing. Ti yw fy ngelyn, Sais. Mae Ceolwulf yn ddyn marw, ond rwyt yn arweinydd ac fe gawn gyfarfod eto, un brenin gerbron y llall." The Welsh prince stared at Ethelred, nodded, and turned back to his entourage, awaiting his fate as hostage or freed prisoner, the sag in his shoulders suggesting that he was resigned to either.

The birds had returned and began to sing once more. Ethelred lifted his throbbing arm and held it to the opposite shoulder, hoping to staunch the bleeding.

Ethelred and Wulf set about assessing the losses and giving orders. Wulf grumbled between instructions. "You, get the Leech to come and look at this wound, it needs binding. I see the slime Ceolwulf lives. If he fell in shit it would turn to blossom. You there, fetch water for this man. And that one needs help getting to his feet." He turned to Ethelred. "What did the Welshman say to you?"

Ethelred ran through the translation in his mind. *'You are my foe, Englishman. Ceolwulf is a dead man, but you are a worthy leader, and you and I will meet again, one king to another.'* "He only said that he would fight me another day."

AD882

Gloucestershire, Mercia

From the top of the ridge, he could see his beloved river shining silver as it trailed its way through the vale. Farmsteads betrayed the position of the wellsprings, the buildings settled on the dry land above and avoiding the old Roman settlements below. Looking northeast, he fixed his gaze in the direction from which he'd come. Last night, in Deerhurst Church, he had knelt and prayed. For forgiveness for all he had done, and for strength and courage for all that he still had to do. Leaving the serenity of the cool stone building, he had looked up at the carved figure of the Virgin, her Christ-child still in the womb, yet to be born. Like his plans, his hopes. Now he turned and looked to the south. In the distance was Stinchcombe Hill, covered with trees that curled its surface and coloured it green and, all around him, the gentle breeze of spring cooled the edges of the new season's sunshine. From here, a man could believe that the Vikings had never been, so settled and unchanged was this view that he had known from boyhood. Except that ghosts trod relentlessly where children once had played and memories lingered near cold cooking-pots, cooling the air where women had once stirred the stews that warmed the house, heart and belly. Scars were in the minds of men, not on the landscape.

Beyond Stinchcombe lay the road to their destination. How different were the marshes of Somerset, where hope had been born anew. Alfred had hidden out in those

31

marshes until he was strong enough to rise up and beat the invaders back. And back they had gone, retiring to East Anglia, only stopping to occupy Cirencester on the way to East Anglia, where Ethelred had no doubt that they would regroup and come again. Now Cirencester was a town in ashes and its name would forever speak to Ethelred of churches plundered, innocents slain, and kings not worthy of the title. If only he had not gone to Wales; disobeyed, stayed at home in his Hwicce lands the day Guthrum's army came back from Wessex via Gloucestershire and found only elders, women, children. If he had been there that day then maybe... He was able to twitch the briefest of smiles, though, for at least he also had the memory of the day when on the bloody ground at Conwy, Anarawd, bereaved son of Rhodri, had silenced any argument that Ceolwulf might have offered against Ethelred's plan. And, standing over the slain king of Mercia, the avenged Anarawd had called out to Ethelred.

'Sais, this man is dead who killed my father. He will feed the fires of hell and I will warm my hands on the flames. But I see that his death brings you no sadness. I think that you understand a little of my loss. There is naught between us, now. Go with God.'

And he did. For surely God was with him, then, and last night. He recalled Wulf's words yester-eve. *'You brood on your thoughts too much. You do not need Alfred's leave to be as a king to us. We have agreed that you are lord of all Mercia and your sword arm will quiet those who disbelieve it.'* Well, they were many who disbelieved it; kinsmen of Ceolwulf, kinsman of Burgred, animals snapping over scraps. But these kings had lost only their kingdoms or crowns, while ordinary men lost so much more... He swallowed against a constriction in his throat. Yesterday he had gathered up those hotly contested scraps, and begun by renewing a grant of land at Cleeve Prior, made in King Burgred's time. The original land-book had been stolen during a pagan raid upon the church where it was kept. Ethelred, in his first act as leader of their kingdom, had confirmed the ownership of those ten hides of

Worcestershire land. The new charter would go out in his name. And now, as lord of Mercia, he sought the hand of Wessex, but even those who might agree that Mercia was better off without a king still believed that Wessex was somehow superior, even if they wouldn't admit it, and feared that the West Saxons would swallow Mercia whole. After all, what hound would settle for a leg bone when the whole carcass was there for the taking? Let them think what they liked then; it was but a hand of friendship he was extending to Alfred, a gesture prompted by the certainty that Alfred would want to see Mercia free of Vikings just as much as the Mercians did. Better, surely, to have all of Mercia with Alfred's help than half of it under the Vikings? He looked again at his beloved surroundings, the stern hills standing guard over the softer pasture lands, the heath land far away on the hillside, the orchard in the near distance. It was all laid out as if God wanted them to have a little of everything. He glanced over his shoulder, thankful to have the Almighty sitting there, guiding him forward. He would do it in His presence then, for there was no other to see. Not now, not since… Wulf said that he dwelled too much inside his own head and it was true, for there were some things now that had nowhere else to live, except to be kept alive as memories. But if thoughtfulness were seen as a weakness on his part, he could at least show the doubters that he was also a man who could act. It would be so easy to blame Alfred for what happened in Cirencester, but the truth was that the Vikings had known they had a welcome in Mercia and Ceolwulf's duplicity had been the cause.

The wind picked up, bringing with it a remembered image of long hair blowing in the breeze, and carried the memory of the scent of herb-water to his nostrils. Ethelred stood up. No man, be he Dane or West Saxon, would take this land from his people again. And the only way for Mercia to remain independent was, perversely, for him to enter into alliance. He strode back to his men. "To Wessex."

The Lord of Somerset's House, Wessex

The wooden practice swords clashed together with a dull thwack and, holding fast to the fence rail where she was sitting, Æthelflæd smiled. Both boys must have felt the jarring to their sword arms, but neither would admit it. Edward feigned a stretch and lifted both arms above his head, surreptitiously rubbing his right with his left. Thelwold turned his back, waggling arms and legs as if limbering up before the next bout, but, watching, she knew he was trying to shake the feeling back into his arm. It was Edward, though, who bluffed his way out of embarrassment.

"Come, Cousin, surely you can take harder knocks than that? My sister there could do better. Show him, Teasel."

Æthelflæd shifted her weight, the better to balance on her perch, straight away miserably aware of the difference between her life and theirs. As she wriggled she felt the linen pads moving around between her legs. Her first monthly bleed was, according to her mother, a reason to give thanks for it meant that she was fertile. But all it seemed to do was stop her from joining in the games. "I will not, Brother, for Thelwold is a head taller than I. Even if you are not frightened of him, I am not ashamed to say that I am."

Thelwold walked over to her and bowed low, grinning as he looked up at her. "My lady, you are as a goddess. Your kind words drip like golden honey onto my wounded pride and heal me so that…"

She burst out laughing. "Oh, how could I do otherwise, when I see before me a god-like man whose shoulders are broad and strong and whose fighting arm is as thick as a tree trunk?"

Edward screwed his face into wrinkles of disbelief. "Beanstalk, more like. And still no hair on his chin, for all he has stalked the earth two years longer than I. Come on, back to it and let us build up those skinny things you call arms. When I am king I shall need fighting-men by my side, not fawning ladies' pets."

Teasel watched as Thelwold's smile froze. His eyes seemed to darken and in less than a moment, though she could not perceive exactly when it happened, the softness of his happy smile set into a cold sneer. He turned away from her, and she knew from the tremor in his shoulders that he wished she had not seen the moment when his happiness had been doused.

"Who says that you will be king?"

Edward brushed his floppy fringe from his eyes and it stuck up momentarily with the rest of the spikes, before slipping to the side of his brow. His action was so slow and relaxed that Teasel knew he was unaware of any change in his cousin's mood. "My father said so. Before he set off he told me that I was named to be king should he fall. I am his son; therefore I will be king after him."

Thelwold's voice rang out on an even, but dangerous tone. "You speak, as always, as if there is no room in the world for doubt. Yet my father was king before yours."

"Yes, yes, but you were only a bairn when my uncle died. You could not have been king then." He grinned and made a patting motion in the air, halfway between his thigh and knee. "Too little."

"I am not little now."

Edward stretched his arms up behind his head and yawned, at ease with the passage of time. "What of it?"

Thelwold hurled a blasphemous response and lunged

35

at Edward, catching him breath-stealingly off guard. Teasel shook her head and slipped carefully from the fence rail. Perhaps it was not so bad to be a girl, for it seemed that the time for games was over just as quickly for the boys.

She stood for a while, watching the old tree-wright who, having long ago given his axe to his son, now helped out by piling the cut logs. He picked up each piece and held it closely to his face, the better to focus on it and gauge its shape and size, and turned with his whole body to put it down on the pile at his side. His son worked rhythmically, hefting the axe aloft and splitting each piece with practised precision, and as he worked at twice the speed of the father, the logs awaiting the pile formed almost as big a heap. The younger man stood up, feigned a thirst and winked at Teasel whilst he sipped his drink and waited, allowing his father to catch up. Teasel grinned. Later, as usual, and as arranged, she would call the old man away, pretending a need for assistance with an easier task. Turning, she looked over to the storage barn where the reeve, checking that his stores were intact, kicked the lazy cat lying at full stretch under the sunshine. The reeve strutted off, issuing muttered threats about bringing in polecats and weasels if the cat would not chase the rats and mice away.

At the far end of the enclosure, a group of women sang as they weaved baskets from the willow that was cut and used in huge quantities on Lord Somerset's estates. The hayward, working on the hedges beyond the enclosure, waved at Teasel and she wandered over to speak to him.

"Good day, Lady. Has their fight become real again?"

She sighed and nodded, folding her arms.

He continued his work as he spoke, cutting the hedge down to shoulder height, leaving tall spikes of the new growth that he could later bend and weave into horizontal supports. "I recall the last time they had harsh words and worse. You did your best to stop them, even threw a pail at them, I think, but at least you have the sense to know when to step back and leave them to it."

"But I always wish I could bide with them and play their games with them."

The hayward smiled and put down his bill. "Little lady, it is a wise woman who knows when to leave the men to their business. When last you saw that they would have blood in spite of your calming words, you came away and helped me to gather the bark from the felled trees."

Teasel laughed. "And I will not do it again, for where was my share of the silver you got for it?"

He winked at her and went back to his hedge-laying.

She walked slowly, with no purpose, over to the boundary fence beyond the hall and stared out over the Levels. The morning mist had lifted and now the sun was sending down shafts of light. The River Brue caught them and threw them back, firing blinding patches of sheet gold across its surface. Beyond the opposite bank, lush summer pasture ran out to the foot of the Tor, whose top was still veiled by the last of the white ethereal vapour resisting the onslaught of sunshine. Teasel took a deep breath and turned her face to the sky. The day would be glorious and if the boys would stop arguing, they could all spend the hours until the evening mealtime splashing in the river and catching fish. It would also please their mother, for the lady Ewith's only concession to the benefits of living in Wessex was her belief that eating fish strengthened the teeth, and anything that brightened their mother's mood could only be welcome. Teasel shifted her weight from one foot to the other and was reminded again of her new limitations. She sighed. No longer would her activities be dictated by sunny days; now she was prisoner to the movements of the moon. The keys she would wear at her belt would open the doors to the storerooms but would lock her childhood away. Via the weaving shed and the bake-house, she would walk the path to womanhood, while the boys continued on their way to becoming men. Her thoughts drifted to images of Edward and Thelwold, helms pushed down on their heads, nose-pieces almost reaching fully bearded cheeks, swords raised ready to fight the fierce demon invaders. Like all lords, they would value their hearth-companions above all others, sharing ale in the hall and watching their backs in the battle, where they would fight against their foe with no fear of death. The pictures sullied her mood and the lure of the river palled. She turned back towards the manor buildings just as a cry went up from the gatehouse. Visitors were approaching. Teasel stopped, one foot poised to take a step, but now she was unsure which way to walk. Her heart rate teased her body to follow its increased speed and break into a run, her new-found dignity as a woman told her to stay on her course, whilst berating the child inside who assumed that with her father away, any strangers would come intent only upon murder.

Lord Somerset, tense-jawed as always, came from the hall and laid a hand on Edward's shoulder. He gestured at his men, armed and ready, and gave Teasel a reassuring wink. It was the only part of his face which moved; his dark hair was shaved close to his head and that, together with his beard bristles and lined face had all combined long ago in the mind of a child, making the young Teasel believe that he had been hewn from rock. Now, older, she clung to this notion and hoped that this sculpted boulder of a man would stand granite-firm against the marauders. She watched him as he stood, legs slightly apart, fists resting on his hips. She tried to forget that the abbey over at Glastonbury had been attacked just a few years before, and to cling instead to the assurance from those in command that here, in Somerset's heartlands where all men were loyal, they would be safer than further west at Cheddar, the royal manor where men at arms were stood down unless the king was in residence. As the strangers came nearer, the thoughts chased round her head. *We are near Athelney, where my father won out. We are near Glastonbury, where the Vikings won out. We are near Athelney...*

Somerset walked nearer to the gateway and his frown melted. "It is your uncle Wulf. It's the Mercians." He turned back towards the hall and his huge voice rolled out across the yard. "Lady Ewith, your brother is here."

Teasel and Edward's mother hurried from the hall, smoothing her veil. She cast a worried glance at her son, then stumbled forward to stand before Wulf's mount. Her voice, always thin, was higher and weaker today; only the urgency of her tone carried the words through the air. "Is it bad tidings? Is the king, is my husband...?"

Wulf jumped from his horse and embraced his sister. "I was not with him. But I have heard that his ships hounded the Viking scum and sent them scuttling back over the sea. We had thought to meet him here. It might be that he has flushed out some more of the heathens on his way home."

Ewith held up her slender white hands and turned to go back to the hall. "I cannot live with it, Brother. My blood runs thin, my heart goes cold. I look old before my time."

Wulf hurried alongside her and made soothing noises as he ushered her inside. Teasel stood with her brother and stared at the visitors. She should have gone to comfort her mother, she knew, but it somehow felt safer to be with the men, not only because they had weapons of protection, but because she felt that here, amongst those who knew, she would find the answers to any questions she might think of. She did not want to be like her mother, sitting inside, wondering.

Two men had ridden at the front of the troop with Wulf. Both were seated in leather saddles carved with intricate decoration and equally adorned with gold, so there was nothing to help her distinguish between their ranks. One, younger than her uncle, with a slim face framed by light brown hair, had smooth sun-warmed cheeks and unusually dark brown eyes. They were shaped like the exotic almonds that one of her father's Frankish friends had brought from over the sea, deep-set and immediately appealing, with an intensity of focus, but above them was the beginning of a deep furrow between his eyebrows and his expression did not invite a lingering look. He had the look of a warrior, staring out from dark eyes that had seen too much of death. Her father always had the same air. Although the reeve had come running, the visitor dismounted and led his own horse to the stables.

The other man, younger still, sat so easily and relaxed in his saddle she wondered he didn't topple over its rump. His blond hair, recently cut by the look of it, was sticking out at odd angles, where curls had been shorn, but not short enough to subdue them. His blue eyes were so pale that the pupils shone uncommonly black. A sprinkling of freckles spilled over both cheekbones and spread over his nose. He smiled at her; a smile which revealed canine teeth jutting slightly forward and as she saw the grin lift all the way to his eyes, she noted that it looked more like the beginning of a laugh, as if he had so much joy in his soul that it was constantly attempting to break out. The contrast with the jaded faces of his companions was refreshing. She felt an urge to smile back but also look away, at once a grown woman yet still a foolish child.

The brown-haired, brown-eyed man came back from the stables and stood with his arms folded, looking around at the hall and the outbuildings and up to the lookout tower.

Wulf strode back from the hall with his sister, pacified, trailing behind him. With his huge hand needing no more than a touch on her back, he urged her forward to stand in front of him while he made the introductions. "My sister, wife to King Alfred…"

Teasel saw her mother wince at the diminished title and recalled Ewith's oft-repeated lament, '*In Mercia I would be called queen*'.

"Here before you are the leading lords of Mercia. Ethelred of the Hwicce, high lord of all Mercia, and this is Alhelm, son of Sigulf of Shrewsbury, newly made ealdorman of north Mercia."

Teasel stared at the younger man again as he lifted his leg forward over his saddle, dismounted and made a pretty bow to her mother, the irrepressible hair bouncing as his head moved, the laugh-smile still teasing the corners of his mouth upwards. So, Alhelm was his name.

Introductions over, the reeve hurried forward with his horse-thegns to take the remaining horses to the stables.

Wulf turned and clasped Edward by the shoulders and then ruffled his hair. The spikes withstood even Wulf's heavy pawing, springing up as soon as contact was removed. "Well, lad, looking at you I think it is time we had a new shield made for you." He turned to shout at his friend Ethelred. "What say you; he is but a head shorter than me now, time for a full-size shield, do you think?"

Ethelred walked over to them and measured the top of Edward's head against his chest. Wulf prodded his nephew and Edward made a jumping motion, fists curled, to joke that he could take on Wulf at any time. The men laughed and it seemed to Teasel that in that moment, Ethelred's face opened out. The vertical frown-line melted away and instead of being closed against the light, his features embraced the day, allowing the sun's rays to paint a sheen upon his cheeks and forehead. His shoulders dropped a little and she understood that the formal introductions at this Wessex court must have been a chore; mock-fighting in the yard was a pleasant indulgence. As the three of them continued to throw punches that stopped just short of contact, Alhelm ran in between them, skipping from foot to foot and challenging them all to take him on. He called out to them with a clear voice, ringing with clarity but a gentle level of volume. It was a bell-chime alongside the blunt-saw tones of her uncle. Teasel giggled. Her body, on stand-down after the alert of the Mercians' arrival, allowed her to slump against the gatehouse fencing. Laughing at the sight of Wulf picking Edward up off the ground and tucking him under his arm, she only belatedly registered the clatter of a shield bouncing off the perimeter fence. Turning her head, she saw Thelwold stomping towards the river, his arms wrapped round his body as if he had been winded.

Ethelred fixed a smile to his face as King Alfred approached. Four or five hours they had been at Somerset's hall, no more. How could they have missed Alfred and his troops on the road when he was so close behind them? It was another lesson to be learned. He waited as the king greeted his wife and eldest children, and, when Alfred turned to him and Wulf, he executed the perfect bow, practised so often since he first decided on his course. Let others think that he bowed in submission; the truth was that he was offering his sword, nothing more. He would fight the Vikings in Mercia with West Saxon help and both he and Alfred would benefit. Alfred laid a thin cold hand on his shoulder and led him into the hall.

A fine feast had been laid out for the king and his unexpected guests. Presented with good food and plentiful supplies of wine and ale, the men mingled easily, Mercian sitting next to West Saxon, arms about shoulders as if they were old friends, with only the occasional jest about a mispronounced word in peculiar accents. King Alfred's scop, clothed more expensively than most of his profession, positioned himself in the corner of the room and played softly upon his harp. The meat was laid before the guests of honour. A plate of roasted lamb lay alongside another of roasted kid. Boiled chickens had been placed next to piles of fresh cheese. Bread was heaped high; the finest sifting producing loaves almost white in colour. Ethelred took out his eating-knife and skewered a chunk of juicy lamb. With his free hand he grabbed a cluster of fresh summer berries and chewed slowly, hooking pips from his teeth with the point of his tongue while Alfred recounted the details of his recent naval battle. Ethelred watched him as he spoke, noticing the care-lines ploughing deep furrows across the older man's forehead. The king's cheeks sported soft whiskers, suggesting that in normal routine, his beard was neatly clipped. Alfred made few hand gestures, speaking instead with measured pauses, but occasionally his long fingers pointed and Ethelred saw that the nails were chewed and ragged-edged. He wondered about the illness which was said to afflict the king in times of strife. He noted, too, the clenched fist that accompanied any mention of the invaders. The king's body would fill in any gaps left by his reserved speech.

When Alfred paused in the tale of his triumph, Ethelred said, "There are Vikings still in Mercia; they hold London." However much he believed that his path was a true one, still he felt that a thousand Mercians back home were turning stares of admonition towards his betrayal of them in that hall in Somerset. "With your help, we can throw them out."

Alfred's face revealed nothing, but Ethelred saw his fingers press together in the smallest of triumphant claps.

The king took a moment before he spoke. "I have driven them from Wessex. Our land, our kingdom; free now of the Viking bane."

"But they will come back. And they are still in London. With your port of Hamwic stifled by their stranglehold, you need somewhere where ships can carry goods, unburdened by heathens bent on slaughter. Together, we can shift them from London, make them think again. Rue the day they sought to take our lands."

The fists had curled again at the mention of Hamwic. Alfred raised his hands in front of his face, not in prayer, but with the finger ends placed neatly together. What need of such deep thought? Did he seek to pretend that this meant less to him than it did to Ethelred?

At last the king spoke. "In Wessex, your Mercian kings are known either for turning tail or for rolling over."

Ethelred fixed a smile to his face, all the while thinking of the blackened cooking-pot that dared to call the bread-oven dirty. Had the man forgotten about his agreement to recognise Danish Law? His failure to come to Burgred's aid? Cirencester?

Alfred spoke on. "I am glad that you came to me. Your kings have let you down. I will not."

"The Mercian folk named me as their leader; they know my thoughts. They know I can beat the Welsh. You are a king, safe home from a victory. Add our strength together and a man would be a fool to reckon against us." He knew what Alfred was waiting for but he would not give it. He had said all that he had come to say.

Alfred moved his head theatrically from side to side, as if considering his options. "You are not anointed by God, not a king…"

And I am the more trustworthy for it.

"But your sword cries out to be bloody. And there is much in Mercia that we admire, for your folk are learned and can read well. This is something that I wish for Wessex, that teaching and learning, the reading of books, can once again thrive. For too long, we have felt alone in our trial. Yes, let us rid ourselves of the bane that irks us still. We will go to London."

Ethelred held in the sigh of relief, just as Alfred affected a smile of benevolence that belied his own desperation. They began to speak of the how, the why and the when. The Wessex fyrd would need to be recalled, the Mercians would need to go home and raise theirs. And as he spoke of the details, Ethelred thought only of the irony: that Alfred spoke as if the whole thing mattered little whilst his body gave him away. Ethelred, meanwhile, had refused to bend his knee to this king, but his words had been enough to make every Mercian believe that he had done exactly that, and given away the last shred of Mercian autonomy. And what could he tell them? That he mistrusted this man slightly less than he mistrusted the Vikings? Well, then, that would have to do. Starving men take scraps where they can and Alfred and he were both hungry. He took a moment to pause and look around the room.

Wulf, his old friend, was cajoling his sister, Ewith, into enjoying herself, without much success. The king's wife looked as if she were involved in some sort of endurance trial, the evening to be borne as graciously as necessary, with the hope that it would not last too long. She smiled politely at her brother's loud utterances, but with almost every blink her gaze went to the door to the private chamber at the end of the hall; her escape route. She'd eaten little and quickly, as if her empty plate would speed the consumption of the rest of the feast. Beside her, an untroubled lake next to a rushing brook, the young girl whom Ethelred assumed to be one of the royal daughters stared with wide eyes that moved slowly while taking in every detail of the feast. Those hazel eyes were dusted all around with delicate freckles, and soft curls of coppery hair fell in tendrils around her face. Her cheekbones were high, but her face still carried the extra flesh of girlhood, even while her bodily curves declared her to be almost a woman grown. She laughed with genuine affection at Wulf's appalling jokes and Ethelred could only admire her maturity, to have learned so young not to groan with every awful pun.

"And she said it was his hair, not his hare, that she thought so lovely." Wulf congratulated himself, slapping his hands against his belly. He carried on laughing whilst he held his cup high for a refill.

The girl picked up the jug of ale and poured her uncle a drink. Still smiling, she came forward and filled Ethelred's cup. The flagon was almost full and she needed her other hand to steady it underneath as she poured, but such was her strength and bearing that she managed to hold it without causing the jug to shake. He watched her walk round the far side of the table, her shoulders back and proud, her free arm relaxed by her side. It must have been one of the first times that she had acted as hostess, yet she looked as if she had been doing it all her life. Her coppery-blonde hair, curling freely around her face, fell down her back in a long braid, but it was neither coiled nor covered. As she took her seat next to her mother, she lifted the plait to avoid sitting on the end and as she lifted it forward over her shoulder, she cast a shy glance back to the head table and quickly looked down, fluttering long lashes down towards her cheeks and taking another fleeting look before returning her attention to her uncle and mother.

Ethelred stabbed at another piece of meat, washed it down with the freshly poured wine and pointed with his knife. "Your daughter?"

King Alfred nodded. "My firstling, Æthelflæd. This is the first time she has sat with her mother and not with the other children. Has she done well, do you think?"

While they spoke, the girl looked again at the guests' bench. Ethelred could not fathom whether she was trying to catch someone's eye, or steal an unseen glance. "Yes," he said, "She is a fine young lady."

Alfred beckoned his scop, who came forward from his chair in the corner of the room and called for silence. "My lord King," he said, "In the stillness of your great hall, I will sing of your mighty deeds."

Waiting for complete silence, the scop stood with his hands down by his side. He eschewed all dramatic flourishes, for the power was in the telling of the tale. His audience had no need to guess the height of the waves that had turned and tossed the Wessex fleet, for the pitch of his voice rose and fell as he drew them in, until some began to sway in time to the lilting of his words, as if they, too, were aboard the ships. Then he spoke in loud rushes, using his skills with alliteration to describe the fierce and bloody fighting. "Then broken, bloodied, the heathen host ran from our mighty king, and those whom God chose not to smite, sank with their serpent ships." Doubtless the scop had some stirring words to finish the tale, speaking of Alfred's glorious return at the head of his victorious army, but they were lost under a final wave; that of the appreciative shouts and jeers from his audience, released from their spell and eager to show their approval. After a suitable interval, the scop sought to lighten the mood yet further. He bowed to Alfred. "My lord, I have a new riddle."

Alfred nodded, leaning forward to speak to the scop, too low for the company to hear. But he must have

46

expressed concern, for the scop said, "No, my lord, not too lewd."

Clearing his throat and now looking a little nervous, the scop licked his lips and began.

"I stand, but have no legs,
And have no bones to make me stiff.
Yet I have the strength that brings hope to a woman,
That laying hands upon me, thrusting back and forth,
She will make a small thing grow."

Whooping and howling, the assembled warriors shouted out their suggestions. "I know what it is. I have one myself." "Yes, but mine is bigger." "Stand aside; let a real man show you what it is."

Reaching forward, Alfred steadied a cup that jiggled with every enthusiastic thump of the table. "He is good at getting them to laugh. But there must be an answer."

Ethelred smiled. Of course there was. "It is a weaving loom."

Alfred inclined his head to acknowledge Ethelred's quick wit. He stood to announce it. "Lord Ethelred has worked out the riddle."

Ethelred laid a hand on Alfred's forearm. "No, leave them. There is more mirth to be drawn out of this thing yet."

Wulf stood up and belched. "He's right. Leave us, dear Brother-by-law. I will settle it for once and for all time when I show them mine." Wulf laughed; Alfred did not.

Lady Ewith blushed and her daughter giggled. Alfred nodded towards the door and said to Ethelred, "I think it might be time to…"

Ethelred nodded, stood up and gave a hint of a bow before approaching Wulf's table and steering his friend away from the mead benches.

Staggering out into the night, Wulf failed to notice Ethelred's sidestep and his boot slid into a puddle of vomit. In the shadows against the fencing where the light of the braziers could not reach, Mercian visitors fumbled their appreciation of the Wessex serving-women, their reward coming forth as encouraging squeals of pretended surprise. Wulf waved his arm in exaggerated gesture and said, "Is all this friendly enough for you?" He thumped his arm across Ethelred's shoulders. "So, what do you think of my Little Teasel?"

Wriggling to avoid buckling under the bulk, Ethelred shifted his shoulders and pushed against Wulf's arm, steering them both away from the wall which had suddenly appeared to veer towards them. "I saw no small child in the hall. All of your sister's younger children were in their beds, or so I thought. I did not see your 'Teasel'."

"It was the young woman who poured your drinks all night. Æthelflæd is my Teasel." Wulf slapped him on the back, the momentum forcing him forward and nearly toppling the pair of them. "Æthelflæd who made cow-eyes at Alhelm all night."

AD883

"That's it. Hold it. Don't let go!"

"No! Lost it! Catch it again."

His sister was sitting amongst the branches of a gnarled oak tree, right arm stretched behind her, hanging on as she leaned forward to help Edward direct their cousin, Thelwold the fisherman. Edward was standing on the opposite bank below, shirt tied round his waist, squinting against the sun stars on the water. He ran his hands through his wayward hair, glanced up at Teasel in the tree and leaned forward again, gripping his knees with tension, only to slap his thighs when Thelwold lost his grip on the fish again as it whipped his hands. Finally the fish shot from Thelwold's grasp, spitting itself in an arc from his hands to the water. He followed it, tracing its trajectory with his body, leaping up and forward and landing slap-stomached in the river.

Edward, too, leaned forward as he watched his cousin's graceless dance, doubling over in a sympathetic curve until he, too, lost his balance. He sat down hard on his knees, then sat up and wiped the tears from his eyes. He glanced up to see Teasel shaking the tree, her shoulders hunched, vibrating with silent laughter.

Thelwold stood up on the river bed and shook his head. His hair slapped round and stuck all on one side, plastered to his forehead and spiked out from his temple.

Edward shouted to him. "Go to it, find another. We're

hungry."

It seemed as if an opaque thought traversed Thelwold's mind, blocking the light from his eyes. "It is your turn now," he said. There were no patterns, no music in his tone.

Edward knew. He'd heard the challenges so many times before; one on the surface, spoken, relevant. The other, buried deep, wrapped in a shroud of resentment yet frightened of its own voice. He knew how his cousin felt about their lives and he felt no inclination to treat it any differently today. "Why howl when we have hounds to do it for us? You are the one in the water, my friend."

Out of the corner of his eye, he saw his sister put her free hand to her mouth. It was just another of the daily stand-offs during which he refused to tread as though on ice while Thelwold's temper snapped as easily as parched twigs and Teasel poured herself over them both like a soothing balm. It was tiresome, that was all. "Come man, do not stand there gaping; find a real fish."

Thelwold sloshed a leg forward to stand square on to Edward. "I said, it is your turn. I have a yearning to laugh at you now." He heaved his other leg round through the weight of the water. "Must I pull you in?"

Edward stared at him; six lanky feet of twitches and chewed nails. "You? Don't make me laugh."

Thelwold thrashed forward. "Bastard."

"Long streak of shit."

"No!"

Edward looked up as Teasel put out her hand as if to stop them. It was her gesturing hand, her sewing hand, her strongest hand, and it was no longer her anchor to the tree.

He ploughed forward across the water, setting off even before the wobble became a fall. He shoved Thelwold out of the way, flat hand to the centre of his chest. The water was deeper under the tree's overhang, but thank Christ there were fewer rocks. Five or six more steps through a river suddenly flowing treacle brought him to the bubbles of wet cloth. Batting aside a floating shoe, he grabbed the centre of the sodden, sinking lumps. *Waist deep only, merciful Jesus, but so many weeds. Come here, girl.* He flipped her over and lifted her clear of the dragging wetness. Legs planted, he centred his weight and brushed the hair from her face. She coughed and he allowed himself to breathe again.

She reached up and brushed the wet hair from his forehead with the back of her fingers, sweeping her hand round until she was able softly to brush his earlobe with a downward stroke. "Silly," she said.

"Silly," he agreed.

He waded to the bank with her, sliding each foot forward to find hidden rocks. They passed Thelwold, who had righted himself and now held a hand to a bleeding gash on his cheek. "You're both silly."

"We know. That's what we meant." Edward set Teasel onto her feet and stroked her head. "All right?"

She nodded.

"I am the one who is bleeding."

"I know that." But he cared not. Let Thelwold see to himself. Perhaps then he would learn to understand what really mattered.

"You should not goad him so," she said to Edward later that day. "He takes everything into his heart and holds it there where it can swiftly be brought forth again."

"Well he shouldn't. He has always looked as if he were weaned on sour wine. Anyway, it is I who should be cross; he was too busy bleating about his own hurt feelings to think of helping you when you fell. How would he fare as a king, who must learn always to put his own feelings aside?"

She looked across at him. They were sitting side by side on the sward in front of the gatehouse. Edward stared straight ahead, no trace of a frown on his smooth brow. His jaw, square and covered with downy pre-beard hairs, was relaxed, with room for a smile to widen it at any moment and there was no tension in the long fingers that rested on his knees. Thelwold would be away licking his wounds

51

somewhere but Edward remained untroubled. Teasel had on a dry kirtle but her hair was taking its time to dry even in the late summer sunshine. She flicked a wet heavy tress at his cheek. "Do not be unkind. You mustn't hate him."

He raised his eyebrows. "Hate? Not I. I will not cower before him nor cringe when he rants, that is all. You are kinder to him than I, it is true, but I do not hate him. I have no time for things like that."

She nudged him. "Feelings, do you mean?"

"Waste of time. They are not real."

"Well, if it was not feelings that drove you to fish me from the water, I thank whatever it was."

"I am here to look after you while my father cannot. As one day I will look after Wessex as my father has not. You are my sister. What else is there to know about why I saved you from drowning?"

She was not persuaded and carried on as if he had not interrupted. "And whatever it was, it must be akin to the thing that drives you to giddiness every time that Gwen walks by."

"Ah, Gwen." He lay down on the grass and put his hands behind his head. "You have hit upon something there."

Teasel nudged him. "So you are not always thinking only of kingship. Not when your thoughts are on Gwen. But beware; Mother will not like it if she hears what you are about."

"Mother need not know." He opened one eye and stared up at her, pausing for threatening effect. "And as for thoughts on kingship, they are with me. I am not sour-lipped and worthy all day like our Thelwold. I am merely playing while I am young. And speaking of feelings, what a feeling Gwen stirs in me. Now that is real; something to get hold of and…"

She put her hand across his mouth. "Spare me such talk away from the mead hall, thank you. I…"

Her silence drew him to sit up. She was glad of his

52

hand on her knee as they waited until the approaching riders came close enough for recognition. Her breath was caught in her chest and she had to fight to exhale. Wariness of strangers was no bad thing, but would this fear ever release its grip? Whenever she and her family arrived at a new court dwelling, she made a show of unpacking, but always kept her most precious possessions in a small, locked chest so that she could be ready to flee the enemy at the next urgent call. The little box, its lid decorated with a carved Celtic cross, stayed by her bed, close enough even for a night-time flight. Even now, as she watched the riders coming closer, she thought of the quickest route to her bower and the box hidden within. "Should we fetch Mother?"

Edward shook his head. "Look. See the hart?"

The riders were friendly and she felt dull-witted for not realising. There was no Raven banner, no shrieks or war cries. Small wonder, for Vikings did not trot blithely up to a Wessex gatehouse in open daylight and stroll in. Looking again and not through silly little-girl eyes, she could see the emblem of the lord of Wiltshire, the red hart dancing on the material through a web of bright green interwoven branches and, held aloft alongside it, a banner with similar colours to that of Uncle Wulf. He was not amongst the riders, but some of the Mercians who rode under the banner were wounded. So, dear God in heaven, what now?

Ewith came running, the younger children tripping to keep up with her. King Alfred's wife had allowed worry to evict dignity. Now Teasel understood that her mother feared widowhood beyond all else. She watched as Ewith wrung her hands in that particular fashion of hers, twisting her little finger in her other fist. Turning to confirm again in her own mind the identity of the lord of Wiltshire, Teasel felt a little of her mother's anxiety and knew for the first time what it meant to fear for someone other than herself, for there, beside Lord Wiltshire, was Alhelm, holding his reins with one hand. His left arm was hanging by his side, a bandage round the wrist. As he steered his horse through the gateway and the mount turned to the left, the dry bloodstains on his breeches became visible. Teasel looked to her mother for guidance. But, having scanned the ranks of the wounded and in the absence of any dead bodies on litters, Ewith threw her hands in the air and went back into the hall. It was almost as though she were disappointed. Of course, Teasel thought. Ewith wanted the worst to happen so that she could cease to expect it. *When my father is dead, she will know peace.*

She bowed to the lord of Wiltshire. "My lord, you are welcome at my father's house. I see that you have wounded men with you. Bring them into the hall where I and the other ladies will tend them." She braved a look at Alhelm and he smiled and shook his head.

"I have been stitched back together, thank you." Once again, he stole her breath with his laugh-smile and the soothing softness of his voice, so surprising for a warrior whom she assumed to be possessed of fearsome prowess.

When, instead of staring, she took note of his actual words, she felt her cheeks grow warm as she realised her stupidity. Of course he had already been stitched; these were the men whose wounds allowed them to travel; any with life-threatening injuries lay in London still. She had much to learn.

Edward stepped forward. "I think what my sister meant, my lord, was that your men must be tired and thirsty and within the hall our women can give them food and ale."

She spoke before Edward had closed his mouth, eager to take the chance he had given her. "Yes indeed, my lord. If you will follow me?" She gave a little bob of the knee and indicated the open hall doorway with a sweep of her arm.

As he passed by, Edward touched her shoulder, leaned over and whispered. "Truly a lady," he said.

"I owe you a boon, Brother. Thank you for saving me. Again."

He smiled. "If not me, then who?"

Inside the hall, the men sat on the benches and Ewith's

women served them ale and the hastily gathered loaves of bread requisitioned from the bake-house. Ewith nodded in response to the lord of Wiltshire's news, but kept her gaze focused on her fingernails as he talked. Teasel listened as the men laughed and jested, making light of their wounds and experiences.

"You think that was bad? See this? It was a gaping hole before it was stitched up. I nearly had to forgo a drink that evening for it was sore when I lifted my arm."

"Ha! It cannot match the bloody new furrow in my leg. See? But you should have seen how I carved my name into the chest of the filth who did this. I might have a torn leg, but at least I can still walk; he cannot."

Teasel slowed her progression with the ale jug, listening to their banter and wishing she could stay with the men, where humour kept death at bay, neither encouraging it by accepting its inevitability, nor by fearing it.

In amongst them, Alhelm held his bandaged wrist away from the ale-splashed table. Teasel dared to scrutinise him for a moment, pleased to note that his curls had grown, softening the edge of his jaw. From shining curls to wounded wrist, right down to his bloodstained, mud-caked boots, he was her image of the perfect warrior; neither grizzled nor ale-soaked, but fearless and couth. He looked up and smiled at her and she hastened away, pretending a need to attend to the dripping jug.

She went to the back of the hall, there to find a full jug. In the darkest corner, a young fyrdsman lay propped on a bench against the wall, his torso sagging under its own weight. His breath was shallow but noisy and he held his hand across his stomach. At first Teasel feigned not to have seen him, but as his distress became more evident, she abandoned the ale jugs and went over to him. He saw her approaching and moved his hand away from his belly. A dark-stained bandage hung loosely, exposing a deep gash. This was not like the familiar cuts and self-inflicted children's scrapes. Teasel had never seen so deep a wound.

The young man looked up at her. "I am sorry," he said. "I think it has opened up again."

She stood for a moment, staring stupidly at him while she waited for her wits to regroup. "Are you one of Lord Alhelm's men?"

He nodded. "From Shrewsbury."

She called out, "Lord Alhelm," and as she stood up, she waylaid one of the other women. "Fetch me the herbs and leech-worts," she said to her. "We need clean linens for the wound and tell the cooks to stew chicken in wine and walnut oil and bring the drink to this man." As Alhelm came to stand beside her, she forced a deep gulp of air into her lungs and leaned forward to unwrap the bandage.

"Thank you for what you did for him," Alhelm said afterwards.

Teasel's intention had been to come out to the yard to vomit up all the foetid air and repellent odours she had swallowed whilst tending the boy's wound. When Alhelm spoke, she managed to find the regal poise so revered by her mother and, long ago, her aunt in Mercia. Standing up straight she swallowed, breathed deeply of the clean fresh air and steadied her shaking hands on a rail post. "I am glad to have done what I could."

She took a few steps forward and he fell in beside her, matching his stride to hers. "You know the leech-books by heart, it seems. And yet you are still young."

Her hand flew up to her veil and she tucked away the unruly strands that had escaped from underneath the linen. "Oh, I am really not so young as you think, my lord." She paused, looking up to see if he believed her. "Besides, my father left word that I and my brother and sisters should be taught to read and write, so I have a little learning."

"So you can read?"

She looked at him once more and thought that he moved his head a little from side to side, as if weighing the information and making much of it. Well then, if he liked clever women, she would tell him. "My teacher, Abbot Beocca, says that my writing is neat and readable." She had always hated her lessons, and in any case was only schooled in English and not Latin, but now she sent silent prayers of gratitude that the long, tedious hours of learning had brought forth the reward that Lord Alhelm was impressed with her knowledge.

"It cannot have been easy, when you have spent so many years running and hiding."

They had reached the green lawn by the gatehouse and he held his arm out, inviting her to sit down.

She spread her kirtle out and knelt on it as gracefully as she could. When he had settled beside her, supple legs crossed, she answered.

"I wake sometimes in the night, even now. Twelfth Night was the worst, for they were upon us before we knew it. Uncle Wulf caught hold of me and Edward and we rode through the night." She hugged her arms. "It was so, so cold. We rode for miles until we reached the safety of Lord Somerset's house near my father's house at Cheddar."

"Is that the house where we first met you?"

She nodded. "There, we could do naught but sit and hope for news, for we knew not how many died that night, nor whether our own father and mother lived."

He leaned in towards her. "It is no bad thing, though, that you have learned a little of what it is to live in these times. In Mercia, too, many have lost fathers, brothers, sisters, wives." He nodded towards the hall. "Every man in there holds his own loss in his heart as he goes out to fight."

"You, too?"

He smiled and although it lifted his mouth, it was weighted with too much sadness to reach his eyes. "Every man."

Something in his expression prohibited further questioning. Instead, she said, "What news, then, of London?"

Edward bounded over to join them, hurling himself on

the grass beside his sister. "Yes, my lord, what news?"

Alhelm spoke then of the siege of London and how the English now had the Vikings surrounded and trapped. It was only a matter of time, he said, before the invaders, weary and hungry, gave in. He had been wounded in a skirmish by the defensive wall, a careless slip during which he let his shield arm lower too much and an enemy knife opened his wrist. "Good thing it was the top side, or I should not be here to tell you of it. Your father deemed that I could be spared, and should be the one to bring your mother news of our undertaking."

"My lord of Wiltshire has already done so, though my mother was not over-willing to listen. But my sister and I are used to hearing our father's words spoken by another."

As Edward spoke, Teasel chewed her bottom lip. So, Alhelm had not needed to come, for Wiltshire, the old silver fox, had been the one to speak formally of the campaign. Was it possible, then, that he had seized an opportunity to visit her? Now, as she stared at Lord Alhelm, she saw not only a softly spoken heroic warrior, but a man who would ride for hours with a wounded hand, all in the name of love. God had fashioned for her a faultless man.

Alhelm continued his report. "To begin with, it all went their way, but my lord Ethelred has many tricks to keep his foes on their toes. Each time we were beaten back, he thought of something new to try."

She said, "But my father, it is he who leads the English?"

"Oh yes, but we fight together, as one."

"Yes, but..."

Edward patted her shoulder. He spoke to Alhelm. "These 'tricks' you spoke of, do you mean that these are new, or..."

Speaking across her, they talked of tactics. Alhelm spoke of the cunning of Lord Ethelred and how the combined forces of Wessex and Mercia had proved to be a match for the invaders, whilst Edward commented now and again. "Once the lord Ethelred had spoken, did my father not think to help him by doing thus? Now if it were me, I would have…"

Trying to avoid staring rudely at Alhelm's beautiful long, graceful fingers, Teasel glanced around the enclosure, smiling at the young men who, under the reeve's instruction, had begun to repair the walkways between the buildings and were singing a ribald song as they worked. The itinerant bone-carver had set a stool outside the bake-house and spread his wares out on the ground before him. As he sat, no doubt hoping for scraps from the bakery, he continued to fashion a comb from the pieces of antler he had grooved, split into sections and fixed together with rivets. He whistled as he trimmed the teeth. Laughter pealed from the wool-dressing shed, where the young girls were wont to share jokes as deftly as they carded the wool.

A young woman made her way to the weaving shed and Teasel laid a hand on her brother's arm. "Edward."

He looked where she pointed and caught his breath. He held up a hand in apology to the Mercian. "My lord Alhelm, with your, by your, leave, if I may; my sister will er, that is, if you do not mind?"

She pushed him. "Go. I am well cared for." *And besides, two is a much better number than three.*

Edward dashed away, his run slowing to a lope until he settled in beside the girl as if he had been walking with her for miles. He reached for her hand so subtly that an onlooker might not see, and she did not even look up or break stride. They walked hand in hand round beyond the weaving sheds.

Their going gave Teasel nothing to observe but the silence they left behind. She smothered it with a laugh. "He will soon be old enough to fight, but he dare not tell our mother of his love for Gwen."

"Is she low-born?"

"No, not really. Her father was steward to my uncle Wulf. As such, she is not high-born enough to wed the son

59

of the king, but Mother is torn and does not like to have to think on it, for Gwen is Mercian and is, therefore, in Mother's eyes, too good for my brother." She bit her lip. How to explain? "She does not wish to see another Mercian woman forced to take on a lower standing than she would have in her homeland. It prods her own bitterness wider awake."

"You speak as if you think she is wrong. Does this mean that you do not mind the thought of West Saxons wedding and bedding with Mercians?"

"Oh, yes, I mean no. That is to say, I..." She hastily found a snagged thread on her kirtle which needed urgent pulling.

While she continued to look down, willing her cheeks to stop burning, she became aware of approaching footfall.

Alhelm greeted the newcomer. "We have not met. I am Alhelm of Shrewsbury."

"Thelwold of Dorset. Son of King Athelred of Wessex, late brother of Alfred. Teasel, was that Gwen with Edward?"

Forced to curtail the study of her own shoes, she lifted her head. "Yes. Soon, everyone will know about the two of them, I think."

"Huh." Thelwold chewed a sliver of skin from his thumb and spat it out. "It is a wonder to me why women fawn over him. After all, he is little more than a child. With most of the men away, I would have thought they might come to the next eldest."

"That would be you?" Alhelm smiled and Teasel stole the whole image to store in her memory for nightly retrieval, scanning the crinkle round the pale blue eyes, the uneven teeth that she found so endearing, the overloading of freckles that made hers seem like just a few specks.

Thelwold nodded. "Of those who are not away fighting, I am the eldest man of the house of Wessex. You have spoken to my cousin of the fight in London. There is no harm in that. But you should have been told to seek me out first." He smiled down at Teasel and just for a moment, the sinews in his neck seemed to loosen. His gaze flicked back to Alhelm. "So will you tell me now, of the tidings from London?"

Alhelm repeated his tales and Thelwold interjected with staccato affirmations. With each 'uh-huh' or 'I see', he danced from foot to foot. Teasel was used to his jerky movements and could not remember a time when he had ever stood still for more than a moment. As soon as Alhelm had finished his report, Thelwold shot away.

The Mercian said, "There goes one who will not wait too long for what he thinks is his due. Something has stirred him up."

"Do you think so? Most folk find that he is always like that. I daresay I have grown used to it. He and Edward sometimes clash, although he is always sweet to me."

"I have seen youths like him before. He covets aught that he cannot have, or that someone else already has."

She smiled. "You think he lusts after Gwen? Well that would answer the riddle. It must be hard to love if you know that your love is to wed another."

He was still smiling at her, but the crinkle had gone from around his eyes. "Yes, I think that it would be."

A loud crash resonated from inside the hall. She stiffened. Dear God, would it ever stop?

Her hand was on his arm. He gently lifted it away, encasing her palm with both his own. "It was most likely a mead bench turning over." He released her hand, but held her gaze with his own, his eyes narrowed with concern. "My lady, you were never safer than in these times. This town lies right between the two kingdoms. Alfred has rebuilt the walls and look, you can see how the river works as a friend, enfolding the town. All of Wessex and Free Mercia stand fast between here and London. My lord Ethelred was right to woo your father, for together we are stronger than any kingdom alone."

He was talking again of the brilliance of Ethelred's

strategies, but he might as well have spoken of the colour of loom weights. She was content to listen to the gentle tone of his soothing voice and to believe in his promises of protection.

"My father has many Frankish friends, but I have never seen a Viking," she said. "What are they like?"

Ready to flinch, she held herself rigid as she prepared to hear tales of fire-breathing demons, blood dripping from the jaws of the hell-beasts that they rode into battle. Instead, he told her that they looked very similar to Angles and Saxons. They wore the same clothes, bore similar weapons, except that their shield decoration usually bore pagan imagery. They were so similar, in fact, that many Englishmen could even understand their language.

She shook her head rhythmically as, detail by detail, he deconstructed her monsters and humanised them. She pointed to his bandaged wrist and said, "Men? Like you, like my father; it was men who did this to you?" She inhaled and puffed the air out sharply, jerking her head in the direction of the hall. "To that poor boy in there?"

"I am sorry," he said, "I sought only to calm your fears. The mind can make things seem so fearsome."

Children feared monsters. Adults must face much worse; she understood that now. "I am old enough to know the truth about such things, my lord."

"Oh, yes, I forgot to ask. How old are you, Lady Æthelflæd?"

She smoothed her dress and sat up straight. She decided to dare a little lash-fluttering as she said, "I am fourteen, my lord."

He seemed satisfied with the answer. Again, she watched as his head moved gently from side to side as he stored away this significant fact. She thought that he might as well tuck her heart inside along with all this newly gathered information; it was already his anyway.

AD884

Malmesbury

Teasel looked up to see what was blocking the light from the open doorway. "Out of the way, Brother; I cannot see the loom."

Edward feigned deafness, putting a hand to his ear. "Click-clack, click-clack. It is bad enough outside, but in here the din is worse. How do you stand it?"

"By keeping busy at it every day. You should find something to do, and then you would not be at such a loss."

He slid his foot along the floor of the weaving-hut and leaned towards her with his knee bent. "Ah, but I have been busy. I have been at the hundred-moot. A youth was sent to ordeal for stealing sheep. He did not have twelve men who would swear to his good name."

She let go of the heddle bar, holding a hand up to stop her companion on the other side of the loom. "A youth, you say? Was he old enough to go for ordeal?"

Edward shrugged. "Twelve, thirteen maybe. Does it matter, if he stole?"

"No. But it does if he did not steal. And if he was younger than twelve he should not have been sent at all."

"He was guilty. I saw it in his eyes. Anyway, it bores me now." He grinned. "And I was not there all morning. I have also been speaking to Uncle Wulf."

She grinned, but refused the bait, taking up the heddle bar again and nodding to her weaving partner to begin again. "He has much to say."

63

Edward danced around her, leaning close to her other ear. "Indeed. He has come from Buckinghamshire, where Ethelred of Mercia has granted him five hides of land and all rights to the salt-workings there. He will grow even richer."

She smiled. "Indeed."

"And you are grinning at his good news."

"I am."

He reached his arm around in front of her and pulled her into a gentle headlock. "And your silly sheep-grin has naught to do with the thought of who rode here with him? Naught to do with an ealdorman of Mercia who goes by the name of Alhelm? Alhelm who comes with news for Mother and then two heartbeats later comes to ask how you fare, are you well, do you ride, can you ride, would you like to ride?" He leaned right into to her and imitated her voice. *'Oh, yes I will ride. Even though I do it badly, I would love to ride with you, Lord Alhelm.'*

She grabbed hold of his arm and swung her torso from side to side. "No, no and no."

He released her and kissed the top of her head. "You are a sweet liar, Sister."

"And so are you if you would have me believe that you have only been at the moot and nowhere near the grain store with Gwen."

Edward chuckled.

Teasel sighed and signalled once more to her companion, who nodded. "I will go and help Gytha to set up her warp threads, my lady."

Teasel turned to Edward and folded her arms. "This is not something to be laughed at. Mother is not strong. You should not be giving her anything else to worry about. Already she is telling all who will listen that Wulf grows richer by the day and if she were still in Mercia and not stuck in Wessex she would match him for wealth and be a real queen to boot."

Edward stepped his right leg out and stood with his

hands on his hips. "Is it wrong for me to love a woman?"

"No, but it is wrong for you to lie to Mother about it." He had some grain dust on his forehead and she brushed it clear with the back of her fingers and reached round to stroke his earlobe with her index finger before she lowered her hand.

"Ha! I know that you are not wroth with me whenever you do that." His smile faded. "I do not lie to Mother, I simply choose not to tell her. I am young; there is time yet for me to play, before I have to..."

Teasel put a finger to his mouth. "Mother is weak and her sleep is troubled. She worries."

"She is married to a king who must bide away from her until the heathen has been beaten. That is her lot in life."

"That does not mean it will not fret her."

He looked puzzled.

She continued. "You do not see it, do you? To you, everything is either right, or it is wrong and you do not stop to think how anyone might feel."

He was still frowning. "If something is wrong, I will fight to put it right. I would do it because it is the right thing to do, not because of how I feel."

"Well, Mother is not like that and I will not..."

Teasel's workmate came back to the loom, adjusted the clay loom weights and took hold of her end of the heddle bar. Teasel copied her, and between them they began feeding the weft threads through once more.

Edward backed out of the hut, hands over his ears in a final protest against the noise of the looms. Before he stepped back through the doorway he held his hand up, four fingers spread out and his thumb tucked under. He mouthed the number at her. "Four."

She put her head down and pretended to concentrate on the red and white checked cloth growing on the loom. Four, indeed. Four times in the last six months, Alhelm had ridden into Wessex for one reason or another. *One excuse or another.*

AD885

London, Occupied Mercia

The young thegn jumped from his horse though the beast had not yet stopped. His cap fell to the ground, but he left it where it lay. Mud streaked his plain-weave tunic and his chest pounded like that of a snared bird. Glancing about him, he broke into a run, looking left and right as he made his way down to the riverbank. Elbowing his way through the throng of soldiers, he said, "My lords, the king? Where is King Alfred? I must find him."

Ethelred had been using the early morning light to inspect the tear in his tent where a careless tilt of a spear had let water in all night. He turned and grabbed the man by the shoulder as he hurtled towards the Mercian encampment. "Hold, lad. What news?"

The thegn gulped air and wiped a muddy sleeve across his brow, distributing, rather than clearing, the dirt there. "I am Ailric of Rochester. A Viking host has made landfall there and is making its way to London. I have come to tell the king."

Ethelred patted the lad's shoulder before releasing him. He exchanged glances with Wulf. He said, "We must not get trapped in the middle, with the horde still in London and these new ones at our backs."

Wulf nodded. He put his arm around the thegn's shoulders and walked him away. "Come lad, let us go to Alfred. You tell him what you know and I will tell him that

66

the Mercians ride out to meet this new host."

Ethelred ducked his head and went into his tent. In the gloom, Alhelm was sitting on a stool, holding his chin in his hands as he listened to his companion. The other young man spoke quietly, explaining the art of fish-tickling, never once using his hands to aid expression. His eyes were a darker blue, almost grey. His hair was straighter than Alhelm's and a dirtier blond. The front strands were caught up and tied with a thong at the back of his head. Ethelred had worn his hair like that as a young man. Was he so much older now? To these two youths, Alhelm barely in his twenties, his friend younger still, he must seem like an old man but no, the truth was that he was not yet thirty and he had much still to do. If his vow was not to rest until the heathens had been expunged from Mercia, then he had no time to dwell on how quickly the days passed. Alhelm looked up and raised an eyebrow. Ethelred realised that his news must be writ large on his face. "There is a new host at Rochester."

Alhelm leaped up and hooked his sword belt from the table. "How soon do we ride?"

"Wulf has gone to tell Alfred. We need his men, so we will leave when he comes back." He spoke to Alhelm, but watched the other man, who stood up slowly, wiped his hands on his breeches and counted on his fingers.

"My lord, the men of Hampshire are great enough in number to bridge the gap that will be left here. With your leave I will speak to the lord Somerset about sparing some Wessex men to come with you. Let us not water down the blend of both kingdoms that has fought so well these past months." He moved out of the tent, neither with insouciance nor urgency, but with the purpose and focus of a blacksmith in the forge, who must make the new weapons, repair the old while fighting raged, but who would not cut short the welding process, knowing the importance of each detail.

Ethelred stared after him. "He is a rare find."

Alhelm, struggling with his sword belt, only glanced up. "Who, Frith? He is a fiend to beat at the gaming boards." Alhelm tapped his forehead. "Sharp mind."

Ethelred shook his head. "That might be so. But what I meant was that it is rare to find a man so keen to stir Mercians and West Saxons together into one brew. I know that he has been fighting with your north Mercians, but where is he from?"

Alhelm gave up the struggle with his sword belt and let the loose end slip to the floor. "Frith is a friend of the lord Edward and his sister and I think he grew up in Wiltshire, but he likes to bring his men to stand with mine at the shield wall."

Ethelred sucked his bottom lip. So he was not the only man who saw the benefits of neighbourly co-operation. The knowledge brought comfort.

Alhelm had resumed his fight with the sword belt and now had it buckled. Ethelred fought against the urge to laugh and wondered if he should point out that the buckle pin had not caught properly.

Alhelm must have sensed Ethelred's scrutiny, for he looked up again. "My lord?"

"Afterwards, I will need someone to ride to Wessex."

Alhelm smiled. "In my mind, I have left already, my lord."

"We have a small fight to deal with first, so you had best stay alive." He returned the smile. "I have too much need of a man like you for you to do something silly like dying."

"Then I must stay by your side throughout, for all men say you are too quick-witted to be killed by your foes."

Ethelred laughed. "Not as quick as you, who seeks to gain by it."

Alhelm's pale eyes seemed darker in the dim light of the tent. He said, "My lord, I would..."

Ethelred's smile slipped a little and he blinked quickly. "I know." *You would stride through fire for me, I know. You did.*

68

They stared at each other for a moment, both aware that there were unspoken words that need not be given air. As he stood, awkwardly shuffling his weight from one foot to the other, Alhelm's recalcitrant sword belt slid silently to the floor and Ethelred's self-discipline failed him. He threw back his head and shattered the uncomfortable silence with his laughter.

The Lord of Wiltshire's House, Avebury, Wessex

The noises of summer drifted through the shutters, the calls of the animals in the pasture, the foot-scuffing of the peddlers taking advantage of dry roads to set out early to markets, but Edward was in no mood to go out and meet the day. Leaning up on his elbow, he lowered his face and bent to kiss Gwen once more. She opened one eye and turned to kiss his neck. Encouraged, he began to slide his hand along her thigh, but she slapped him gently away and sat up, shaking her hair back over her shoulders. He stroked the golden strands, tucking them behind her ear as he did so. "Come, Gwen, we have time for one more, do we not?"

"No, my love, lie still and rest now and I must be about my day. If your mother even knew that I was here, she would throw me out of her household."

"And I would bring you right back home again, for you are seventeen and your own woman." At moments like this, when he was bodily at peace, his mind railed against his mother's ridiculous notions of Mercian pride.

"Your mother has been good to me since my father died. I would not wish to upset her. Besides, my love, you have things to do."

He sat up fully, put his arms around her and pulled her to him until her head rested against his chest. Closing his eyes, he breathed deeply, enjoying the scent of her hair. Honey and what was it? Rosewater, yes, and the faint trace of the straw, where she'd lain with him since just before dawn. He kissed the top of her head and sighed. "I do not see why it is wrong to spend more time with you, out in the open, where all can see how blissful you make me."

She twisted her head and looked up at him. Her eyes, those beautiful eyes, flecked like golden sand, gazed wide, round and sad. He felt a lurching somewhere in his chest and felt faint from the strength of the movement. "I love you," he said, and kissed each eyelid.

She straightened until she could meet his eye level. With a hand on either side of his face, she kissed his mouth. "And I, you. I will soothe you where I can. But you are the king's son and your life's path will not be as mine. I can never be your wife, but your love keeps me alive and warm and that is all I need."

"I know what is marked out for me. But I am not my father. When I am king…"

She put a finger to his lips. "When you are king your mind will waver even less than it does now. Your kingship will be all. So it is best to keep me hidden; that way it will be easier, after."

He smiled, but his skin no longer felt like it was a good fit. He began to fidget, trying to scratch an elusive itch. It spread to his mind, where his thoughts echoed her words and bounced around his head to maximise his discomfort. He knocked them aside and gave her a gentle squeeze. "It is true, though, that when I am with you my hands begin to wander. And should I not strive to make the best of the freedom that I still have?"

He nuzzled her neck and she began to laugh. The sound always made him think of the water in the brook by Fisher's Meadow as it chuckled its way over the rounded pebbles. Perhaps, for his sixteenth birthday, they could go there and savour a day in the sunshine, playing in the water and lying on the bank. The thought aroused more than his body and he felt the need to hold her tightly. Scooping underneath her, he lifted her, still wrapped in his arms, and rocked her close. She had stopped laughing. He laid her back down on the straw and moved his hand over her breast.

The barn door crashed open.

"No, he is not here. Wait, over there. Edward, is that you?"

Scrabbling to his feet, Edward placed himself in front of Gwen as they both brushed at their clothes. He blinked in the intruding sunshine. "Frith, Lord Alhelm. On any other day I would be thrilled to see that you both still live."

"How churl-like he speaks to us. And we, the heroes of Rochester, who rode in last night after little boys had gone to bed. It will not do, not at all." Alhelm held a straight face for a moment and then laughed.

Edward shook his head. "Rochester? The last we heard, you were still in London." Dear God, could he dare to hope that at last there had been a proper fight?

Frith stepped forward. "We were there when tidings came of a new host and..."

While Frith told his tale, Edward listened and nodded. He tried to concentrate, but was still uncomfortably aware of Gwen's hand slipping from his and the sudden darkness as the door shut quietly behind her.

Teasel wished that the child would sit still. The kingfisher settled on its perch for only a moment before the noise blew it back into flight. Teasel blinked as the flash of blue shone brilliantly then disappeared. "Fleyda, stop that. You might fall in; come back from the edge."

The girl looked up, poised with another twig in her hand ready to throw into the pool. She frowned and her pretty features narrowed into something nastier. Teasel was shocked to see what looked like hatred on her young charge's face and wondered if the girl had ever been told off before. So close to the edge of the pool, where there was a gap in the canopy, the sun shone down on Fleyda's hair, drenching the blonde with streaks of copper. Teasel felt uneasy staring at the mix of purity and petulance. The child was only seven or eight. Not enough time spent on earth yet, surely, to become so cross? But the girl spoke and she had her answer.

"My father says that now my mother is dead, I am lady of the house and I can do whatever I wish."

And I am the daughter of a king but I cannot do whatever I like. But who was she to know what the loss of a parent felt like? If it felt like fear, or the panic of separation, then she knew how rough its touch might be. She tried hard to focus on the little chin, jutting out but quivering, betraying the nugget of goodness which Teasel was convinced resided within the child still. "Come, then, away from the water, for he would be wroth with me if I were to let you fall in, would he not?"

The girl shrugged. Teasel had seen the gesture many times when her own younger siblings had the sting removed from their tests of authority. She offered Fleyda back her pride. "Which do you think we should do now, gather some bluebells or go down to the weir?"

"I say we go to the weir, for if we gather them now, the blooms will wilt ere we get them home."

Teasel nodded. "You are right. How bright you are to think of it."

Laughter and shouting bounced in echoes from the trees on the incline behind them and Teasel put her head to one side, lifting her ear the better to identify the voices.

Edward and the lord Frith came stumbling like hound-pups down the slope, slithering sometimes on both feet, sometimes down on one knee, leaving trails like drunks' cart tracks scuffed through the moss and undergrowth and laughing all the while. Behind them Alhelm came more steadily. His hair was longer than last time she had seen him, the curls licking round the underside of his jaw, where a shadow of a beard lurked. He held his right thigh, as if protecting it against a fall. When Frith reached the level ground, he stood up and, without turning, held his arm out straight at shoulder height and Alhelm used it as a prop to bring himself to a stop. Teasel inhaled deeply, and only then did she become aware that she had been holding her breath since the men hove into view. If she spoke now, her words would be as intelligible as those of old Mawa, who sucked fish whole into her toothless mouth and laughed whenever she had to be reminded of her own name. She was grateful when Edward stepped in front of her and began the conversation.

"Teasel, where is your knee-bend? Here, before you, stand two men who have killed almost every Viking in the land with their bare hands."

Her laugh mingled with her question. "What?"

"It is true." Alhelm grinned. "Although, we had some help. Word came of a new host in Kent and…"

She put her hands to her mouth to stifle the gasp. "Another?" She shook her head. "How could my father have ever hoped to be in so many places all at the same time?" He had struggled for so long; at least now, it seemed, he had friends.

Alhelm continued with his tale. "Lord Ethelred knew right away that we must not get trapped between them and the heathen still holed up in London. At once he…"

She smiled and nodded as he spoke, but all she could think was, *but what of you? You are hurt; I saw it when you held your leg.*

"And when your uncle Wulf slipped, it was my lord Ethelred who pulled him from the path of a spear."

"Ha," said Edward, "As well he did, for if Wulf had sunk to the ground, there is not a man in the land who could get him up again."

"And who is this?" Frith pointed to the girl who stood by Teasel's side, chubby child-arms folded across the pre-pubescent forward jut of the stomach.

Teasel tugged her gaze from Alhelm's face. "Forgive me, my lords, here is Fleyda, daughter of the lord Wiltshire, who is our kinsman."

"I am bored. You said that we could go to the weir."

Teasel forced a smile. "So I did. With your leave, my lords?" But she tilted her head to one side and made no move to leave.

Frith held out his hands, palm up, and turned to his companions as he spoke. "Why do we not all go?"

Teasel's shoulders, held tense, slid down again. "A good plan, my lord. I do not know why I did not think of it myself." She smiled her gratitude and received a conspiratorial wink in return.

Down by the river, the trees were more closely packed and the sun could do no more than dapple the occasional patch of gold onto the woodland floor. Teasel sat far enough away from the water's edge to keep her feet dry, close enough to supervise Fleyda, who resumed her stick-throwing. The little twigs whooshed along the higher level, before becoming trapped at the base of the weir. "And that is why you must not play in the water near here," Teasel told her.

"They are."

Teasel looked further upstream, where her brother and his friends had taken off their tunics and were swinging on an overhanging branch, kicking out and then letting go. "Well, they are old enough to be silly. And there are three of them, so if one gets into…" It was Alhelm's turn. Months of camping out on the outskirts of London had left him browned by the sun. Teasel stared at his naked torso and felt a fluid sensation in her stomach, similar to nervousness, but not quite the same. As he jumped to catch hold of the branch, his muscles flexed and she had to swallow, her mouth suddenly dry.

Fleyda said, "Edward is younger than them. He is not so much older than me."

"Oh, yes, he is a bit." Eight years or so. But what did a difference in age matter?

Alhelm slid into the water and Frith waded in to help him out, stepping a leg into the flow and holding out an arm

75

for Alhelm. Alhelm stood, found his balance and reached one hand out to meet Frith's, pushing the other hand through his wet hair to smooth it away from his face.

Fleyda continued to chatter. "He is already fine-looking."

Yes, he is. "Hmm? Oh, Edward? I cannot see it, for he is my brother."

They came dripping and laughing to throw themselves down beside her. Again, she was reminded not so much of mighty warriors as young hounds, shaking themselves dry after a swim. Watching him with her brother, she had to force herself to remember that Alhelm was an ealdorman, and had many responsibilities. It was so cheering to see him like this; she wondered if there were any moments to match it in her mother's early life with her father, before the heathens came. "But it will be better now, now that he is not alone. Now that the Mercians are here."

"Life is always better when the Mercians are here." Alhelm smiled at her, the two rows of small white teeth separating, as if his jaw were ready to break open in laughter.

She felt her cheeks growing warm. "Oh, I am sorry, I was but thinking out loud."

"Thoughts as good as those should always be shared." He looked about and behind her. "No food?"

"No, my lord, we did not think to be away from home for so much of the day."

"Nevertheless, you are kind to offer to spend your day with young Lady Fleyda. I think it shows how good you will be with children."

She looked down at her hands, wondering why they did not visibly shake, even though she could feel them trembling enough to jump from her lap. He was pleased to see her maternal attributes; it could only mean one thing. She dared to glance up and found him smiling at her.

"A song then, to sate us instead of meat, even if it will not slake our thirst. Frith?"

His friend nodded. "But it will be a good old southern song, of winsome Wiltshire women, who are the most lovely." He smiled, a superior monk-at-a-feast smile, while they disputed his claims and, when they had finished hurling their light-hearted insults, he began his song.

Alhelm sat forward, rubbed the last drops of water from his feet and began to put on his boots. Teasel looked at his ankles, both covered with reddened, bumpy, almost scaly skin. He caught her staring and said, "Others have suffered more than you or I can ever know."

Only the echoes of her mother's endless words on decorum prevented Teasel from hugging him. This brave, gentle man had been hurt, badly, but even now he sought to make light of it, brush it away. He would not speak of his own pain. Only a child would press the matter. She bowed her head in recognition of his modesty, and to show that she understood his reticence to speak of the past.

He leaned closer to her and whispered. "Do you like to hear songs, my lady?"

She, thrilled that he should ask, nodded. She hugged her knees, closed her eyes and listened to Frith's voice, flowing smoothly but strongly, ringing out above the grumble of the weir. If they could only stay a few more days; she could endure many hours of this simple happiness. She felt the sun's warmth across her cheeks and brow and was glad to know that it was still early in the afternoon. The evening meal was hours away and there was nothing pressing.

"I am bored. I wish to go home now."

Teasel reached her hands out along the earth, clawing her frustration and, gathering up a lump of moss, squeezed her clenched fingers around it. *I am the daughter of a king but I cannot do whatever I like.* She sighed, and put on her fixed smile, the one she had been taught to use during feast times and all formal occasions when she represented her kin. But a tiny portion of peevishness remained and she threw the moss. It thudded against Edward's boots, knocking one over.

Alhelm nodded his appreciation. "Good shot, my lady."

Her anger melted, though she remained warm. Her cheeks felt flushed, her breathing was rapid and her heart was hammering. It was bliss.

Edward poked Frith in the ribs. "Young Fleyda wishes to wend her way home, for she was not wooed by your winning words of winsome Wiltshire women." He retrieved his boots and pulled them on.

Frith groaned, stood up and gently cuffed him round the head, unbalancing him as he struggled to put his newly booted foot back on the ground. "Good word-craft indeed, youngster. But it would not have been witty word-craft that won the day for us at Rochester."

Edward rose to his feet, and to the challenge, and sped off after Frith. He caught up with him and they began to mock-fight their way along the path to the outer edge of the wood, staggering to avoid taking the direct line that would lead through the ancient stones, steering wide as soon as they broke free of the trees to pass clear of the malevolent, godless symbols. Fleyda followed them out of the wood, crouching every now and then to collect twigs. Teasel and Alhelm slowed their pace so as not to tread on the hem of the little girl's kirtle and Teasel let her arm hang loosely, occasionally swinging it high to make him notice that it was his to hold if he chose to.

But he was looking ahead, laughing at the antics of his fellows. "You were right, my lady. It was a great day when my lord and your father began to fight together. The team they are building might yet win. Lord Ethelred says that oxen pull stronger when they are yoked together. He has given us hope."

She pointed up the track. "And time for Edward to live a little freely yet." It was a shame that Gwen could not have shared their afternoon, but Teasel knew he would seek her out as soon as he was able. Who knew, perhaps he would not be the only one to hug a secret to his chest that night.

"You and your brother stand fast together, do you not?"

She nodded, though he did not see, for he was still looking ahead. "Each of us is the rock for the other. With Father always off fighting and Mother, well, for some years now, she has been a little like that elm up there. It can be seen, you can stand next to it and yet you cannot reach it."

"And so you had to learn early on how to run a house, welcome guests to a hall, lead the cooks?"

She was so flattered that he had noticed that she fired her words out to deflect the compliment before embarrassment could take hold. "Yet it is good to throw cares away for a while, do you not think, my lord?"

Had she planned to do it, she would have found herself too timid, but without thought, she stopped on the path. Courtesy forced him to stand still, too. She smiled up at him, not daring to breathe, telling herself that whatever else, she must notice every detail of this first kiss, so that she could relive it a thousand times tonight. An ant tickled over her foot and she tried to ignore it. She did not want any tainting her memory of this moment, even though the itch was now working its devilment up her leg.

He looked down at her and gave a closed-lipped smile. He licked his lips. Should she do the same? Was this what one did before a kiss? "My lady, I am glad that you share your father's thoughts on the fellowship with the Mercians, for it is…"

Was he always so talkative before he kissed a woman? If he didn't hurry, her heart would burst right through her chest. Unbidden, her foot moved nearer to his and she resumed her wait, trying hard to keep her thoughts away from the hard stone under her shoe.

"Lady Teasel, I wish you to carry these, for they are too heavy for me now. And I wish to hurry so that I can walk with Lord Edward."

Fleyda had turned to face them and was holding out

79

her bundle of twigs. Alhelm swooped forward and bowed low. "Let me, Lady Fleyda."

He shrugged his apology to Teasel and walked alongside Fleyda. Teasel stuck her royal smile on again and wished she could tell little Fleyda how much better off she would be to drop her queenly ways and behave as freely as a churl.

"I am sorry that Fleyda took you away yesterday." She was standing behind him, watching him. Every now and again she glanced up, squinting against the low morning sun to look past the gate and defence ditch to the straight road beyond. The horizon was interrupted by the dark mound of Silbury Hill, where he would stop to collect more men to swell the ranks, leaving a few behind the palisade to light the beacon if necessary. His men moved to and from the hall, snatching a last drink of ale before the journey, stuffing chunks of bread and cheese into their packs, collecting repaired and sharpened weapons from the smithy.

He put down his own saddle pack and came to stand alongside her on the hall steps. He swept his arm out to the side, indicating the yard full of soldiers packing up to leave. "I am always being taken somewhere I do not wish to go." He gave a little smile. "I live in hope of finding something sweet when I get there, though."

He looked down and would not meet her gaze. For all he was the elder by eight years, it seemed that he was as nervous as she.

"I dared to hope that you had already found it, my lord?"

The little laugh he gave was far removed from his usual robust chuckle. "I must always be on the road, my lady."

"But surely you know?"

Now he coughed. "Know what, my lady?"

His question made her falter. She said, "That I, that is to say, I think it is understood."

He stopped fidgeting and looked up at the sky. Then

he looked at her with the same expression as in the woods. But he could not kiss her here, surely, not with everyone looking?

He took her hand, instead. "My lady, you are sixteen now and old enough." He coughed again. "Old enough to know that you have my heart and I will always be nearby to do your bidding."

He bowed and went to rejoin his men.

Frith came out from the hall, with Edward a step behind him. Frith put a hand up to greet Alhelm and said, "I must find my father."

Teasel watched as he walked towards the forge. Frith's father emerged, deep in conversation with the smith. Frith bowed his head, said a few words, and then father and son embraced, the elder patting Frith's back and placing a kiss on each cheek.

Teasel felt Edward shifting his weight from one foot to the other. "Too much," he said, too loudly, as if extra volume would lead her to think that he believed his own words and dispel her knowledge that Alfred was never like that with him. "Who wishes to see such things out here in sight of everyone?"

She smiled and wrapped her arms around her middle. "Oh, but you might have to get used to such sights, Brother. I think I am to be wed." She turned to face him, giving a backwards nod.

Edward looked over at Alhelm and arched his eyebrows. "Really? He kept that well hidden. I must ask him how he does it, for it seems the whole world knows about me and Gwen. Mother, I have been told, is fit to burst. If she asks, you have not seen me all day."

She laughed and nodded. She would watch until her love was out of sight, on the other side of Silbury Hill, and then she, too, would avoid her mother, for she did not wish to be reminded of the pain of separation. She wanted to spend the days until Alhelm returned hugging herself and dreaming of him.

AD886

The vivid banners flapped in the breeze and the sun shot sharp spears of reflection from the burnished helms. Alfred's purple cloak flared out behind him and billowed around his horse's hindquarters. The men rode tall, their cloak pins shining and the reins hanging loosely in their hands. The men on foot shouldered their shields, heavy though they must be after so long marching, but they stepped easily, every so often falling out of line to take a playful lunge at a neighbour. Even now, within sight of the royal manor, this fyrd came at a leisurely, triumphant pace. Fyrdsmen, having given of their prescribed service days, peeled off to take the tributary paths which would take them home to their villages. Back on home ground and no longer united against a common enemy, they traded good-natured tribal and territorial insults at those with whom they'd fought for so long and were now leaving behind as they went home to see to the harvest and resume their role as husbandmen. Mercians walked alongside the remaining West Saxons, laughing and joking, like brothers now after time spent together in battle. Bunched behind King Alfred, the lords of Somerset and Wiltshire, the first dark and square-jawed, the second smaller, thinner, white-blond, rode next to their Mercian counterparts: Wulf, most revered leader of the Gaini and Alhelm, ealdorman of northern Mercia. In the middle of the group, comfortably astride a tall black stallion, rode Lord Frith, newly awarded lands in

Buckinghamshire, who literally could now put feet in both kingdoms and call the land his own.

They began to file through the gateway, bringing a seemingly solid noise of hoof beats, clanking bits and creaking tack. The familiar scent of sweaty horses and men, so lacking when they were away, filled the courtyard, as welcome to those waiting as a swarm returning to cheer the beekeeper waiting by his empty hive. Teasel, standing beside her mother, glanced sideways. Ewith was breathing quickly, but was it through relief, or the deeply held belief that this was but a respite, a cruel glimpse of happiness before Alfred returned to battle and certain death? Teasel could not know the answer, but knew that she could not suffer to live that way, with a bereavement settled in her heart years before the death. And, relieved as she was to see her father home safe, there was only one face she wished to see. They were too near now, the great bulk of the horses too close for her to find him without straining her neck. She must wait, as her father dismounted and allowed the rest to follow. Alfred slipped from his horse, embraced his wife with a formal kiss which neither required nor received a response from Ewith, and turned to address the assembled household immediately, leaving the other lords to listen whilst still sitting in the saddle.

"We have ridden from London, where, with God's might and the help of our Mercian friends, we have driven the heathen away across the sea. London was once in Mercia and I have given it to the lord Ethelred, where it will be safe in his keeping. The roads and waterways into the south are free once more." He took a deep breath and turned slowly to look at all those clustered about him. "We have been blessed and this is a great day. I wish to mark it with a token to show the deep and abiding friendship of our two kingdoms. Once, I gave my sister to wed the king of Mercia. Now, I will give my eldest daughter to wed a Mercian lord."

All her life, Alfred had been a hazy figure, a father who rarely came home and had not the time to speak much to her when he did. But, this once, the king's daughter did not mind that he had not spoken to her first. Teasel's breath caught on the lump in the back of her throat. Her father was about to tell the world so there was no need for discretion. Craning her neck, she stared up at her future husband. Alhelm sat elm-straight, his gaze fixed on Alfred. No matter, he would turn to look at her when her father spoke his name. *Speak, Father, say the name, so that I may breathe again.*

"This righteous and God-fearing man has shown steadfast belief in our fellowship and has fought with the strength of a bear and craftiness of a fox, the fearlessness of a hound and clear sight of a hawk."

Alhelm's cheek twitched. Teasel smiled and loved him a little bit more; for his modesty, for almost containing all reaction to such praise, but for being human and humble enough not to quite manage it.

Alfred continued. "This man will be not so much son, but more like a brother, to me and to Wessex. I am proud to name Ethelred of the Hwicce, lord of all Mercia, as my friend, and give him my daughter as bride."

He had said the wrong name. Still she gazed at Alhelm and still he stared at Alfred. The cheering and shouts of joy pummelled her senses but she stood, rooted. Alhelm did not move. *Turn to look at me. Tell me with your eyes that my father is mistaken.* Hands patted her shoulders, fingers stroked her hair, palms squeezed her hands, but they were but to the side of her, he in front of her. Slowly, as if he did not know that it hurt her more that way, he turned his head and looked across at her. While she blinked stupidly, waiting for it all to be said again, but correctly this time, he raised his hands as if in apology. She saw his face. The gentle curls of his soft blond hair, the dark shadow on his chin. The blue eyes, so pale, like one drop of ink swirled through a trough of clear water. She saw the sadness there, she saw the smooth cheekbones, crease-free because there was no smile there today, and she saw his beautiful mouth set in a straight line. But she did not see surprise.

"And now, let us eat. Let us drink. Let us thank God for all we have." Alfred spread his arms wide, bowed to his wife, and the courtyard bustled once more like a barn on fire. Riders dismounted, grooms ran to fetch the horses to the stables and the men who dismounted back-slapped with those who had been standing during the king's speech. Children tugged at Teasel's skirts and women, old men, lords, uncles and anyone who could vaguely claim kinship pushed a kiss onto her cheek. Before all could squeeze into the hall, those at the front were back out again, slopping ale and shouting toasts. Her feet were still rooted, her knees too weak to lift them. *I am the daughter of a king and I cannot do what I like.* Alhelm walked past her, close enough for her to breathe his scent, close enough for her to touch. But not now. Not ever.

She was not to serve at this feast and nor, it seemed, was her mother. They sat with the men at the head table. Alfred spoke, not of war, but of forging stronger links with Mercia, of borrowing learned clergy to come and raise literacy levels amongst his subjects. "Soon, the churches and abbeys will be strong again and all will be able to read, like we and our dear children."

Teasel stared without hunger at the boards laden with food. Her mother was far more animated than usual. Teasel had expected her mother's misery to expand and incorporate her daughter's. But of course, it was the opposite of the situation with Gwen; Ewith would believe that Teasel's status would be elevated in Mercia where, she said, they knew how to treat their women. Ewith laughed at her brother's jokes and drank more wine than usual. Lord Frith commented on her unusual brooch and the king's wife giggled like a girl.

"This? Oh 'tis an old brooch of my mother's, mine since my wedding. But I thank you for your kind words. Do you think it looks well on me?" She leaned forward, thrusting her torso nearer to Frith. "See the craftsmanship.

Mercian." She nudged him with her elbow.

"Mother, stop it." It was said quietly through clenched teeth, but it should have not been said at all and she was instantly sorry. It was merely a cruel mistiming that had brought her mother back to her cheery old self when Teasel herself felt so dispirited. She opened her mouth to apologise.

But Ewith, replacing her empty cup on the table, put her hand on her daughter's and said, "I am making merry on your behalf. You are going home, and you will be a queen in all but name. She reached for the jug and refilled her cup, waving it around as she spoke. "You will have a fine hall, better than this, with salted herring from the eastern sea and with, oh, spilled a bit, gold wall hangings and lots of…" She laughed, too high and too loudly and folk from the other tables turned to look. Then the elation, stuck there only by alcohol, melted from her face. She slopped some more wine into her cup and took a large gulp, the drink driving her spirits down with it. "Whereas I, I will be forever…" She seemed to lose the thread of her thought, and fell silent as she held up her cup for a refill.

Teasel leaned across to her brother and said, "As if my heart were not already cleft in two, she must stamp on it now by being so glad for me."

Edward, chewing on a chicken leg, said. "It might be that it will not be as bad as you fear. He is not an ogre, at least."

She had been blinking quickly all evening, but knew it was as a thin linen veil against a thunderstorm. The tears were mustering, hot enough to burn. Think, then. What was he like? She had only seen him once and all she could recall was the sombre face, but there was naught unusual in that. She had spent her childhood thinking that all the men of Wessex had been born with that same solemn countenance. His eyes, she remembered, were a soft, dark brown, like honey when the bees had been feasting on clover. And his smile, when it came, was open and unreserved. But it was not Alhelm's. What else was there to know? "It is of no help to me." Ogre or not, he was simply the wrong man.

Edward put the chicken leg on the table and wiped his mouth with the back of his hand. "Then cling to what you already know. Of who we are." He took up his ale cup and swallowed hard. "Of what we must become when we are no longer children. Mother does as she must. So will I, and so must you. If it is good for Wessex that you do this thing, then you must do it. We are all of us yoked to that burden." His mouth settled into a grim, thin-lipped line, as if he were clasping it shut to trap unspoken words.

"You mean that I must wear a silly grin and not show the hurt?" Even as she spoke, her voice cracked and she knew he was right, for deep beneath the humiliation of this day, her old self, her royal self, was ashamed at the outward display of weakness.

He shrugged. "Children of the house of Wessex are not free."

But royal or not, brothers were made to argue with. "Oh, well spoken, proud Atheling. But I am not bound yet." She pushed back her chair and hurried from the hall. She was mindful of her age just enough to refrain from running, but her cheeks burned and every slow step seemed no more than an inch as she passed tables suddenly grown longer in her effort to get to the door and be free. Perhaps, afterwards, she would remember that not many folk turned to look, but now it felt as if every gaze in the room was focused on her as if she were not merely walking, but lit up by green flames.

Outside, she leaned with her hands pressed on the wall behind her. The thudding, pulsing sound in her ears gradually gave way to the music of birdsong and the noise of the mead hall retreated as the comforting sounds of the forge and farmyard grew louder. Now, with no-one to see, she allowed the tears to fall, jumping with a guilty rush that put a flutter of embarrassment in her guts when she heard the door slam.

Thelwold edged towards her and put out a hand, tentative like a small child testing to see if the cooking pot were still hot.

"I will not bite," she said.

His hand reached her arm and he patted it. "I came to tell you that I am sorry," he said.

She sniffed, raised her hand to wipe her nose and thought better of it. Then, she thought, *it is only Thelwold*, and she put the back of her hand to her face and wiped it sideways across her nose. "I thank you for your kind words."

But her automatic and polite response obviously did not satisfy him, for he gripped tighter on her arm and said, "No, I mean it. For I know what it is to have your hopes ripped from your heart. I…"

The noise from the hall grew louder and fell away as the door opened and closed once more. Edward was standing with Alhelm. Thelwold's grip on her arm increased.

Edward said, "Come away, Thelwold."

"But I am only trying to…"

"There is no need. I have brought Lord Alhelm now."

Somewhere beneath her misery, she was aware that she should step between them. Both were thinking only of her, yet Thelwold was misconstruing Edward's words. Why could Edward not simply say, 'I know you are trying to help, but here is the only man who can help her now'? Why could Thelwold not understand that he was not useless simply because he was not, right then and there, the best person to help her? And who could she blame for the fact that her sorrow was so deep that she had not the energy to put them right, this one last time before they all had to grow up?

Her fingers twitched, wanting to reach out to Thelwold, but her arm remained heavy and she let him go. Somewhere near her lips there quivered a rebuke for her brother, so caring but so tactless. But she remained silent.

Alhelm came to stand in front of her. He reached out, but his hand hovered, shaking, before he retracted it, folding his arms instead. "Edward has told me what you thought, but it was never said. I did not say…"

For the first time, the soft timbre of his voice did not soothe her soul. She said, "But you followed me out here. So that must mean that you care." Why could she not say something grown-up instead of behaving like a sulky child?

He shifted his weight from one foot to the other. "As always, I am making sure that you are all right. That is all I have ever done."

Even as he spoke, she was shaking her head. "No, no, it is not true."

His hand was on her arm. His tone was insistent. "My lord sent me. I was his eyes, there to watch over you and speak to you, learn your thoughts and speak his name to you as often as I could."

Louder now, she said, "No, you were not, it was not like that." But was it? All those visits, always with tidings about the wars, but especially he came with tales of Ethelred's bravery and skill. All the questions he had asked her, taking careful note of the answers not, as she had thought, to keep safe in his own memory, but to pass on to his lord. It was true that he had never spoken any words of love, never, even when she had told him of her feelings towards him. And yet…

She sniffed and stood up straight, pushing away from the wall and standing as steadily as she could. Tilting her chin to look up and meet his gaze she said, "You would need to have a heart hewn from stone to do all that, to be like that and not…" She inhaled. "Tell me that you do not love me." She held her breath.

He shook his head and began to walk away.

She exhaled and words came out unbidden. "Say it," she shouted at his back. "Say that you do not love me." He kept walking and she raised her voice again. "Say it, and then I can hate you."

But he did not turn. He did not say it, and she could not hate him.

Part II – Wifmann (Woman)

AD887

London

Æthelflæd, daughter of Alfred, king of Wessex, wrinkled her nose. Even indoors, the strange smells of London assaulted her nostrils, reminding her how far she was from home. Seething piles of fish wriggled on the quayside, unloaded next to casks of brightly coloured, unfamiliar spices. Even the folk smelled odd, of salt sea air and foreign habits. Away from the water, the townsfolk displayed differing attitudes towards strangers, welcoming the sailors and traders, but feigning ignorance of any West Saxon dialect. They wore scent which she could not recognise and cooked odd-smelling delicacies which gave off aromas that left her longing for an honest Wiltshire pottage. For so long, all that her kin and countrymen had wished for was to be free of the Viking scourge, but never had she thought that such freedom would see her wrenched from her home like this. Sighing, she banged the shutter closed and her mother looked up and tutted.

Ewith indicated the pile of linen in front of her. "How can I see to these now?"

"Oh why bother? Must I take them? Surely they have sheets in Mercia." *And beds to put them on.* The thought warmed her cheeks and she swallowed down a writhing coil of worry. "Mother?"

Her tone must have changed, for Ewith looked up, her expression kind yet quizzical. "Yes?"

Teasel dragged a stool nearer to her mother's seat and sat down opposite Ewith. "I have been told that it will hurt."

Ewith sniffed and continued folding the clothes. "It might. But it is soon over. Until such a time as any bond grows between you, he will waste little time whispering words of love." She waved a hand towards the window, as if they were still in Wessex surrounded by lush farmland and grazing stock. "The first time will be no more than as a ram to a ewe. Then, in time, a kindness will grow, maybe even love, and it will become something more tender."

Ewith paused and an embryonic smile raised the corners of her mouth, as if she were pondering the love between her and Alfred. But almost straight away her lips sank into their downward curve and she leaned forward over the linen to tap her daughter's knee. "Never forget that you are a daughter of a king. When you wed, he will still be an ealdorman, but you stand higher yet than he. He will know it." She sat back. "Come, then, do not rob me of my day. What? You think this is only about your wedding? No, my girl, queen or not, I will shine when I give my daughter as bride to Mercia."

Her dress was made of the finest linen, dyed with madder root to a beautiful shade of red. Her coppery-blonde plait, brought over her shoulder and lying against her chest, looked so pleasing against the deep crimson hue that she had not been able to help but look down at it every few minutes, stroking the smooth braid with satisfaction right up to the moment that her ladies had placed the veil upon her head and secured it with a gold headband. But she knew that her appearance was as a deep puddle to the sunshine when she saw her betrothed.

Ethelred was wearing a vivid green tunic, cut from the most expensive imported silk. The neck opening was edged with a band of yellow silk, shot through with strands of gold. This gold banding also draped round the tunic hem, which hung just an inch from the floor. Teasel considered this man, who could afford a floor-length tunic made entirely from, and not just edged in, silk and wondered if Ewith had underestimated his wealth. At his waist, his belt buckle, heavily gold, twisted within its own shape with curves and coils of intricately worked metal. The swirling shapes wound into a knot which ended with a hound's head, its eye stamped with a deep red garnet. There were mosaics of more garnets inlaid around the outer edges of the buckle. Ethelred wore a light woollen cloak, caught at his shoulder with a gold clasp; two gold triangles studded with yet more garnets and decorated again with the intertwined metal knot-work. He put a hand up to flick a curl of hair loose from his collar and she caught a glimpse of his gold arm-ring, given to him by her father. His arm dropped quickly and she mused that he was not happy to be wearing this expensive gift. He might have been content to add another gold arm-ring to his collection but this one carried with it the burden of being named Alfred's man and although Teasel did not know much about Ethelred, she could tell that the symbol of submission sat tightly on the Mercian's arm. This day, he was clean-shaven. If it was an affectation, designed to make him appear more youthful, then she deemed it a success. Looking at him while the bishop of London droned his Latin, she noted again how his face remained free of the lines which had taken lodging on her father's face, where, even in this new time of peace, Alfred's expression was one of permanent worry. Ethelred, obviously understanding the bishop's words, nodded every now and then, and mouthed brief, soundless prayers. His jawbone moved forward slightly and she saw a small scar on the edge between face and neck, but although she knew the deep furrow was still there between his brows, she could find no trace of a line or crease on his now smooth cheek. Spending her formative years petted by giants, first Uncle Wulf and then Thelwold and latterly Edward, who seemed to have grown a foot in the year before his seventeenth birthday, she had viewed Ethelred as being of inconsequential height. But standing next to him now, she felt the straining in her neck as she looked up at him and guessed that his shoulder was further from the ground than was the crown of her own head. Feeling brave, she leaned in a little closer and breathed in deeply. He smelled neither clean nor dirty and her only awareness was of the warmth radiating from his body. She shivered, though, and stood tall and straight, concentrating on the foreign words instead of on the foreign sensation of being so close to a man who was not of her own family.

In this game she was but one of the prizes, a token to be held up and admired. Her worth was in her status, not in her looks or accomplishment. She understood this, as the daughter of a king and of a disappointed mother, and she was not surprised to find herself virtually ignored at the wedding feast. Ethelred spoke to her father and Ewith responded graciously to the many compliments and deference due to her as mother of this precious daughter, whose wedding symbolised the success of the new peace. The older woman had her hand constantly at her veil, smoothing and checking it. She appeared to be wearing her entire collection of jewellery, but, so adorned, looked a little out of place, where the other ladies of the court had chosen, like Ethelred, to demonstrate their wealth through the fine cuts and fabrics of their clothes. Remembering the gold arm ring, Teasel noted that although he was almost certain to own many such valuable items, today Ethelred had chosen to wear only the one which was relevant to the day's proceedings. But whatever the cause, Ewith was attracting many glances and comments and was blossoming like a flower under sunlight.

Teasel put on her smile, lowered her head so that the flowing sides of her veil masked her face a little, and stared at the food in front of her. In common with all the folk about her, it was not her wont to waste food. Who knew when the next harvest would fail, or when the murrain would come again to decimate the cattle stocks? She had been no more than five and better off than most, but she still remembered the hunger she had endured during her first experience of widespread famine. Standing beside the head table, a serving-boy carved the meat. The roasted lamb, boiled bacon and spit-cooked chickens barely left room for the piles of freshly caught cod and salted herring. The sight of the herring made Teasel smile; no doubt her mother would be impressed with the fish that was so expensive and highly prized in the West. The regaining of London had meant that supply trains were no longer interrupted and one could only gaze with gratitude upon the variety of food on the tables. The cheese was soft and fresh and the bread served with it was made of the finest sifted wheat. Yet she had no appetite and, raising her cup to her lips for the toast, she found that a mere sip was enough to wet her mouth. Discomfited by the thought of wasted food, she dared to touch her husband's arm.

"I find that I am not hungry. May I ask that any leftover food be shared out amongst the folk of the town?"

When first she spoke, he looked at her with what she feared was disapproval. But then he smiled and she thought, again, how his countenance opened out, the lines smoothing into an expression so honest and trustworthy that she understood how this taciturn man might inspire such loyalty among his men as Alhelm had shown. He said, "If that is your wish, then it will be done."

The intimacy of looking so closely upon his face served only to remind her of what was to come. "I thank you, my lord," she said, and turned to look at her mother. Within seconds she heard him resume his conversation with her father and she gazed around the room, searching for distraction. If she concentrated hard enough, then surely she could find something interesting enough to divert her mind from its double misery; the fear of the impending bedtime and the desolate knowledge that it would be with the wrong man. But her wandering gaze betrayed her and all it showed her was that he, Alhelm, was not in the room and it would let her think of nothing else. Now, she was grateful that no pretence was required of her; this wedding was no love match, her husband craved alliance not affection, so she was free to journey with her thoughts and speak only when spoken to.

At least she was not ugly. Ethelred had heard tell of one particular Frankish princess, married off for political gain, whose husband had accused her of standing upside down, so much did her face resemble her backside. Perhaps it was good, too, that this was no love match. Alfred's sister had loved Burgred with all her heart and they had lost much of their bargaining power because of their love for one another. Better that Alfred knew Ethelred kept his daughter on sufferance only, a token to be treasured only as long as their fellowship prospered. A shame, though, that she was not better company. A warm presence by the fire on a cold night and a companion to talk with was no less than every man's basic desire. Even the expensive herring, there to satisfy Ewith's taste for luxury and to show her daughter that she was not being sent beyond the bounds of civilisation, had failed to stir the girl's appetite. But leftover food and the prospect of a cold hearth constituted a small price to pay for Alfred's co-operation, and he had harboured few illusions about how she would feel towards him.

He was standing in the courtyard, waiting for her to reappear from the ladies' bower with all her belongings to take on the journey back to Mercia proper. Wulf staggered outside and slapped him on the back. "So, you will take her back to Gloucester and hope she warms to your ways, eh?"

Ethelred grunted. "It does not seem likely. It was a fitting name that you gave her, for she is, indeed, prickly." He nodded back towards the hall. "She spoke to me but once in there and that was only to tell me that she was not hungry."

Wulf stroked his beard and frowned. "Prickly? I do

not..." He slapped his forehead and laughed. "I see, I see. No, you have it wrong. I named her Little Teasel for she would come always to sit upon my lap, and there she would comb my beard for me. And what is another name for a teasel? Wolf's comb." Now he was laughing so violently at his own joke that he had to lean forward and rest his hands on his knees. "My friend, you will have to find another reason for her lack of warmth towards you."

Ethelred pushed a silent laugh through his nostrils. Oh, he knew the reason. What did they think he was doing, he that spoke little? It was known to all that he would rather kill a hundred of the heathen than make a speech; did they think, though, that he never used his eyes or ears either? He did not need any answers, but he could give his new young wife the information that she sought. He was not blind. She had searched with her gaze all around the hall but she should have been looking along the road to north Mercia, the road that Alhelm had taken just the day before, back to his lands in Shropshire, citing manifold reasons why he could not stay to witness his lord's wedding. No, his lord was not blind. He had seen.

All day the clanking of the baggage cart had given her a steady beat to listen to, a rhythmic lull that overwhelmed the sound of her agitated heartbeat. When they stopped for rest and relief, she had the calming presence of Lord Frith, so that although the pounding of her nervous heart grew louder again, she was not completely alone amidst these unknown Mercian faces. Frith gave her small smiles every now and again, and when the wind caught his long hair and played with it, she saw him again in his carefree moments by the river and it brought Edward and Alhelm closer to her. She shivered and pulled her cloak tighter around her body. It had been so warm, that day by the river, but now, here in some strange land, the light was fading and any heat from the sun had long since passed into the earth. To one side of the road there were dense trees, to the other was an open expanse of grass, inhabited by one lonely oak. She sat with her back against its trunk, knees drawn up under her cloak, trying to keep warm and out of the wind.

They were not resting for long, she had been told, so there was no need to light a fire. Ethelred had ridden ahead, bored, no doubt, by the slow procession of the lady and her belongings. Her silence must have conveyed her thoughts, for Frith, squatting beside her and balancing his weight on his heels, told her that the lord had ridden ahead to ensure that all was ready for her welcome. She smiled, but turned to stare at the woodland beyond, as she pictured the welcoming scene at Ethelred's hall: a nail, high up on the wall of his great hall, where he could hang her, his trophy, like a prized shield or expensive embroidery. The chill of the dying day covered her face, shroud-like, and then it began to leach into her bones. The dark lines of the trees became blurred in the gloom, merging as the light disappeared from the gaps between them. But the darkness did not fall so much as flicker, for the shadows between the trees moved, dark shapes rising and falling. She sat forward. Blinking to clear her vision, she looked again at this unnatural dusk-fall. She reached for Frith, but he was gone.

She heard a high whining in the air and spent a slow moment trying to think what would make such a noise. She realised what was causing the sound just as another arrow flew past her and embedded itself into the tree behind her. Scrabbling to her feet, she did not stand up, but ran, crouched, to the other side of the tree. There she sat, knees to her chest and hands to her ears, her heart thumping and her bowels threateningly loose.

For years, her nightmares had brought visions of Viking attack. Now she heard the noise of battle and it was more terrifying than anything her mind had conjured up. Men died silently in dreams, but here the screaming of death rose up sharply to pierce the evening air, as if splitting the very sky. The clash of metal rang out in two distinct tones, the higher song reverberating when sword sparked off

100

sword, a duller tone falling quickly away when axe met axe. Unable to see whether her escort was strong enough to fight off the attackers, she allowed her hands to slip down and she clasped them in prayer. A strong odour wafted around her nostrils and she opened her eyes. One of the assailants had his face before hers. He stared at her with his dark eyes and as he smiled she experienced again the strong, sweet stench of his breath. He reached out and clamped a hand upon her shoulder, pulling her to her feet. Frith appeared behind him, there was a small sound which she could not identify, and the man's grip loosened. He sank to the ground in front of her and even where she could still feel the pressure on her shoulder, the hold was replaced by a gentle squeeze of Frith's hand. She looked up and he nodded at her before wiping the sweat from his eyes and hurling himself back into the fray. She sank to her knees, her hands in front of her chest in full supplication. Mouthing as many of the Latin prayers as she could remember, she tensed against the involuntary flinches that made her upper body collapse every time a blow rang out.

The screams gave way to moans and the clanging of metal faded away to be replaced by the sounds of skin thwacking on skin, as, she presumed, knuckles and fists pummelled prostrate foes. A hand, gentle, raised her to her feet and she stepped round the tree. Instantly, the cold seeping through her bones awakened her senses and she became aware that her toes were frozen almost beyond feeling. Yet there was a warmth rising up from the spread of bodies on the ground, and the air was thick still with the heat, sweat and blood of the fighting just moments before. The mixture of cold and heat, the thick odours hanging in the air, and the sudden release through a body held so tense drove the contents of her stomach towards her throat and she put her hand to her face. Swallowing forcefully, she turned her head, for although the darkness was fast stealing vision, still she did not want to look upon the faces of the dead men. Frith had ordered someone to calm the frightened horses; another was commanded to deal with the dead.

Frith walked past her and she stopped him with her hand upon his forearm. "Will there be more of them out there? Vikings?"

"No, they were not..." He wiped his hand-sæx on the hem of his tunic and looked down at her. He inhaled as if he were about to speak on, but then he sighed and shook his head. "No," he said again, "They were not part of a bigger host. And we left none alive."

As they resumed their journey she reflected that in the half-light she had seen so little of the ambush that she would still not be able clearly to identify the Viking enemy. But, as each mile they travelled was another mile of safety between her and the heathens, she allowed herself to relax a little, and eventually felt a small smile hovering on her lips. When she told Edward about the night's events, she would at least be able to boast that she had not screamed once. Then, overcome by longing for the brother she would not see again for years, she gave up all resistance to fatigue and slept.

Gloucester

Frith had already made his report to Ethelred. She needed
no words to tell her; the look on her husband's face was
enough for her to be sure that he knew what had happened.
His cheek was twitching and she wondered if this were a
frequent affliction, or one that arose purely from tension,
which, so far, had accompanied their every meeting. She
thought that Frith's friendly hand on Ethelred's arm was
perhaps there to restrain, but she did not know her lord well
enough to know if that would be necessary. And now,
despite that ignorance and the night's events, she must face
the Mercian witan, and greet all the lords who lived in this
proud, strange land. The task would not be small. She had
barely learned the names of her escort, but now she must
differentiate between those who were the men of Ethelred's
hall and who travelled with him, and those who attended the
Gloucester witan because they owned lands nearby. Then,
no doubt, there would be others here this night who had
come from other districts, solely for the purpose of meeting
their new lady. She stood as straight and still as she could,
making sure that the long skirt of her kirtle was at no point
touching her body. She would not let them see that she was
shaking. Neither the ambush nor the introductions would
reveal the Wessex princess as a frightened girl.

The hall looked as any other; the central hearth glowed
with a welcoming fire and at first glance she would not
know that she were in another kingdom. But the unfamiliar
smell which had accosted her nostrils when she arrived was

wafting in from outside and the hanging hooks for swords and shields were empty, for tonight no man would find himself unarmed after what had happened. Then the leading men of Mercia came to make their greetings and their accents betrayed their origins. One by one they stepped forward to where she was standing by the head table and pronounced their Mercian names in their Mercian accent and, though she knew that their solemnity owed as much to the attack as to their sense of occasion, nevertheless it added to the picture of foreignness being laid before her. These Mercians, whose origins lay in another part of the old country, did not look particularly different to her as individuals, but a glance round the hall showed a scene filled with men whose colouring was predominantly lighter than in Saxon Wessex. These descendants of the Angles were deferential, but not welcoming, and it was obvious that their lord had delivered a damning verdict on their failure to protect their charge.

Without smiles, they presented themselves. The first, Thelwold, looked less like her cousin of the same name and more like a goat, for his beard grew to a curly point just below his chin. Next came a man whose name was Alfred and Teasel's pride began to rub the wrong way up her nerves. These folk were so careful to accentuate their otherness, yet here she was in a court where there lived a Thelwold and an Alfred. This Alfred, though, was small and barrel-chested, nothing like her willowy father. After Little Alfred had stepped away, two huge men came forward. They must have been higher in rank, for their gold-edged clothing spoke of their wealth. She wondered if they had been more affronted by the attack upon her royal person, for theirs were the sternest faces of all. Both had long grey hair, but the first, Eardwulf, wore a beard that was almost as long, while the other, Eadnoth, was bare-chinned. After them she was introduced variously to men called, she thought, Wighelm, Luda, Wilferth, Ecghun and Acha and she knew that she would spend a month, at least, irritating them by asking them to repeat their names. When her mother's household had lodged at Lord Somerset's house, Teasel had made friends with old Sæxferth, who was always at a loss to see distant objects with clarity and often asked her to help him identify high-flying birds, so she was accustomed to the notion of blurred vision. Never before though had she known that sounds, too, could blur.

Ethelred stepped forward. "My lady is tired."

She thought perhaps that it was trickery but no, those four simple words were enough for the room to empty. Even after a declaration from King Alfred, the halls of Wessex were usually slower to clear than that. Grateful for Ethelred's intervention, she sat down on the mead bench. The hall door flapped in the night breeze and the odd smell increased in pungency. She had smelled it before, but not in her everyday business and it continued to puzzle her.

"They will wish to come back in shortly."

Startled by the broken silence, she turned to look at him.

"To sleep. Some of them will wish to come back in."

She stared at him. Of course, it was bedtime. And how foolish she had been to forget that yet another ordeal awaited her before she could call the day her own and sleep. Whatever small spirit of rebellion dwelled within her, it was far too insubstantial to prove potent. She could already bear witness that here was a man who had little difficulty commanding the folk of his kingdom. He was not to be gainsaid. In any case, her fear would control her voice and she would not have him know it, so she merely nodded and stood up, waiting for him to show her the way.

He took a step towards her and held out his hand. As she took it he said, "You are unharmed?"

And she nodded again. The steadfast Lord Frith had delivered the goods in one piece.

But Frith could not be constantly at her side. Certainly not this dark night, when the only candle lighting the way to the bedchamber was held by her husband.

The dawn light seeping through the cracks in the shutters opened her eyes and she looked around without moving her head. She was alone in her bed, as she was used to being, ever since she had stopped sleeping with her nurse when still a tiny child. Familiar noises from outside floated into the room; the ox-herd shooing his bellowing charges back to the ploughman after watching them overnight, the cockerels crowing and the looms clattering into life. She considered the possibility that the previous night had been but a dream, but she knew that she was no longer in Wessex, for how else to explain the subtle difference in the tone of the lowing and bleating outside that came from beasts unfamiliar to her, of voices she did not recognise, or this new chamber, with its door to the right of the bed not the left, and the different scent to the bedcovers, which smelled more like the mead hall than her own bed, freshened every morning with herbs. Her mother had led her to believe that Mercia was a civilised land, yet here she was in a smelly room and no women to attend her. Her clothes from last night still lay in the heap where they fell. No indeed, she was not in her own bed, for the clothes spoke their tale, as did the slightly bruised sensation between her legs, but it was naught that could be described as pain. He had been tender with her last night, and given the lie to more of her mother's words. Ewith had told her that it would be brief and perfunctory, but that over time the love would come. Last night it had not been brief and it had not hurt. Ethelred had placed the gentlest kisses on every inch of her and had fallen asleep with his arm around her. It was not the animal coupling to which her mother had alluded, but it was all done with total detachment, an extraordinary display of physical kindness, but without any affection. If rough lust were supposed to turn eventually into love, what sort of journey began with tenderness but no warmth?

She had come to Mercia knowing that it was the beginning of a life of loneliness, wed to a man who had no interest in her beyond her worth as a bargaining tool. But even if he forgot it, she was the daughter of a king and could not lie abed feeling sorry for herself. She had been thrust, willing or not, into a grown-up world and there must be much to discover. Clasping hold of the top of the linen sheet, she pushed it down as far as her knees and sat up.

Now, she saw that one of her travel chests lay on the floor and she swung her legs over the side of the bed, walked two steps and opened it to rummage for an under-dress and a kirtle more suited to an ordinary day than the expensive red gown. She slipped the linen garment over her head and then pulled on the plain woollen dress and as she smoothed it over her hips, she looked at the smaller wooden box next to her clothes chest. It was the little trunk with the Celtic cross carving which contained a bag of coin, a warm cloak and a blanket; the chest which she never unpacked, except to replace the dried herbs that kept the clothing fresh. She was now wife to a man who ruled a kingdom where she believed that the Viking presence might fade to just a memory. Frith had told her that the men last night were all dead, and that they were not from a larger host. Did she need the box, still? "We'll see," she said and pulled her hair over her shoulder to braid it.

She opened the bedchamber door and peered out with a shy glance into the main hall, letting out a breath of relief to see none but servants dragging the trestles away from the wall in preparation for the midday meal. When each table was in place, a serving-woman spread fragrant meadowsweet leaves on the floor around it. So, they did know then, these Mercians, how to sweeten a room. She crossed the hall, pushed against the heavy oak door and gave entry to the beam of daylight, letting it fall into the mead hall as she stepped outside. She had no plan and she paused on the step, but Lord Frith was standing by the door and immediately stepped towards her. "How timely to find you here," she said.

One side of his mouth lifted into a smile. "Not really, my lady, I have been waiting for you. I am to show you your new home."

He bowed and put out his arm to the side, allowing her to walk in front of him. The odd smell drifted into her nostrils once more and she put her head up, sniffing. "What is it?"

He shook his head, as if he could not detect it, but then he laughed and said, "I think that you mean the pigs in the woods over there." He jerked his head to the side in order to flick his hair from his eyes. "I, too, wondered what it was when first I came here. There are pigs in Wessex but..."

"My father does not like them and thinks them not good meat for kings." Did Alfred have any real idea where he had sent her?

Frith drew alongside her and put a hand to her elbow. "This way, my lady."

Teasel followed, looking at the town as if through her father's eyes and wondering if he would be pleased. Through the gate, Frith led her away from the hall and towards the crossroads in the centre of the town. From here it was clear that one quadrant was occupied by the hall and its various accommodation buildings. In the next quadrant, the church dominated, while the other two served the townsfolk and held a mixture of dwellings, sheds and small plots given over to farming. Beyond the town gate, near the river, a cluster of dwellings was visible and Teasel thought that she could see the watermill turning. She followed Frith as he walked each branch of the crossroads. Introductions were not necessary, for all the folk would know who this stranger was, but Teasel noticed that though they bowed, they did not smile. She knew that they would be sombre after hearing of the attack last night, ashamed, even, that it had been allowed to happen. Well, at least these less than welcoming Mercians might have to learn to live with the fear, just like the West Saxons had done for years.

Completing their circuit and walking back towards the hall, they walked past a retting pit, where flax stems were being soaked. A brief glance told Teasel that the process here was the same as in Wessex. There was a fence around the pit and leaning up against it were the mallets and boards which would be used once the stems were dried to remove the fibres. Beside them were the iron-toothed heckling tools which would clean and separate the fibres ready for spinning.

Frith was pointing. "Over there is the..."

She turned. "The tannery. Yes, I know." She could see the scudding area where the skin and hair were removed from the hides and, next to it, the frames over which the furs were spread whilst the fat and egg-white preservatives were spread on the flesh side. But even without these visual clues, she would have known the building. Digging their way from the very back of her mind, memories were emerging, of folk who must long since be dead, like old Higbald the smith. She had been here before, as a child at her Uncle Burgred's court.

By the forge, and looking nothing like she remembered old Higbald, a young man was leaning against the wall. He held one hand across his waist, the thumb tucked into his belt. The other hand was at his ear, tugging and stroking the lobe. As Teasel and Frith walked by, he pushed his torso away from the wall, but did not bow.

Frith said, "This is the lady Æthelflæd. You should bend your knee."

The young man sniffed. "I know who she is."

"If that is true, why were you not in the hall last night to make her welcome?" Frith took a step closer to him. "And since you were not in the hall, the lord will want to know where you were. Indeed, he will be more than ready to hear of your whereabouts."

"Then there is no need for me to waste my breath speaking to you." The youth peeled himself fully from the wall and walked off.

Frith turned to Teasel. "My lady, I am sorry for the slight. He will be made to pay."

She gave a dismissive wave. "It is no matter." She

stared after the young man, who seemed so familiar to her. No, not familiar, more that he reminded her of someone, but how could he, when she had never before met a man with such red hair? "Who is he?"

"That is Brihtsige." Frith's tone suggested an exasperation which was born before this day's insult.

"And who is Brihtsige, who makes you wroth?"

Frith ran his hand across his bearded chin. "He is a youth who believes that Lord Ethelred has no right to Mercia. When Burgred was king, Ceolwulf came and shrewdly or unwisely," he laughed, "Choose which way you want to think on that one. Shrewdly or unwisely, threw in his lot with the Vikings and took the king-helm. Burgred fled. He had kin, one of whom was Lord Ethelred's friend, Beornoth. But when Ceolwulf died, Beornoth gave up his right to the kingship and, along with every other man in Mercia, named Ethelred as the man to wrest his kingdom from the Viking grip. Beornoth had a right to be king, but bowed to a stronger fighting-man. A week before your wedding, he retired to a monastery."

Aware since childhood of the alliterative names of the English royal houses, Teasel needed no prompting. "And Brihtsige is kin to Beornoth?"

Frith nodded. "You miss little, my lady. He is his son. And Brihtsige burns with a twofold flame. Not only does he feel cheated of his rights, he does not think that Mercia should ever clasp the hand of Wessex. You will find no friend in Brihtsige, I am sad to say." He glanced over to the royal enclosure and raised his arm in a wave of greeting. "There is my wife. I said that I would help her this morning to heave the big loom away from the weaving-shed wall, but with your leave I will bring her to you this afternoon. Alyth will be more than willing to be your new woman."

She nodded to give her permission for him to leave, but he hovered on one foot, hesitating. "My lady, will you walk with us? For I fear that there might be others as uncouth as Brihtsige."

But she waved him away and he showed her a full, deep bow and ran with easy long strides until he caught up with his wife. Teasel sighed. His full given name, Æthelfrith, meant Noble Peace. This was all one needed to know about such a man. Benign and calm, always on the side of truth, he and men like him would be the glue that held Wessex and Mercia together far more than kings or princes, whose bonds were sealed with symbolic weddings. Watching him walk off, his hand lightly touching the small of his wife's back, she longed to feel that same assurance, in such a minuscule gesture, that all would be well.

But as she listened again in her mind, she heard his words more clearly. Brihtsige might have spoken rudely, but he showed only the same contempt that she had seen on every face that she had looked upon this morning. This was not the reverential country of her mother's memory. If she could turn her nose up at mere Mercian smells, then why should the Mercians not turn their backs on a West Saxon princess? *My sweet Lord, how deep the hatred lies. I never thought.* Even among those who were not, like Brihtsige, openly hostile to Ethelred's leadership there had been naught more than a dutiful nod of the head. Eardwulf and Eadnoth, the Goat and the Little Alfred, the men whom she had met the previous evening, had all stared at her with little more than disdain. Hard enough to be in a foreign land against her will, harder still to be where she was not wanted. And this thought, striking her for the first time, smote her hard.

As if he had heard her thoughts, her beloved Alhelm appeared alongside her.

She stared at him as her cheeks warmed and her pulse increased. *Where have you been? Why were you not at my wedding? Did you stay away the better to ease your pain even though it made mine worse?*

He said, "It will be hard for you, at first, while they know you only as a daughter of Wessex. But Frith will see to your every need."

"He cannot see to all my needs." She bit her lip. Why

did he always pull forth words which she had not considered before they were out of her mouth? And why, when in less than two days she had become wed, been attacked and lost her maidenhood, why only now did she find herself blinking back tears?

"My lady, all here is new and it will take you some time, but things will not seem so hard once you begin to feel at home."

She had enough self-control to refrain from berating him for breaking her heart. Instead, the overwrought child, having gathered and nursed every perceived slight, shouted at the injustice of it all. "Home? How can I ever feel at home when none will make it so for me? When I think of all that I have lost or left behind; my mother's houses, the kingdom that I have known as home, my father, my kin…" Her voice, having risen to the pitch closest to sobs, fell away.

He laid a hand on her arm. Wishing only to savour the warmth of his touch, she struggled to heed his words.

He said, "There are many here who could speak your words. My lord Ethelred, to name but one, would tear off his sword arm to have back what is gone."

I need not be reminded how a new wife will stifle his ways. "Would that we could all have the freedom of staying unwed."

Now he looked at her and his face was devoid of all light, as if, in the dark, someone had carried a candle past him and left him once again in the shadows. He released her arm. "It is not what you have lost, but what you will not give up which might hinder you in the days to come." He turned as if to go, but balanced momentarily on one foot, tilting his head first to one side and then the other. Again, he pivoted on his supporting leg and made to leave, but span round again and said, "But I will be here, to do whatever I can to ease your worries. I would lay down my life for you."

"There you are." Ethelred, his clothing bloodstained

and grimy, strode up to them and took Teasel's hand. He lifted her fingers to rest on his forearm and held his other hand over them. "I have the bishop of Worcester in the hall. He has letters from your father and he has also said that he will bless us during a service in the minster."

She felt the pressure on her hand, a firm grasp where a moment ago she had felt Alhelm's gentle touch. If Ethelred had known what had passed between them, she might have interpreted this strong grip as deliberate, territorial. Probably he did not know his strength. Odd, because he had certainly known to be gentle with her the night before.

"Come; the bishop says he will bless us tomorrow, but you should meet him first." Before Ethelred led her away, he nodded at Alhelm. "You should be there, tomorrow, for you missed being witness to our wedding..."

Teasel looked up and saw that the muscle in his cheek was twitching.

"And I will see you at the witanagemot the day after that."

Alhelm stared, unsmiling, back at him. "My time is yours now, my lord. Lately I have been busy tending something of great worth, but I am back now." He glanced down at Ethelred's tunic. "Is it done?"

"It is. Most of it was seen to last night, but today it has been finished."

Teasel followed Alhelm's gaze and noticed his tiny nod as he observed Ethelred's bloody clothing. She could only wonder what it was that they were hinting at.

Ethelred pulled lightly on her arm and she walked with him, but dared to twist her head back to catch one last glimpse of Alhelm. She was in time to catch his heavy-lidded blink as he looked first down at the ground and then away from her, and she sensed that whilst they might have been alluding to whatever caused the bloody clothes, their words to each other had been as double-edged as their swords.

113

AD888

Capricious clouds had been playing across the sky all morning and now they danced away again to allow a bright block of light to beam into the hall. The whitewashed walls took on a heavenly glow and the gold plate on the head table glistened. A young warrior, seated on the bench by the central hearth, was whittling away on an arrow shaft. A small child, watching, tugged on the warrior's leg binding. The young man scooped up the toddler, sat him on his lap, and allowed him to examine the carving. Seated on the longest of the mead benches, where all the older, doughty, warriors sat, Eadnoth and Eardwulf flanked Uncle Wulf and punctuated their lively debate with percussive thumps of their fists upon the table, adding to the rhythm by crashing their ale cups down after each drink and embellishing the performance with loud belches.

Teasel picked up the stiff piece of vellum lying in front of her and held it to the light. She ran her finger over every mention of her name but then she shook her head and placed the document back on the table.

Bishop Werferth smiled, nodding at the charter. He did not move his arms to gesture; he never did. Amidst the arm-waving and noise of the witan meetings, he always sat with back straight, commanding attention when he required it merely by standing up and waiting for quiet. "Would you like me to read it to you?"

"I thank you for the offer, but no. I witnessed the gift of land to your church here in Worcester, and it was the first time that a gift was made in both mine and my husband's name. I will not forget that, even if I cannot read the words when they are written down."

The bishop took a step nearer the table. "If you look, you will see. There is Ethelred's name, and mine, and down below, it speaks of the church of Saint Peter."

She sighed. "You must think me such a dull-wit, but although my father was keen for us all to be taught, my learning was broken up by so much moving and hiding from the heathens. And I only ever learned the English; I am but a woman, you see."

Werferth sat down and placed his hands lightly on the edge of the table. "There is no shame in it. Mercian learning has suffered too, with each Viking raid on our churches. He smiled. "And, although he was an outstanding scholar, Lord Ethelred would oft-times use his quick wits to wriggle from his lessons. Once, there was a loud bang outside the window, a tree falling, I think, or maybe far-off thunder. Ethelred told the young monk teaching him that it was another blast-blaze from the mill and that he should run and see if help were needed." The bishop chuckled. "It happens often enough, so the monk believed him. Ethelred then went off fishing. It is a wonder that he ever learned to read." He patted her hand. "But I have seen how hard you work alongside your husband in the witan. Others have seen it too, for only yesterday Bishop Deorlaf said the same to me."

The dearth of kindness shown to her recently left her curiously ill-prepared to accept his compliment and she put her hand up to silence him. "You are both men of the Church; you have to be kind. The truth is," she glanced around the room and, as usual, found that many folk had been scrutinising her, but turned away as soon as her gaze met theirs. "The truth is that I have much yet to learn, besides my reading. I am no longer a child." She fumbled for the parchment and squinted at the neat script, willing herself to read and understand the Latin. If she concentrated, perhaps she would be distracted from the discomfort. Her mother's predictions of a fruitful womb had proven as ill-founded as her pronouncements on the golden land of Mercia. No, she was indeed no longer a child, discovering instead just how long a woman will bleed after a miscarriage.

Werferth sat quietly by her side. The only indication of his presence was a small rhythmic whistling with his every exhalation. The door banged open; Teasel scrabbled to her feet, but Werferth only turned his head and tilted it, enquiring.

A messenger hesitated in the doorway, one hand still on the door, one foot hovering to come forward. "My lady, forgive me, I had not known that you would be in here." He folded into a deep bow.

Teasel stepped towards him. "Think naught of it. Stand up and let me see you. It is Tidulf, is it not? You are one of my father's thegns. You have word from Wessex?"

Tidulf reddened round the neck. "Yes, my lady, but my letter is for the bishop of Worcester. All others have been handed to Lord Ethelred."

She beckoned him into the room, concerned not to let the disappointment linger too long, too visible, on her face.

Werferth held his hand out and took the proffered letter. He scanned it quickly and looked up to smile at Teasel. "Your father begs me go to Wessex to speak about how best to teach reading and writing to all who dwell there."

She stretched the forced, fixed smile and gave a brittle laugh. "So, it is not only me who is lacking in that way?"

As she spoke, she turned to see why Tidulf had bent to the floor again. Ethelred had stepped through the doorway and was followed by Alhelm, Frith, the Goat and Little Alfred.

"Up, up," Ethelred said, striding past the messenger and nodding to Teasel. "My dear, it is merely proof that Mercian learning is the best and your father acknowledges this. Why, we even have a Mercian now as archbishop of Canterbury. We are spreading out; maybe we will take over all of the English kingdoms?"

Werferth bowed his head. Looking up, he said, "Bear in mind, my lord, that Alfred also has the monk, Asser, with him, who is, as we all know, a Welshman. For all we know, he might have the same dreams for the Welsh?"

Ethelred laughed and Teasel marvelled still at the change that it wrought. This man had been so solemn when she first saw him and so dour at their wedding. Now, his cheeks lifted and his eyes glittered, but his smile was not for her, and he turned away to join the debate among the doughty warriors. She cast another glance around the hall and saw them all, exchanging light-hearted insults and slapping each other on the back. Growing up in the courts of Wessex, she had accepted the familiar vision of sombre faces. Now she realised that Uncle Wulf, so loud and brash when he was with her mother, was not unusual nor out of place in his native Mercia. Were the West Saxons too sober, too willing to allow their cares to weary them? Or were these Mercians too blind to the dangers all around? But then of course, they had not suffered, as a nation, the way the West Saxons had. If these folk had lived through the fear, the terror that had coloured her childhood with its vile hues, they would not laugh. Not if they knew of Alfred's struggle, every new incursion threatening to extinguish his hopes of a free island. She looked again at the small child, being dandled on the young man's knee. Shifting in her seat, she was uncomfortably reminded of her own, dashed hopes.

She felt the pressure of Werferth's hand upon her own, his skin cold but dry, his grip gentle but reassuring.

He leaned in to direct his words to her ear. "You should seek something to soothe your soul. I have my bees; is there something you could do, somewhere you could go,

117

other than the church, when you seek true stillness?"

Something to give me purpose, he means. Somewhere where I will not see how my lord shuns me. She shrugged. "He is so much less, gloomy, when he is not with me. When I see him now, with them," she shook her head. "At our wedding, with my father he was so glum."

She felt movement and turned to see Werferth chuckling softly under his breath. "He is in his own home, with his own folk. You should also bear in mind that your lord, much like your father, has had to keep both his eyes on the fight, but now, with London won back, there is a little time to soften the eyes and let the lips take over, to smile, talk and drink. And there is something else that you should know. Lord Ethelred is," he leaned in again to whisper, "Shy. He was ever thus. Even with Lady Mildrith."

Turning fully, staring, she belatedly recovered her manners and closed her gaping mouth. After all, why should it be a surprise that a man of Ethelred's age had a past? She repeated the name. "And where does she live?"

Werferth's brows moved together and a furrow appeared across his forehead. "My lady, do you not know? But then, why would you, for he would never speak of it; has never spoken of it." He looked around and then lowered his voice again. "Some years ago, King Ceolwulf called all the men of Mercia to fight the foe in Wales. Ethelred rode out with Alhelm's father, Sigulf of Shrewsbury. Alhelm, too young to go, stayed behind with Ethelred's father who was too old and lame to fight. While they were gone, the Vikings came, in the night, bent on thievery and murder. The hall was set alight; Mildrith and Ethelred's father were within. Alhelm hurried into the flames, but could not save them. He was, himself, badly burned. He bears the scars to this day."

Teasel, numb, could only nod. She had seen those scars, that day in the woods. She managed to turn her face to look upon the group of younger men. Frith was goading Eadnoth, who needed little more spinning to send him into a dizzy rage. Alhelm cuffed Frith round the head and Ethelred sat, his own head back, his mouth stretching to let out a full-throated laugh.

"Little wonder, then, that they are bound by strong ties." Her voice sounded odd, not echoing in her head as usual, but falling dull into the air.

"Stronger than you think. There is yet more to this tale, for while Ethelred was away fighting, he had put himself between Alhelm's father and an axe. Ethelred, too, carries a scar, but Alhelm's father lived."

Did he have a scar? She had not seen it, but then the bedroom was always dark, and she had not reached out to touch, or feel, only yield.

She stared again at the fighting-men. Alhelm was seated beside Ethelred, hands drawing shapes on the table to illustrate his points as he talked. His soft blond curls lapped around his jaw line and even though he was focusing, the beautiful soft roundedness of his face remained unlined. Ethelred interjected occasionally, adding his own refinements to the imaginary sketches and using hand gestures to point out the flaws in Alhelm's ideas. When Ethelred leaned forward, their shoulders touched. How foolish she had been. No person on earth would ever get between them. Not now, not after what had passed. She was beginning to understand, but the image of Alhelm as heroic champion, striding into a conflagration, did nothing to diminish the glow of the candle that burned in her heart for him.

"Like this, do you see?" Alhelm had hold of Frith again, but this time he was pretending to punch him full in the face.

Teasel strained to listen, as Alhelm described a fat fellow in Gloucester, telling his hearth-companions that the man's face resembled a punched pillow.

Ethelred chuckled. "I wish I had seen that. I have not met the man, but I will know him if ever I see him. And he will wonder why the mere sight of him makes me laugh when I do."

Wulf said, "Fat can be good. In the hunt, a fat beast would be slower."

Frith leaned forward and stroked Wulf's belly. "Whoever saw a fat beast? All I can see is a fat man."

Wulf bellowed a laugh. "Well then, I must let it all down with ale." He held up his cup and waited for it to be refilled. Next to him, Eadnoth and Eardwulf began to raise their voices, but their tone was sharp, not jovial.

Eadnoth said, "It was not. My father was there and he told my mother..."

Eardwulf slammed his fist down on the table. "Oh, your father was it? Known for his good word? Ha! I do not think so. It was my father who saw it and he said..."

Frith laid his hand on Eardwulf's arm and held it down on the table.

Ethelred leaned forward and said, "My friends. Sour words make sour ale. Your fathers are dead, and we mourn them both. But, being dead, they cannot settle this for us. Let us not waste good drinking time."

It was said quietly, but every man had listened. Within seconds, the older men were hugging each other and joining back in with the laughter and jokes.

Bishop Werferth patted Teasel's hand and stood up. He went over to the mead bench and touched Ethelred's arm. Werferth bent and whispered into the lord's ear and Ethelred's smile dropped away. He stood up and walked over to Teasel.

He held out his hand. "Come; walk with me."

The smile had left as quickly as it came; a brief ray of warmth that left a cold expression behind, much like the racing clouds that had allowed a glimpse of sunshine. It was plain that he had no real desire to leave his hearth-mates and spend time with his wife instead. Knowing this, she hesitated, and, unsure what to say, said nothing.

Werferth, walking back to the dais with light, measured steps, swept her cloak from her chair-back and draped it around her shoulders. She thanked him with a smile and followed Ethelred from the hall.

They walked in silence towards the gateway and out onto the path beyond. He said, "I have had tidings from your father. Your aunt has died in Italy."

She did not stop, but walked with head bowed. "I am sorry to hear it. I was fond of her when I was a child in her house."

"She had a sad life."

Teasel sighed. "My mother would say of her that she, at least, was a queen." She tried to bring to mind her recollections of King Burgred's wife, but all memories were faint and the only thing she could recall with certainty was the smell of the queen's perfume.

Ethelred touched her arm. "This way."

He stepped off the path and she followed him into the wood, where swathes of bluebells were hiding their bright cheeriness from the outside world, catching the early spring sunshine before the canopy leaves opened out and drenched them with shade. Accustomed now to the silence of Ethelred, where speech only punctuated the pauses and not the other way round, she settled her stride to a gentle stroll and found her thoughts returning to the last queen of Mercia. Poor woman, to die in exile, alone. Teasel felt closer to her aunt at that moment than ever before; news of her death brought her nearer and at a time when Teasel, predicted never to be a queen, held that title in all but name. She was lady of the houses where her aunt had held sway and Teasel smiled at the thought. Her father had promised to write to her aunt and tell her of her niece's wedding, so perhaps, at the end, she knew and it would have comforted her.

Ethelred, no doubt assuming that she was grieving, lifted a hand and squeezed her shoulder. His pronouncement on the dead woman's sad life would be his only words on the subject. Just as his only comments on her miscarriage had been the occasional enquiry after her health.

121

She chose not to take this as a slight, grateful that at least he had not castigated her for losing the child. She glanced sideways at him. Acceptance of her circumstances had been seeping into her bones slowly, month by month, sitting alongside her love for Alhelm but never pushing it away. It had helped to think upon the new life growing within her, but now that hope was gone. Ethelred's company was dull, but bearable. Bishop Werferth's assertion that her lord was merely shy would have been a comfort and a plausible explanation, but now she knew of Ethelred's terrible loss and she had not the skills to know how to react. Their marriage was such a formal affair that she was not even sure if she should mention it to him. *Besides, if he has lost a wife whom he loved, then what hope for me? He is not shy; most likely, he hates me for even having to be here.* Best, she decided, to continue with her quiet obeisance, performing her duties as wife and lady. At least she would leave him no cause to upbraid her. She would become expert now in subjugating personal longing, expediting her duty with her special smile. *Aunt*, she thought, *you may yet look down and be proud of me.*

She walked with him out of the wood, passing clumps of greater stitchwort at its edge, and onto a grassy path which led the way up a gentle slope, cutting a route between two meadows. The grass there was interspersed with buttercups, clover and yarrow. Below them, to the left, the ruins of a burned out church stood host to creeping ivy, wayward grass and birds' nests. Under Teasel's feet, delicate ribwort plantain encroached onto the path and Ethelred stooped to pick two spikes of the white flowers. He handed them to her. "There is nowhere more lovely than this at springtime," he said.

Lovely, with those charred, crumbling walls below them? A small, devil-propelled version of her inner self wanted suddenly to walk alone in life, instead of always alongside another. It was no good his trying to be nice to her now, and she felt a compulsion to push him away. "We have these in Wessex, too, my lord. My brother, Edward, often brought them to me. Edward and I saw many sights in Wessex that stole our breath. Mercia has naught that we do not."

He stared at her as if without comprehension. "But I know this; I know *here*." He walked on again, but looked over his shoulder and said, "Besides, you will not have Edward so near from now on and will need to loosen those ties now."

She followed him up the hill and he unclasped his cloak to spread it on the ground for her. She thanked him and sat down beside him, where they stared out across the countryside below. Lambs wobbled to keep up with the grazing ewes and curlews swooped up and then low, searching, she thought, for nesting sites. A curl of smoke rose from a shepherd's hut. She sniffed and picked at the flowers in her hand until her fingers became sticky. She saw naught that she could not find in her homeland. Fields were fields, were they not, unless he knew of some that were blue? And why should she think of cutting the ties that bound her to Edward? These folk, and Ethelred himself, expected her to become instantly Mercian while all the time not accepting that she was a West Saxon.

He was lost in thought and she knew that he did not want to be rescued and so she waited, until he nodded, sounded a small "Hmm" of satisfaction, and stood up. He offered his hand and she took it, trying to stand up in such a way so as not to dislodge the linen wadding between her legs.

They retraced their steps, returning to the town by way of the wood. One tree was very much like another, but this little wood seemed familiar. A well-worn path cut between the ancient trunks and forked off further ahead. Teasel grasped Ethelred's arm and said, "There is a stone, over there, a tall one. At least, I think there was a stone, once."

He led her along the right-hand branch of the fork to the eastern edge of the wood. "Is this the one you mean?"

Surrounded by clumps of wild ramson leaves, and

protected by the last line of trees, a burial stone stood like a sentinel, its carvings deep and sharp, sheltered as it was from the excesses of the weather.

"It marks the burial of a great Mercian lord," he said. "He died fighting the Vikings. The field where he fell was a long way from Mercia but his last wish was to be brought home."

"Yes, but, it means that I have been here before. For otherwise, how would I have known?"

He shrugged. "With your aunt, I would guess. When you were little."

He turned to find their original route but she stared at the gravestone, shaking her head. Embryonic memories unfurled in her mind, opening up like the wings of new-hatched chicks, of games played among the bluebells, of hiding behind trees and the threat of a scolding if she were late home. Yes, she had been here before and the closeness she felt to her aunt was not because of circumstance, but the abiding, if unrecognised, memory of happy, carefree childhood days. She knew this place. She opened her mouth to speak, but he had gone on ahead. No matter; she only wanted to say that she now had an inkling of what it was he felt about his homeland. How memories could linger, even when unacknowledged, how the longing for home could last beyond a lifetime, and how a man could travel many miles to fight the heathen who threatened his freedom, but still want to be laid beneath his own soil. She laid the flowers on the grave and walked quickly to catch him up, warmed by her new-found understanding.

It took only three more steps before the realisation thumped into her head, as if the fat pillow-man had rolled down the hill and crashed into her. Smugly noting that Ethelred's beloved Mercia was blighted by an ugly ruined church, she had not afforded any significance to what she had seen beyond the burned out shell: holes in the ground where once had been upright timbers, lines carved in the fields where once had been wooden fences. A whole village had once stood there and had been destroyed. By chance, perhaps; an untended candle or a spark from a hearth-fire? There was comfort to be had from that thought, but she knew the truth. Vikings had been here. Vikings had razed a village, plundered its church and set it alight. How could she have thought that the Mercians knew naught of fear? Her own dear dead aunt had to flee from the heathens, after all. Why should the Mercians not be as fiercely jealous of their independence as Wessex, when they too were fighting for their very lives? Poor uncle Burgred had lost his king-helm and his kingdom; Wessex at least had benefited from five members of the same royal house, reigning one after the other. Succession struggles, Viking raids; Mercia had, indeed, suffered. She had carried her hurt and perceived suffering, turning her haughty nose away from the pig smell, little knowing that Mercia was mourning. Mercians were mourning. She had spent so many nights lying awake through fear when she had no idea what that truly meant. And when she heard about Mildrith, about Alhelm and his father, her first emotion had been self-pity. No wonder Ethelred hated her. She was naught but a silly child.

He should have waited for her, he knew that, but surely he had given her enough time? Not just this day, but since she came to Mercia as his bride. That first night, she had been scared, twice over, but he had admired the way she tried to hide it. He'd been careful not to hurt her and then he'd backed away, giving her time to grow accustomed to her new home. But now it was she who stayed away whenever possible. Werferth had warned him that she knew about Mildrith and so he had walked with her, away from the rowdy members of his witan, to give her the chance to speak to him about it. Talking of her own loss, of the death of her aunt, might have given her an excuse to speak to him of mourning. He might have answered her questions, had she had any to ask. He would not have minded talking for the first time what happened, for it was with him every day anyway. If she had worries, he could have eased them, could have told her that this was just how it was; he lived with it every day. But no, she had not chosen to speak. A loveless marriage could still have its uses, companionship being the main one. No man wished to live his life alone, unless it was to answer God's calling. Another voice by the hearth and another warm body in the bed was rarely a bad thing. Yet she refused to offer even this much. Scarcely a word passed her lips, and she looked too frequently upon the wrong lord. Did she think that it went unnoticed? The trick, as he could have told her, was to carry the hurt where others could not see it.

Nearing the enclosure fence, he saw Frith's wife. It reminded him that his wife was also mourning another recent loss, a being whose life had not yet been lived. He called out. "Lady Alyth."

Alyth approached him, put her hands on the fence and bobbed her head.

"I would have you be more than a waiting-woman to my wife; I would have you be a friend. And I would have her be more than the woman wed to the lord. Can a way be found?"

Alyth smiled. It lifted her plump cheeks and brought creases to sit around her pretty green eyes and for a ridiculous second he begrudged Frith his great fortune.

She said, "I will do what I can."

Teasel walked back to the hall, stamping her feet like a child wishing someone to notice its sulk. It was easier to hide her embarrassment; she was cross with herself and so walked as if cross with others. But there was no Edward to tease her out of her mood and give her a few moments of patient understanding while she forgave herself, and to allow her the time to buy back her dignity. She was alone.

Rounding the corner from the church, she saw Bishop Werferth and he beckoned her. She greeted him outside the brew-house and he held a cup out to her. She took the proffered drink and sipped it.

"What is wrong, my dear; do you not like it? Have you never tasted mead before?"

Having taken in enough air to shout, she now exhaled heavily. She must not be rude to the bishop. "I had thought it to be wine. It was a shock. And yes, I have tasted mead. We have such things in Wessex and as you must know, I am half West Saxon." She had failed in her effort not to be discourteous, for this last comment had been delivered with the whining tone of affronted pride.

He smiled. "You might wish to say instead that you are half Mercian. But what do you think of the brew? This is made with honey from my bees."

She licked her lips, considering the sweet liquid and its aftertaste.

"What is it; did you not like it? It is good honey that my little striped friends make for me."

She shook her head. "No, it is good. But…" Since her arrival there had been few ceremonial meals and she had not supped with mead for many months. And now she recalled the sweet-smelling breath of the man who tried to abduct her on her wedding day. He had been drinking mead, and as far as she knew, the Vikings did not make the brew. Were those men, those attackers, Mercian? If so, her husband had many, many more worries than she had thought. *He does not need a sad, lovelorn child adding to his woes.* Thank goodness, then, that she had resolved to stay out of his way.

AD889

Gloucester

Spring was coming; there was strength in the early morning sun and the trees and hedgerows quivered constantly as the birds flew back and forth amidst the flurry of nest-building. The beasts were back out in the pasture and soon there would be fresh milk to drink for a while before, later in the summer, the process began of turning the glut into cheese for the winter months. She smiled to recall that when she first came here, she assumed that Mercian habits might be different and was left feeling foolish when the dairyman explained patiently that they, too, turned the milk from the cows into butter and used the creamier sheep and goat's milk for cheese. Teasel felt herself blush at the memory as she walked across the small sward between the hall and the clutch of sleeping-bowers. The tanner's son was sitting on a stool outside his father's workshop, working on the intricate decoration to a sword-belt. Teasel felt sorry for the wool-carders, who had to sit and work inside to dress the wool. It was the sort of morning to cheer the soul and she was glad to be abroad. Having stepped around the ladies who sat weaving their baskets she waved to the wood-turner, who had set up his pole-lathe at the far end of the yard, where the sun's rays could reach his back, unhindered by obstructions such as house roofs. He went back to his task, turning the unseasoned wood on the lathe and she walked on towards the hall. The reeve strode from the bake-house and held up a hand. Teasel waited for him.

He puffed as he walked, and began to speak even before he stopped to stand in front of her, arms pointing at the wood-turner. "What is he doing? I have need of more boards and benches."

She laid a hand on his arm. "I will call the tree-wrights to you. Speak to them about it. How are the fences?"

"They are all mended, my lady. But the hayward's wound is no better and it hinders his work."

She fumbled for the keys at her belt. "I will unlock the store." While she clanked the keys, finding the right one for the locked spice boxes, she tried to recall the treatments for dog bites. No doubt they had already made a salve from boiled burdock and butter. Sometimes the application of bruised betony would soothe the wound. Plantain might work. But no, there were no expensive spices that would help. "Never mind," she said, "I will go and see him and then we will think about the best way to heal the wound."

She knew that the reeve still had other work to do, but he seemed reluctant to leave, shuffling from one foot to the other and fingering the hem of his tunic. She looked beyond him and saw Ethelred walking towards them. She spoke to the reeve. "Is aught amiss?"

He scratched at the back of his neck. "My lady, I need, daily, to be in the stores, but you are the key-holder."

She shook her head. "How did you fare before I came here?"

"There was no lady then."

She said, "I understand. But I have to hold the keys. It is what it means to be the lady of the hall."

The reeve stood with legs parted, as if to plant his feet. Did he think she was intent on barging him out of the way? He was letting her know that he would not give ground, but surely he must understand, particularly in the presence of Lord Ethelred, that neither could she?

Ethelred stepped forward. "Why do you not agree to meet every day, say, straight after sunrise? My lady can then unlock the stores for you and you can take what you need for the day's work. Then Lady Æthelflæd can shut the lock again."

He walked off, leaving Teasel feeling foolish and the reeve looking as though a bee had stung his tongue.

The reeve bowed. "Then with your leave, I will go and look at the threshing floor and see if the oven and kiln need mending. Better to see to the work now, before we need them."

She nodded and tarried a moment, watching him walk away. She held her face up to catch a little of the sun's warmth. Guilty for the indulgence, she walked on.

In front of the stables, a group of thegns and ealdormen were passing the time before the witanagemot. The elderly ealdormen, Eadnoth and Eardwulf, stood on one side, close to the Goat and Little Alfred, surrounded by their personal thegns, the retainers who rode with them, acting as both bodyguards and servants. They made a point of halting their conversation, turning unsmiling faces towards her and Teasel adjusted her head so that her chin lowered, though she kept her gaze focused on the path ahead. Her mother had been so proud of her Mercian heritage, assuring Teasel that she would be treated like a queen, here where the men had a higher regard for their womenfolk. Ewith's memories were obviously addled. As Teasel approached the group, Eadnoth's thegns, Luda and Wilferth, stood back, one to the left and one to the right and made accentuated, mocking bows. Wilferth said, "My lady," and the thegn Acha snorted as he suppressed a laugh. Another voice, which she recognised as Eardwulf's, rang out above the sniggers. "A freeman may wed a slave, yet his bride will still be a slave. A lord may wed a churl-born woman, yet he is still a thegn and she is still churl-born."

He fell silent, but she knew there was more to come.

"Therefore, it follows that a Mercian may wed a West Saxon, but he is still a Mercian and she will still be a..." If he finished his sentence, she did not hear, for the laughter crowded the air around her ears. Her cheeks felt as though they were on fire, but she kept walking, staring straight ahead. If they were bent on hating her merely for the colour of her blood, she could do naught.

She saw that Frith, her uncle Wulf and Alhelm were over by the gatehouse, while at the same time she became aware that one of the pack of jeering wolves behind her had peeled off and was now loping along just beside her. A sideward glance told her that it was the red-haired Brihtsige. She stayed on her course, refusing to look at him, and tried not to flinch when she felt him come nearer.

"You are right to look upon your path, my lady. There are great men dwelling here upon whom your eyes should never dare to rest."

Despite the punctures to her pride, there was a small pocket of brave indignation left inside her somewhere. "How dare you? When I wed the lord Ethelred…"

"What? You sought to bring Wessex ways to Mercia? To drag us all onto a higher path? Oh, yes, you are a high-born lady, indeed. You hold your nose even higher, as if Mercia is one bad stink. Yet it is odd, is it not, how one thing smells sweet to your nose. But, listen well, lady; that is one bloom that grows higher than you could ever hope to reach, however high you stick that pretty nose in the air."

She looked across and saw that he was shaking his head slowly, his mouth lifted in a mocking smile. He wandered away and she turned on the spot in a slow circle. Ethelred was nowhere in sight. Then she clutched her stomach, for it felt as if her insides had been plucked up into her chest. Despite the heat in her cheeks, she felt cold and all she could hear was the sound of her heart hammering as if it, too, had risen and was now lodged in her ears. They knew. They all knew. She stared, wondering, at Alhelm. No, he would not have told them. She had given herself away; avoiding her husband whenever possible and being stupid enough to assume that her longing glances at Alhelm had gone unnoticed by all others. All others. Ethelred, who had only moments ago helped her with the reeve, must have been struggling daily not to show his distaste for her. A sharp pricking flowed down her nostrils, her throat tightened and her eyes became watery. Afraid to blink, lest the tears fall, she looked into the middle distance. She saw Alhelm slapping Uncle Wulf on the back and heard them both laughing and she straightened her back, sniffed, and began to walk on. A tiny voice of outrage began to whisper in her head, testing its right to be heard. Then as she stalked off in as queenly a manner as she could, it screamed out in her thoughts. *How can it be fair? It was Alhelm who made me believe that he cared for me. Why do they not turn their backs on him, too?* Because he was a lord of Mercia. Because he had proved himself loyal unto death. Because he was more precious to Ethelred than she would ever be.

It was not like the first time. Then, there had been no pain, just bleeding and a small object, unidentifiable as more than a blood clot, which might or might not have been the beginnings of a bairn. The second time she had been more sure of what was happening, feeling a dragging sensation, and a cramping of the stomach, followed by the inevitable bleed and the expulsion of a larger mass. But today there was pain. It burned her with its heat, scraping her insides as if with an antler comb, deep rhythmic scratches that clawed from the top of her swollen belly to the base of her back. Alyth held her hand, saying nothing. Frith's wife was too sensible, too much a true friend, to lie to her. It would not be all right; she was losing this babe too, and there was naught to be gained by saying otherwise.

Another row of sharp pins rose up, pricking and scraping, and Teasel gasped. "It will come, soon, will it not?"

Alyth kept hold of the clasped hand and patted it with her other hand. "I think so, yes. Let me fetch you another drink; your lips are dry."

Alyth went to the table and poured a cup of ale. Teasel

watched her, envying her freedom to move without pain around the room. A curious wave seemed to build in her belly, moving along and down, until she felt pressure on her bowel and understood what the older women meant when they spoke of bearing down to give birth. With two involuntary pushes she sensed that it was over. She lay back and stared at the ceiling. Alyth wrapped something small in a cradle blanket and walked towards the door. "I will tell Lord Ethelred," she said.

Within minutes, Ethelred came to her bower. He sat on the edge of the bed and he took her hand in his.

The tears fell sideways from her face, dripping down and wetting the fronts of her ears, moistening her hair. "I have failed you once more, my lord."

He squeezed her hand tighter. "No, you have not."

She lifted her shoulders away from the pillow. "But you must have a son."

He pushed her gently back down with his free hand, all the while shaking his head. "No. In Mercia we do not always yearn for sons. It is understood that when the time comes, the witan will name the next king, and he might or might not be the son of the last king." He smiled. "And I am not even a king." He leaned forward and kissed her forehead. "It is sad, but it is God's will." He sat up and patted her hand as he let go. "You. You are all that matters. And you must get well soon."

He left her then, and she turned onto her side to curl up. He had been kind to her and again, she was grateful that he had not been wroth with her. Nor would he be, as long as she remained well. His trophy, his key to the fellowship with Wessex, she was useless to him if she were unwell, or dead. Alive, she was as precious to him as his kingdom, for she gave him the means to keep it free. God help her for a poor, barren failure if her father ever cut her, or Mercia, loose.

Alyth came back in, her long blonde plait brought forward over her shoulder. As she re-tied the end, she said,

"Your lord is upset. It is a bitter blow for you both."

Teasel turned her face back to the wall. "For me, yes. For him, no. He told me; I am the thing that binds the tie with Wessex. Children will not matter." And, she thought, he had simply just walked away. How strange that it had been Alhelm who always paid her such close attention, yet the one who really wanted to wed her was the one who showed only indifference to her.

She felt the bed dip as Alyth sat beside her.

"You are wrong, my lady. I have known Lord Ethelred for many years. He grieves this day, believe me." Alyth sighed and leaned over Teasel, touching her shoulder and pulling her onto her back. "You will be out of bed soon enough and then you must…"

Teasel sniffed. "Must what? Forget?"

Alyth sucked her bottom lip. "No, not that. But, well, what did you do when you lived in Wessex? I mean, is there something at which you were skilled, or…?"

The words of the old hayward at Glastonbury came back to her then. *'The last time they fought, you knew it was wise to leave them to it and you came and helped me with the bark from the felled trees.'*

She sat up. "I was good at knowing when to leave the men to their business." She shook her head for she felt as if only now were she coming awake. "So I used to help the folk with the milking and the sowing. I helped wean the bairns and helped to fill the haylofts."

Alyth patted her hand. "Tomorrow, then. And you will feel better in no time."

AD890

Droitwich, Mercia

"They say that the lords Eadnoth and Eardwulf have ridden in to ask Lord Ethelred to settle their newest wrangle." Hild, thegn's wife, picked up her spindle and wound the thread round it to spin once again, allowing it to dangle just above the blanket on the grass where her baby lay, kicking his legs out frog-fashion. "My Wiglaf has gone up to the hall to see if he will be needed as a witness."

Teasel scooped out another handful of soil, pushed another seed into the new hole, and glanced up at Alyth, sitting on a stool beside her. She knew that Alyth would understand why she smiled; it was a true freedom, to be outdoors and away from the politics of the hall. "I am glad not to have to hear any of it, for their shouting goes through me like a hammer onto a wooden peg."

Alyth gave a small chuckle and reached over her expanded belly to pick up the scissors and cut the thread on her mending. "You do not need to tell me, for the light in your eyes is brighter when we are here."

Teasel nodded. "I believe it. Besides, it will be the same as always. Eadnoth will stick out his chest and bellow, Eardwulf will fill the air with his loud oaths and curses and my lord will hear them out, and then hush their din with but a few wise words." She laughed and pressed her fingers into the cool soil once more, pushing until the loosened clods yielded no more and compressed and compacted against her

135

probing. She held the grin while she worked, picturing their frustrated splutters when Ethelred, with his quiet quick wit, burst their pride with his sharp wisdom.

Alyth put aside the torn under-shirt and leaned forward as much as her bulk would allow. "You are even more carefree than usual, though. What is it that makes your grin linger?"

"Oh, 'tis naught. I was thinking," she shook her head. "I cannot say." *For I have found myself thinking with kindheartedness upon my husband and it is shaming that this is the first time I have done it.* "You are right. Being here is good for me."

Hild snorted. "Ah, will you bide a while longer, then, my lady, and help me with the washing; help me fetch the wood ash for it, and then make ready with the roots for dyeing, the madder root, the..."

"Yes, if it will lessen your burden."

Alyth and Hild laughed.

"What is it? I mean it; if I can help, I will."

Hild sent the spindle down once more. "I know, my lady. But I was only teasing. Forgive me."

She accepted the joke with good grace. It was cheering to hear the sound of Hild's laughter, as the older woman emerged, like spring from winter, from a period of mourning two of her children. Teasel thought that perhaps her own spirits lifted when she was away from the hall simply because out here, with the folk, she was reminded that they suffered hardships far worse than miscarriage, or being shunned by the hearth-thegns. Working alongside them, she could learn, as they did, to make the best of her situation and it gave her solace.

Teasel resumed her sowing, hollowing out the loose soil and pressing the seeds deeply into the earth. "These will grow in no time, you'll see. And then you will have your wort-bed near enough to the cooking-fire without having to walk so far. Whenever you need some chervil, dill or feverfew it will be here for you." Head down, she continued to speak whilst planting. "You will need to spread a little water on these for a day or two but they should take well. This is good earth. You will…"

Two crows flew down, audaciously attempting to pick up what she had just sown. She grabbed at her left shoe, took it off and hurled it at the birds. "Off with you! Hild, you must keep a look out for them, for they will be back." She looked up, wondering why Hild did not answer.

Hild had put down her spindle and Alyth was on her feet, head bowed. She indicated with a sideward glance and Teasel turned to look behind her. Ethelred took two steps along the path and motioned with a wave of his palm that they should resume their tasks. How long had he been standing there? Teasel's mouth went dry. It was bad news; why else would he come himself, instead of sending one of his thegns with a message? But if that were true, then why was he laughing?

She looked stricken and he could only wonder why. He had merely come to tell her that a merchant was at the hall with gossip from Wessex, and to find a moment's peace for himself before the council meeting. Perhaps she thought he would be wroth with her for neglecting the guests up at the hall. Perhaps she was unaware how much he admired her for helping the folk as often as she did. How little they still knew of one another. But instead of reflecting on that sad situation, he felt his grin spreading his mouth open even wider. Kneeling in the flowerbed, she had wiped her forehead but, instead of using the back of her hand she had, with childlike instinct, rubbed with her palm and now stood blinking at him, one foot bare, completely unaware that her brow was covered with dirt. Tendrils of copper hair curled around her face and they, too, were bobbled with bits of soil. He recalled the first time he saw her, sitting on the fence while her brother and cousin clashed swords. Here was a girl who had spent her years wishing to join in, knowing that she couldn't, and learning, instead, to find her own freedom. He looked beyond her, at Hild who was now cradling her wailing baby, and Alyth, whose stomach bulged with the evidence of new life. He felt the disappointment stabbing at his gut and wondered how his young wife could bear to be among them. He took a step towards her. "You have more strength than I thought," he said. He lifted her chin with his forefinger and wiped her brow with his other sleeve, and chose not to disabuse her when she misunderstood him and told him that sowing required no strength at all, really.

Thegn Wulfgar knelt before his lord and held out his right hand. Ethelred placed the symbolic twig onto the man's flat palm. It was the last business of the day and the land gift was straightforward. Ethelred, procurator of Mercia, granted to Wulfgar fifteen hides of land at Walden in Hertfordshire and the boundaries of that land were read out slowly and carefully before all those present bore witness and gave consent. Ethelred topped the witness list, followed by his wife. After them, the bishops; Teasel smiled at Werferth as he affirmed his assent. She stood up, bowed to her husband and walked softly towards the door. Uncle Wulf gave her a wink and a nod, as if reading her thoughts. It was probably obvious to all, but the lady was bored and sought escape.

She had come to hate the silence of a churchyard. That was a shame, for this one was beautiful at this time of year. Brambles curled round the walls and grave markers, showing their small white flowers. Bumblebees droned in and out of the clover and butterflies moved quickly overhead, like the shadow in a blink. Shy sweetbriar and sweet honeysuckle bobbed their fragrant flowers in the gentle breeze. May blossom gave a white softness to the hedgerows beyond the wall and nesting birds darted in and out of their homes, be they stone or wood. If only she had not buried so many bairns; bairns who would never be brought here to be received into the Church. At least she did not have to stand now, as she had only a month ago, smile fixed, while Alhelm walked through the church doors at Shrewsbury with his new bride. His lady was small, with pale skin and slender shoulders. Teasel had hoped that she would not walk too close by her, if for no other reason than that she would feel like a hefty workhorse alongside such a delicate creature. Alhelm had looked like one of the Greek gods whose stories Werferth taught her in his attempts to educate her. His hair was long, resting on his shoulders. His curls bounced blond, kissed by the summer sun. His lovely blue eyes, so pale with their pinprick black pupils, squinted against the brightness and the creases around them deepened as he smiled at his wedding guests. Teasel, unwilling to meet his gaze, had been content to torment herself by giving him only sideward glances and wondering which would hurt more: if he had been happy to wed, or if he had not.

With too many cruel memories lurking among the benign flowerbeds, she took the path to the salt-works instead. Passing by the scriptorium, she smiled at a young novice monk attending to the strips of vellum stretching on their frames. He poured cold water on them, a job which she witnessed often; when a smooth sticky surface appeared, he and his fellow novices would bring their stools out into the sunshine and shave the skins with their little half-moon knives. Nearing the salt-works, she stood for some moments while she smelled the air which reminded her of seaside trips in Wessex. Ethelred could boast all he liked about his precious Mercia, but he had no coastline south of the Wirral to show her and she missed the drying but invigorating sea breeze upon her face. Once, he had had taken her to see the huge wave that washed up his beloved river. Near the full moon in March, she had stood with him by the riverbank and nodded as he pointed out the stillness of the air. A moment later, the leaves had begun to shake and an eerie shriek, like a whistling wind, built up to a frightening volume and the river took on the appearance of the sea as the huge wave rumbled along the water, pushing on towards Gloucester. It was a sight to behold, but it was not the same as the sea. At least here she could smell the salt.

She breathed in deeply, giving silent thanks to God that, after two hard years, the folk had once again survived the hunger gap between the last of the autumn stores and the first of the spring produce.

Turning back towards the centre of the town, she paused by the forge. A group of children had gathered around the smith and his apprentice, who had taken a break from their sweltering work to come out into the yard and were now taking turns to throw horseshoes at a twig planted in the ground. The children cheered them on, shouts of encouragement turning to groans of sympathy when the metal failed to hook round the target, missing by only inches. As Teasel approached, the children fell silent and stood aside to let her through.

Sensing that they were waiting, hoping for words of approbation, she laughed and clapped her hands. "May I?"

The smith grinned through stumped teeth and handed her a shoe. "Here's a lighter one for you, my lady. Aim steady."

She closed one eye as she had seen the bowmen do, and shot the horseshoe towards the target. One end of the arc connected with the twig, sending the shoe spinning round before it landed wide of the mark. One of the children scuttled to retrieve it but she said, "No, no, let me do it." She strode forward to pick it up, bending down to scoop up the u-shape and return to her mark. But as she reached for it, a soft leather boot trapped it on the ground. She glanced up. Ethelred bent down himself, gathered up the shoe and handed it to her.

"So you do sometimes miss your mark, then?" His face was settled into its usual non-alignment, neither angry nor happy. But as he released the metal toy into her hand, she was sure that he twitched a smile before he turned away.

She played a few more rounds before she went to find him. He was seated by the table on the dais at the far end of the great hall. In one hand he held a letter; his other held a drink to his lips, hovering, while he laughed out loud.

As she approached, a servant darted forward to put another cup on the table and a slave boy rushed over with a jug of ale. She sat down and waited until he had poured her drink and then she took a large sip. "I hope I did not make you wroth by leaving the witanagemot early, my lord."

"You did not." He picked up his cup and drank, swallowing several times before setting the empty cup down and signalling for more. He slapped the letter with the back of his hand. "From Anarawd of Gwynedd. You would not believe what that Welsh hawk has done now."

She spoke at the same time. "I grew bored and a little restless. I felt the need to be outside."

His mouth was open and he seemed as if he would tell her of this Welshman, but instead he said, "Come then." He left the drink on the table and stood up, holding out his hand.

She grasped his fingers and allowed him to help pull her up. "Where to, my lord?"

"Let us ride. You are not...?"

She shook her head. No, she could not yet be sure that she was with child again. As if it mattered. She might as well cause a miscarriage as wait for the inevitable to happen.

On the way to the door he paused and looked at the game-board where the pieces remained as she and Bishop Werferth had left them the previous week. He studied the position of the pieces for a moment, then picked up her 'king' and moved it across the board.

"I have been brooding over that for days," she said.

He smiled, winked, and bowed to allow her to leave the hall first.

They had ridden away from the town along a deeply wooded track. His stallion was a stride ahead of hers and she looked at his back for a while, noting, not for the first time, how well he sat in the saddle. His cloak covered his

141

broad shoulders, draped over his straight back and rippled into folds with each rhythmic movement of the horse's haunches. His hair, greying a little now, fell in soft waves around the nape of his neck and there was a broad angle between neck and shoulder. He was relaxed. But, never comfortable astride a horse, despite what she had eagerly once told Alhelm, she was glad when Ethelred suggested they stop by a pond to allow the horses to drink.

Teasel sat by the water's edge. "Look, minnows," she said. Reaching forward until she was resting on one elbow, she slid her hand into the water and held it steady, trying to catch one of the tiny fish. She remembered from her fishing trips with Edward and Thelwold just how long this might take, so she stuck her tongue to the corner of her lips to aid concentration, summoned up all her reserves of patience, got herself comfortable and waited. She knew he was watching her and when she took a moment to look up, she found that he was smiling at her. She grinned back at him and looked down to regain her concentration.

She was so close to the ground that she felt, rather than heard, the hoof beats pounding along the path behind them. By the time she had scrabbled to her feet, Ethelred was by the roadside, sword drawn. She remained where she was, hoping that she was out of sight and therefore at no risk to herself, nor a burden to him. Then she laughed out loud, for the leading horseman was Uncle Wulf. He came ungracefully to a halt in front of his lord, out of breath and belly wobbling. Her smile froze when she saw his companion coming to an equally ungainly halt behind him.

She grew warm, even here among the trees where the sunshine could not reach.

Alhelm kept his gaze upon the road ahead.

Her uncle said, "Young Wulfgar told us of a cousin of his, getting wed this day here in the woods." Wulf leaned out of the saddle and nodded for emphasis. "He says the ale will flow all night, so we are like the hawk to the hare. Coming?"

Ethelred turned to his wife. "We should go to give our blessing, I think."

Praying that they might go at a more sedate pace than the speed which her uncle favoured, she allowed Ethelred to lift her back onto her horse and they rode on, deeper into the forest.

In a clearing they came upon the wedding party. Ribbons waved and flapped from the branches of the tall oaks and in the centre of the glade an archway, woven from withies, had been decorated with garlands of wildflowers. The bride was wearing a similar crown of twisted flowers and woodland greenery. The couple bowed before Ethelred, who laid a hand on each of their heads before entreating them to rise up. The bride's father thrust a dripping wooden ale cup into his hands and they drank a toast. Tumblers turned cartwheels one after another across the floor of the clearing and a whistler struck up a tune, encouraging the younger folk to dance. Ethelred offered his arm to Teasel as they stood watching. Wulf and Alhelm propped themselves against a hollowed tree trunk and nursed jugs of ale to their chests.

Wulf said, "This will all be fresh still, for you. It must feel like yesterday since you were wed. How goes it with your lady?"

Teasel convinced herself that there was a flatness in Alhelm's tone as he answered, his voice even quieter than usual.

"She is well. Life has settled down once more, for it has been longer than you might think."

Wulf nudged him. "Thrill of the hunt died down already, eh? Ready to stalk another are you? Lust for blood up and flowing again?"

Alhelm smiled up at Teasel, but it was no more than a simple silent expression of their common understanding and tolerance of Wulf's verbal excesses. She accepted it as such and managed to return the smile. Once, she might have entertained the notion that he kept his wife tucked away on

143

his Shropshire estates because he was still in love with Teasel, but now, whilst the idea floated across her mind, she acknowledged it as fantasy and let it pass by.

Whatever the reasons, there was no indignant wife looking on and, when Alhelm stood up to join the dance, Teasel was free to gaze upon him without guilt. He was not the same man who had courted her at her father's houses; the absent flattery of pretended interest had left nothing in its stead but at least she did not have to suffer the pain of seeing him with another woman, and for that, she was grateful. He danced as if he knew he were being observed and was the less graceful for it, making self-mocking gestures and grinning at Wulf rather than paying rapt attention to his dancing partner. She watched his blond curls bouncing as he jumped around and felt the inside of her belly lift up as she stared at the droplets of sweat forming by the opening of his tunic, where the collar bones lost their definition in the centre between his chest and his throat. He broke away from the dance, ran back to snatch a mouthful of ale, then, laughing, skipped back into the dance.

Her belly ceased its fluttering and her breathing slowed. She would waste no time examining thoughts, happy merely to watch him as he leaped and laughed. Each time he turned she saw his smile, and the sight was as warming and welcome to her as the first sunshine of spring.

A young village girl skipped up to Ethelred and asked him to dance. She curtseyed low and looked up through a thick mass of unrestrained tawny hair. "Will you, my lord?"

No, of course he would not. *If she seeks to make merry, then she has asked the wrong lord.* But Teasel was left to gape like a fish on the bank while her husband bowed and held out his arm to lead the girl to the circle of dancers. She watched as he turned and jumped, twirling the girl around and then pulling her to him and pushing her out again at arm's length before the dance moved on a step. All the while, he bent his head close to the girl's and spoke into her ear, laughing at her responses. Teasel folded her arms across

144

her chest. How could a man of so few words have so much to say to a churl's daughter?

She flung herself down next to Uncle Wulf and took a mouthful of his ale. "Shy, is it? I would not call a bishop a liar but..."

Wulf took the ale from her, downed a mouthful and wiped his mouth with the back of his hand. "What?"

The music was loud, but she was reluctant to raise her voice. Instead she spoke in a loud, forced whisper. "Werferth told me that my lord was shy. He does not look it now."

Wulf's laugh exploded from his mouth as if some powerful mule had kicked it from within. "Ha! Shy? Never. Young Ethelred always had an eye for the pretty women. Like a fox in a hen house. Well, not so much after Mildrith." He winced and gave her a questioning look.

"I know about Mildrith."

He sighed his relief. "Then I have not misspoken." He chuckled as if the joke were now his alone, to keep and repeat for his own amusement. "Shy, eh? That is a good one." He took another drink. "I have seen more timid boars."

Ethelred had slowed his steps to match the music and looked at the young girl as he held his hand out for her, holding her gaze and no doubt making her feel flattered. Teasel folded her arms across her chest. *I have seen less attentive mother hens.*

She sat back against Wulf's bulk, and reached up to stroke his beard, the soothing habit so old that it required little conscious thought. "He is far less forward when he is with me."

Wulf reached round her head to scratch his nose and then belched. "To me, he has always been as you see him now. He likes to put folk at ease. More so if they are pretty. Now that I think on it, he might hold back with folk whom he does not know, but he knows you, little one, eh?" He nudged her as he had done Alhelm, with, she was sure,

145

exactly the same force.

While she tried subtly to rub her throbbing ribcage, he chuckled again.

"From up here, it feels like an early frost. What is really wrong, my pretty; is it that you fear having a cold bed tonight?"

She opened her mouth, but no words came forth.

Wulf slapped his big paddle of a hand on her thigh. "Cheer up, Little Teasel. If this is the first time you have suffered a night's sleep without him, then be grateful it did not come sooner."

Still her mouth hung open. Perhaps Ethelred had other women from the moment she wed him; she had never considered it. How little she knew of him; had bothered to learn.

She turned to look at her husband, watching him as he leaped with a lightness of step that belied his years. His face, thrust wide open in that rare but attractive smile, banished the deep furrow above his nose. His cheeks, lifted by the upturned corners of his lips, in turn pushed up to draw his eyes half closed, and creased the skin around them.

She wondered if Wulf might have unintentionally spoken a truth; did Ethelred indeed view her as a stranger, was that why he was so cold towards her? She was no wife left at home; Ethelred walked with her, sought her out when he knew she was bored, showed her his river with its peculiar tidal bore and allowed her to accompany him wherever he travelled. He had arranged to have expensive food served at their wedding and she had thought him to be showing off. But perhaps all he really wanted was for her to become part of his world.

He laughed again at some witty remark the young girl simpered into his ear, then he bowed and walked over to the tree stump and sat down beside Teasel. His body radiated its warmth and she found her breathing synchronising with his as he inhaled and exhaled deeply through his mouth. The calming effect made her pause to consider, and she remembered his ability to silence an argument with a few quiet words, and even the air of controlled composure which he spread through the hall on the night of the attempted abduction of his bride. Putting folk at their ease, exactly as Wulf had pointed out.

One of the young men still dancing appeared to stumble over his own feet and turned a half-circle before landing on his backside. Ethelred threw back his head and laughed. Teasel recalled the few moments when she had heard that laughter and realised that it had much to do with the things which Ethelred saw, be it the sight of Edward's wooden-swordplay or a dizzy dancer stumbling to the ground. A half-formed thought about his expression at the horseshoe-throwing made her open her mouth to speak, but Alhelm was approaching and Ethelred had already begun to address him.

"I should leave it to the younger men," he said, still breathing noisily.

She had been about to ask if he would allow her to dance with him, but all that emerged was "Oh."

When he had caught his breath, Ethelred said, "Time to go," stood up and held out his hand.

She glanced again at Wulf, who merely winked and slapped her rump as she stood up. She smoothed her skirts and took Ethelred's proffered arm, grateful that he had not humiliated her further by going off immediately with his new conquest. With her head high and her queenly mask in place, she waited for Wulf and Alhelm to escort her back to the town, but her uncle was caught in a burping fit and was in no hurry to rise and allow her a quick and dignified exit.

Ethelred lifted her into her saddle once more and jumped onto his own mount. "Let us not wait for them," he said, and looked down at Wulf. "He, for one, could do with sleeping it off."

She blinked and then stared at him. "You mean you are coming with me?"

He frowned. "Why would I not be?"

He clicked his tongue and his horse moved off. She followed him, slinking low in her seat as her whole body sagged with sudden and unexpected relief.

Ethelred propped himself on his elbow and looked down at her, wondering. All the way home to Worcester he had mused over what was wrong with the woman. He had suggested that they go along to join in the festivities because he had noticed how she loved to be outdoors and he thought it would prolong the day for her in an enjoyable way. So he could not then fathom why, when he walked over to her, she played with her uncle's beard as if she were still a child, and looked as if she had swallowed a bee.

Now a strand of hair lay like glowing copper across her forehead and he reached over with his free hand to lift it away. He felt the droplets of perspiration which still dotted her forehead. He smiled, for whatever it was that had held her tongue on the journey home, it had not tied her limbs and she had still been willing to come to his bed. Even more so; for this woman who had sulked all the way home, had joined with him in a way that belied her earlier, silent indifference.

She opened her eyes and smiled at him. He pondered this sudden thawing; after sensing the sweet tightening of muscles that told him of her pleasure, he had relaxed his entire body, daring to believe that, in life as in bed, he could let down his guard. Viking activity had faded away to almost nothing; was it possible that they could look forward to a lasting peace, that he could share a battle-free life with a woman who might become his willing companion? With the raiders quiet and his marriage successful, the gainsayers, too, would be silenced. Could he dare to hope?

She wriggled her shoulders and said, "I am sorry that I slept."

He shifted his weight, stretching out his cramped shoulder before leaning again on his elbow. He studied her face. She was almost frowning, as if she intended her words to convey a deeper meaning. Yet he could discern none. He said, "You are free to do as you wish. I am rarely wroth."

She reached up and scratched her nose. "It is a soft bed, my lord. I have oft-times thought so, but wonder if I should have said so before."

He lay back and put his arms up, hands under his head. "There are many words that are better left unspoken."

She turned towards him. "Deeds, then. That must be the way of it."

It seemed that she was offering something else to him along with her body. It was a strange gift, for he could not decide whether it was an apology, a promise, or some statement of intent. But in this night which seemed to herald the end of solitary nights when sleep had hitherto been held at bay by worries of Vikings, insurrection and loneliness, he accepted it gratefully.

Wulf, Eadnoth, Eardwulf and the other doughty warriors were seated on a bench outside the hall, drinking, gaming and arguing. Teasel waited until Wulf looked up and she waved before moving on. The others would not welcome her presence. Beyond the enclosure fence, the thegns Acha, Wilferth and Luda were honing their fighting skills. They threw spears at a stuffed sack and hefted their axes aloft, crashing them together with such a loud clang that she blinked involuntarily with every blow. She noticed that their axe blades, whilst evidently sharp, had none of the intricate engraving that graced the blades of the noblemen's weapons. Her uncle Wulf's, in particular, boasted swirling patterns with twists and turns which began as abstract shapes but ended in depictions of animal heads. By the fence, the thegns' helms lay, only slightly dented but again devoid of any patterned engraving. Acha and Wilferth began a swordfight and Teasel turned one side of her mouth up into what she knew was now a smug, proud smile. Their scabbards were plain, with no decoration, nor were they lined with sheep's wool to prevent rust. As they touched blades and began to swing as if drawing a number eight, she noted that their swords were dull; Ethelred's blade was one of the finest in the land. The only other man whom she knew to possess one of such quality was Alfred of Wessex. The thegns' blades glinted in the sunshine, it was true, but she had seen the reeve polishing Ethelred's sword and she knew its worth, how the weapon had been made from many strands of twisted iron rods which had been heated and beaten together with steel to marry the strengths of each metal. The craftsmanship had produced a blade which carried waves of swirling patterns across and down its length that shimmered as they caught the light, and dazzled. Only the richest, the most successful men, could afford to commission such war gear. A terrifying agent of death, that identified itself immediately on the battlefield, it was also a thing of immeasurable beauty. And they, pale shadows of the man they followed, would never own such a prize. Never would they be as rich, nor enjoy the same social standing. Men would never look up to them in quite the same way. They would not be feted for their skill and cunning and bravery the way men spoke with awe of Lord Ethelred. And he was her husband.

Sitting on the grass outside the chapel, Brihtsige tossed a gold penny from hand to hand, his gaze flicking from one group to the other. Teasel, already insulated by the previous night's rapprochement, felt her blood warming further as her childhood came back and flooded her head with soothing memories. And, despite his ruddy colouring and his occasional harsh words to her, she knew in that moment that Brihtsige reminded her of Cousin Thelwold. Cross-legged on the ground, here was the familiar fidgeting misfit whose misery she felt, but was powerless to ease. Many years ago, she had spurned Thelwold's efforts to comfort her because her heart was aching for Alhelm. She had pushed him away when he needed to feel useful, trusted.

She sat down beside Brihtsige, pulling the folds of her long kirtle around her knees. Thelwold had often been soothed with a loving touch of a hand upon his arm, but this morning all she dared to offer to Brihtsige were words. "Since I came here, I have often felt like I sit outside the hall, looking through the doors at the warmth of the hearth," she said.

He continued to fiddle with the coin, turning it over and over between his thumb and middle finger. "So?"

"I was cursing folks for not trying to get to know me, but all that time, I was guilty of that same crime. I have come to understand that now."

Now she had his attention. He slipped the coin into the purse at his belt and sat forward, twisting his upper body so that he could look directly at her. "How?"

"I think I can tell you, for I believe that you and I both know the coldness beyond the hearth and I would welcome more friendships. My lord and I have reached an understanding, now, and it gives me a little hope for my life here."

She looked up to see Alhelm walking with Frith across the front of the hall. They sat down on the bench alongside the older men, making great play of shoving their bulky-framed elders along and wriggling their younger, thinner backsides into the space. The companionship of the warrior was a bond that no woman would ever experience. Teasel knew that she would never be allowed to step between two hearth-friends and she might as well make the best of a bad situation. Despite her best intentions, her heart had leaped at the sight of Alhelm and it caused her voice to tremble a little. "They will all go back to their own lands tomorrow when the witan is done. You should not sit here on your own; why not come with me?"

He stared at her. "Where to?"

He was still wary of her and she did not blame him, but his guarded expression could not dispel her new found optimism. "I go to make my farewells, for if the men and the drink spend the night together, I daresay that I will not get another chance." Her resolve seemed solid enough, but it was new and untested and she was not sure how long it would last, so when Brihtsige merely shrugged, she moved quickly to the bench by the hall before her new untried bravery dissolved.

Ethelred kicked a stray stalk of straw from his boot. He left the horse-trader in the stables with the horse-thegns, the grooms responsible for his mounts. They would test the horse for him and if they confirmed his thoughts, he would buy it and have it sent back to Gloucester. But for now, let the merchant think he had no interest. Drunken shouts from the direction of the hall told him that some of the men had already gone in to await the start of the witan session. He rubbed his forehead. A land dispute had taxed all the best legal brains in Mercia and was still not resolved and they had but one more day to settle it. He craved just another moment of calm out here in the sunshine, before he entered the realm of darkness and din. He had thought to find her in one of the small gardens which she helped to tend, but wondered if she had gone instead to oversee the food preparation. In front of the bake-house he saw Brihtsige, who hastily withdrew his hand from underneath the skirt of the slave girl standing next to him. She bobbed her head and ducked into the building.

Ethelred beckoned Brihtsige to stand from his bow. "I seek the lady Æthelflæd. Has she been this way?"

Brihtsige shook his head and Ethelred took a step to move past him.

"Although," Brihtsige, as if just waking, sprang away from the wall and stood beside his lord. "I was with the lady earlier."

Ethelred sighed. It had only been the promise of a snatched moment in the sunshine and already the vision was fading from his mind's eye. Why could the man have not said so before? Swallowing his impatience, he tried to keep his tone even and pleasant. "But do you know where she is now?"

Brihtsige shrugged. He examined his nails and did not look up as he spoke, imparting his information as if it were of no importance, but shifting his gaze upwards with the last word. "She went to speak to the lord Alhelm. She said she was guilty of not getting to know him better and that there was something she must say to him before it was too late."

Cushioned by the comfort from her new-found familiarity with Ethelred, Teasel had felt brave enough to say goodbye to Alhelm and hint of something in the way of a more permanent farewell. But by the time she'd reached the bench where he had been standing only moments before, he had gone.

She knew that her temporary courage would desert her if she pursued her quarry, and having lost the bravery born of impulsive whim, she had stopped and sighed. Looking out towards the river she saw him, on the quayside, talking to a boatman. She presumed that he was overseeing the delivery of merchandise and, without any realistic idea of what she was going to do when she got there, she ambled out of the town and down to the river. Perhaps he would see her and talk to her, perhaps not. And so, leaving events to unfold as they might, she kept to the path which would, if necessary, steer her away from the quay and left to the mill, which stood as a reasonable excuse for her presence by the river that day. The sun's rays bounced blinding darts off the surface of the river and Teasel squinted as she approached. Alhelm was deep in conversation, inventory in hand, discussing the quality of the cargo onboard the boat. She had to shield her eyes with a raised hand and could not be sure whether he had even noticed her and so, when she came to the bend in the path which led to the mill, she had no choice but to follow it, or stand before him looking foolish until he chose to speak to her. Unable completely to abandon the enterprise, she walked with poise as she turned and made her way to the mill. Perhaps he had looked up, perhaps he had seen her after all and if he were indeed staring at her back she would walk tall and with grace. Just in case.

She stood for a while outside the mill. Her breathing slowed and her mind was becalmed by the sheen on the millpond. Contained by timber edging, the water was held, still and polished as ice. She rested her foot on the upper edge of one of the planks and looked at the covered chute which took the water away to where it would push against the horizontal wheel below, forcing it to turn. For a moment she mused on how the wheel would fare if it tried to resist. This day was the first of her life in Mercia where she had felt calm acquiescence washing past her, as, like the wheel, she accepted the things that came her way, instead of refusing to acknowledge her circumstances. Happiness might not yet be hers, but after the previous day's revelations, she felt certain that life would ease, for both her and Ethelred. If only she could have conveyed all this to Alhelm, instead of having to pretend some urgent business with the miller. She bit her lower lip. She might have succeeded in making Alhelm believe that she had a reason to be at the mill but it was another matter to think of something plausible to tell the miller. As freemen, the churl farmers would negotiate their own terms, but the lady would not; the reeve would have been here earlier to check stockpiles and convey the town's requirements. With each creaking revolution of the wheel, she thought of ever more outlandish reasons why she would be here in the reeve's stead, as if he had forgotten something on his first visit, but when the story became a tale of how the reeve's leg had been crushed under the weight of a collapsed ox-cart, she smiled and accepted that she had no option but simply to call 'good day' as she walked past before returning to the hall.

Still being careful to act with purpose, she nodded, so that an unseen observer might assume that she had been assessing the efficiency of the wheel or checking the depth of the pond water or even the state of repair of the chute.

She walked briskly round to the door of the mill-house. The sound of the miller's voice, raised in agitation, made her hesitate, with her mouth open but her greeting left unsaid. The miller was imploring someone to leave, and Teasel stepped back, assuming that this other person would appear by the door at any moment. The unwelcome person was impossible to identify beyond his gender, for his voice was soft, his words murmured, and his low tone sent out little more than an audible hum underneath the miller's timorous entreaty.

"I must ask again. Leave, I beg you. And take that away."

A mumbled response brought Teasel a step further forward as she inclined her head and tried to make sense of the interloper's words. Shaking her head, she stood back, once more expecting the stranger to come through the doorway.

The miller shrieked. "No you must not! The flour dust will…"

An unseen force pushed hot augers into her ears and shoved her backwards onto the path. Teasel sat on the ground and stared around in panic. The thunderclap had been louder than any tempest she had ever lived through. But on a day as bright as this, where was the storm? As her senses regrouped and relayed what they knew to her addled brain, she stood up and shouted. "Fire!"

Alhelm and the boatmen came running with pails of water. With a few shouted commands, Alhelm had them all in line and Teasel was second in place in a chain passing buckets of water and throwing them into the burning mill-house. Alhelm stood in front of her and as he turned to take each new bucket, he spoke his thoughts. "What was the miller thinking; did he light a candle in there? Amidst all that flour dust." He shook his head.

"It might not have been the miller. There were two men in there and I think the miller was wroth with the other one." She took the next bucket from the man behind her and coughed as a cloud of hot dusty smoke billowed out of the mill.

Alhelm, eyes streaming, took the pale from her and threw its contents through the doorway. "Then we will look for two bodies. I do not think we are winning here."

But the flames began to shrink, the plumes of smoke rose lower in the air and the water made a comforting quenching noise as he flung it. Alhelm stood still, assessing, and called out to the end of the line. "More water; take it round to the window." He turned to Teasel. "My lady, stand here and keep throwing the water. I will go in and see if I can find the miller."

Teasel nodded and took his place at the front of the line. The heat of exertion added to the raised temperature of the air from the mill and she reached up and ripped off her veil, using it as a cloth to wipe the sweat and muck from her brow.

Alhelm called out to her. "My lady, will you come in? It is safe, for the fire is out."

She stepped into the gloom, edging one foot in front of the other. Blinking until her eyes adjusted to the reduced light, she stood still until she could see Alhelm. He was kneeling by the upright shaft which connected the millstones to the wheel below. Behind him, the piled sacks of milled grain had been stored before distribution. Teasel offered up a silent prayer of thanks that they had been far enough away from the centre of the blast to remain intact. The wooden shaft was charred and Alhelm put a hand out to test the residual heat. Satisfied that it was not still smouldering, he stood up and wiped his hands on his breeches. He pointed to the far wall. "Over there."

Underneath the largest of the windows, as if he had been trying to escape through the opening, the miller was lying on the floor, face to one side, one arm outstretched. Teasel knelt and put her hand against his nostrils, feeling for breath. She shook her head. "I think the blast took his wakefulness and then he breathed in too much of the smoke. There is naught I can do for him." She stood up and made the sign of the cross. "God will tend him now. Where is the other?"

Alhelm pushed sweat-soaked hair from his face. He wiped the back of his hand across his brow, smearing streaks of soot over his forehead. "Lady, I cannot say. There is no-one else here."

She frowned. Had she misheard? Perhaps there had been only one voice, and maybe she had heard naught else but the rumble and drone of the mill machinery.

Alhelm stepped forward. "Maybe he was speaking to someone at the window. Come, lady, the reeve can deal with the body. I will send for him when I take you home."

Outside, the crowd had grown. Folk who had no doubt heard the explosion had come running, seen that the fire was out and now stood and stared at the charred walls of the mill-house. Ethelred was standing at the front of the group.

She waited. He would do naught so silly as to enquire whether she were hurt, for he could plainly see that she was not. He would only ask questions to which his eyes and ears gave no ready answer.

She stepped aside and Ethelred looked from her to his ealdorman, standing behind her. She saw the scene through his eyes; his wife and Alhelm together in the mill, she with her veil off, hair loose. She stepped forward, opening her mouth to tell him that they had not been in the mill together when the flour dust ignited. She turned briefly to Alhelm who gave the smallest shake of the head, enough for Ethelred to know that he was innocent and completely loyal. Even so, Teasel knew that she stood in a dangerous place that posed a greater threat than any blast-blaze in the mill, for Ethelred was not the only witness to her apparent shame, although he alone among the crowd seemed unsurprised to encounter the lady and the ealdorman together in the mill.

Brihtsige, having no better reason for being down at

157

the mill than she, sauntered past the onlookers and addressed Ethelred. "You found her, then?" He smiled as he walked past Teasel and then strolled on, whistling. He found reason to linger on the path, examining what she was sure was a pretended splinter in his palm.

Now she understood that Ethelred was not here because he had heard the explosion but because Brihtsige had told him she was following Alhelm. He might have come running when he heard the noise, but thanks to Brihtsige he already knew whom he would find inside the mill.

Ethelred turned to the side and Teasel saw the muscle twitching in his cheek. His hands were clenched in fists and she knew that however cross he might be with her, he was even more wroth with Brihtsige.

She was hurt by Brihtsige's actions, having tried only that morning to dispel his wariness of her. Why would he and his ilk not accept her, even now? And why seek to goad Ethelred with mischief-making? Her father had never had to face such treachery and nor should any leader. She had been foolish to trust Brihtsige with her thoughts, but her embarrassment, her self-loathing, sat small against her indignation on Ethelred's behalf. She made fists of her own hands, but kept them clamped to her sides. Instead, she stepped forward and addressed her husband.

"My lord, all is done here that needed to be done." And perhaps more besides. "I would be grateful for your arm to lean upon; will you walk with me back to the hall?" *Dear God, let him say yes. For if he will not walk with me now, then I have nowhere left to go.*

His dark eyes were hidden beneath heavy lids that seemed weighted with sadness. But he smiled, and offered her his hand. As they walked away, she turned and caught Brihtsige's gaze, smouldering with its own ferocious heat.

It was not the first time that she had seen a would-be mischief-maker undone. But Brihtsige's scowl spoke of more than annoyance that Ethelred had not, like some helpless fish, snapped at the bait. Brihtsige would naturally be wrathful that she had escaped a public admonition, but his gaze had conveyed his wish to burn her face with his stare where the fire had not. *'Maybe the miller was speaking to someone at the window'.* Alhelm had thought no more upon his words. But how could Brihtsige have known that she and Alhelm would be in the mill together, unless he knew what would befall the miller, that a fire would bring them both running? Had Brihtsige sent one of his henchmen to follow her; had that man been at the window, ready with a flame to throw, intent on more, much more, than mere mischief? She dared not turn back to look at him, but although she shook off the suspicion, she still felt cold despite the heat of the day.

AD891

Teasel held out her hand and gripped Alyth's elbow, supporting the other woman's weight as she stepped down the slope onto the path to the village. Alyth smiled her thanks and smoothed her dress over her swollen belly before walking on. Two steps further on, the swish of leaves underfoot fell silent as she stopped and handed her basket to Teasel.

"Sorry, my lady, but this one sits on my bladder in a way that little Athelstan did not."

Teasel waited while her companion squatted down by the side of the road. She herself had been feeling sick these past few mornings and looking now at Alyth struggling, even with assistance, to stand up again, she wondered which discomfort she had to look forward to; the drawing agony of miscarriage or this ungainly bloating while another being took control over its mother's body. Alyth bent from the knees, leaning backwards slightly as Teasel helped her up, handed her the basket and they continued their journey. With the woodlands close to their left, its trees deep in the autumnal act of disrobing, they followed the path to Wormelow, occasionally hearing the hue and cry as the hounds led the hunters nearer to their quarry. Teasel exchanged glances with Alyth, who sighed. The hunt was always exciting, but at night, when the nets were laid out for mending, walking in front of the buildings became hazardous for a pregnant woman who could barely see where to put her feet.

Teasel held out her arm for support. "It could have been worse; we might have come here tomorrow and you would have to take care not to get knocked." Today, the lords hunted, the animals being driven by beaters into nets to be killed by archers or spearmen while at the meeting place, the folk gathered for the market fayre and the hundred-moot on the morrow. After that, the very highest of the nobles would go hawking with their sparrow hawks and goshawks. She was right to insist that she and Alyth came to make their purchases before the crowds gathered in full the next day. "At least for the now, we will be able to walk and buy without worry."

Alyth waited while the next round of baying and calling from the hunt subsided and nodded, although it was clear from her tone that she was unconvinced. "You might be right."

Out from the woods, they followed the path to the ancient burial mound, where tomorrow Ethelred would sit in judgement at the court. Today, there was a loud excitement that would be hushed on the morrow by the legal proceedings. Teasel and Alyth walked between the ramshackle buildings and covered stalls that sprang up regularly around the site, some abandoned when the court moved on, some hastily rebuilt when the tradesmen and women arrived back again. Sitting in the first covered stall, the bone-worker from Worcester touched his cap at the ladies. He sat huddled against the late autumn wind, a piece of half-worked antler in his hand, a pile of deer skulls behind him, and his board laden with objects which were finished and available to buy. Alyth selected two combs while Teasel asked the man how his wife fared.

"She is better, my lady. I did as you bade and had my sister boil the marshmallow root. We gave the drink to my wife and it soothed her bad throat. And the meadowsweet blossom-water washed the fever out."

161

"I am right glad to hear it." She had not been convinced that her remedy would work; nearer the coasts of Wessex she would have recommended a soup made from easily digested winkles with peas, but had offered the other remedy as one less tried, but with more easily obtainable ingredients.

A four-sided pen constructed of willow hurdles had been erected to house a gaggle of geese and they began to honk and hiss as Alyth and Teasel walked by. Teasel laughed and shook her head, holding up a hand to the goose-herd to indicate that she would not be taking any of his birds and they moved on the next stall. Here, Grim, a local leather-worker, clutched coins given to him by his father with which to buy some finished and treated hides. "I have only a few sceattas," he said, opening up his sweating palm and briefly showing the silver coins, before making a fist again and scowling.

The women chuckled and Teasel said, "Your father will be proud of your bartering skills, Grim."

The youth flushed from his forehead to the back of his neck and Teasel bit her lip, hoping that she hadn't distracted him from his task.

She moved on quickly to one of the more permanent structures, wherein a fire blazed and a grey-haired woman was selling bowls of warm pottage.

The woman bobbed a knee when she saw Teasel and shoved her other two customers further along the bench to make space for her honoured patrons. "Oh, my lady, I have not seen you for a twelve-month." The last word caught in her throat.

"Your cough is no better. This will be your second winter with it. You must take care."

The old soup-seller recovered her voice and wiped the corner of her mouth. "The elves do like to shoot the illness into me. It makes me bent-backed, but I have become used to it and it does not bother my sleep. God bless you for your kindness, though, my lady."

After a warming bowl of the thick vegetable broth, Teasel and Alyth stepped back into the chill air. Alyth went to relieve herself and Teasel wandered over to the jewellery stall. She smiled at the young woman seated behind the table laden with brooches and cloak pins, necklaces made with strung beads, and metal purse fasteners.

Alyth came to join her and whispered, "These are not fit for you, my lady."

Teasel continued to run her finger over the engraving on a circular brooch. "I was drawn to look at the fine working," she said. She knew, as Alyth did, of course, that these pieces were made from pewter and in some cases tin itself, but they were prettily worked and would suit the purse contents of those who would come to the market tomorrow. She looked up at the woman again. "Thank you for letting me look at these."

As they turned to leave, Alyth said, "You always have a kind word for the folk."

Teasel offered her arm once more as they negotiated the rutted path. "My riches might mark me out as a high-born lady, but fine clothes did no good when the Vikings came. Then, I was a child whose father was away fighting and my mother hid her face in the pillow. It was folk like these who offered me comfort."

Alyth smiled. "Well at least we can be thankful that those raids are no more. There are children in these steadings who have never heard of Vikings. Long may that be true."

"Amen." Teasel linked her arm through Alyth's. "Come, we should be away before the cooks get too busy." A celebratory meal would be required tonight if the huntsmen were successful, even though a pig slaughtered from the herd would provide more meat than the hunters would likely bring home. Even so, Ethelred's place as lord, and therefore, by definition, provider, would once again be reinforced, and from the noises they had heard earlier, he might well be on the trail of a deer. Teasel put her hand to her own belly, the thought of food bringing on the misery of sickness once more.

Along the woodland path, the sound of the hunt grew louder. The two women passed a low gate which served as an exit route for the animals from the enclosed land where the hunt took place and Alyth ducked her head, hurrying past it. "Come, lady."

Teasel said, "It does not sound to me that the hounds are so near that they will send a deer over the leap-gate." But she, too, instinctively hunched as she walked past the gate. She paused to see if there were any sign of the hunt, but though the hounds' calls floated on the slender breeze there was none in sight. "You see, there was naught to be afraid of."

Turning to move on, she bumped into Alyth, who was standing motionless in the road. Ahead, standing on the path, was a boar, doubtless roused by the din of the hunt. Mercifully, they must have been upwind of the beast, for it had its head down and was sniffing the ground, unaware of the humans nearby. But this was a beast used to foraging at dusk and dawn, not in the height of the day. Who could guess its mood? Teasel pulled gently on Alyth's arm. She whispered. "Go back to the leap-gate and go into the woodland. The huntsmen are nearby. See if you can get help. Go now, slowly."

Alyth's shoulders moved up and down, following the rhythm of her rapid breathing. She scratched the path with her shoes, sliding her feet slowly back until she was level with Teasel. "My lady, I cannot leave you here on your own."

Teasel swallowed in a vain attempt to lubricate her mouth. When she tried to speak, her top lip stuck to her teeth and she had to run her tongue along them to free it. "I would sooner face this boar than Lord Frith should aught befall you or your bairn."

As soon as Alyth was off the path, Teasel began to retrace her steps. Her mouth moved in silent prayer.

Almighty God, let Alyth get her legs over the gate. Give us the time that we need to get her to safety. Blessed Lord, give me the strength for what is to come. Would it be frivolous to pray also for her heart to beat more quietly? Surely the boar would hear it hammering upon her chest. The animal stopped its foraging and lifted its head. There were no visible tusks so she knew it was a female, but if it saw her, it would still charge and its bite was powerful. Her breathing came swift and shallow and in her efforts to keep even that silent, she barely took in enough air. Beginning to feel light in the head, she swallowed hard in an attempt to fight the nausea, but now her legs were weak from fear and she began to wonder if she could run at all. She edged cautiously backwards, not daring to turn her head and wondering how far she was from the gate. Looking down, she peered between her feet, to keep check on the lie of the land as she stepped back. A loud noise broke the silence; a scraping, scratching, scrabbling sound, it filled the space hanging empty in the air and she screamed and covered her head, convinced the beast was on the charge. She turned and ran for the safety of the gate only to be met by the mounted huntsmen as they urged their steeds over the gate. Three of them skidded to a halt in the lane, blocking her view of the boar. Someone threw a spear and a screech rent the thickening air. Now the riders dismounted and loud conversation floated around her ears, yet she could not discern the words. A hand was on her shoulder and a voice cut through the babble.

"My lady, are you hurt?"

She looked up and blinked hard to refocus. Frith was peering down at her, frowning, worried. His breath came in uneven bursts, the sweat hovering on his brow.

"I am unhurt." Even as she spoke, she looked over her shoulder to see the three others to whom she owed a debt of thanks. Old Eadnoth crouched down on one knee, examining the carcass while Alhelm and Little Alfred stood behind him. Alhelm had the spear in his hand and he was wiping it clean on his breeches. She cringed. Let it not be

Alhelm who had thrown the spear. Her standing amongst these men was low enough without her having to bow to her first, not-so-secret love, to thank him for saving her life. She looked back at Frith. "Was it him?"

Frith squeezed her shoulder. "No, my lady. It was Eadnoth. Eadnoth saved the woman who stood between my wife and a wild boar."

She slumped forward and rested her face against his chest. His long blond hair felt soft against her cheek and his body was warm and yielding. Yet she knew however hard she leaned upon him, he would never sway. *Almighty God, I give thanks for my deliverance this day, and God, thank you for giving me Lord Frith.*

She sat in her bower and wiped the tears with the back of her hand. Ethelred had gone to receive his guests and she knew she had but moments before she was expected to make her appearance in the hall. The visitors from Wessex, sent by Alfred to question Bishop Werferth further about education and literacy, would be keen to greet her, he had said. *'And all will wish to drink to your name, after what you did this day. We are all proud.'* He had said no more, but patted her head and left her alone. And she had remained in her chair for a while, rocking slightly as the lost child bled away from her.

Outside, the chill night air immediately tried to grab her bones and she pulled her cloak tight over her woollen dress. The smell of the roasting pig wafted from the spit outside the cook-house, the cooking-fire lighting up the enclosure and speaking of warmth and sustenance. At this time of year the odour of slaughter was everywhere and in her pregnant state her nostrils had been under constant attack, receiving the normally inoffensive aroma and turning it into a noxious stench which tipped her stomach upside down. Perhaps now she would be able to walk past the butchers without covering her face with her veil and holding her breath. She stood for a moment outside the hall door, breathing in the warm scent of the horses, tethered against the rails because the stables were full. Catching hold of the bridle of a brown gelding, she stroked the leatherwork, finding it smooth and devoid of all decoration. This was a thegn's mount, then. The visiting noblemen's stallions would all be stabled, their gold-adorned tack hung up on the stable walls, guarded by the horse-thegns and the visitors' servants. The gelding snickered and butted its nose against her chest and she held it there, listening to the shouts and whoops emanating from the hall. She patted the horse's neck, trying to draw some of its powerful strength and turn it into the courage she needed to enter the hall. She took one more gulp of the clean, fresh, dark air and stepped inside.

The din made her want to cradle her ears with her hands. Every seat on the mead benches was taken, and Mercians and West Saxons were sharing drinking-horns while they swapped lewd jokes. With relief, she realised that she had chosen wisely when she dressed that evening, for the ealdormen and leading thegns were in their finest woollen tunics, but the garments were not silk-edged. No high feast this, then. Scanning the throng for familiar faces, she saw at once why this was considered a slightly less prestigious occasion, for there were no ealdormen from Wessex amongst the visitors. The only laymen amongst the guests were the retainers of the churchmen who had come to speak to Bishop Werferth. They were many in number though, for churchmen followed the same expediencies as noblemen, riding out with enough men who could form an effective bodyguard. Foremost among the religious deputation was Abbot John of Athelney. Known as the Old Saxon, he hailed from the old country across the sea, whence Alfred had invited him, and Teasel remembered his arrival in Somerset just a few months before her marriage. Doubtless he brought news of another exile, Plegmund, Mercian born, but installed as archbishop of Canterbury, also at Alfred's behest.

Uncle Wulf was in position on the bench reserved for the doughty warriors and he shared a horn with Eadnoth, Eardwulf, Little Alfred and the Goat. The other ealdormen and leading thegns were sitting on the bench along the other side of the dais, and among them she saw Frith, Alhelm, Acha and Brihtsige. Brihtsige glanced up at her but his expression was unfathomable. No matter; she would not dwell on it, for any feelings he evoked belonged to a self-pitying newcomer with whom Teasel was becoming less acquainted. Behind the table on the dais, Ethelred was seated beside Werferth, who in turn was next to Abbot John. She walked forward and took up her seat next to her husband, nodding to him and Werferth as she sat down.

The roasted pig was brought to the tables, along with hard cheese and bread, although only the top tables received loaves made from finely sifted flour, while the warriors on the lower mead benches were served with batches of wholemeal loaves. Plates were brought in piled high with autumn fruits, apples and pears and the first of the dried hazelnuts, and bowls of warming cereal-brew puffed out their scented steam, hinting at the flavouring of onions, garlic and cabbage.

Teasel waited to be served by the little slave hovering behind the high table. By custom, she should herself have served wine and beer to the guests, but since they had begun drinking long ere she entered the hall, she saw no need to observe the usual code of behaviour. Aware that her physical discomfort might be obvious because of her slumped posture, and anxious somehow to assert her credentials as a worthy lady, she raised a hand and beckoned the reeve, instructing him to bring the highly prized pepper mill and offer its expensive contents to their guests. As her own plate was being filled, Uncle Wulf raised his hand in greeting to her and called for quiet. Only those closest to his table heard him, but those who did hear put down their drinks and eating knives to listen.

"Friends and hearth-kin, drink with me this night. I

give you the lady Æthelflæd, who faced down a wild boar, standing between the beast and the lady Alyth."

The toast raised, all who were listening responded with the traditional "Be hale," raising their drinks and holding them in her direction. Teasel looked down at her hands. She felt Ethelred's hand squeezing her knee and managed a small smile for him. Looking up, she gazed across at the ealdormen's table and saw Frith holding his ale cup in salute. He mouthed, "Thank you" and grinned at her. He set his cup on the table and put both hands to one side of his face, to indicate that Alyth was still sleeping.

Among the doughty warriors, most were turning the event into a personal triumph for Wulf, slapping him on the back and congratulating him. She smiled at this demonstration of the power of kinship, watching her uncle shamelessly taking all praise that came his way. But both Eadnoth and Eardwulf glanced over to the high table and each gave the smallest of nods. This time she laughed aloud. How strange that she should have gained even the tiniest amount of their respect for thinking like a woman in order to protect another woman. It was hardly the stuff of battles, of scops' poems.

With that thought, she looked over at Ethelred's scop, plucking his harp gamely, the music staying well below the level of noise and unheard by all except those seated at the end of the nearest table to him. With no recent raiding to provide inspiration for a tale, she wondered what he would sing of instead. When finally he was summoned to come before the dais and face his audience, she hoped for his sake that he had something suitably stirring, for the hall was in no mood to listen to mere folk-tales; these men wanted descriptions of valour, blood and victory, plenty of gore which could then be washed down with yet more wine and ale.

The scop cleared his throat and called for silence. Those nearest to him responded, though not immediately, taking time to finish their conversations and call for more drink. As they began to quiet, so the lull moved as a wave across the hall, until even those by the door realised that the entertainment was about to begin, and fell silent.

"I see many worthy stalwarts seated in this hall," his audience cheered and applauded itself. He encouraged the roar with an upward sweep of his outstretched arms, bringing them down and once more indicating the need for quiet. "And I would not dare to tell a tale of any lesser bravery than I have witnessed among the men in this hall." He took a wide stance, spreading his weight evenly and settling in for a retelling of an old and familiar tale. "Listen."

And listen they did, shouting, groaning, and cheering as he stirred their warrior spirits with his words. He lifted his arm high. "He whirled his blade, swung his arm with all his strength and the ring-hilted sword sang a greedy war-song on the monster's head." They banged the tables and bellowed, encouraging him as he continued with his tale until, exhausted, he sat down on the floor, legs crossed and head bowed.

Ethelred stood up, holding up his hand. A semblance of quiet followed, allowing him to thank the scop.

Before he had finished, a shout came from somewhere near the doorway. "Tell us another. How about one for those of us who are so far from home this night? A tale of the mighty King Alfred?" It was spoken in a Wessex accent, and Teasel thought it might have been a gesture to her, the lady, far from home.

On the next table, a Mercian thegn replied. "Is he the only mighty one?" The thegn held his drink aloft and nodded at Teasel. She swallowed and widened her eyes in surprise. It was as if they were both laying claim to her; that the Mercian was saying, '*She belongs to Mercia now. We did not want her, but if we think that you seek to claim her back, then we will hold on to her.*' He shouted at the visitor. "We do not need such things, for there are many doughty men here in these lands. We could sing for hours of their great and daring deeds."

A West Saxon thegn whose face seemed familiar to Teasel stood up and thumped his fist on the table. "Yet your scop does not sing of them, for he knows that without the strength of Alfred's fyrd, you would be singing Danish songs around your hearth this night."

A thegn from Wulf's Gaini tribe leaped up. "You will take back your words or you will swallow them through a hole in your belly." He drew back his fist, but a thegn on another table was the first to throw a punch, upending the table as he did so and beginning an all-out fight.

Ethelred nodded at Frith, who nodded at Alhelm and gradually the Mercian nobles stood up and began to edge out, positioning themselves behind the scrapping drunkards.

Teasel watched the scuffle with increasing irritation. *Silly puffed-up men with their easily bruised pride.* She felt the discomfort between her thighs and wondered if these fine warriors would cope with the endless disappointment of miscarriage as bravely as they seemed to defend every imagined slight. Embarrassment at the behaviour of her countrymen, the West Saxons, gave way to an irritation that revealed her loyalties to be torn. She stood up and banged the table with her cup. When this proved ineffective she began throwing the heavy metal plates and cups, noting with satisfaction that many made contact with the protagonists' heads. Bishop Werferth looked across at her, his eyebrows raised. He rose to his feet, ready to speak, but she shook her head. She threw a few more missiles until the men began to stop, turning to see the source of this new onslaught.

When she had their attention, she clutched the table's edge with tightly gripping fingers and raised her chin. "God help us all if the Vikings ever do come back. Look at you; you are like children fighting over a silver penny." She put her hands on her hips. "Hearken to me, all of you. I was sent here as a token of the will between the folk of two kingdoms to stand as one against the foe. If that foe could see you now, it would bring shame on your heads. I fought tooth and nail with my brother but let no man stand

171

between us. This is how it should be between Wessex and Mercia. I am half West Saxon." The Mercians who had been most hostile to her, Eadnoth, Brihtsige and their followers, jeered, but it was quieter, perhaps tempered by some small embarrassment at being chastened. "And I am half Mercian. I might be the daughter of a king but the blood of the Gaini flows also through my veins and I know at what cost these folk have fought the heathen." She glared at the visitors. "You have come from Wessex and we have been your hosts. This is no way to repay our kindness and I will not have fighting in my hall." She sat down and put a hand to her head. Her temple throbbed and she wished only to leave to seek sanctuary in her private bower. She must have stunned them with her words, for they were silent now. Not even daring to look at her husband, she put her hands in her lap and gazed at them, wishing her cheeks would stop burning and regretting the tired impatience which had led her to speak so out of turn.

Someone in the hall began to thump his hand on the table and soon after, others joined in. The rhythmic banging grew louder and then was accompanied by shouts. "Stand for the lady Æthelflæd." "The lady is a true Mercian to speak so." "Be hale, Lady Æthelflæd."

She braved a glance out at the room and saw that old Eadnoth was smiling at her. This was enough. She turned to Ethelred, who smiled and let his face open up.

"It was well said. They love you for taking their part."

She looked across at Bishop Werferth and he returned her smile, nodding his head to show his approval. "Good words, my lady. Good words."

The fight forgotten, the drinking resumed and all was as before, except that when she looked up again, one final cheer rose up and she blinked hard as they saluted her. "Lady Æthelflæd. Lady of the Mercians."

AD892

It was going to be a good day. Teasel liked the town; within the defensive ramparts, the burh echoed to the sounds of carefree commerce. She particularly liked to listen to the clinking and hammering emanating from the town's mint, occasionally asking if she could rub her thumbs over the newly pressed coins. Since the Vikings had been ousted from London, much of the settlement here had been fortified and remodelled and Ethelred had personally shown her around when she first came here, walking with her up and down the neatly laid out grid of streets. Today, the harvest was in but the sun was still shining and the warmth of its rays seemed to imbue the townsfolk with an added vibrancy as they went about their work. The carpenters had been working their pole-lathes, turning the unseasoned wood and not allowing it to dry out as they fashioned the backs for the new chairs. The reeve of this town was an ill-tempered individual whose shouting had punctuated the morning's toil and reminded all who heard that he would have to shoulder the blame if the new furniture was not ready for the lord's hall, but the men ignored his ranting and blunted his sting by hurling good-natured abuse at him. The salt-peddler from Droitwich had arrived and, on his way to the market, had stopped off at the kitchen that served the great hall, finding time to tell Teasel that his son was now fully recovered from his sickness and to thank her for her help. Furthermore, he had praised the effectiveness of the alliance and told her that it was a pleasure to take the long journey now that the roads in this part of Mercia were safe and she had glowed with associated pride that her husband and father were the far-sighted men who had achieved this.

Walking back from the cook-house she had met Alhelm. Their conversation had been brief and awkward, as usual, but no tears had burned her eyes. It was such a small thing, but it was a sign that she was learning to live with the knowledge that he now shared his life with another, the way he had never had a chance to do with her. She hummed a little tune as she made her way back to her bower.

She let the door go with a clatter; the door closed and the latch clunked down a moment later.

Alyth looked up from her sewing. "Now that is a wondrous sight. Have you had good tidings?"

Teasel put her basket on the floor and flung her cloak onto the bed. "No. The sun is shining, the folk are cheery, and I did something that made me proud, that is all." She sat down on her bed. *I saw him, and I did not cry.*

Alyth put away her stitching. She paused, as if unsure whether to continue. She shrugged. "Why not?" Sitting forward, she settled down for a gossip. Teasel leaned nearer in response.

"I have heard whispered words about the wife of Lord Alhelm."

Teasel put a hand to her veil and fiddled with the linen. "Really? I saw him only a short while ago."

If Alyth noticed her discomfort, she chose to ignore it, for she barely paused for breath before continuing. "Folk say that his wife is sad. She weeps when he is not at home and she weeps even more when he is."

"He does not love her?" Teasel slapped down a nasty urge to be pleased by the news.

"It is not that." Alyth looked up. "I mean, I would not know about that side of things, my lady. They fight a lot, I believe, over the long nights he spends drinking with Wulf.

174

But that is mild news when you hear about her sister. She, it seems, loves her husband but not the bed they share. Or rather, what goes on under the sheets."

Teasel put a hand to her mouth. "No. How do you know this?"

"Oh, the same old way. My sister is friend to the sister of Alhelm's wife, and she told me. You know how these things spread. But my lady, think on it. Not to love bedtime? I cannot think how sad that must make her. I can think of naught else that is as welcome at the end of a day sewing and weaving. I could not bear to say no, or go without. Could you?"

Teasel felt her cheeks warming a little. Dismissing any feelings that had bubbled up in response to the revelation that Alhelm's marriage was not perfect, she thought carefully about Alyth's question. From that first time, when he had destroyed the expectations of pain and disappointment planted in her mind by her mother, after every failed pregnancy, and not just at night with the candles snuffed, Ethelred had always been kind, loving even. Whatever their mismatch, the bedroom had become a place where their silence had not mattered. And now that she thought on it, she acknowledged that there was no dread, only pleasure. "No," she said at last, "I could not bear to be without it."

Alyth giggled. "Come, we will be needed in the hall."

Outside, they met Frith. "Ah, I was on my way to find you." He kissed his wife and held out a letter to Teasel.

Sending silent thanks to her teacher, Werferth, she read it quickly. "Oh I knew it was going to be a good day. Did I not tell you it would be, Alyth? My brother has a son. He has named him Athelstan."

The Royal Manor of Cheddar, Wessex

The muscle in Ethelred's cheek twitched with a new ferocity. He fixed his gaze on the horizon and Teasel forbore to beg for a rest, even though her legs were aching after the lengthy ride. It was she, after all, who had asked to visit her brother, even if the latest news had overshadowed that of Athelstan's birth. Not one, but two Viking armies had established fortresses in Kent and now a whole Mercian fyrd rode to Wessex along with the visiting kin and Teasel knew when to hold her tongue. Wulf had no jokes for them and even Frith kept his thoughts to himself and offered no words of comfort. The year was fading and it felt as if the sun were dying, too, retracting its warmth and leaving in its place a bitter, chilling wind.

Falling back on the privileges of her sex, Teasel left the men to worry about the coming fight and as soon as they arrived at the king's manor at Cheddar she sought out her brother. He was standing outside the hall, spine erect, broad shoulders relaxed and hair still sticking up as if he had slept upright every night of this life. Suppressing the urge to throw her arms around his neck, she reached out and touched the side of his head with her cupped hand, bringing her fingers down to stroke his earlobe just as she had done when they were young. It was more of a stretch than she remembered and she joked that Edward seemed taller now that he was a father.

176

He leaned forward and kissed her forehead. "If you think that a man grows every time he fathers a child, why is our father not ten feet tall?"

She smiled to think of her father growing taller with the birth of each child. But she did not want her thoughts to linger on her younger brother nor yet on her sisters, one sent to a nunnery and the other to a marriage in a foreign land before they grew up and had a chance to know her. Now, as then, there was really only her and Edward, whether her father had grown taller or not. She linked her arm through his as they went to see Gwen. "Maybe he once was. Maybe fighting the Vikings all the time robbed him of his height. Let us hope that none of you shrinks this time."

His smile faded. "Father had not thought that they would come again. Not in such number. Whereas I..."

She put a finger to his lips. "Let us not speak of it before we must. As for you, I only meant that you stand proud now, as a father should, and it gives you a look of loftiness."

He bent down, leaning close to her ear and said, "Or do you think merely that you have not seen me in almost five years and that I have really grown?" He nudged her before he straightened up again, laughing.

Teasel laughed too. She had yearned to come home for so long and now she was holding her brother's arm, and wherever she looked she saw folk whom she'd known since childhood. Outside the hall, the lord of Somerset was talking with the king, while Wulf stood by a bower, hugging his sister Ewith, who endured his molestations with the indulgent expression she had once reserved for her youngest children. Lord Wiltshire made his way from the latrine, bowed to Teasel, and waved his arm in greeting to his daughter.

Teasel stopped, jerking Edward's arm back. "Is that Fleyda? Now there is one who really has grown."

Fleyda had indeed grown taller. Teasel recalled the small girl with regal pretensions who had marred her day in

177

the woods with Alhelm all those long years ago and it was hard to trust her eyes and believe that this was the same person. It was no surprise that the protuberant tummy redolent of childhood had slimmed away, but now this young woman was tall and slender, with barely a curve showing through her lightweight summer kirtle. But then she turned towards the royal siblings and though her facial features had also slimmed, losing the childish roundness and gaining definition, there was still no mistaking the cat-green eyes, the regal tilt of the chin and the small thin nose above which two small lines seemed to have been formed by the habit of pulling the eyes into a frequent frown. Yet when she looked at Edward and smiled, it was as though a wrinkled blanket had been smoothed with a heated stone; her frown lines vanished to be replaced by dimples pushed into her cheeks by the pressure of her wide smile. Her chin dropped and her eyes seemed to widen, despite the smile. Teasel said, "She has become winsome indeed."

Edward made a show of rubbing the front of his shoulder as if it had hurt when Teasel yanked upon it. His head was down and the back of his neck reddened. "Never mind about her. Come and see Gwen, who craves to see you."

At the door of the guest bower, Teasel stopped again, putting her hand over Edward's as it rested on the latch. "Has Mother fully welcomed Gwen as kin?"

Edward shrugged. "We are ever hopeful."

Teasel moved her hand away from the door and squeezed his forearm. How perverse that Ewith envied her own daughter for marrying a Mercian, yet would not countenance allowing her son to do the same. She took a deep breath and lifted her smile, walking into the room with arms outstretched. "Gwen, it is lovely to see you. And this is my little nephew?" She kissed Gwen and swooped to bend over the cot. Baby Athelstan lay on his back with his arms above his head, blinking blue eyes and kicking his feet against the folded blankets underneath him.

Gwen propped herself up on her elbows. "I had hoped to be up to greet you, but I took an illness after he was born. He is strong though, and feeds well."

Teasel stroked the little round cheek with the back of a crooked finger. "He is wonderful," she said. "May I hold him?"

As she cradled the tiny creature in her arms, a burning sensation travelled down her nose and she sniffed, but was too late to blink the tears back. Blink she did, but the action only caused them to plop from her cheeks to the floor. "Forgive me, I am overwrought from the long ride and the bliss of seeing you all again."

Gwen put a hand out and stroked her son's head. "You do not need to say sorry for spilling tears." She winced and lay back down. "I am beginning to think that fathers have the best of it; someone else to give birth to their children." She covered Teasel's hand with her own. Lowering her voice further, she said, "Your time will come. Meanwhile, you are free to hold him any time you wish to. And if he is crying, then so much the better; I will be glad of the rest."

The baby seemed contented but even if he were not, Gwen was not a woman to be knocked from her serenity by an irritable babe. Teasel was grateful for Gwen's pretence for it softened the knocks of envy that hammered her heart as she held her little nephew. She put the child back in his crib, sniffed and stood up. She crooked her finger again and brushed it past Edward's ear. "Look after your woman. There is none better."

In the yard, she met Ethelred. She guessed he had only just come from the stables; even though the reeve would be responsible for providing horse stalls, Ethelred would want to check that his valuable animal was suitably housed.

With eyes downcast, she said, "The horses are well looked after, my lord? I know how you like to oversee the stabling of the steeds yourself."

"Yes, they are. Have you seen the child?"

She could hardly bear to look up and see the

disappointment on his face, for if the sight of the baby brought forth her own tears, what would it do to his pride? He had never reproached her for her barrenness, but when she did look up, he was looking at her with down-turned mouth, eyelids blinking slowly, and what she could almost have imagined to be a tear glistening in the corner of one eye, if she believed that such a man could ever cry. She could think of nothing to say but, "I am sorry, my lord," before she bobbed a curtsey and ran off to pay her respects to Ewith.

Sent on a chase to rival any hunt, she was directed first to the hall and then to the cook-house, but her mother, having previously endured Wulf's mauling, was hiding well that day. The noise from the mews suggested that the fowl-keeper was in his hut, feeding his birds and Teasel walked past the building, beyond the food store. She walked in a wide arc to avoid an area of raised ground, rumoured to be the grave of a traitor, executed in her grandfather's day and buried by his reeve away from the churchyard. Casting a glance out of the gateway along the path that led eastwards, she saw plenty of folk in the vast leek gardens, tending the tasty vegetables which, when cooked with the onion and garlic in the stores, would bring flavour to the winter meals. More than a few ladies of the manor were in the gardens, but there was no sign of the lady Ewith.

Teasel walked back towards the great hall and climbed the two wooden steps to the outer door. Standing outside it was a man with hair darker than any she had ever seen. His face was wider than that of most Saxons, his eyes were round and brown and he had a distinctive cleft in his chin. He was, perhaps, two or three years younger than Ethelred, the beginnings of lines around his eyes, but absence of grey in his hair, indicating that he might be a year or two into his thirties. His clothing was slightly odd, for he wore a leather jerkin over his tunic and trousers with no leg bindings. She realised that she was staring, and bowed her head.

He said, "Lady Æthelflæd?"

He spoke English, but with a strong accent. She looked up and, rudely, she spoke her thoughts. "You sound like Asser, the Welshman."

He smiled, showing her a full set of teeth, unlike Asser the monk, who had lost most of his top set and whistled as he talked. "I am Anarawd of Gwynedd. And you are sad."

His forward remarked relieved her of the need to apologise for her own lapse in manners. She stood up straight, the better to seem regal. "You are my husband's foe. I should not speak with you."

He grinned again. "But I have bent my knee to your father. His friends are my friends now."

She found it hard to know what to say to this strange man. His looks were so exotic, his speech so foreign and his reputation so large in her mind. Whenever Ethelred spoke of him, she pictured a handsome man, a little wild, perhaps, who fought valiantly to protect his birthright. Why would the son of murdered Rhodri and killer of Ceolwulf submit to her father? She remembered that Ethelred had started to speak to her of some outlandish act of Anarawd's but that she had thought it too dull to be worth listening to. But had he really bowed to her father, or was he teasing her?

Puzzlement must have shown on her face for he said, "I needed your father's help to fight the South Welsh. Men do what they must to save their kingdoms."

Oh, but there was bitter truth in his words. She let out a harsh laugh. "And what did you take as a token of my father's friendship? Alfred has already given away his barren daughter. 'Tis well that Edward's woman has borne only a son, who cannot be bartered."

The Welshman stopped smiling. "All men. All men do what they must for their kingdom; your brother might yet have to yield in ways he might not like. Besides, your husband keeps you, does he not? That must mean that he does not mind your childlessness. Myself, I like a woman thin, for they go fat and lumpy after childbirth."

She could not help grinning a little at the unintentional

compliment and she slid her hands over her slim waistline. Then her thoughts caught up with her ears and she said, "What do you mean, that my husband 'keeps' me? He can do little else, or risk my father's wrath."

Anarawd shot out a Welsh word, which sounded as if it might signify disparagement at her remark, then he said, "Wessex is as beholden to Mercia as Mercia is to Wessex. I have stood against your husband in battle and there is no better man in a fight. He is a worthy foe, and an even better friend. We had something to bind us, for we both blamed the same man for the death of our kin. Ethelred is a great man. If he keeps you as wife, it is not through fear of your father."

He grinned again and reached up to brush hair from his eyes. She watched him, daring to meet his gaze and wondering idly if his hair was as soft to the touch as it looked.

He leaned forward and said, "He keeps you because you are 'prydferth'."

She took a step nearer. "What does that mean?"

The smile vanished and he looked at her, the large brown eyes unblinking. "Beautiful."

Her blood flowed warmer around her body and she tried to slow her breathing to normal pace. The Welshman was looking over her shoulder and she turned to see Ethelred approaching the hall.

Anarawd raised his arm in greeting. "Sais."

Ethelred nodded and returned the acknowledgment. "Welshman."

"I have met your lady and need nothing more from the day. Englishman, I must tell you that your wife is modest, loyal and lovely. You are a man to be envied."

Ethelred cast a look at Teasel, the same look he gave her whenever Alhelm was nearby, then he turned back to the Welshman. "Dw i'n gwybod."

Inside, the men went upstairs to join the meeting with her father and she wandered over to the far end of the hall to the temporary scriptorium. There the monks scratched away in flustered candlelight, writing up the agreements of the previous day's witan meeting. Hunched and squinting, they looked up only to give a cursory nod before continuing with their work. Only one, more relaxed, worked in colour. He used yellow from arsenic and orange derived from toasted lead and Teasel paused to watch while he fashioned an intricately swirling capital letter for what she assumed was one of her father's translations. Seated at a larger table, with a huge book opened in front of him, the Welsh monk, Asser, held a quill hovering over the vellum, waiting to add the next correction to the script in front of him. When he saw Teasel, he laid the pen aside, and sat up straight, hands disappearing into his cavernous sleeves.

"I have met another Welshman," she said.

He sniffed as if she had brought with her the smell from the latrines. "There is Wales, and then there is Gwynedd."

"King Anarawd," she emphasised his rank, "Said some lovely things about me and my lord answered, 'Dw i'n gwybod'. What is this in English?"

Asser's face remained as expressionless as a carving on a wall. "Your lord said, 'I know'."

Teasel was sitting on the little rise to the west of the manor. It was not very high, but from her perch she could see enough of the surrounding countryside, part of her beloved Wessex. Folk continued filling the storage barns, and she knew that up in the lofts the apples would be turned every day, to keep them from mouldering while they were stored over the winter. Cart wheels were being mended and strengthened to cope with the hard, frosted ground. All was playing out below her as it should. Yet her world was not the same, and she found that she was only missing the place now that she was back. Lately, she had been busy making a life in Mercia and had barely given a thought to home, apart from when she thought of Edward. His life had changed and she recognised that hers had altered, too. Now, even her knowledge of men had grown, for she had discovered that Alhelm was not the only beautiful man striding God's earth. The Welshman seemed to have reached with his eyes into her chest and pulled all her breath out of her. She tried to compare the appraisal he had given her with the way Alhelm looked at her but had to acknowledge that Alhelm had never looked at her that way. Her cheeks grew warm even though no-one was there to witness her embarrassment.

It had all been a story in her silly, little-girl's head. It had been she who gazed upon Alhelm's beautiful face, imagining that she saw her love reflected there. Never had she seen anguish in his eyes, for his loyalty was always to Ethelred and Alhelm was untroubled by what had passed between himself and a love-struck girl, beyond, perhaps, a slight guilt at having misled her. His beauty had availed her naught beyond giving her something to rest her eyes on. He had done his duty by his lord and probably thought no more on it, despite her unfounded beliefs to the contrary. His lord, her husband.

Her husband. She was aware that she had been growing fonder of Ethelred, savouring the moments when his sober manner gave way to indulgent laughter, admiring his keen wit, and relishing the comfort of being soothed merely by his being close by so that she need not look upon his face but feed from the warmth of his presence, but still she had held to her belief that he kept her only through obligation to her father. Now Anarawd had told her different and she thought instead about the look that Ethelred had given her when he happened upon her speaking with the Welshman, and wondered if it did, in fact, betray some other emotion beyond that of mere proprietorial indignation. She had for so long looked upon Ethelred as a replacement father, but he was different from Alfred. For one thing, he had hardly been away from her side these five years past, whereas her father was little more than a stranger to her. That was all about to change though, for she knew that below her, in the great hall, the men were planning for war. While the women would be… She slapped the heel of her hand against her forehead. "Mother. I must find her."

She ran down the hill, tacking first to the left and then the right, until she came to the level ground. Rushing into the yard, she grabbed the guard and said, "Do you know where Lady Ewith is?"

"I saw her go into the bake-house, my lady."

"I thank you."

Almost the whole of the bake-house doorway was obstructed with the extra loaves piled up along the outer wall. Teasel squeezed through sideways into the hot gloomy bakery. "Mother?"

Ewith had her sleeves rolled up and was kneading a large chunk of dough. But whereas the other baking-women pummelled and punched, looking all the while at their dough, the king's wife stared at the back wall.

Teasel laid a hand on her arm and the older woman stopped kneading but continued to stare straight ahead. "Mother, come with me. We will be needed in the hall."

Ewith shook her head. "Only afterwards. Then we are needed to bury the bodies and stitch the wounded, hush the fatherless children when they wail."

"Mother, stop it. Father is alive. He lives." She reached round to hold her mother by the shoulders, turning her to face her. "While they live, there is hope."

But Ewith's eyes suggested no more perception than if she had been blind. Teasel left her and went to join the men.

She took her skirts in her hands and trotted up the stairs to the upper hall, entering in time to hear the end of her brother's speech. He spoke eloquently and gave many insights into the best strategies to be used for the upcoming campaign. And while he spoke she looked beyond him, to the lords of Somerset and Wiltshire, and then to the farthest end of the room where she noticed a young thegn sitting by the hearth, brown bloodstains on his cloak, a chunk of hair missing from his head, and a dirty bandage wrapped around his hand.

Edward was pounding his fist into his hand and as she stared at the thegn she half listened to, "Must not get caught sleeping. We should split up, half to fight, half to build." He ended with a declaration. "I will fight, Father. You cannot say that I am too young, for I have a child of my own now."

"The less said about that, the better."

Teasel turned when she heard Ewith's voice and saw her mother standing in the doorway. She grabbed her hand and led the lady into the room, seating her in a chair and patting her knee. She went to stand by her husband and braved a smile. Ethelred looked surprised, but smiled back at her. She nodded towards her mother, and then looked up at him. "You and I, we will work together. As one."

His brown eyes narrowed as his mouth turned into the suggestion of a smile and he gazed down at her with an expression that she thought might signal his approval. For no reason that she could fathom, her thoughts wandered to the day he had found her digging in the dirt at Hild's house.

He gave her the details of their discussion. "We have heard that not only are there new hosts in Kent, but now the old hosts in East Anglia and Northumbria have broken their oaths to your father."

"But Guthrum swore?"

Alfred said, "Guthrum is dead. God has given us long years to make England strong again. We have retaken London and the years of peace have meant that we have been able to build burhs. Now, like crows for meat, they come to take what we have grown."

Alfred looked stunned. Even now, it seemed that he struggled to accept that men could act so dishonourably. Teasel took a step forward, reaching out to her father.

Ethelred held her back. "There is more." He beckoned the young thegn forward. "Can you bear to tell your tale once more, for my lady's ears?"

The young man approached the nobles. His shoulders

hunched forward and his chin drooped. His upper eyelids sagged and the inner corners of his eyebrows were angled upwards. So much sadness was written on his face that Teasel held her breath.

"It was at Andrædsweald, my lady. Their leader is named Hasteinn. They brought their ships, laden with men and steeds, came up the stream as far as the woods, and we were halfway through building the burh and the outer walls were nearly up. There was a breach and they rushed through like a beck that has burst its banks. Some of us had only the wooden poles we had been hammering. I speared a few. It was..." He shook his head, and then looked down at the floor, holding his wounded hand in the crook of his other arm.

Ethelred stepped forward. "They are many. But we are no longer few. Now we show them what fellowship means."

They began to discuss more detailed plans and Teasel signalled for food and more drink for the thegn. While she waited to see him settled once more by the hearth, she looked around the room. Despite the circumstances she was still glad to be back amongst them, friends and kin almost all: the lords Somerset and Wiltshire, loyal and steadfast, her father and her brother. And one other, whom she had not yet had time to greet; her cousin Thelwold, standing at the back of the room, arms folded, listening, but saying nothing.

Part III – Wif (Wife)

AD893

Milton, Kent

The chill February wind blew across the flat meadow; it was a breeze whipped up into something a little stronger and it felt like it was slapping Ethelred's face. Alhelm came to stand by his side as they watched the ritual being acted out in front of them.

"Is this wise, my lord?" Alhelm's hand hovered near his sword hilt.

Ethelred puffed out a silent laugh. How would he explain it to a child? Two Viking armies were dug down in Kent and a massed force of Mercians and West Saxons stood strategically between them, in reach of either fortress should the enemy choose to move out from behind their barricades. But then would not the child say that there was no point in being between two camps if you forgot to look behind you? Perhaps an innocent would concur with Alfred's belief that all men would be bound by their word. Surely only such childlike trust could have led to this agreement between Alfred and the Viking Hasteinn, an exchange of gold in return for promises of peace, secured with oaths and hostages? The king of Wessex might hold to his faith, but Ethelred could not shake the memory of Guthrum's assurances of peace followed briskly by his occupation of Cirencester. He shook his head. "No, I do not believe that this is wise."

The Viking had knelt before Alfred, accepted the

191

chests of gold and now turned to beckon his hostages forward. Edward, standing beside his father, leaned forward and whispered into Alfred's ear. The king paused before nodding and Edward walked over to the Mercians. The wind blew through the younger man's cornstalk hair, rippling the spikes, but it was not strong enough to blow away the care-lines drawing two grooves across his brow.

"Lord Ethelred, Hasteinn has given us men and women from amongst his own kin. I do not think that we can send them to my mother; she is not, well enough, to oversee their care. May we send them to my uncle Wulf in Mercia?"

Ethelred nodded. Edward's relief was obvious as his frown gave way to a grateful smile.

Alhelm sucked air through his teeth. "Wulf will not be happy about that."

"Nor will my wife." Ethelred turned to go back into his tent. No, she would be less than happy. Wrathful, frightened even. Had he done the right thing by agreeing to Edward's request? He waved at his servant to begin packing the chests and sat down on a small wooden stool. He could only hope that, despite his wife's fear of the invaders, she would understand the decision, not least because she, more than perhaps her father, was aware of the delicacy of Ewith's mind. And she would know that it was a mark of his faith in her that he trusted her with this task, an important aspect of this war they were now waging against this new pagan threat. He smiled to think of his good fortune and her words to him before they parted. It was a relief to know that she understood the difficulties he faced. Her childhood years left her terrified of the Vikings but being Alfred's daughter also gave her an insight into the struggles to rid England of the heathens. She had always known what it meant to be the kin of kings and now she appeared to be learning what it was to be the wife of Mercia.

He turned his attention to his personal belongings spread out across the small table. He picked up an ivory comb, a gift from his wife. As he stroked the smooth spine and then flicked the teeth-ends, running his finger across them, he allowed his mind to wander until it drew a picture of his wife, gazing up at him as they lay together the night before he left. This was his first enforced absence from her and he had not expected the separation to affect him. After Mildrith, the only thing that mattered to him was freeing Mercia and so he had remained indifferent to his young bride. Despite Wulf's advocacy of her charms, he had found her somewhat aloof, and she was acquiescent, rather than responsive when first she came to his bed, but at least her remote manner had meant that he did not have to talk endlessly to her. Now she had made it clear that she stood not merely behind him, but with him, he could be satisfied that they had an affable and workable relationship on which to build. He smiled, silently congratulating himself. He had been right to stand back, to say nothing, and wait for her youth-lust for Alhelm to flow out of her veins. His silence had been repaid. She was grown-up now, wedded to Mercia. And, as that last night together had suggested, giving a glimpse of happiness and the possibility of deepening their understanding, she was now fully wedded to him.

But he could not hide from his own nagging doubt that her interest in Alhelm might be replaced by a lusting after Anarawd. Alhelm had never been a real threat and Ethelred had only to battle her imaginings, growing smug in the knowledge that his strategy of non-intervention was beginning, at last, to pay off. Anarawd was a different matter. As with Alhelm, Ethelred could match the Welshman for valour but he could not match him for word-craft and easy charm. And it surprised him to find that it was a force other than pride compelling him to do something more substantial than waiting if he were not to lose her a second time. Putting the comb aside, he pressed his forefinger to the bridge of his nose and tried to rub away a tiredness there. If only he could mend the sadness of her lost babies, for he recalled not only her words of support, but the unshed tears in her eyes after she had looked upon the baby Athelstan. With each loss his admiration grew, that she could bear the heartbreak with such outward strength. He wished he could help her, but all he could do was try to give her what she wished for. His wooden cross lay on the bench and he reached out to touch it. Perhaps he had left a new seed planted in her belly the night before he left her. Not being a king, he had no hopes for a dynasty; life in the here and now was all he could think about, but a living babe would ease her hurt and for that, he could only pray.

He looked up to see who had blocked the light from the tent flap. Edward pushed through the gap, followed by Frith and Alhelm. He looked at their faces, stood up quickly and said, "Tell me."

Edward was shaking his head. "The Northumbrian Vikings came down from the north, met those settled in East Anglia and went off to do their worst. My father is leaving now to follow them."

"Where?"

"Headed for Devon. Exeter, we think." He touched Ethelred's arm. "There is more. Those we should have been watching, behind us at Appledore? They have broken out, gone to harry Hampshire."

Ethelred swore and ordered the packed chests to be taken outside. Gathering his personal belongings he wrapped his cross in a soft leather cloth and tucked it into the otter-skin bag hanging from his belt. To Edward and Frith he said, "Follow them. Alhelm and I will take Hasteinn's women back to Mercia and then we will come to find you."

"But my lord, all the men of Wessex and half those of Mercia will be elsewhere. Do you have enough to fight, should you need to?"

"Alhelm and I will be all that each other needs."

Frith laid an arm on Edward's shoulder. "Do not worry, friend. These two have an understanding that goes beyond steadfastness."

Alhelm looked at Ethelred, as if staring out across all that had been left unspoken. "My lord knows that I would die for him. He needs me to say naught else."

Ethelred nodded. "I know it. No other words are needed." He turned back to Edward. "Go now." As Edward held the tent flap for Frith to duck under, Ethelred said, "My Brother of Wessex, keep this always in your mind. Watch them. Know where they are at all times. And if you can keep them from knowing where you are, so much the better."

"Alhelm told me of your sharp mind. I am keen to learn from you." Edward bent to duck through the opening, but he hesitated, placing his hand on Ethelred's arm. "I have no wish to live my father's life, always running, catching but letting go."

Ethelred was cautious. Alfred was his ally. "I understand. But we must fight them."

Edward stepped back into the tent and stood up. "Fight them, yes, but to the bitter end. Guthrum was an oath-breaking swine and I would not be minded to leave even my turds in Hasteinn's keeping."

Ethelred laughed in surprise. "We will work together well, Wessex. Nightly do I pray that Guthrum burns in hell for what he did to my lands. Do not worry; first let us deal with this new threat, then we will build such a strong England that they will never dare to come back."

"What am I meant to do with her?"

Teasel stared at the Viking woman, who was wearing a striking boat-shaped brooch. But this was no ordinary decoration; its design incorporated every menacing detail of the hated longboats, including the dragon head and even a tiny face, depicting the lookout at the top of the mast. Below it, a pendant shaped like a hammer moved up and down in rhythm with the woman's breath, glinting in the reflected light from the hearth-fire. Her serving-woman sported a bear's tooth as a pendant and her hair was tidied behind an odd linen cap, tied under her chin. Teasel looked again at the woman, whose breath flowed in fast waves, forcing the hammer-pendant in a shallow upward movement as her breath came in ragged snatches, but whose face showed only haughty disdain. Teasel noted the woman's silver spiral arm ring that seemed to coil into a serpent's head, and she shuddered. She turned back to the hapless escort. "Tell me, and tell me plain."

While he spoke, she continued to steal brief but frequent glances at this living breathing enemy. The woman's brow was set in a frown; her sullen face, filthy, was framed by braided hair. Her plaid cloak was like any that one could see on the backs of English women. The most striking aspect of the woman's appearance, save for her strange metal adornments, was her height, for she was only as tall at Teasel, who had long imagined that these foreign invaders stood eight feet tall or more.

The road-weary thegn had hardly stood from his bow, remaining in a cringing lunge as he told her, "Your father took this woman and the rest of them as tokens of the heathen Hasteinn's goodwill." He flinched. "He also gave them gold, my lady. Lord Ethelred was not glad."

"No, I can believe that my husband is far from glad." She glanced again at the woman, whose arms were folded, and then back at the messenger. "Speak on."

"Your father is in Devon fighting the settlers from the north and east and your brother is following the host from Appledore. Your husband was on his way to bring these hostages to you when we had word that Hasteinn has already broken his oath and gone from Milton to Benfleet to seek out more riches. My lord has gone to deal with him."

Teasel put a hand to her throat. "Who is with him?"

"Lord Alhelm and all the north Mercians. And as I left them, word came in that King Alfred has sent half his fyrd to help them and, as far as I know, that means that the lords of Somerset and Wiltshire are with them now."

Teasel shifted her gaze yet again to the ragged woman standing by the fire. She wondered if she dared to take a step nearer to ascertain whether these foreigners had a different smell about them. "You tell me of all the harm that this woman's kind has unleashed on our land and look how she stands with her head high. What manner of beings are they, these Vikings, that they have no hearts? Do they even know our words?"

"The high-born one does. Her women have but a gossip of English. What will you do with her, my lady?"

She had no idea. The woman's life should be forfeit, for her husband had broken his oath, but it was not for her to mete out the punishment. She would happily send the woman for ordeal, by fire or water, or throw her into one of the jails on the royal manors, but it was not her right. Until told otherwise, she would have to show her the hospitality and respect due to a high-ranking hostage. "I will feed her. I will clothe her. I will hate her. But I will not fear her."

197

Farnham, Surrey, Wessex

Edward rode alongside Frith. They kept their heads down in a futile attempt to keep the squally spring rain from pummelling their faces. Their moods were grim and well matched; Frith had left a pregnant wife at home and Edward rode away from his own woman and child. But Edward felt the strength of providence as he urged his mount forward and knew that in England, at this time, there was no other reason for his existence than to be here in this place. The thought turned his mind to the shaming events at Milton. He and his father spoke to the same God, but Alfred deeply trusted that faith-driven benevolence would win over these heathens. Edward believed that God's purpose for him was to drive the scum back across the sea, wasting no time on preaching or converting. He could only hope that Ethelred had received his message and was even now on his way to deal with the duplicitous Hasteinn. He, meanwhile, had studiously followed his brother-in-law's advice, stalking the host from Appledore, sending small bands of men to skirmish with them as they tore their way through Hampshire and Berkshire, but keeping his main force well out of their sight. He lifted his head and glanced across at Frith. "Far enough?"

Frith put a gloved hand to his face and wiped it across his rain-soaked cheeks. "I think so. We are well ahead of them; if we turn and stand now we will have time to ready ourselves before they come upon us."

Edward wheeled his horse around and gave the order to halt. A shiver of doubt ran down his spine, washed along with the penetrating rain. Watching, unseen, they had waited until the Vikings, loaded with booty, began their return journey. Edward had ordered his men to leave before them, thus staying ahead of the enemy. Now they would turn, send their horses to the rear, stand, and surprise the bastards. But should they have acted sooner? Were they still undiscovered, or were their foes already swinging their axes, ready for a fight? Edward looked about him. They had come up to the top of a low ridge, lined with trees. Here, they could hide, but still come forward with enough time to line up the shield wall. The ridge was not so high that the foreigners would attempt to go round it and by the time they saw the English forces, it would be too late for them to turn and run. As long as they were still unaware of the English presence.

Frith slipped from his saddle and led his horse up beyond the line of trees. Going to each group of men, their division dictated by their tribal inclinations or geographical origins, he established the identity of the archer snipers and ordered them to the edge of the trees, where they could be ready to attack the flanks of the enemy. Edward noted his friend's actions, and took comfort from knowing that Frith would anticipate any order he might think to give, working efficiently for the good of the whole company. He caught, though, the expression on the other man's face, which betrayed his inner sadness. This was a man determined to busy himself and take his thoughts away from home. Edward, atheling, heir to the throne of Wessex, knew that he would have to go one step further and push all thoughts of Gwen and his boy out of his head altogether. Here, now, naught mattered but the winning of this battle.

Perhaps an hour passed, maybe a little more, the rain eased, but he was right not to let the men start fires for cooking. He heard them a moment before he saw them, for they were singing. The words were unintelligible, but for Edward the meaning was clear. Strolling along, walking with the horse-drawn cartloads of looted treasure, voices raised in song, this was an army marching triumphant, relaxed, off its guard. The Vikings had no idea that Edward was ahead of them.

The Vikings were armed, but their swords were sheathed, their axes tucked through their belts. Several of the men had hitched a ride in the back of the carts and were swigging ale from pilfered jugs and leather bottles. One man at the front of the group was walking backwards, exhorting the others with his whirling arms to keep up the singsong as they ambled. Edward turned and motioned to his men. This could be a rout, if they only held fast until the right moment. It was up to him to judge when that would be. Keeping his arm raised to hold his men back, he waited until the staggering, swaggering raiders were too close for retreat. He saw the last of the carts come up the slope and waited until the point at which it would roll backwards if momentum ceased to pull it. The wheels rumbled slowly over the uneven ground and the stolen goods jangled and clanked with every bump. Gold chalices, plates and cups, jewellery, coin and holy relics jostled and jumped as the thieves hauled them towards the ridge. In front of the biggest cart, a horse caught sight of movement in the trees and snickered loudly. A few of the Vikings stopped to look up and Edward brought his arm down, signalling to the men behind him. The Englishmen burst from their shelter, forming a line with their shields pressed hard together and ran down the hill as one, battering the stunned raiders at the head of the convoy and standing to do battle with the rest.

The drunks slithered from the carts and only then cast about for their weapons, slung carelessly into the wagons when first they'd boarded. Scrabbling to find them, they were no help to those engaged with the Saxon shield-bearers and some of them gave up the hunt for arms and began instead to attempt to drag the carts backwards in a bid to escape with their booty. A stand-off at the shield wall left one Saxon with a shoulder wound and another with a slashed cheek, but seven Vikings lay on the ground, dead or dying. But others in their line began to turn, slipping in the wet grass now churned to mud, and saw their comrades making off with the spoils of their earlier raids. Anxious not to lose all, they deserted the front line and ran to join those in retreat, either to assist, or fight for their share.

Edward shouted out. "After them!"

Caught in open ground, with no hope of forming a wall, the raiders had to stand and fight on their own, and the meadow was dotted with pairs of men, fighting hand to hand, one on one. Edward stood back from the prone body of his challenger and assessed the scene before him. Only a few of his men were still engaged in battle. The main group, no longer required, stood safe behind the wall. Two of the enemy broke away from the individual combat and one was brought to the ground by an axe flung through the air after him. Edward signalled to the archers to pick off the few who were still fleeing, but he saw no point now in pursuing them on foot. He allowed a few stragglers to escape, and turned his attention to the carts. Let the few who lived keep their lives and so tell a warning to others; they had naught to show for their scavenging and England's riches were back in the hands of the English.

He went back to the shield wall and was content to find that no more of his men had been injured. Nodding towards the fallen foe he said, "Bury them." He held out his hands to Frith and they locked arms, each gripping the other by the forearms. "A good day's work, my friend. Now, let us get warm and dry."

He tensed when he heard a cry from behind the ridge. Dear God, had he underestimated the slack rabble? Had they regrouped somehow and come up behind him? No, not enough had been spared. He squinted through the misty dampness and relaxed when he saw that it was a lone rider, a messenger he had sent out for news almost two weeks ago.

The man tumbled off his horse and staggered forward. "My lord, grim tidings. King Alfred is still in Exeter and cannot gain ground against the heathens there. He has sent half his men to the Mercians, to aid the fight with Hasteinn at Benfleet. And there is talk of another host, gathered at Shoebury and digging in." The man gasped and filled his lungs, panting most of the air straight out again.

Edward turned to Frith. "God help us, they are at us from all sides. Can we hold?"

Gloucester

Teasel tucked the basket of loaves under her arm and made her way to the hall. Despite the warming spring sunshine and the cheering sight of the white may blossom, a fleeting wave of sadness washed through her mind, but she stood up straight and brought her shoulders out of a hunch. This day was like every other; bread must be baked, stores checked, cows milked. But the sense of loss would not go away and she ceased the attempt to fool herself. It had little to do with the emptiness, yet again, of her womb. The basket of loaves was not so full as usual, not all the tables in the hall would be fully laid. Apart from Wulf, who was too old now, and Brihtsige, who was in mourning, the men were gone. The steading was empty and now she knew how her mother had felt for all those years, when Alfred was away. Well, she would not retreat into shadows where darkness fed the monster of fear. She shoved at the hall door with her free hip and dumped the loaves on the nearest table. There was work to be done and she pushed her sleeves away from her wrists and hauled another trestle away from the wall.

"Let me help you."

She swallowed to push her heart back down from her throat and put a hand to her chest as she spoke to Brihtsige. "You made my heart leap. I thought I was alone in here."

He smiled but did not reply. He took hold of the table and pulled it with ease, sliding it next to the first one. He pointed to the batch of loaves. "On here?" She nodded and he took four of the loaves and placed them in the middle of the second table. "Shall I take some to Gunnhildr?"

Teasel stared at him. Even at his most well-behaved, Brihtsige had never been more than frostily polite in his dealings with her. At his worst... She could never entirely shake the notion that he had sought to wreak more than mere mischief the day the mill caught fire. Now, only a few weeks into mourning for his father Beornoth, he was pretending friendliness and offering to take food to the principal hostage. Sensing that not all was as it appeared, she nevertheless could think of no reason to refuse him. Furthermore, she welcomed the excuse not to go herself. "Why not?"

He lowered his head in a semblance of a bow and the sunlight from the window revealed motes of dust dancing around his copper mane. As if sensing her scrutiny, he looked up and said, "She tells me tales. Sagas, they call them. It eases my pain."

Sad enough about Beornoth's passing, she hung her own head in sympathy and let all ungenerous thoughts fly from her mind. He gathered up the bread and left her alone in the hall. She turned her attention to the benches and the shaft of sunlight, unimpeded now by the blocking figure of Brihtsige, led her gaze to the jugs of ale on a small table by the back wall. "Brihtsige, wait!" But he was long gone and she set about lining up the benches and laying a jug upon each board. A girl from the dairy came in with the cheeses and two slave boys arrived to wait on table for the diners. They stirred the fire into angry life and the dairymaid reached up to straighten a wall hanging. Teasel thanked her, noting that the cloth was fading from constant visits of sunlight upon its edge, the once vibrant red now a rusty hue. Resolving to set time aside to switch all the hangings around, she continued to busy herself, but the remaining ale jug was always in her peripheral vision, reminding her of her task. Sighing, she scooped it up and went to the Viking woman's hut.

Gunnhildr, dressed in ill-fitting Mercian clothes but still wearing her own goatskin boots, was standing by the hearth. Brihtsige, the man who was in mourning, was sitting with one foot crossed over the other knee, laughing while the Viking woman told him a funny tale.

"So that is how he got his name. He never forgave us, old Hare-hugger. He sent the girl a birch-bark scroll, writing on it how he loved her still, but she'd upped and wed another by then."

Brihtsige chuckled again, but the woman's mouth straightened into a wistful line. "I should send a birch-bark to my man back home, to tell him I live."

Teasel thumped the jug down on a wooden chest. "And would you write it in your heathen rune marks? Your husband will know that you live for we do not kill women. And he is not 'home', for this is our land, not yours. You have no right to it."

Gunnhildr looked at her, in a way that reminded Teasel of the kitchen cats disdaining sour milk. "Your land? Ask the Welsh what they think about that. See this brooch? See how what we call the gripping beast grabs at his own throat? In throwing your words at me, you only choke yourself." She turned back to Brihtsige. "I said I would show you a game of Hefntafl." She clicked her fingers and her serving-woman darted forward. "Bring my gaming board."

The woman brought the square wooden board and placed it on the table. It was edged with decorative carving and the centre was punched with holes which would hold the gaming pieces. From two of the sides, carved wooden heads protruded, one larger than the other. Gunnhildr turned the board so that the larger of the heads pointed towards Brihtsige. "Let us begin."

Teasel stared at the exotic board but as the two players began to move the pieces, she scoffed inwardly. This was naught more than a different version of their own game of Tables and the aim of the warrior pieces to trap the king in the corner was exactly the same. She opened her mouth to say as much, but without a backward glance the woman held up her hand indicating that she required silence in which to concentrate, while Brihtsige leaned in over the board and supported his chin with his fist.

Teasel, forgotten, slammed out of the hut. *'Ask the Welsh what they think about that.'* How dare she speak so? Teasel was not to blame for her forefathers' settlement of British land. She had not even been born then, whereas Gunnhildr was fully involved in the attempted takeover of Saxon England. Damn the woman, for seeking to shift the blame and for beguiling Brihtsige. Ask the Welsh, indeed. She could not think about past wrongs, only the here and now and fighting for what was right at that moment. And thinking of that ancient race made her think only of the wild Welshman who taught her to appreciate what, no, *who*, she had already in her possession. She stopped in the middle of the yard and slapped her hands on her thighs. "Enough." *Home.* That had been the word that fired the anger, the indignation, in her heart.

Turning on her heel, she marched to her private bower and knelt down by the side of her bed. *Lord God, be always with my lord Ethelred and give him the strength to smite down our foes. And let my faith in him bide unwavering in my heart.* Reaching under the bed, she pulled out the locked travelling-chest and took a key from her belt. Opening the carved wooden lid, she took out the contents one by one and separated them into different chests. The bag of coin slid down the side of a larger box containing currency and jewels. The cloak, folded tightly, just fitted into her clothes chest. She took the blanket, shook it to air it, folded it once and laid it over her bed. She stood up. "I will never run away. This is my home and here I stay."

Long ago, she had learned that the common folk suffered far more than she ever could, or would. In that knowledge, she had found that it was best always to hide the fear that had stalked her every moment, asleep or awake.

She had learned to make the best of every situation. She did not want to be left behind; she would rather be where the men were, where there was no wondering, no worrying. Here, she was too close to the enemy with no power. This was a woman's fate, then. But she would not cower in a corner, nor wring her hands in premature mourning. Gunnhildr would have one attendant only, from this day onwards; an ever present companion who would teach her to forget Hefntafl and say 'Tables'. The board might be different, but the game was the same.

Back outside in the yard, she walked taller, shoulders back, the crown of her head reaching towards the sky. She saw one of the Vikings' horses, and recalled that when the hostages arrived she had asked why their bridles had been stripped, only to be told that they had no pendant ornaments handing from their bridles. The only metal which adorned the horse-gear had been the odd and uncomfortable-looking iron stirrups. Teasel laughed. What poor, plain, ugly monsters these heathens had turned out to be.

Alyth waved and came to speak to her, her baby boy wrapped tight against the cold and snuggled against her breast. "There is a shadow on your chest my lady; what has lifted your chin so high to do that?"

Teasel took a long breath in, feeling the cool air in her nostrils. "That Viking woman is fond of playing games. So now she and I will play a game. But when it comes to showing the most pride, she will have to settle for being a sorry loser."

Benfleet, Essex

Ethelred watched the ships burning. The flames coiled hungrily around the timbers and reached eagerly to devour the masts. Like hounds at feeding time, they ate noisily, spitting and cracking. A serpent-shaped wooden figurehead lurched up, its mouth spewing fire, the eye eerily alight, its last hiss impotent in the seconds before it was consumed by its own furnace flare. A flake of paint lifted from the beast's neck, curling up and dancing in the heated wind, before breaking free and flying off into the ember-strewn sky. The smoke reached the shore and Ethelred had time to see the vessels fall in on themselves, no fuel left for the fire as the skeleton ships folded into the water, before he turned, wiping his stinging eyes.

As the last dragon-prow plunged into watery oblivion, Alhelm came to stand alongside his lord. "Their 'wave-walkers' do not look so proud now, do they? The only shame is that the swine Hasteinn is not here to see his fleet go under."

Ethelred wiped the back of his hand across his eyes again. The high summer heat had left him sweating and the salty moisture mixed with the thick smoke was an irritating brew. He did not care about Hasteinn; he would come back from wherever he was raiding and find his camp destroyed, his ships sunk and all the treasure so far amassed restored to the churches of England. And he would know that wherever

208

he went from now on, the English would hunt him down.

Alhelm pointed to a solitary boat anchored at the far end of the harbour, safe from the reach of the licking flames. "What about that one?"

"I am sending it to Alfred at Exeter. A gift; of hope."

Arm in arm, they walked back through the remnants of the Viking camp. The few remaining livestock, the beasts that had not run off, had been rounded up and tethered, to become future food stock for the English troops. Deep trenches ran from one side of the enclosure almost up the harbour's edge. The labourers worked loudly, Mercians working alongside West Saxons, asking questions of each other.

"Do they bury their dead like this?"

"Who cares? Lord Wiltshire said to do it, so we do it."

"Should've burned the scum with their ships."

Alhelm chuckled. "They work well together against a common foe. If any ever had doubts about this fellowship, they need look no further than here to breathe new life into their faith."

"Pray God it lasts. We are not done yet." Ethelred ducked ahead of Alhelm into his tent. "First, I will wash the sweat away."

Alhelm followed him in and let the flap fall behind him. "And then?"

"Then we go and find the rest of them."

Buttington, River Severn, Mercia

The scop was sitting with his legs crossed and his slender hand cupping his chin. "Tell me that bit again, for I must have every part right before I can begin to make up my song."

The soldier sighed. "I thought you scops were quick-witted? I'll begin again. The English were all away fighting. Alfred was in Exeter, Edward at Farnham and Ethelred at Benfleet. News came that a Viking host had come to Shoebury." He paused. "You have, I take it, enough about the great wins at Benfleet and Farnham? You know that after Edward took back the gold from the thieves he chased and besieged them? Then I will carry on. From their stronghold at Shoebury, these Vikings sailed along the Thames where they gathered to them more heathens from East Anglia and Northumbria, swelling their number threefold. Then they sailed along the Severn and came to this place." He rubbed his nose. "I must say, you might wait until we have won here, or else died, before you begin to write. Ah, Lord Ethelred, forgive me, I did not see you there."

The soldier jumped up and lowered his head to hide his flushed cheeks, but Ethelred signalled for him to sit down.

The scop was braver. "My lord, do you have aught to add to the tale? If I am to sing of your greatness I need every…"

"There is naught." Ethelred agreed with the soldier, that it might be better to wait until the story's end before writing it. It was true that the poet would need more detail, but it was not for Ethelred to tell him. Why have a scop and sing yourself? Besides, his adornments to the tale would consist only of strategies, of lessons learned and never forgotten. As soon as he had been able, he had taken his forces along the Shoebury trail. Never again would men of Mercia be caught off guard; this he had sworn the day he met Anarawd in Gwynedd. Wary ever since of ambushes, he had kept outriders on the road, who had shadowed those Shoebury Vikings as they made their way to meet their reinforcements. And after the humiliation at Milton, he had made sure that he knew where the enemy was at all times, with a network of messengers scouring the country, keeping track of all hostile activity. And so, knowing that there were no other hosts nearby to help them, he had followed them here, to Buttington, watched as they dug themselves in and then begun his siege, damming the river beyond the meadow so that the little stream could be diverted away from the Viking camp. As the enemy who sought to hide changed into the enemy trapped within, Ethelred made sure that they knew they were surrounded, sending men to camp on the west side of the river whilst he remained on the east. They had no water, and no escape route. It had been three weeks now and the smell was getting stronger. In battle, he used his ears to listen for when the music changed. Here, he was learning to use his nose. The heathens had killed most of their animals for food but now the stench came from the carcasses left rotting for lack of speed in butchery and a new odour rose on the late summer wind, telling a tale of sickness. Of death.

Leaving the scop to extract what information he still could from the weary soldier, Ethelred walked away from their little campfire towards his own, where Alhelm was keeping watch over the spitted mutton while the lords

Somerset and Wiltshire cradled their ale cups and dozed in the midday sun. Ethelred turned to look at the beleaguered fortress behind him. Noon; nearly time for food. All men grew vocal at mealtimes. He'd been wrong to think that only his nose was required here. There was a song of siege; and it was silent when those besieged were starving.

Ethelred tucked his foot under a stool and dragged it nearer the fire. Alhelm looked up and asked the question with his raised eyebrow.

"Soon. They are dying."

Somerset snorted himself fully awake. "They like it not when the arrow turns in flight and hits the bowman. How long have they used these strongholds as bases for their thievery and bloodletting? Now they are as a trap to them."

Wiltshire said, "Do we have enough men to overcome them when they do come out? They will be weakened, I know, but even so…"

Hoof beats pummelled the dusty ground beyond the stream. The men labouring on the earthworks by the river came running, but their faces showed no alarm, the sweat on their brows indicative of naught more than the effect of labouring in the hot sunshine.

Ethelred stood up. He recognised the newcomers and allowed himself a smile. "We have more than enough men now." He walked forward to embrace the leader of the new arrivals, who returned the hug and draped his arm around Ethelred's shoulder.

"Riding is thirsty work, Sais," said Anarawd of Gwynedd. "I hope you have plenty of your weak English ale waiting for me."

After the days of church-like quiet, the single shout was a powerful, unmistakable signal. They were coming out. The English and Welsh gathered, waiting beyond the gate in the palisade, curious to see what the enemy would look like after five weeks of starvation and privation. Hairy and smelly, Wiltshire had said. Naught new there, then, Somerset had replied. But now all humour was put aside, as shield walls clattered into position, Mercian linden wood butted up against Welsh shields, Wessex bowstrings taut to protect Hwicce spear-throwers.

The wooden gate opened slowly, the unseasoned wood giving a high-pitched creak as it yielded. They came out in a straggle, shoulders rounded, cheeks fallen in after weeks without food to fill them out. But their heads were not heavy and they carried them proudly, with chins up and jaws jutting forward. These were men determined to die well. Ethelred thought idly about singling out their scop, or skald as they would call him, to find out how he would sing of this shambolic ending.

The Vikings arranged themselves into a shield wall and began their advance towards the English line. Ethelred braced himself for the impact, waiting for the instant when the two lines smashed into each other, forcing a moment of impasse where neither side could move forward, nor would move back. The clash came, the dull thud as shield hit shield, and Ethelred caught the foetid breath of the man opposite him, but he was able straight away to take a step forward. Glancing sideways, he saw that the other men in his line had all felt the weakness in the opposing line. With another push, the defenders were forced back another few steps and a few of them stumbled.

One of Alhelm's thegns leaped from his position at the end of the shield wall. Leaning over a fallen Norseman, he said, "Thank your gods that you did not starve in there. Off you go now instead to your Valhalla." He sent him there with one sword thrust to the chest. Other Englishmen had broken away to despatch the rest of the fallen men, but now the lines regrouped. These Vikings were not about to give up.

The English pushed forward again, this time shattering the enemy wall. The starving men scattered; some scrabbled to their feet, some ran. Ethelred stepped from the shield wall and smashed his shoulder against the man with the foul-smelling breath. The man raised his shield against Ethelred's sword, lowered it as Ethelred tried to slice into his thigh, but was too slow to raise it again and Ethelred brought his blade down on the man's shoulder, driving deep towards his neck until it severed the ties of life. Beyond him, the lords of Somerset and Wiltshire stood in front of the men, slashing and parrying, protected at the back by their faithful retainers, meeting little resistance to their front. A cry rose up from the Welsh and Ethelred was sure he heard Anarawd exhorting his men to earn their supper. The men of Gwynedd loosed a torturous and constant chain of arrows upon the enemy, whooping and cheering whenever they hit their targets.

Alhelm came, panting, to Ethelred's side. He waved his sword towards those who were fleeing. "Shall we follow?"

Ethelred inhaled through his nose, instantly regretting it as blood and sweat surged up his nostrils. He threw down his helm and wiped stinging blobs of moisture from his eyes. "Leave them. They are too few."

"But if they think to try again?"

"We will beat them." He walked over to the West Saxons and clasped hands first with Somerset, then with Wiltshire. "It is done, my lords. Pray God that our win here does not mean Alfred's loss at Exeter."

He strode back across the bloody field and motioned to a thegn to detail a digging party. Turning back towards their encampment, he saw the scop. The poet was counting the numbers of dead. Ethelred said, "You can sing it this evening, if you have it ready."

"Yes, my lord. How does this sound? All before him, dead and crushed. His death-bringer sang as it cleaved their skulls. He left none alive…"

Ethelred put his hand out to stop the gyrating arms. "Do not sing of the death of all Vikings. We won this day. There will be others."

"Ah, but such a day, my lord." He began again. "Blood ran over the earth, seeping from their wounds, their eyes saw only death…"

Ethelred left him to it.

Alhelm came to find him in his tent and handed him his abandoned helm. "They will come again, you know. We should truly have left none alive."

Ethelred put down the helm, sighed and stretched out on his bed. He waved at his boy to pull his boots off. "They will come again anyway. This day was but a beginning. It is not yet over."

Alhelm sat down on a stool and leaned his elbows on the table. "So where do we go now?"

"Speak for yourself, but I am going to go home." He looked up at his friend. "To my wife."

Alhelm held his gaze and stared at him for a moment before nodding his head. "She will welcome it." He called for ale and then said, "You are my friend and my lord. You must know that when I am in the shield wall at your behest, I will never step beyond the line without your leave."

Ethelred stretched his arms above his head. "I know it. Truly." *You have never stepped in my way. Your shadow, though, is another matter. Let us hope it has shortened while we have been away.*

Gloucester

She awoke, cold. Now began a fight, between her desire to stay in bed, the warmest place in the room, though still chilly, or get up and poke the fire to life, thus getting colder in the process, but with the promise of being able to sleep again, warm. The dawn came later now that it was autumn, and so the chill of the night retreated more slowly in the mornings. Conceding that she would not feel comfortable again without stoking the fire, she leaped from the bed, jiggled at the dying embers with the poker until a curl of flame began to twist around the half burned log and then she scrambled back under the blankets and furs, desperate to snuggle back down before the warm space grew cold in her absence. Curled into the smallest possible shape, she waited for the shivering to subside. Only then did her mind take in what her eyes had seen. The cots beside her bed were empty, her women gone. Even Alyth, who slept with her when Frith was away, was absent. Sighing, she accepted that her attempts to heat up were in vain. She sat up and grabbed at a fur cloak, slipping it round her shoulders before making her way to the hall. There, she found more activity than among Bishop Werferth's beloved bees. A spit had been assembled just beyond the hall steps and a side of beef was already basted and ready to turn. An ant-line of cooks came from the bake-house, carrying baskets of loaves. Inside, Teasel's women darted between the servants setting

216

up the tables, barking orders to the bakers, baxters and dairymaids. There was also a carpenter's din inside her own head. She put a hand up to her temple, then reached out with the other to slow Alyth as she hurtled past. "What is going on?"

Alyth, her arms full of napkins, stopped and released a girlish smile. "Forgive us, my lady. A rider came in before dawn with news that the men are on their way home. You were so tired after last night that we thought to let you sleep on."

Last night. Staying up with Gunnhildr and, because despite her misgivings she felt sorry for him, Brihtsige. Playing board games; no enjoyment, just determined to win, a point of pride. She'd retired late, too late, victorious, but with a head too full of wine, hence the hammering now in her head. Silly. "When are they due?"

Alyth stepped towards the door and squinted up at the broadening sky. "Soon." She bobbed, and hurried off to unburden herself of the napkins and find another job to do.

Teasel waylaid a young man on his way to the blacksmith's lodge. "Will you go to the church and tell the bishop that Lord Ethelred is on his way home? We would welcome his grace and blessing at our hall this day."

Standing still, she felt for one moment as if she were at the centre of a whirlpool; calm and unaffected. Yet as soon as she stepped to one side, and narrowly missed knocking into another consignment from the bakery, she became part of the eddy, swept along on the excitement with no time to think about how she felt. The men were coming home and it was simply a good thing.

The fear had long since left. She could look out at an approaching army without feeling compelled to turn and run. Standing on the hall steps, waiting to welcome her lord, her husband, she had a moment now to consider what it meant to her. Not the leaping stomach that used to await Alhelm, but a comforting, soft relief that all were home and well and that there would be an end to loneliness and cold sheets. She hoped that she did not look as worry-worn as Alhelm's wife, brought to Gloucester when the hordes came too close to her lands, but growing paler by the day since her arrival.

The Mercians rode into the yard, their vibrantly painted shields grubby, top-coated with browned blood and ready-to-crumble black mud. The banners flapped their tattered edges, one displaying the perfect outline of a boot print. Spears appeared twice their normal weight and even the horses walked with their heads low, barely picking their hooves up above the fallen leaves. Yet as the men filed into the enclosure and spotted their loved ones in the welcoming throng, they stood taller, smiles breaking across the mud-lined, sweat-streaked faces.

The ealdormen had thegns to attend to their horses and they walked to the steps where their ladies awaited them. Frith, blond hair hanging long and dirty, said nothing, but took his youngest child from Alyth's arms, kissed the boy's head and reached over the infant to kiss his wife, wrapping his free arm around her waist and leading her away. Alhelm had nothing more than a perfunctory, "My lady," for his wife, before he began his enthusiastic retelling of the siege of Buttington, still at loyal pains to point out the brilliance of his lord's manoeuvring. "We had begun to give up hope, but my lord Ethelred came to us, with stirring words…"

Ethelred stood in front of Teasel. He, like Frith, had nothing to say. He looked at her, his irises quivering as if he expected her to turn to look at Alhelm, but she could not take her gaze from his face which looked so desperately fatigued. His cheekbones stood in sharp relief, above the hollows where once there had been well-fed flesh. He smiled at her, but his eyebrows did not shift down towards the rising mouth, so that his eyes hardly moved, remaining vacant and watery below heavily blinking lids. She put her arm out, and brushed a fall of hair from his brow, sweeping

218

her hand down to stroke his earlobe. If it felt odd to him that she gave him the touch usually reserved for her beloved brother, he did not show surprise, and the movement felt natural to her. She took a step towards him. "Welcome home."

She held her arm out to him and flicked a glance at the assembled noblemen. Wulf stood amongst his brethren, and all the old guard smiled benevolently, as if, in that one gesture, she had erased all their memories of her disloyal heart, and earned, at last, their approval.

Ethelred had yet to step into her embrace and he was looking down at her belly. She shook her head quickly and he nodded. Coming forward in response to her outstretched arm, he slid his hand around her waist and led her to her bower. His grip was gentle, and the warmth of his hand radiated through her woollen kirtle and warmed her still-chilled bones. She was used to his touch, neither welcoming nor rejecting it, at ease with the familiar. But today she felt the urge to respond to him, today she wanted to tell him how she beat the Viking woman at the gaming table, how she was happy and proud to fight, in whatever tiny way she could, in his name. Standing beside her bed, she helped him to remove his sword and belt and knelt to pull his grimy boots off.

Childlike impatience willed him to notice, but she knew that a man would never see the detail in a room. So she pointed to the travelling-blanket, laid out neatly on top of the bed. "I have unpacked. My home is here with you. I had faith that you would win."

His eyes registered surprise, his brows lifting for a second. He smiled.

Feeling stupid in his silence, she said, "You did? You won?"

He sat down on the bed and swung his legs round onto the covers. Leaning back, he put his hands behind his head. "Yes, we won. This time."

She sat down beside him and dared to touch him,

stroking his thigh. He did not move. Her cheeks warming, she said, "Do you not want to?"

"I am tired. You do not have to."

The disappointed child, silenced once, now returned to have its little whine. He had not noticed the significance of her unpacked chest, was blind to her freshly combed hair and had not noticed her scent, bought all those years ago in London and saved for special occasions. His first homecoming since their wedding and all her efforts to be a good wife had gone unnoticed. She had been wrong. He was as indifferent to her as he had been on their wedding night and now she felt a fool. "*Have* to? From duty, you mean? My lord, only duty would make me come to you now, for you have shown that you do not want me willing." The devil-child within was in full, sulky attack. She stood up, came round to his side of the bed and folded her arms across her chest. "I wonder if you would even know who it was beneath you, so little do you look at me."

He leaped up to stand before her and she flinched. He took hold of her wrist, forcing her arms away from her body. "Do you want it? Do you want me?"

Beneath the dirt, penetrating the layers of worry and weariness, his expression showed. She had seen the look enough times now to recognise it; whenever Alhelm was nearby, when Anarawd spoke to her. Now, she understood what it meant. "Yes," she said, "I do."

She flung her arms wide and he stepped nearer. Hugging him tight she reached up to kiss his neck. He pushed her back to arm's length and took her hand, pulling her back towards the bed. But she resisted. Putting a hand to his face, she stroked his cheek and said, "But I would know. Do you want me? Always you seem unmoved by me, our time together."

"I was waiting," he said. He looked around the room. "And now I see that there are no shadows here."

Puzzled but content, she shook her head and raised her face to his. He bent to kiss her, gently as always. But then he gripped her more tightly and the kiss became something deeper. He stepped his body against hers and they tumbled onto the bed. She raised her pelvis to his and wrapped one leg around his calf. He kissed her earlobe and said, "My God, how I have waited for this. For you to want this."

Her stomach lurched and the sensation slid all the way down to the tops of her thighs. The child within was banished, neither to be seen nor heard.

He was lying with his arm under her neck, his hand dangling but just able to reach to stroke her arm. A trickle of sweat still held its line down his breastbone and she wriggled closer to him, blissful to be warm again. And what a way to be warm. She smiled at the memory and looked up at his face. He was staring at the ceiling. "Tell me now," she said.

"The scop has it all for you. You will hear it tonight."

She propped herself up on her elbow. "You are weary; you must sleep."

"I will sleep when I am done, for it will be the sleep of the dead." He turned onto his side and looked into her eyes. "For now, I only want it to stop. For a little while, so I can believe it is all finished. With you, lying here with me, I can believe that the world has gone and it is all over. But not if I sleep."

She stroked his eyebrow smooth with her little finger. "I wish you had spoken to me before of your worries."

He shrugged. "It was not the right time. I was mourning. You were young."

She moved her hand to the other eyebrow. "And I was part of your worries; the Wessex woman who did not belong. A token of a friendship that none believed in." Perhaps now, after his victory at Buttington, the doubters would believe. And if he would make use of her as a haven from the battlefield, from the reality of the heathen incursions, then she would do that for him and with pleasure, for she had need of him too. Then she remembered that she had the gift of a tale for him. She explained to him how she had beaten Gunnhildr at the tables. He laughed.

"Good girl. I must release them and send them back to Hasteinn. What?"

She had forgotten how a genuine laugh transformed his face. "Naught, my lord. I am a little, that is to say, I have a need, too."

"Tell me, then."

Lying on her back with her head resting on his chest, she told him of her fears and horrors when the hostages arrived. "At first, I was frightened. Then I was eaten up by feelings of wrath, that this woman could stand at my hearth as if she owned it. I heard her speak of our land as if she owned that too and I watched as she bewitched Brihtsige. It was as if she were all the ghosts that stalked me in dreams, the seed of all my hatred and fear and I knew I had to belittle her, somehow. That is when I hatched my plan to beat her. She taught me her way of playing Hefntafl and I won. It felt good."

Her head wobbled as he chuckled. "So, what is your need?"

"To share the feeling. It was frightening; as if I walked along the edge of the world, all alone. I could stand it for so long, but then I had a need of warmth, a need to speak of what I had done." *For someone to put their hand on the small of my back and tell me that all will be well. As you did, today.*

He pulled away from underneath her, sliding her so that she was fully on her back, and leaned over her. "Then give yourself to me, and I will shield you with my life."

"I will. I have. I do."

Lady Æthelflæd was sitting on her own specially carved chair, next to the lord of Mercia in his great hall. Just on the edge of the table, he held her hand in his, fingers interlaced. While he talked, ate and drank, he stroked her palm with his thumb. Around them, sharing their food, family and friends were all enjoying the celebratory meal. This was not her entire family, but all her kin and companions here were loved. She felt at home. Glancing across at Ethelred, she thought of what had passed earlier and smiled, reminders of how he had made her feel causing a pleasant sensation to rise up from her loins and nestle as a warmth in her stomach and inciting the desire to reach across and kiss him. He had not spent hours talking to her about his battles; that was not his way, nor would it ever be. But he had opened up a place for her in his life and welcomed her in. It was only her perception, but it felt right and it felt comfortable. As if aware of her scrutiny, he gave her hand a small squeeze.

Further along the head table, Uncle Wulf chewed on a chunk of the spit-roasted beef, wiped his mouth and delivered the punch line to his joke. "She said it was a fear of snakes that had sent her running to his room in the first place!"

Alhelm and Frith both smiled before the delivery and Teasel suspected that they had heard the tale before, but she loved them for being kind enough not to say so. Wulf was ageing. As his body diminished and his deafness increased, his spirit grew; his voice grew louder, his jokes cruder. It was second nature for younger men to cosset the old, doughty warriors, but she was still grateful for their indulgence.

Beside her, Bishop Werferth coughed and she turned to him. Werferth, too, was an old man, but he sat with his back straight, no forward roll to his shoulders. His chest was broad for a man who often rode but seldom fought. After her momentary worry about Wulf, Teasel returned to her life-held assumption that men could live forever away from the battlefield. The bishop coughed again and she said, "I am sorry for my uncle's coarseness, my lord."

"Think naught of it, my dear. I had a crumb stuck in my throat. It must be hard for your uncle, having missed the fighting. This is but his way of telling the world that he is yet alive. As I shall tell your father so when I go to Wessex next month, it is a proud time for all Mercians, whether they fought, or not."

"Not *all* Mercians." Ethelred pointed at Brihtsige, who sat with arms folded, staring at his food and frowning as if he thought it poisoned.

Werferth said, "He mourns Beornoth, as we all do. He was a great and mighty man."

"I think there is rather more to it, my lords," said Teasel. "My lord husband, you have sent away the Viking woman."

He let go of her hand to spread his arms in gesture. "You think I should have bid her share my mead bench?"

"No, God forbid. All I meant was that Brihtsige has lost his heart to Gunnhildr. He spent almost all his waking hours with her."

Wulf leaned across. "And I reckon he craved to spend some of his sleeping hours there too."

Ethelred's cheek twitched. He said, "Then he has loved unwisely. He will learn."

Teasel watched as the young red-headed man fidgeted in his chair. He put a finger to his mouth and chewed at a loose piece of skin and, though he looked nothing like her dark-haired cousin, nevertheless the thwarted Brihtsige reminded her again of Thelwold. But it was another affinity which drew her sympathy to this outsider. The faces of the men around her conveyed only their scorn, but she looked across at Alhelm and thought that unrequited love was no easy thing to bear. She flushed to ponder that she had borne hers with as little dignity and discretion. She sensed Ethelred's gaze upon her and turned to face him. She opened her mouth to speak.

Wulf stood up. "The scop! The scop will sing of our great leader."

Teasel leaned to whisper in her husband's ear. "Will he sing of the things that I now know of you? And will he be brief so that you can show me again?" She wanted to speak her apology, her shame, her guilt at making him suffer for her childish desires, to thank him for his kindness, his patience. He smiled and squeezed her hand and she knew that she had travelled at least part way there with her flirtatious words.

The scop brought his little stool and placed it before the dais. He went back to the corner of the room and fetched his harp, tested the strings and sat down. He cleared his throat and began his tale of Ethelred's triumphs, from the taking of hostages at Milton to the victory at Buttington. "And there, by the broad water flow, the gleaming swords struck their lightning blows..."

Ethelred began to fiddle with the embroidered edging on his shirt cuff and Teasel smiled. The man was as the scop described; fearless, patriotic, loyal and inspiring. But he was also, as Werferth had told her long ago, shy. "This makes you squirm, my lord. I see that now. I am beginning to know you; one day, I will know your deepest thoughts."

He coughed. "Right now, they would not be hard to fathom." He stood up, thanked the scop and announced a reward. "Tomorrow, at the gift-giving, you will not be forgotten."

Cheers went round the room as the warriors looked forward to the next day, when their lord would grant gold and land for services rendered during the campaign.

Ethelred pushed back his heavy oak chair. "I must, er," he gestured to suggest that he was on his way to the latrine. "I will see you after." He nodded towards the bedchamber and left the hall.

His exit was well-timed, taken by many as a cue to leave. Those who had private lodging in the guest bowers made their way into the cold night, while others waited for the tables to be moved back so that they could stake their claim on the benches nearest the hearth to guarantee a warm night's sleep. Frith and Alyth took their leave and escorted Alhelm's wife from the hall. She had lost her youthful bloom and turned to her husband as she left the room, showing a wan face and blue-shadowed eye sockets. Alhelm stayed to assist Wulf to his quarters, shoving his hand under the bigger man's armpit and hauling him from his seat. Wulf craved a moment to speak with Bishop Werferth and Teasel found herself standing alone with Alhelm.

"Your uncle wished to speak to the bishop."

"Yes, Bishop Werferth is going back to Worcester tomorrow. Your wife looked tired this evening."

"She is with child."

The new-found heat which had warmed her belly all evening had softened it too and left her ill-prepared for this knife thrust. How silly to imagine that the warmth of entente would act as any kind of shield. But if her understanding with Ethelred was as an untrained child against the doughty might of her love for Alhelm, she must protect it or let it die. So the lady of Mercia smiled, ignored her body, clutched hold of her thoughts, held her chin high and said, "I am glad for you both. May you be as blissful to be with one another as I am with my lord."

"Truly?"

She nodded. "I am glad to be his wife."

Alhelm's frown softened and his shoulders relaxed. "Then I am free at last to love you and I will. I love you as my lord's wife and my sword belongs to you both. Let me bow to you as I would do a queen."

She allowed him his extravagant gesture and replied with a regal bow of the head. So, there it was. He was not wounded, but relieved. What she had perceived as her answering blow had not even winded him. As he stood up, she turned away and let the smile fade, holding her hands to her stomach. She was no queen, but a fool who had imagined that one love would die simply because another love had been born.

She had counted every upright timber in the hall, and if she closed her eyes she would be able to point to every protruding nail, name every bunch of herbs hanging from them and direct a blind man to the besom propped up against the upright nearest the door. She could describe every dent in the cauldron hook above the hearth and if asked to say what else lay forgotten about the room, she could name the wooden bucket and clay pot on the floor and the pair of gloves on the table. She muttered as she scanned the room again in search of something new to look at. "Wearisome. Dreary. Dull."

Ethelred picked up another vellum document, holding it at an angle to read it in the light from the window.

She clapped her hands and sat forward. "Come, my lord, even a great leader such as you needs to rest."

Without looking up, he held out his arm, waited for her to walk to him, and then brought her onto his lap. Continuing to read the charter, he nodded in the vague direction of his sword and shield. "I am at rest."

She lowered her head, trying to get between him and the document. "You mean that you are not fighting. That is not rest. You have been at home for three weeks now yet you still go to witan meetings, you see the bishop every day..."

"That is what I do. I lead Mercia."

"Hmm, Mercia. Your great and beloved land." She twisted around and leaned back, so that he had no option but to put the vellum down and support her back lest she topple from his lap. As his arm tightened around her waist she said, "Show me it then, my lord, I dare you. Where is it, where is she, this other lover of yours?"

He leaned over and pressed his brow to hers, wiggling his nose against hers. Then with an exaggerated sigh, he lifted her up and onto her feet, snatched his leather gloves from the table and yanked on his boots. "Come then."

They rode out of the town, for a time staying on the road, before turning back and following the course of the Severn for many miles, all the while travelling south. Letting the horses gallop whilst in the open countryside, they slowed through the hamlets and, in these small communities, the folk that they encountered showed a reverence for Ethelred that surpassed anything she had witnessed in the towns of Gloucester or Worcester. "We are in the Hwicce heartland," he told her, as she watched yet another churl lay down his hedging bill and drop to his knees as the lord and his lady rode past.

And so they came to Deerhurst, the ancient centre of the Hwicce people, where a modest hall stood alongside the church and as they drew near, Ethelred pointed towards the top of the church wall; a winged angel, carved in relief, hovered above the ground, unable to fly away. Assuming that they were about to go into the church to pray, Teasel prepared to dismount, but Ethelred swung his horse round and she followed him through a small wooded area and down to the river. Somewhere among the trees, an amorous male fox screeched its distinctive mating cackle. Slung between the lower shrubs, hammock webs cradled the spiders which were more evident at this time of year. It was clear that the river level was usually higher; on the far bank, the neat round holes that formed the entrance to the water vole burrows were visible above the water.

Pointing, Ethelred said, "Down there. I want to show you something." He dismounted and helped her down from her mare.

Walking her to the water's edge, he said, "Look up."

228

On a branch overhanging the river, a frayed end of rope dangled in the breeze, out of reach of even the tallest man. "I tied that there when I was ten years old."

She looked up at the tattered remnants. "No you did not. How did you reach?"

"I climbed up. As high as the angel in the church. There is always a way to get what you crave."

She laughed. "I was not born then. What an old man you are."

He tilted his head to one side and stared at her.

"Oh, forgive me. I should not have spoken thus."

He took her hand and they sat down. "It is all right. It is only that you have never thought to tease me before. I always found you, er, cold."

Teasel raked her hand through the grass, tugging clumps of it from the earth and squeezing it between her fingers. In all the years she had sought to keep out of his way it had never occurred to her how her actions might have been interpreted. He had always been eager to show her things, in order to make her feel at home, or so she thought. Perhaps it was more than that; in seeking to make her love the land perhaps he sought to make her love him? "I think I was frightened."

He shuffled round to sit cross-legged in front of her. "Of me?"

She shook her head. "Never. Of becoming like my mother, maybe. Then, well, after I found out about Mildrith. And, there was Al…"

He put a finger to her lips. "I know. We shall not speak of it again."

He had not ever spoken of his loss, or his feelings concerning Alhelm. And now she was sure that he had been trying to communicate with her in other ways.

"You know, my lord, I wonder if we should waste any more of this afternoon speaking at all?" She wriggled until her face was free of his hand. "I have often found myself wishing to see you laugh more often, too. For when you do," with her teeth tugging again at her lower lip, she stared at him, hoping he might guess the rest of her thought. Spurred by the urge to make him laugh, she contemplated making a reach for the rope swing, wondering how deep the water was if she were to slip. Her mind made up, she moved forward to stand up, but he reached out and held her arm.

"Will you lie down with me on this *Mercian* grass?"

She returned his grin. "Now it is you who does the teasing. Today I will have naught but Mercia. Without and within."

"Wisely spoken, my lady."

He laid his hands on the front of her shoulders and leaned over her, pushing her onto her back. Lying on a bed of fallen leaves and warmed by his body, she took one brief look at his precious Mercian sky before she closed her eyes. It might be beautiful, here where the clouds were high and the earth smelled of mushroom spores, but she would not dare to tell him that for all she cared, she might as well be in the boggiest marsh of East Anglia, as long as he was with her.

They rode home in silence. She looked across at him now and again, returning his smiles and that was all that was needed. Even if he had the words, he could tell her nothing more, for there was naught else to know. She had been wrong to think that his passion was reserved solely for Mercia. She was content to spend the rest of the journey planning the meal for next week's feast day and trying to decide whether she should order the purchase of new table linens.

At home she slipped back into her domestic role, ascertaining the yardage of cloth produced that day on the looms and checking the kitchen stores, and after the evening meal she slipped into her husband's bed. In the morning she awoke to feel his body pressed against hers, lying behind her and wrapped around her like a protective cloak. Her mother must be truly mad not to consider moments like these as worthy payments for the months spent alone. She thanked God that Ethelred had been patient enough to wait for her truly to appreciate the gift.

She listened to the noise from outside, establishing the hour by what she heard. There was no mistaking the clanking and rattling sounds as the ploughman yoked the oxen. The beasts had been watched all night in the pasture, then watered and brought back by the ox-herd, who signalled the dawn to the sleeping occupants of the houses scattered round about. Very soon he would bring them in overnight and be able to sleep with them in the barns through the winter, but today he had been awake all night and was now declaring loudly his intention to sleep until midday.

Teasel did not immediately take account of the knock on the door. When it came a second time she sat up and took notice, nudging Ethelred out of his slumber.

He sat up and spoke out in a croaky morning voice. "Come in."

The young messenger was sweating, the beads of moisture hovering on his brow. "My lord, it is not good news. With a heavy heart I have come to tell you…"

"Go on."

"Those who did not lose their lives at Buttington, the wounded and the weak, we followed them as you told us to. They went back to East Anglia, took their wives and children safe into Viking land there and then went on their way."

"On their way?"

"My lord, they have bolstered their number with fresh men and ridden to Chester and are holed up behind the old city walls."

Ethelred lay back upon the pillows. "Bastards."

Chester

Ethelred stamped his feet on the hard ground in a futile attempt to warm his toes. What kind of fool campaigned in the middle of winter? A fool who would not settle until the only Vikings in Mercia were those in slavery or graves. But every successful Viking raid against Alfred had been launched in wintertime, so let them now swallow their own vile brew. He watched the smoke rising from the chimneys of the newly reoccupied city of Chester and looked back at the small brazier outside his tent. They had not long since had their noon-meat but the low, weak midwinter sun would soon drop. He must order the fires lit.

Frith came to stand beside him and gave him a cup of wine. "I have told the thegns to light the fires," he said.

Ethelred snorted his silent laugh. The man's ability to mind-read was almost unholy.

"Some of the men have asked if we will take a day's rest for Christmas. The priests are willing to say a mass."

Bright against the darkening sky, a flaming arrow rose up from behind the city wall and sang past their heads. They retreated towards their encampment, out of reach.

Ethelred said, "Will they let us rest?" He knew that inside the city, the heathens would already have prepared their Yule logs. Feeling warm and safe, they would let them burn for twelve days and not worry about the Christians beyond the walls. Vikings sat around Mercian fireplaces while Englishmen were deprived of the comfort of the hearth. He thought about those huge logs, glowing in the Chester grates. He looked again at the smoke hanging above the houses. He drained his cup, wiped his mouth and said, "Burn it."

"My lord?"

"The fields, the cows, the crop stores. Burn it all."

They tore the sleeves from their tunics and tied them across their faces, but the smoke attacked their eyes, provoking stinging tears. Ethelred knew that they were suffering, but he wanted the fires controlled. They could spread towards the estuary, but not too far inland. One of the thegns came to him, his voice conveying the scratching effects of the smoke on his throat. "The beasts, my lord. All of them? Could we not butcher some for our own needs?"

Ethelred shook his head. "No. Let them think that we do need them. It will make their hunger worse." He stood back. The heat was extreme, but concentrated. His face was uncomfortably hot, but his feet were still chilled by the hard earth beneath them.

It was not only the heat which was intense. The noise was startlingly loud as the flames crackled and snapped, working their way across the fields, devouring the slaughtered cattle, the abandoned huts, the fences and hedgerows. Ethelred went back to his tent and ordered his belongings packed.

Alhelm looked up, eyebrows raised. "Should we not finish it with a fight?"

"It is finished. They will starve." And now they knew that wherever they went, he would be on their tails, ready to fight or starve them depending on where they holed up. It was a risk, but he wanted them to know that he believed himself superior. He would not take any cattle and he would not see the siege out to the bitter end. They had to believe that he was so sure of winning overall that he did not need to secure every bout. And there would be no peace treaties.

233

He tensed his hands, curling his fingers into tight fists and punching towards the ground, then he knelt and lifted his hands in prayer. God grant that he was right. If he were destined to spend his life fighting the hordes, then let it be for the good of his kingdom. Could God hear him? So many good men stood by his side; Alhelm, Frith, Wulf, the men of Wessex: Alfred, Somerset, Wiltshire and Edward. Surely all these were not wrong? And now he knew that his wife stood alongside him. That even when they were apart, she stood defiant on his behalf and knew that he spared many more than just a passing thought for her. She was half West Saxon, but now thought of herself as wholly Mercian. His dream was hers. The knowledge did not change his purpose, or his behaviour. But it wrapped his nights in soft wool, whereas he had only hitherto known scratchy blankets. On his last homecoming she had reached up and touched him with affection and a gesture which hitherto she had spared only for her brother. Her love, her allegiance, brought an additional comfort to his life. He had begun to tell her so; when he got home, he would tell her more. He stood up and spoke to Alhelm. "Home, my friend. Until the next time."

Worcester

"It was as if twenty-four months were shoved into a gap only big enough for twelve, beginning with Farnham and ending in Chester."

Bishop Werferth smiled. "Yes, my lady, but that was last year, not this. And this poor fellow will need a little more than that, if he is to write it all down and take it to our friend Asser." He reached out to touch her arm as she made to leave. "And, it would be as well to have the Mercian side to the tale, before those in Wessex write their own."

She could not straighten her arm any further without wrenching it rudely from Werferth's gentle grasp. She was far better employed helping the reeve as he distributed what food they had to the folk who had none; the hungry gap in the early spring had not been successfully bridged and with more than a year of fighting, and a mediocre harvest, food was scarce. But spirits would sink further if the military successes were not broadcast. She sighed and sat down again. "Well, if you will hear it from a woman, I will tell you what I know."

Werferth slipped his hands into his sleeves and chuckled. At a volume fixed between too quiet to be heard and too loud to cause embarrassment, he said, "A woman. Merely a woman. Merely a woman who has helped me and her husband to strengthen my beloved Worcester and build strong walls around the town. And that is before we speak of how much wealth she has bestowed upon my churches."

Teasel coughed and batted his words away with her hand. "If you swear not to write any of that," she glared at Werferth before turning back to the scribe, "Then I will tell you what I know."

The buck-toothed scribe spoke wetly of his gratitude. "If you would, my lady, then I can mark it against what I already have written here." He pointed at his wax tablet and sucked spittle back into his mouth.

Teasel took a sip of wine to wet her mouth and began. "At the beginning of the year of our Lord, eight hundred and ninety four, the Viking horde left Chester. Starving, they went into Wales and began raiding there. My lord Ethelred, who had burned them out of Chester, followed them there, and helped his great friend the king of Gwynedd, Lord Anarawd." She took another sip, for her mouth was very dry. It was always difficult to pronounce the foreign name but if the effort also made her breathing more shallow and her heartbeat quicker, then she affected not to notice. "The heathens, finding no succour in Wales, went back to their strongholds in Essex but," she leaned forward. "They moved north through Northumbria and back through East Anglia, for they did not dare to come back through Mercia, so frightened were they of my lord and his fyrd."

She sat back, waiting for the young monk to commit her words to the wax. He scratched away with his stylus, the calligraphy less than perfect, for these were notes only, to be transferred at a later date to intricately decorated vellum pages. He looked up and signalled for her to continue.

"Now they have rowed up the Thames and up the Lea. They look like they plan to overwinter there. My husband has men watching them." He would be home from the hunt soon. She must ready the hall and speak to the cook. "What do you hear from Wessex?"

Werferth said, "As you might guess, my lady, all talk is of Devon and how, much like your dear husband, your father was able to starve the heathens out and they left

Exeter. We have heard that on their way back to the east they harried Chichester. But the men there stood fast against them, killed many hundreds of them and took some of their ships."

She nodded and sighed with satisfaction. Once, and it seemed a lifetime ago, one man stood against the Vikings. Now, Alfred, Edward and Ethelred, with aid from Gwynedd, swept over the kingdoms of England and North Wales like malevolent clouds, leaving the enemy little chance of predicting where they would rain down their retaliatory blows. And while the building of burhs continued, so the chances of successful reprisal diminished. And hope bred quickly, for the folk who dwelled within were now finding the courage to fight back instead of waiting for assistance.

She said, "Lord Ethelred told me of Chichester. He said that these Viking sailors would hear a new sound of water; that of the tide turning against them."

AD895

Near Hertford

"Brother, I have been here but a few hours and now I am scratching too." Edward raked his fingers through his cornstalk hair.

"Lice," Ethelred said.

Edward slapped at an itch on his leg and cursed. "For a man of few words, you would do well not to waste them by telling me what I already know." He scratched again and said, "My sister used to give the little ones a brew of ale with oak-rind and a little worm-wood stirred into it. I see that you do not even have a bowl of water."

Ethelred stood up. "We have been here a long time, Brother. Washing has not been our first..." He saw no need to finish his sentence. His infestation and grubbiness had evidently told Edward all he needed to know.

"Not for much longer, though." Edward was grinning. He was still a young man, full of enthusiasm, enough to overlook the defeat of the summer as a small setback.

Ethelred knew that he had to believe it, too, but he had become weary now, more cautious. He had marched with the men of London to the enemy fortress on the banks of the Lea, but they had been repulsed. His faith had slipped, but now, with the harvest safely gathered, Alfred, with no repeat of Exeter to distract him, had come with men and bringing hope. Ethelred allowed himself to smile; Edward's cheerfulness was spreading as quickly as the fleas jumped

238

and the lice crawled from head to head. It did feel different this time. They were three armies, not one. And that fact, along with the beacons that flared across the southern kingdoms, meant that the Vikings had been deprived of their most lethal weapon; they could no longer mount surprise attacks and run away confident that there would be no pursuit.

Edward thumped his legs onto the table and crossed his ankles. Swigging a large cup of ale, he spoke between mouthfuls. "Any day now, my father will send word. All we need to do is be ready to see what the scum do next."

When Ethelred remained silent, Edward lunged forward. "You are as bad as Frith. How can you bide so still? Does it not clutch your guts?" He sat back. "It must be the wisdom that comes with your greater years." He chuckled. "Two, mind, not one, but two."

Ethelred could only nod in agreement. Alfred had spent the autumn building two fortresses lower down the river. Any day now, the Vikings would realise that they could not get their ships back out and onto the Thames. When they returned, he would strike. Until then, he must sit and scratch.

He had slipped into a light sleep after the evening meal when word came. Grateful for his ability to get adequate rest with his boots on, he moved through the camp as word spread. Edward, too, was cheerfully mustering his own men, passing on orders and keeping the news moving along the lines. As he came in front of the tent nearest to the Mercian camp, Ethelred heard him say, "They've run and left their ships behind. Those of you who went with Lord Ethelred to Benfleet two years ago know what must now be done. Take their ships, burn those that cannot be brought away. Men of Wessex, to me. They've run off overland, so we must be as hounds to the boar."

Ethelred met him at the far side of the camp

Edward said, "You'll take the London men with you?"

"Yes." Ethelred grinned, renewed. "My scop has taken

to calling me 'fire-lighter'. I must not let him down."

Edward swung himself onto his horse. "You know, I am beginning to feel that we can beat them back for ever. Meet me on the road when you have set your fire and burned their leavings." He gave a wide grin and tapped his finger to his temple. "Building, you see? Like they do; only better."

Ethelred heard his words over again as he mounted his own stallion. He urged his horse forward to the front of the line and saw his scop running towards him. "Come and see me, after. But be ready to write the story's end."

The scop ran alongside his lord. "Wrath of the righteous? Sailors worthless without ships? Fires of hell? Christians burning the walls of Valhalla?"

Ethelred punched the air and let out a war cry. "Yes," he shouted behind him and his warriors took up his chant. "Out, out, out, out, out!"

AD896

Gloucester

They stood together looking out towards the rich pasture. Whatever had caused the deaths among the herds, it was not the paucity of the grass and the livestock numbers would recover. Time was the thing, and if it could pass slowly, left to its natural rhythm, it could heal most things. Only this morning, she had watched as Ethelred silenced an argument between two neighbours, commissioned the carving of a new chair for his scop and beat Wulf at a game of Tables. There had been spare moments in which to walk down to the river, and to speak to the women who were sitting on the bank, slapping the linen against the rocks and launching the clothing back into the water, watching it bubble up like upturned sails. Yes, the pasture was lush and with time and the warmth of the strengthening sun, all would be well.

The muscle just above Ethelred's jaw line was twitching, but Teasel knew that this time he was not fighting anger, but laughter. She lifted her head, offering her face to the sun, and breathed in deeply. She wanted to twirl and skip; there had never been such an occasion as this, but probably she should behave with a little more dignity.

She took his proffered arm and they walked together to the witanagemot. She had overseen the preparation of the hall and was sure that all the council members would be impressed with the show of wealth. New wall hangings, embroidered with the finest gold thread, fluttered from their fixings in the draught from the open door. Strewn across the high roof beams, fresh flowers had been hung alongside the dried herbs, and ivy leaves trailed down the upright timbers. Candles of the finest beeswax burned in delicately worked iron wall-sconces. The head table was covered with a linen cloth and laid with gold cups and plates. The other boards were bare of cloth, but loaded with bread and fruit and jugs of ale and Teasel had ordered silk-covered cushions to be spread out along the benches for those who chose to sit more comfortably. Ethelred patted her arm. He walked to the edge of the hall, picked up his shield and hung it ceremoniously on the wall, initiating the ancient tradition. All the other witan members took the shields still leaning against the foot of the wall and hung them high, those who carried swords adding them to the hooks. This was a moot-hall and there would be no fighting.

She allowed Ethelred to lead her to her seat and watched him as he stood to greet all the members of his council. Some were missing from the throng; Little Alfred, the Goat and Eardwulf had all died. Of the old stalwarts, only Wulf and Eadnoth, greying and frayed, remained. Frith was absent, too, having gone to see Edward and to attend to his lands in Wessex. Alhelm took his seat at the head table, next to the bishop. His blond curls had lost a little of their youthful lustre and the angle from neck to shoulder was less defined now that he carried a little extra weight in middle-age. Ethelred had on one of his finest tunics, an emerald green silk, edged with panels of embroidery. The gold stitching coiled along the hem, around the cuffs and down the neck opening. His leg bindings were fashioned from new cloth and looked uncommonly white against his brown breeches. He was wearing his favourite garnet-set belt buckle and his empty scabbard reflected the candlelight; the decorated silverwork glittered as it swung up and back when he brushed it aside to sit down.

Bishop Werferth stood and offered a prayer. Teasel was aware of Ethelred's swallowing as he prepared for his speech. The prayer and blessing completed, the lord of Mercia lifted his head and addressed the witan.

"Here have I gathered all the Mercian council, the bishops, my ealdormen and all my thegns. This I have done with the leave of King Alfred. This day, we will speak of the best way to lead our folk, both in their daily lives and in the matter of their souls."

He moved his hands forward and laid them on the table. "From this day on we shall be free to right all wrongs, give back all lands unlawfully taken, and begin to build anew." He stood up. "Let us drink to our free land, and if any man here does not yet know of it, let us say again that the last of the Viking hordes, that which fled from us at the Lea and dug in at Bridgnorth, has gone back to the east."

The finest nobles of Mercia began cheering, swearing and throwing cupfuls of ale to the back of their throats. Ethelred said "And most have gone from there over the sea," but Teasel doubted that any but she and the bishop had heard him under the din. She let the tears flow and Bishop Werferth squeezed her hand. Ethelred allowed his fine warriors to behave as a drunken rabble, while he sat back in his chair and closed his eyes.

Teasel reached over and placed her hand on his thigh. She whispered in his ear. "Well done, my love. Breathe it in, for you have earned it."

When he judged the moment to be right, Ethelred sat forward and called for the drinking-horn. The giant aurochs horn, filled with ale, would be passed around, enabling the men to continue drinking, but would force them to concentrate, for the horn could not be put down. Once the horn had travelled round the entire room, Ethelred waved his hand. "Let us to business."

Bishop Werferth began with the first land claim. Teasel sat back, knowing that his would be followed by many more; disputes which had festered during the war years, with no-one in government having the time to pass judgement.

Werferth sat forward, tucked his hands in his sleeves

and stated his case. "I wish to tell you of the woodland at Woodchester, gifted to us at Worcester in the time of King Æthelbald, given to the bishop at that time for mastland and woodland and as a gift for the good of his own soul."

Werferth's claim was against the current holder of the land and when the defendant stood up, Teasel smiled. His name was Thelwold, but he was a short, balding man who looked nothing like her tall, lissom cousin. This barrel-bellied man would not be the one to sour this day of all days, and he agreed that he would never argue against claims brought by the Church. "Further," he said, "My man, Ecglaf, will ride with the priest Wulfhun and mark out all the edges of the land, and match them to the grant of King Æthelbald."

Priest Wulfhun sat up in his chair and sorted through the pile of documents at the scribes' table, hurrying to find the charter in question.

"But, my lords," Thelwold said, "I would beg a boon. Will the bishop and his flock let me have the use of the land for my lifetime? I offer that neither I, nor my son, would withhold from the bishop the swine pasture at Longridge, which has been gifted to me for my lifetime."

For a few moments, Teasel could only see the crowns of heads, as the men of the council bent low in discussion. Consulting the clergy, Ethelred took but a few more minutes to give his judgement. "The offer shall stand. But should Thelwold's son die before him, then all the aforesaid land will go straight back to the Church. Should Thelwold or his son fail to keep friendship with the bishop, then again, the bishop will have all his lands, spoken of here."

He sat back whilst all the leading nobles and clergy gave their assent to the judgement. Despite the freedom to conduct peacetime business, which had long been neglected, he did not look free from worry. Perhaps he would rather be celebrating than working. Teasel turned to him and said, "How hard it must be for you, when all you wish to do is keep your ale cup filled."

But he shook his head. "No, there will be time a plenty for that after. I was thinking on the matter of land and how ownership of it is like a key to a strong lock."

Teasel sat back in her chair and crossed her ankles. As she moved, she felt a patch of moisture between her legs. "My lord, with your leave, there is something I need to see to."

His glance contained a question, eyebrows drawn together in enquiry, but she merely bobbed her head and walked with deliberate slowness towards the door. Outside, she ran to her bower and pulled her linen pads from the chest by the bed. Truly it was God's curse that caused all women to measure their days from one bleed to the next. She pulled the skirt of her kirtle around, checking to make sure that no mark had been left grinning through the woad-dyed wool. She was still inspecting it by the window light when Ethelred came in.

"You left early. Is all well?"

She sighed. "Walk with me?"

They left her bower and walked back along the street past the great hall. Passing the church on their left they walked towards the main town gate via tilled fields and out to the river. Boats moved up and down the waterway, breaking the surface of the water and causing the reflected spring sunshine to bounce and splinter. She knew he was waiting for his answer. "All is well. But once more I find that I am not with child."

His hand, holding hers, relaxed. "Is that all? I thought you might be unwell."

"My lord, you are kind to me. But in nigh on ten years of being wed to you I have not…"

"It is God's will."

A young couple alighted from a fishing boat and ran, laughing, towards the town. The youth made as if to chase his girl, while she repaid him with squeals of faked protest, allowing him easily to catch her and clutch her to him, lifting her from the ground and spinning her round. Teasel and

Ethelred had never behaved in such an unfettered way. Once, with Alhelm, she had thought about such games. Her marriage had been grown-up from the beginning. Was it because he was so much older than she? Or was it due to his reserved nature, which left no room for frivolity? No matter, for their life was not dull and they had shared moments of true pleasure. He never told her, but she knew that in his own way, he loved her. And he was like the walls of Werferth's cathedral, a protector, a buffer against the cold wind of life's uncertainties. Even so... She took his hand and held it to her breast. "It must grieve you though?"

The young couple had stopped to chat to a friend but laughter continued to punctuate their conversation.

Ethelred retrieved his hand and, reversing the grasp, held her hand in both of his. He said, "When your Uncle Burgred fled, we lost a king. My whole life has been a fight, a fight to hold on to a kingdom. I am not a king; my sons would not be kings. Mercia is what matters, Mercia and you. There need be no 'house of Ethelred'."

The young couple moved away and their companion walked past Teasel and Ethelred. He gestured a bow as he crossed in front of them. "A great day, my lord. The first witanagemot in a free Mercia. We should drink to it."

"Yes, Brihtsige, we will."

Teasel, unacknowledged by the redhead, had no need to reply. In any case, she was too lost in thought. It was not the first time that she had seen Brihtsige smiling, and, like every man in Mercia he had good reason to be happy. Yet there was something in the smug way his smile turned one side of his mouth more than the other that left her wondering if he was cheered by something else. Whilst he had ignored her, he continued to smirk at her as he walked past, thumbs tucked in his belt and legs kicking out in a slow swagger, as if he knew something that she did not. She shook her head at the notion. The monsters of her childhood had gone away for ever. How silly to invite new ones to take their place.

AD898

Teasel stood in the yard and took a deep breath. The new day's sun shone across the autumn morning and the air was sharp enough to cut her breath just a little as she inhaled. Above her, the chitter-chatter of the swallows grew momentarily louder as they flocked directly overhead, then fell away again as they flew off in their large arc, calling for more to join them. They would leave any day now, although nobody knew where they went. Some believed that they lived under the water of the large lakes in the north, others that they lived at the very back of the deepest caves, but all that could be said for sure was that they would leave soon, to come again in the summer. Only yesterday, she had watched as Bishop Werferth moved his hives to the west wall of the abbey gardens, where they could be sheltered from the prevailing winter wind as the temperatures dropped. To the side of every building, the lean-to stores of hay were stacked high, and in the barns, the lofts were engorged by bountiful stores of food and with the Vikings gone, come summer, this yard would come alive to the sound of contented children, running with full bellies. Teasel smiled.

She had promised to help in the bake-house that morning, but had made her excuses, finding the atmosphere too hot and stuffy. Deciding to try her hand in the kitchen, where myriad salting and preserving tasks awaited, she walked around the front of the hall and across the far end of the weapons field. Sidestepping an adventurous goat, which grinned at her before attempting to take a mouthful of her skirts, she called out to a churl in the field beyond the chapel.

"Huna, your goat has slipped its tether. There are sacks of dried peas beyond the cook-house, you had better come and get it before it eats our winter stocks."

Huna raised his arm in acknowledgement and Teasel was aware of another movement in the far corner of the weapons field. Not having heard the clash of any practice weapons, she turned to see who was honing their battle skills so early in the morning. She saw Brihtsige talking to two other men, and she went on her way. Two steps nearer the cook-house, she stopped and moved back again. She did not recognise the other men and at first had not thought it odd, assuming that they were his retainers. But these men were dressed in fine clothing, and if they were thegns, they would have been at Ethelred's house many times before. One of them had a decorated scabbard hanging from his belt and she could see an uneven line of white below the sword hilt, suggesting that the scabbard was lined. Here was a rich man indeed, if his sword were precious enough to be wrapped in lanolin-rich wool. She turned to steal a glance at their horses, tethered at the far end of the paddock. Both bridles and saddles were richly adorned, but one of the horses carried distinctive markings, with three of its fetlocks pure white against its black coat. A white blaze on its face extended over one eye. She waved her arm in greeting. "Brihtsige, bring your friends to the hall after."

He must not have heard, for with a quick lean forward, as if he were whispering, he lingered for a moment with his hand on his rich companion's back, embraced him and walked with his distinctive jerky stride back towards the great hall. The other two men walked to the far end of the enclosure and mounted their steeds.

Teasel shook her head and turned round. Frith strode

across the yard and she reached out to touch his arm and pull him towards her. "Do you know those men?"

Frith put his hand to his brow to shield his eyes from the sunshine. "I would know that steed anywhere. Unless he has stolen it from its owner, that rider is Sigehelm of Kent. So saying, I would think that the other rider is Thegn Edwold. He is a friend of your kinsman, Thelwold."

She swallowed, pushing down the feelings of hurt that Thelwold had not sent greetings. "They are a long way from home, then."

Her hand was still on his arm and she felt his muscles tensing. "Indeed they are, Lady. You will forgive me, but I need to find Lord Ethelred."

She watched him go, his always steady gait betraying naught of his mood. She continued on her way, aware that even if there were cause for concern, Ethelred would not tell her. He would not wish to trouble her. Not now that...

It took her a moment to catch her breath. The force of the bump was not great, but had surprised her. When she regained her composure, she saw from Brihtsige's face that he was as surprised as she to collide as they each moved round the corner of the building.

Concern wafted briefly across his features, before his face settled into its usual mask of indifference and his perfunctory enquiry was delivered in a tone as flat as an unleavened weekday loaf. "My lady is unhurt, I hope?"

She nodded, but rubbed her stomach, as much from habit as worry, but he noted the action and a crease appeared above his eyebrows.

He stepped forward. "You are with child."

She nodded. His question was, in tone, an accusation. She said, "And you will share in mine and Lord Ethelred's gladness?"

He shook his head, and shifted his weight to and from his back leg. Teasel was reminded of her little brother and sisters and the way they used to dance when their bladders were full. He said, "But you are barren. Your husband said

249

it. I heard him. He said that there would be no 'house of Ethelred'."

For over four months she had held her tongue, waiting for the familiar pains and bleeding to announce her failure yet again. But this time, the sickness had persisted, her body had begun, slowly, to alter, and then, last week, she had felt small flutters of movement. This babe was alive. And Teasel's world had immediately shrunk, as all else floated away and all that remained was her and her child. She hugged herself, she smiled, she noted every tiny kick, welcomed every wave of nausea. Yet now the protective weave was torn, for here was someone who was not happy for her. She tried to deflect the blow; if the talk was not of her and her child, then he could not infect her bliss. "Will you bring your friends to meet us?"

He rubbed his nose as if the worst itch known to mankind lay tormenting him there. "They are not, er, they have gone." And Brihtsige backed away for two steps, before turning and emulating them.

Alhelm and Wulf came from the hall, running across the yard. Wulf said, "We saw him knock you. Are you hurt, little one?"

"No, I am..." She sighed. The walls around her secret happiness had been breached and soon the world would know anyway. "I am with child."

Wulf roared his delight. "No. Truly? God's blessing indeed!" He took her hands and danced round with her in a circle, taking care to keep her at arm's length, and his bulky frame away from her body.

And, spinning, she kept her gaze focused on Alhelm. His beautiful pale eyes had widened in surprise, and then narrowed into what she might have perceived to be sadness, if she had not long ago put aside any hope of his loving her. Wulf released her, but put his arm around her shoulders and patted her. She continued to stare at Alhelm.

He was blinking quickly and he shook his head to flick a curl from his eye. He lowered his chin and stared back at her. He held her gaze for a long few moments while Wulf continued to paw her with gentle strength, and then he said, "All is well?"

She nodded. "All is well."

He looked down and began to scuff the dirt under his foot. "You are far enough along for it to live?"

"I am. It cannot be undone now."

Still he had no smile for her. He flicked his foot sideways so swiftly that he left a line in the dirt. He looked up. "No going back."

She watched him as he returned to the hall and she softly repeated his words. "No going back."

AD899

Worcester — February

She listened to the ringing of the bells and then wiped her brow as if, once the sweat was gone, her mind would once again work properly. It had begun just before dawn on Wednesday, when she had bent to put on her shoes before yet another visit to the latrine. Her waters had burst forth and as she stood back up, a dull ache began in her lower back. She had memories, thereafter, of cycles of low abdominal pain and of desperate tiredness. But could it truly be Friday now? The stomach cramps had come and gone, but the backache was constant, and she recalled Alyth's pronouncement that the baby was all 'withershins'. The bairn's back was nestled against hers and this was the reason for all the pain. So the child would be born back to front. If it were born at all; the lady Æthelflæd, so long a failure, had begun to believe that she would never be delivered of a living baby.

She stood up to try to massage some feeling back into her legs but a new sensation brought a wave of cramping across her stomach and she clutched Alyth's arm. "I think I need to empty my bowels."

Alyth caught hold of her hand and gently pushed her into a squat. "No, my lady, you need to push."

How do I do this? I have never been shown what to do and yet there is no way back, only forward. Who could have foreseen that I, leaving the men to their work, would at last have this, real women's

252

work, to bring about? Here it is, then. With God's help, I will stride
into the unknown and do what I must.

Alyth had combed her hair for her, fanning it out over the
pillow. Putting the antler comb onto the clothes chest, she
had then reached up and hung a potent mix of herbs above
the bed to ward off the elf-shot which might attack a
woman recently delivered of a bairn. She had helped Teasel
into a clean under-shift and wiped her face with a warm
damp cloth. Then she had gone to fetch Ethelred.

Now he sat next to her on the bed, holding her hand
and stroking the back of it with his thumb. His face,
beautiful to her now, laid bare his emotions for her to see.
But she could not share his bliss, for she could not
understand why he was not wroth with her.

He reached across and stroked the baby's head. His
hand enveloped the tiny, almost hairless skull. "She is pretty,
like her mother."

She sighed. "She is a daughter, not a son."

He sat up straight and peered at her. "So?"

For many years, the likes of Alhelm had spoken to her
of her husband's superior wisdom, his skilful battle
strategies and his ability to endear himself to his men. She
had seen with her own eyes how he had many times
resolved an argument with words as sharp as a sword. Why,
then, must he be so dull-witted now? "A daughter cannot be
a leader. She cannot be named as 'atheling'." She struggled
to sit up. "She cannot be a king." Exhausted, she lay back
on the pillow. "You need a son to follow you." *And I do not
think that I will ever be able to do this again.*

He shook his head and picked up her hand, holding it
to his mouth and pressing his warm lips against her palm.
He set it down on the mattress but kept tight hold as he
said, "Have you not yet lived in Mercia long enough to
know that we are not the same as the West Saxons? Your
father was king after his brother who was king after his
father. But here we always give the king-helm to the man

253

who will wear it best." He coughed. "Well, at least that is ever the hope. Even if this were my son lying here, he would be only one of many athelings and would not, by right, be king." He leaned over and kissed her forehead. "I have a daughter and I have a wife who lived through childbirth. It is enough."

He went, then, to speak to Bishop Werferth about the baptism and, no doubt, to drink to the baby's health until none in the hall could recall why they were there. Staring at the pink, hairless creature who had made such a fight of getting out into the world, she thought of her own family in Wessex. She considered the use to which she, as the eldest daughter had been put, and how Edward, the eldest son, derived strength from his absolute belief in his destiny to rule. In these darkened times, Mercia would have been more secure if Ethelred had a living heir. And this child, sweet though she might be to look upon, would bring joy, but little worth. Wessex ways were seen as naught but a threat, but they might yet have been a girl-child's salvation. *And knowing this, my love, I find that the Wessex blood flows through me yet. For I, at least, am the daughter of a king.* Her daughter was not; what would become of her?

Winchester, Early November

The streets of Winchester were crowded but quiet. So many West Saxons stood in the streets that there was barely room to move a horse through the throng. Farmers used their hoes and shovels as crutches, leaning silently on them, while the women planted their feet wide, steadying themselves for the long vigil in streets where the trading stalls were all closed and sustenance would be hard to procure. All the while, the gates of Winchester stood open, as more folk came in from villages and towns all over Wessex. Most were dry-eyed, but their faces were pale, their mouths pulled down by the heaviness of their mood. Turning the corner that would take them to the king's great hall, the contingent from Mercia continued to move their horses forward slowly, guiding the beasts through the press of people. All the riders stared straight ahead, a need for decorum and observation of protocol keeping their expressions neutral. Where they could, the folk on the streets moved back to let them pass, pushing their backs against the timbers of the houses, pressing against the fastened shutters and leaning on the locked doors.

The struggle for dignity seemed to have been won, and the hall was in sight, when a woman broke away from the crowd, ran in front of the horses and dropped onto one knee.

"God bless you, my lady."

Teasel breathed in, found her throat constricted by a sob, and let the tears fall.

Edward was standing on the hall steps, with Asser and several of Alfred's Frankish friends and Welsh allies. Anarawd of Gwynedd stood with legs apart, firmly planted, hands folded in front of him. His dark eyes glistened as if with moisture, his brows were drawn together in sadness. He glanced at her briefly, before lowering his gaze. Ethelred nodded to him and squeezed Teasel's hand before going off to see his horse properly stabled.

Edward stepped forward and embraced his sister. "Come, my love, there is no shame in weeping. I, too, have shed tears. The whole kingdom is bereft."

He beckoned for a servant to take her cloak, but she shook her head. Unlike the Vikings who seemed to delight in raiding during the winter months, she was still unused to travelling in winter. "I will keep it with me a while longer, thank you." She blew on her fingers and looked beyond her brother and into the hall. "In there?"

He nodded and stood back to allow her to enter the hall. Clutching her cloak tightly around her body, she stepped inside where the only light came from candles, for the shutters were pulled closed and the hearth was unlit. Even in the winter months, her father's body would deteriorate rapidly and although she had cursed the churned muddy roads and the icy wind that shadowed every step of the journey, she was thankful that he had not died in summer and been buried long before she could reach his court to pay her respects.

Alfred, king of the West Saxons, lay in his finest clothes; a garnet-red silk tunic edged with gold embroidery and a pair of soft woollen breeches. His sword, the top of the hilt decorated with delicate patterns worked in silver and in-filled with the expensive niello which produced a strikingly beautiful black and white effect, lay across his chest, his stiff fingers curled around its handle. Below his hand, someone had placed his ceremonial king-helm on his lower chest, and two gold coins had been pressed onto his closed lids. She thought stupidly that someone should be standing by to trim his ever neat beard. How odd that her first thoughts of her dead father should be of his predilection for personal grooming. But the truth was that she barely knew the man; he had sent her to be fostered by her aunt and now, as a mother herself, she realised that this was because Ewith had become ever more fragile with each of her subsequent childbed ordeals. Yet even when Little Teasel had returned to the Wessex court, Alfred was away trying to stave off the heathen onslaught. She knew of his attempts to re-educate his people in the wake of the destruction of the Church and its institutions, but most of the detail of that reform had been relayed to her by Bishop Werferth. Only recently had she learned to understand Alfred's trials, when she had tried to be both a solid rock and a haven for her husband as he, too, attempted to stem the spread of Viking encroachment upon English soil. In truth, she had only known her father through the words and deeds of others. To Ewith, he had been a figure so strong, so immense, so loved, that she could not bear the thought that one day he must die. Fear latched onto her love like a parasite and would only die upon the death of its host. To Edward, he had been a man who saw a way to defeat the hordes, but allowed his Christian decency to weaken his resolve. To Ethelred, Anarawd and the others, he was the hub of the wheel by which spokes could be attached to make common cause. To the Church and the folk, he was the saviour of the cultural traditions that marked the English from the heathens. Teasel's impression was of a weary life, bravely lived.

She stepped away from the bier and took a cup of wine from one of the steward's thegns. Edward moved to her side and the rest of the high-born mourners gathered round the body. They stood with wine cups in hand and drank to the memory of King Alfred, first of that name.

Asser, the air whistling past his remaining teeth as he

spoke, was the first to drain his cup. "I can only thank God that I was able to finish my book of the king's life some years back. At least it has all been written down, so folk will know of this great man, his great deeds, and how he won out over the..."

Edward had been shaking his head as Asser spoke. Now he said, "No. The story is not ended yet."

Many of those gathered turned their faces away, no doubt startled at Edward's gainsaying of a religious man, held in such high regard by the late king, but keen to make allowance nevertheless for his grief. They found convenient snagged threads on their clothing, itchy legs which needed scratching, something arresting to look at on the floor or among the roof timbers. Anarawd, alone amongst the men, took a step forward, tilting his head as if to hear the better, and Teasel watched, intrigued, as Edward stated his case.

"It is not ended as long as those scum still bide on our land," he said. "They have not all gone back over the sea and until they do, there will be no story's end." He looked at his sister, staring into her eyes as if trying to convey a message. "I will finish it, God and the witan willing. I am glad that the lord Ethelred could be here; I would like to speak with him, after." He held her gaze a moment more, gave the tiniest of nods and snapped his fingers for another drink.

Teasel stepped towards him and brushed his hair from his forehead, finishing the gesture with a soft stroke of his earlobe. "I will tell him. First, I must find Mother."

Ewith, too, was sitting in a darkened bower, her head bowed and her hands in her lap, neatly laid, one on top of the other. The only light came from a solitary cresset, the oil burning unevenly and causing the flame to flicker as the draught from the opening door disturbed the air in the room. Teasel sat down beside her mother and put an arm around her tiny shoulders. The older woman's breathing was shallow but even. If she had cried, she had long since dried her tears. And Ewith bore her sadness strangely; it was as if she had left behind her flesh and bones and withdrawn to a safer haven, to an alcove of dark calm deep within her mind, where she sat with her thoughts, at peace. "It is over," was all she would say and Teasel knew that for her mother, this came as naught but blessed relief. At last, she could mourn, having lived through his death so many times already.

Edward lay down on his bed while his servant pulled his boots off for him. The funeral had sapped his strength, but he could not take the time to sleep. Archbishop Plegmund's words had been both stirring and calming in equal measure and Edward twitched a smile to recall his sister's comment that such eloquence could only come from a Mercian. It provided a moment of welcome levity as he considered her husband and his lack of poetic articulacy and concluded that his pillow-talk must be fluent indeed for her to have such a high opinion of Mercian expressiveness. But Plegmund also spoke of continuity and the duty of kings to serve and protect their people and Edward could not afford to nap. He must persuade the witan to elect him as Alfred's heir, to offer him the kingship. He would be thirty come next birthday, the age at which bishops were consecrated; it seemed a good age to wear a crown.

Unbidden yet unerring, Frith appeared in the doorway. "Ready?"

Edward swung his legs from the bed, feeling with his feet until he located his soft leather slippers. "I am. But what if they do not name me?"

Frith barely paused to blink before replying. "Why would they not? You are the first-born son. All will stand behind you."

Edward tightened his sword belt and straightened his tunic. "But who are they? New men, all of them. Somerset, dead. Wiltshire, dead." God and Edward's friends might declare for him, but were the new untested men listening? "Thelwold will not name me, but will put himself forward as atheling in my stead." He gripped his friend's arm. "Will you stand with me, Frith?"

Frith pushed a strand of long blond hair behind his ear. "Behind, beside, before you, wherever you have need of me, unto death."

Edward stared at his friend, feeling a deep and abiding love, but also an urge to break the solemnity of the moment.

Frith laughed. "But only when your sister does not need me, for she is the prettier of the two and I would rather spend time with her."

Edward smiled and punched Frith on the arm, before tugging him into a headlock. "What need have I of Vikings, with a friend such as you?"

The sound of a cough brought them both to standing, uncomfortably back in their adult world, aware that they had been caught in a childlike moment. Edward looked towards the door and spoke in his deepest voice to the thegn standing there. "Yes?"

The thegn stepped forward. "My lord, the witan is ready for you now."

As Edward had expected, Thelwold was already whinging to all who would listen. Teasel was patting his arm, no doubt making soothing noises. The gentle touch of a woman was always welcome, but in Edward's opinion, Thelwold needed harsh treatment, for pandering to his whims only made his whining louder. Edward sighed and took his place at the centre of the head table. His father's hall was decorated as it had been when Alfred was alive. His favourite wall hangings, swathes of yellow cloth overlaid with chevrons of red, fluttered shyly every time the huge oak doors opened and closed. A servant brought in a basket of flax, used for fire-lighting, and stayed near the hearth, kneeling to smooth out the ash in the long fire-pit, where, when the nobles had finished their meeting, some of the food for the evening meal would be cooked. Edward leaned back and felt the cut-out crucifix shape at the back of his father's chair pressing into the base of his neck. It was all as if naught had changed save the face of the man who occupied the chair. But continuity was not enough. And, as if heaven were in agreement with him, the sun broke through the window and anointed his thoughts about the need to come out from the shadow and into the light. He opened his mouth to address the gathering, but Thelwold's voice rose above the general hum of pre-meeting chatter.

"Why, then, was Alfred buried here in Winchester? If his kingship had truly been within the law, should he not have been laid to rest in the burial home of our kings? Why does he not now lie with his brother, my father, at Wimborne?"

Teasel put a hand on Thelwold's knee and Edward was sure that he saw her purse her mouth into a shush, as if soothing a fractious child. He raised his arm and caught his cousin's attention.

"Lord Thelwold, you have something more that you wish to say?"

Thelwold gave a dramatic shrug. "Naught really, save that my father, King Athelred, was a great man who fought the Danes eight times and died of wounds, fearlessly begot and bravely borne. His sons should have been kings after him."

Edward snorted. "Your father sat on his knees praying whilst mine went out and won the fight at Ashdown. It was the great King Alfred's wish to be buried here in Winchester."

"Because he knew he had no right to lie with the great kings of Wessex at Wimborne."

Edward resisted the urge to shout back at him. Thelwold might not have realised it, but although the witan meeting had not formally begun, all those who were listening would now consider that their genealogy had already been established. Edward was aware that those who had been chatting were now quietening, interested in the debate. Gradually they fell to silence, turning their faces towards either him or Thelwold, chins cupped in hands, heads to one side. The bystanders had become an audience and the manner in which the argument was conducted would give the council a good measure of the athelings' strength of character.

Edward said, "Alfred did enough in his lifetime to earn the right to be buried wherever he wished. And I know how doughty a man he was, for I was with him, fighting by his side." He left the declaration hanging there, seeing no need to add, 'You were not.'

The hall door opened again and Gwen slipped into the room, holding tightly to Athelstan's hand. As she took her seat, Edward cleared his throat, ready to cite the boy's existence as further evidence of his suitability to take the king-helm. But he said nothing. There were too many in the room who would use the phrase 'Mercian whore' and Gwen was too much more than that to suffer such abuse. He looked slowly around the room, at the faces of the council members, trying to see if he had yet won them over. Alongside the men of Wiltshire, Fleyda, the late ealdorman's daughter, was sitting with her back straight and her neat little hands placed, one palm over the other, on the table. Her cat-eyes blinked slowly and prettily, and each time she opened them she looked directly at him. He smiled, knowing that the Wiltshire vote was important, particularly as Fleyda's father had claimed a link to the royal house. Edward felt the back of his neck redden as he looked again at the young beauty and then across to Gwen and the child who was, for the time-being, although deeply loved, of no use to him. He looked away, aware that his heartbeat was accelerating. The only reality was in this room, his only guide, God.

For distraction, he rested his gaze upon his guests, these Mercians whom his council members might decry as their social inferiors. Uncle Wulf, more the size of a bear now, was hoary but hearty and still held the younger warriors in awe. Alhelm, greying a little at the temples, wore his tunics a little more open at the chest these days, for his neck was thicker than in his youth. Frith's hair was still blond and longer than was fashionable. He was lithe, sitting in his chair almost as if he had been poured into it, and his face remained unlined. A red-haired man was sitting next to him, fidgeting almost as much as Thelwold. His restless leg-crossing and uncrossing gave Frith's composure, by comparison, a languid air, though anyone who knew him and had fought alongside him would know it to be an illusion. And at the end of that bench was Ethelred, beard flecked with white specks, but sitting straight as an ash spear; the victor of Buttington would only need to raise his arm and every Mercian in the room would willingly die at his command. *And that is what I need.* Forgetting his speech about duty, destiny and dynasty, he sought the words to show the witan the man he promised to be, instead of merely opening his veins to show them whose blood flowed there. Let all thoughts pass from dead kings and hand-fast women to the here and now, to the men in this room. He stood up.

"It is true that my father won the fight at Ashdown. But mostly he gained peace through land settlement." They gratified him by reacting as he thought they would, with a collective gasp of outrage that he would now begin to destroy his father's reputation. Kings were not made in such ways.

But speaking over the grunts of disapproval, he said, "My father settled the Danelaw on the Vikings that they may call English land their own. From there they harried and raided, stealing from our churches and monasteries. Every good oath they swore was worthless." He paused and looked at them all again, in turn. "I am not my father. I would drive them all from our shores, not give them leave to stay."

For a moment, there was no reaction, as if it had taken longer than usual for his words to reach their ears. Then a Wiltshire thegn called out. "They are not in Wessex. They are not in our kingdom. Is that not enough?"

263

Edward slammed his fist down on the table. "They are on our island. They are in England. For Alfred, it was enough to be king of a small kingdom fighting only with the help of others. I would not have that." Friendship, marriage alliances; these all had their place. Alfred had been a king, yet still he had been reliant on those expediencies. He, Edward would be stronger yet. "Look to these Mercians; they will fight alongside me and I with them. They will fight for Wessex if Wessex is Edward. And let there be no mistake; Edward means to fight."

The members of the witan copied him in slapping their palms down on the tables. They cheered and roared and a chant began. "Edward, Edward, Edward." He stood, breathing hard and grinning. When he and Thelwold were boys, they would wait until the men were away, and then sneak into the goose pens. They would chase the geese and each other. He could not recall all the rules of the game now, but the important thing was to win by being the speediest. One day he had picked up a gosling and run to the far end of the enclosure with it. He looked over at his cousin now, wondering if he, too, remembered that first time, when Edward had used his initiative and left Thelwold standing.

Thelwold got to his feet now and threw his comments across the clamour. "My lord, to see you named as king is as welcome a sight to me as if a farmer were to see a cockle in his wheat field."

"Better to be that than a grain weevil."

Whatever Thelwold had prepared as his follow-up remark remained half formed and unsaid, as his mouth changed shape from its intended utterance, opening wide, then clamping shut. He heaved himself away from the table, setting it wobbling, and rushed for the door. Edward glanced around the room and saw that, even if any had their doubts about their decision, Thelwold's final outburst had dispelled them.

But amongst the faces that stared at Thelwold's back

with disgust and then turned to smile and wave at Edward, there was one whose features were creased with lines of worry, and, as she walked towards him, his sister's frown of disquiet changed into a scowl of disapproval. She embraced him, touching his ear in her usual way. But the stroke turned into a tweak and she wore a stern expression on her face. "Tread with care, Brother. You speak of being more to Wessex than was our father and your words bring hope to your folk. But they knell a warning sound to Mercians. They ring of more than the mere hand of Alfred's friendship. You are fighting for a belief, a dream. Mercia fights to keep itself; as a name, as a kingdom, as a homeland. If you mean to swallow Mercia, you will need to chew well, for it will wriggle."

Ethelred came to stand by her and Teasel placed her arm on her husband's. Edward wondered if she envisaged a borderline on the floor between them. Let her. Lines could be stepped over.

He spoke to Ethelred. "You have no kings. You always knew it would come to this."

Ethelred bowed his head and conceded the point. "It is true. Once, we had too many. Those who were of Burgred's line fought endlessly with those of Ceolwulf's. Now, there is none left of those houses. None fit to be king."

The wall hangings behind Edward's chair wafted up as the last men left the hall and set the door banging. He noticed that it was the red-haired Mercian who had stayed until the last, slamming the door petulantly immediately after Ethelred had spoken. "No man clouts a door when he is blissful. I might almost think that he did not like hearing what you said. Do all Mercians stand with you? And therefore, will they stand with me?"

"Enough will. And although I am not a king and have no sons, I will fight for Mercian freedom until I draw my last breath." Ethelred waved at the spot in the room where, moments before, Anarawd had been standing. "And we have Gwynedd standing alongside us. King Anarawd stood as your father's man and has fought by my side."

Edward sniffed. The Welshman seemed always like a wolf on the prowl. Time would tell whether he would prove to be a boon or a bane.

Teasel had been staring at the door and now she stepped forward and touched Edward's arm. "That man who left with Brihtsige?" As he shook his head, she explained. "The redhead. Who was he speaking to?"

"I had not been heeding much other than winning my fight. But I think he was with Sigehelm of Kent. Why do you ask?"

His sister rubbed her arms as if she were cold. "I do not know."

Wimborne, Dorset

"What kind of unholy madness is this?" Edward felt his jaw clamping shut with unnecessary tension. He had always dismissed his cousin as inconsequential; did the fool now have to prove him right?

Thelwold stood at the gates of the royal manor of Wimborne and screamed at the new king of Wessex. "I will live here, or by God I will die here."

Edward clenched his fists. He said to Frith, "More likely the latter, if I have aught to do with it." To his cousin, he raised his voice and said, "See you in hell, then, you streak of shit."

Edward and Frith made their way back to the camp. The men were entrenched within the old hill fort of Badbury, where the timber palisade had long since disappeared, but the vantage point remained useful and the lie of the land gave them a strategic edge over any forces that Thelwold might have secreted within the manor itself. Edward waved to one of the advance party. "Tell the lord Frith what you found when you got here."

The man bowed and made self-conscious attempts to wipe mud from his breeches. "He has a woman in there, a holy sister from Wimborne abbey. Some say that he has wed her already."

Frith let out a low whistle. "A nun? Why?"

Edward tapped a finger to his temple. "Got stones

where his brain should be. He has ever been thus."

Frith accompanied him along the length of the ancient outer defence. The wind whipped his long hair across his face.

The same wind could do no more than ruffle Edward's straighter, shorter hair, but he felt the chill blowing through it nevertheless.

Frith pushed his hair back behind his ear. "We know that Wimborne holds great meaning for him, but what does he hope to gain by being here?"

"His father is buried there. In this hallowed spot he will name himself king, knowing that men's minds will be drawn to think on the great days of his father's kingship."

"Your father was greater still. Men will think on that and naught else."

Edward grunted a reply. Election by the members of the witan gave legitimacy to rule, but Thelwold was playing to a deeper sense of destiny. Edward would not fear to lose his crown to such a dull-wit; his latest actions would merely confirm the witan's choice. But to come from a long line of kings gave strength to a man's claim; to declare it from a royal burial ground made it stronger still. How easily men turned, when not presented with their hearts' desires. He only wished that he had kept more of a watch on his disaffected cousin, for this was an ill omen for the beginning of his reign, a moment when Thelwold might succeed in garnering the support of the folk in the fields and burhs whose knowledge of the lore surrounding dead kings was greater than their familiarity with the current athelings. He sighed. "If the folk show me their backs, whom can I truly lean on, my friend, besides you?"

"Your witan stands firm behind you and my lord and lady in Mercia are stalwart and steadfast."

Mercia. He felt his back teeth clamp together, drawing a pain into his lower jaw as it tightened. Much as he admired Ethelred, he still bridled against the fact that he needed Mercia every bit as much as the Mercians needed him. "Wait

268

though. You said, Ethelred *and* Teasel? She loves me as a sister should, but I speak of the world of men."

"She lives in the world of men. She believes whole-heartedly in the bond made between our two kingdoms. I love her, as does every man in Mercia, for not only is she lovely to look upon, she is ever willing to learn, of Mercian ways and laws. She learned to read Latin so that she might fully take part in witanagemots, and she hides any sadness so that no man will see her cry. To know what she has suffered is to be in awe of her strength."

Edward stopped and stared out down the slope towards Wimborne as he considered Frith's words. He had always loved his sister simply because she had always been in the world and it was odd to hear Frith giving voice to the reasons why such a woman should be loved. The behaviour he described was nothing more than Edward would expect from a king's daughter, yet Teasel had nevertheless inspired love and respect by her conduct. She had been married off as a symbol of an alliance and somehow found a role for herself. It would prove useful for him to know that women wedded for politics might nevertheless find a way to endear themselves to the folk. He tucked the knowledge away at the back of his mind. "But does she love Mercia more than Wessex?"

"She might. But she does not love Mercia more than she loves you."

"Good. I will have need of that love before the year is out. There might be none forthcoming from elsewhere." *And, God help me, I shall deserve none.*

She was the most beautiful woman he had ever seen. He thought it when first she came to his mother's house and he had loved her since that moment. Motherhood had given plumpness to her cheeks and a little more flesh on her hips, but he would never be aroused by another the way he was when he looked upon her body. Her son ran round her legs, overjoyed to see his father but unable to express his elation except by excited animation. Holding his father's crown on his head, Athelstan dashed round, spinning faster and faster. Gwen stood in the centre of his whirling circle, a patient hand outstretched to stop the boy crashing into the hearth, a serene smile on her face. Once he had told her of his plans, Edward knew that she would never look that way at him again, so, like his cowardly cousin, he ran away from his task and spoke to her of other things, selfishly prolonging that smile on her face for a little while longer, putting off the moment when he destroyed her world. He reached out to catch a falling melt of wax from the candle, and began to fiddle with the candle-staff, twirling it in a circle and watching the flame as it flickered its protest at the disturbance.

"I am back from Wimborne sooner than you thought?"

She nodded, stilled the boy by placing her palm on his head, and walked with Edward to a bench by the hearth. "I prayed that you would not have to fight for long."

"The turn-tail's gut was so weak that he fled in the darkness. He left the nun, soiled now with their sins, and ran away to the north. I did not have to fight at all. At least, not with my sword. It was over in a blink." She was still smiling at him. "You do not speak, my lady. You know, do you not?"

She dipped her head to one side. "I think that you have something to say to me. You have needed to say it ever since you were named king. Yet you are finding it hard to speak of it."

How well she knew him. That knowledge had always been a blessing. Now it was a blight. "I have to put you aside, Gwen." He opened his mouth again, to let his speech flow. He had lain awake all night, searching for the best way to explain his deep sense of duty. God wished him to act only in defence of his kingdom and he must not allow any more challenges to his authority. Therefore he would take a wife, of royal blood, to strengthen his hold on the kingship. With carefully chosen words, he would make Gwen understand. But he got no further than, "My love, I must," before she stood up, kissed the top of his head and went slowly to the door. He scrambled to his feet, stumbling in his haste to follow her, to stop her. "I must tell you…"

She turned and put a finger to her lips. "No, there is no need. Have I not always known that this day was coming?"

He took a step towards her but she put out a hand. "No. This must be the end of it all. Do not be fretted, my love. I cannot but love you, so you must not hate yourself."

She was forced to take a sidestep as the door opened; a messenger knocked but simultaneously rushed into the room.

"My lord, I bring tidings from the north. Thelwold has been welcomed by the Northumbrian Vikings and they have acknowledged his kingship of Wessex."

All his life, the Vikings had hovered on the edge of his awareness until he was old enough to fight them physically.

271

Upon taking his father's crown, he had vowed to drive them from every kingdom of England. He curled his hand into a fist and knocked his knuckles against his forehead. Why had he not taken Thelwold more seriously? Why had he not seen that peace could be threatened as much from other Englishmen? His father was dead, his mother was ill. So far, the witan was supportive but the men within, Frith excepted, were not yet friends. A habit of fifteen years lifted his hands and he reached out to his only source of comfort. But his crown was on the table, still rocking slightly, and Gwen and Athelstan were gone.

AD901

Winchester

Fleyda tapped her fingers on the table. "Why is my name not being written down?"

Edward tried to keep his sigh a silent one. "You are not a queen, my dear. Athelstan's name is not on there either, but your son's name will be. That is enough." His leg began to jiggle as his impatience found a physical outlet. "I want this thing over with as soon as can be." The recipient of the expropriated land had shown heartfelt gratitude, but as Bishop Æthelwulf of Ramsbury bowed before him, Edward now thought only of his uncle of that name, in Mercia. Wulf was dying and Edward craved only to end the meeting and get to his bedside.

It was the last business of the day. He was happy to grant the ten hides of land forfeited by one Wulfhere and his wife. They had paid for their treason with more than their land but their executions had given him no satisfaction. He pictured the gallows, high on the hillside of an old earthwork, on the border of the hundred of Kinwardstone, the bodies swinging as a warning to all that wrongdoing would result in the end of life, poised between heaven and earth, neither in one territory nor the next. Edward would shed no tears for hanged men. One more man on the gallows was one less to crowd the prisons on the royal manors. But how many more were there like Wulfhere? What more did he need to do to win over the hearts of the

273

folk? A shrill reminder of the steps he had already taken penetrated his thoughts.

"But I am your wife. I am the mother of your son. I am kin to the house of Wessex."

And so she liked to remind him, daily. There was no need. Would he have married her for any other reason? He turned to look at her, his little Needle. She remained slim, despite the birth of their son. Her nose was long and straight, thin. The edges of her cat-eyes were starkly defined, her lashes too pale to soften their outline. Yes, everything about his royal wife was sharp, from her features to her voice and constant whining.

He caught Frith's attention and signalled to him that it was time to leave, and then answered his wife. "Let us speak of it at another time. I must get to Mercia and God knows which end of that forsaken land Teasel has ridden to. When we find her, you can whinge to my sister, who also is not a queen." *And maybe she will teach you how to suffer it with a smile.*

Shrewsbury, Mercia

The lord and lady of Mercia also had a grant of ten hides to approve. Edward stood in the doorway and waited while they endorsed the gift of land to the holy community at Much Wenlock and granted a gold chalice in honour of the Abbess Mildburg. A thegn began to walk briskly from the hall but Edward touched his elbow. "Do your lord and lady often make such gifts?"

The thegn bowed as best he could at such close quarters. "They do, my lord. They are great friends of the Church."

Edward nodded and let him go on his way. Good, Christian people, with a small child playing nearby. That must be Elfwen, the babe who was too tiny to travel to Alfred's funeral. His sister was devout; she would understand his need to put his house into godly order. But she was a mother, too. And she loved Gwen. He let out a quiet wry laugh. Edward, king, victor of Farnham, was scared of his big sister. He might well laugh, but he knew that the sweat running down the back of his tunic was only partially a result of the sticky summer heat.

When the business of the day was over, Teasel came to welcome her brother. She had scooped up the child and now held her on her hip. Elfwen's arms only just reached around her mother's neck, and Teasel had to put her head to one side to see round the child's head.

Edward embraced his sister gently, at arm's length, struggling to reach round the sleepy girl in her arms. He kissed her cheek and said, "A gift from God. Well done, my love."

She smiled back at him, her joy lifting her cheeks and dusting them with a pink blush. "This then, is my Elfwen. Who would have thought it, after all these years and me past thirty? I had begun to think myself to be beyond such things, yet here she is." Her beatific smile crumbled before turning into a massive yawn.

Edward gave the child a cursory glance so as not to offend, but truthfully, she looked like any other youngling. And he was not comfortable with the thought of his sister as a victim of constant miscarriage, preferring his long-held ideal of the companion who fished with him, played with him, conspired with him. However, even that version of his sister was not without her harsher side. He coughed, and spoke slowly, for his words might bring on that harshness. "I have brought my sons with me. With Father gone and Mother ill, at least we have the new batch of our kin ready to grow." But his words had brought them both to think of the reason for his presence, for her smile faded and he said, "How is he?" Admonition for his wrongdoings with Gwen would have to wait.

She reached up as if to stroke his ear, but changed her mind, it seemed, and clasped his forearm with a squeezing grip. "You have come in time; that is all I can say."

Almost as if the priest had absolved him without prescribing penance, Edward felt somehow robbed. He sought to push against a locked gate. "I would have walked through fire to get here. I strive to hold on to small bits of my life as a man; Wulf has ever been a part of that life."

"As against your life as a king?" She handed the child to one of her women. Watching them as they left the hall, she opened and closed her hand in a straight-fingered wave at the child who looked over the women's shoulder. She said to Edward, "The birth of a child can never be a bad thing. It helps us to bear the death of loved ones, knowing that new life will always come. Therefore, Brother, you will have to wait a while ere I give you my thoughts on poor Gwen. For now, I welcome your new son and say to you let us go to Uncle."

As they walked, her comments indicated frustration at having to stay beyond the allotted time of the witanagemot here at Shrewsbury, but Wulf had fallen ill and could not be moved. "And I am sorry to say that you will find here a badly kept hall."

He shook his head. This was no royal manor, staffed by servants. This was someone's home, and he could not believe that any of Ethelred's lords would allow their wives to make the visitors feel that their welcome was fading, nor that their housekeeping would be found wanting. She was grief-stricken indeed, for he had never heard her speak so disparagingly.

"Whose lands are these?"

She moved ahead of him. "Lord Alhelm's."

He followed her to the back of the hall, where a small room offered privacy behind a separating door. Inside, the chamber had been darkened. The shutters were pulled and only one candlestick was in use. Edward wiped the back of his neck and dried his hand on his tunic. Uncle Wulf was lying on the bed, covers pushed back. Droplets of sweat on his forehead glittered in the candlelight and his breath fought its way noisily in and out of his shrunken body. It was this last that shocked Edward. The huge beast of a man was now no more than a stretched skin covering a load of thin bones. "Is he hurting?"

Ethelred came to stand behind them in the doorway. "We think not. Even now, he would yell about it if he were."

Edward turned. His brother-in-law was blinking through wet eyes and Edward considered that Ethelred had known Wulf the longest of any of them. His sorrow was eased by the realisation, that here was another kind of kin, built as much on friendship and mutual trust as it was tied by blood; Wessex and Mercia, united by marriage, comradeship and common cause. Wulf's withered chest rose up with a struggle one final time, gasping the air in, rasping it out. The silence that followed was an unwelcome peace for those still breathing and they all gave expression to their grief, filling the air with the sounds of the living. Teasel sobbed, Ethelred coughed before allowing his tears to fall and Edward bowed his head in prayer.

Outside, he blinked in the sunshine and mopped his eyes roughly with the back of his hands. Fleyda was in the yard, snapping instructions to the woman holding her baby son. Athelstan, his pale hair streaked with mud, was digging in the dirt with some of the local boys, pretending to be soldiers digging up Viking treasure hoards.

One said, "The heathen forgot their buried stolen gold. Take this to the king."

"I will use these as gifts for my fighting-men," said another.

Athelstan paddled more of the soil away. It flicked up behind him and spattered over his stepmother's skirts.

She turned to chastise him, saw Edward approaching, and spoke to her husband instead. "Tell him, my lord. He must take more care. The bairn…"

"Looks safe enough with your woman. Do not be too stern, my dear. Athelstan is only eight and is eager to make friends, that is all."

Fleyda fussed once more over the baby. "Well, he is looking in the wrong place. He is a king's son, and not free to make friends wherever he will."

Edward listened to the clack-clacking of her voice, but looked over at his sister and Ethelred. Teasel was holding Elfwen in her arms and Ethelred stood with his arms around them both. They wept still, drawing strength from each other. He had been ready with his defence, but Teasel had not reproached him about Gwen. Not yet, anyway. He looked back at his wife, who fussed about a child she scarcely touched. "We are none of us free to make friends where we will," he said.

"Well I am free to say this, at least." She pointed at Athelstan while she spoke to her husband. "Get this Mercian by-blow out of my sight."

Edward felt no better for having escaped the reprimand from his sister. He could feel his temples pulsing. His thoughts still swam through a mind mirked by the bloody issues of kingdoms, friendships and kin. The torment of duty and destiny were hard enough and now here was racial hatred even within his own family, between the royal wife and the king's son. He raised his hand, but held it in mid-air. Then he, too, pointed at Athelstan. "His mother is more queenly than... Never mind." He turned on his heel and marched away from her.

"My lord, whither do you go that makes you turn your back to me?"

"To speak to the only one who knows the meaning of truth." He slammed back the chapel door and stepped from the hot day into cool sanctuary.

AD902

"No, by God, I will not. And I will hear no more of it. Do you understand?"

Upset by the shouting, Elfwen began to cry and Teasel scooped her onto her knee and rocked her. In fifteen years of marriage she had seldom heard Ethelred raise his voice, but these days yelling seemed to be the rule by which the men of Mercia lived.

"I hear you," said Brihtsige. "I hear that you are not man enough to stand up and take Mercia once and for all. You are free of your bond to Alfred. Do you not yearn to be free of the yoke of Wessex?"

"I said, enough." Ethelred stood up. He strode forward as he said, "Get you gone from here until your blood cools," and Brihtsige retreated.

All but two of the other thegns and nobles had already discreetly left the hall, having no wish to bear witness to Brihtsige's challenge. Elfwen was red in the face from screaming and Teasel could do no more with her. She looked across at Frith, who bowed and left the room. Moments later, Alyth appeared and took the distressed child out of the hall. Frith returned, stood in the open doorway, beckoned the remaining thegn, and allowed the man to walk in front of him before he closed the door quietly, leaving the lord and lady alone.

Ethelred kneaded a sore spot on his temple and reached for a drink.

Teasel walked over to him and pulled him to a bench. She laid a calming hand on his thigh. "Will he let it lie, do you think?"

"Whether he does or does not, I care not. However much I am goaded, I will not break my fellowship with your brother. That way lies ruin for us all."

"Brihtsige is a man who will stand at a crossroads and see only one path. He thinks that Mercia's only worry is the harm that could come from Edward's dreams for England. Does he even know?"

Ethelred poured himself another drink and finished it in three gulps. "About this new threat from Ingimund? No. I bade Frith and Alhelm not to speak of it for the time being." He rubbed his forehead again. "Dear God, will it never end?"

She wriggled to the edge of the bench so that she could turn and face him. She took the wine cup from his hand, placed it on the table, and took his hands in hers. "You could not have known. How could anyone have known that Norsemen would come from Ireland to threaten us? But I saw Anarawd's letter and it seems that he is winning out on Anglesey against them. We do not know what it means for Mercia, but if they come nearer to Chester then at least they will not catch us sleeping."

"Sleeping? My head hurts too much for sleep."

Still she sought to comfort him. "Then come to bed anyway. Alyth has the bairn and there is naught to keep you here."

He stood up and held her to him. He leaned down to kiss her and said, "I thank God for you." He ran his hands down her body and round her hips. She stepped away. He said, "What is it?"

Silly, that was what it was. Elfwen was nearly three and, now that she was weaned, Alyth looked after her so that Teasel was largely spared the trials of soothing the ill-

281

tempered girl. Despite the strictures proscribing such acts, Ethelred had scoffed at the notion that he must stay away from his wife's bed until the child was weaned, so even before Alyth took over, he had insisted on using the expedient by which all the nobility circumvented the rules and the babe had been nursed by a child-feeder. Teasel's life, therefore, had few extra demands now that she was a mother. And yet, she had never felt fully comfortable having him near her after the birth. When she first came to his court, she thought of herself as a token, a trophy, and was unhappy until Anarawd had shown her the measure of her true worth. She had begun to value herself in that new mould, expecting little ever to change. When the babe came along, there was another role to play, and a daily reminder whenever she looked down and saw the changes wrought in her body, for Anarawd had also made her aware of the difference between youthful winsomeness and the rounded-hipped homeliness of motherhood. "I would rather go where we can find some darkness; that is all." She tugged at his arm but he would not be shifted.

He groaned. "Not that old tale again." He pulled her nearer, kissing her forehead. "Listen to me, woman. You are a mother, not a shape-shifter. I will not say I would have you no other way, for I would. I would have you any way. We must take each other as we are. Always." He kissed her again, this time on the mouth.

She put a hand against his chest in what she knew was a futile gesture to keep him away. Reassurances from men who generally never discriminated did little to assuage a woman's shyness. She sighed, not the least comforted. "Then I will yield, for if by yielding I can ease your worries, I am still of use to you."

"Yes." He nodded in mock solemnity, but his face widened as he broke into a smile. He stepped in closer and kissed her neck. He laughed softly and his breath warmed her shoulder. "Oh, yes," he said, "I think you should yield."

"How is your headache now?" She stroked his temple with her little finger, then kissed the soft indent between the top of his ear and his upper jawbone.

He smiled. "Eased. You are skilled at healing."

"I am glad." She smiled and added a teasing subservience. "My lord." He chuckled but she sat up. "Truly, I mean it. Let your worries be mine. For I have none of my own and have room to store yours, if it helps."

He reached his arms around her and pulled her down on top of him. "It does. You do. The world has sharp edges, but knowing that your softness is biding at home for me, brings comfort." He lifted his head, pulled her head level with his by gently pushing his nose against her face and kissed her.

She slid down to lie by his side and wriggled away from the fire, lifting her hip to drag the rug with her and straighten out the ruckles she'd caused by moving. Frith would have ensured that all knew not to disturb them, but she was still grateful for the bench and board placed between the hearth and the door. Ethelred was still on his back and she draped her leg over his and settled her head on the pillow of his shoulder and upper arm. This was so much nicer than the ever more frequent bouts of shouting. Not that he had ever raised his voice to her, but the men were all of short temper, the child had responded with peevishness and she had spent what felt like weeks doing nothing but attempting to soothe a querulous infant before handing her to the ever-patient Alyth. God grant that this day could last, these feeling of bliss linger.

She laughed when she heard the knock. "Hush my thoughts, for they are too loud." Perhaps if they kept low, hid behind the bench?

Ethelred sat up, pulled his wife to her feet and smoothed her dress down. He reached out and tucked an escapee strand of hair back beneath her veil. She kissed his fingers.

He adjusted his belt, checked his tunic and said, "Come

in."

Thegn Ordgar was a man of long-standing service in Edward's fyrd. Teasel stared at his impassive face. *Hush my thoughts, for they were indeed too loud.* "You bear bad tidings."

"Yes my lady, I do. The lady Ewith is dead."

Winchester

She knew that Edward had ordered the new minster built to honour his God and family, a new resting place for Alfred and his descendants, but as Teasel looked around the cold stone building she struggled with the urge to run outside. Every sound, be it a footstep or an uttered word, bounced from wall to wall and hung in the air. Even if the sun shone through the windows, there would be no comforting sigh from timbers creaking with the changing temperature. There could be no intimate, whispered conversations in a building such as this, with naught to catch the words and deaden them in the air, keeping them private. She stamped her chilled feet and as she missed the forgiving yield of wooden floorboards or even impacted earth, she thought that this church had not stood long enough, had not yet housed enough folk to warm it through. Her mother would forever be cold in this place. Yet, she would be at peace. Ewith no longer had to worry about her husband or be fretted by her children. On the day of Elfwen's birth Teasel had vowed that she would never lose sleep over her children in that way. Losing sleep to their cries was enough. Oh, that birthing-day. She would sooner have been lying on some battlefield, stabbed and dying, than in childbed. She clamped her arms around her middle in an attempt to warm up and felt again her thickened waist and splayed ribcage. After all those years dreading her monthly bleed, she was now grateful to have it. She would take up arms against the Norseman Ingimund himself than toil in childbirth again.

Her mother was laid to rest alongside her father's re-interred body and Plegmund finished the service with a prayer for all their souls, living and immortal. Teasel looked again at Edward, who seemed even more anxious than she to get out of the minster. His fidgeting suggested more than mere cold, though. Occasionally he exchanged glances with Frith, as if the loyal nobleman was party to whatever was causing Edward's anxiety. If they had more tears to shed for their mother, they would have to hold them back for now.

Outside, Edward stood with Frith and told her and Ethelred. "Thelwold has teamed up with the East Anglians and has been harrying Mercia while you have been away. I am told that he is now to be found in Wiltshire."

Ethelred reached for Teasel's hand. He gripped her fingers with a strength that made her wince and she felt the anger shaking through his arm. "I will take my wife home and see what he has wreaked behind my back. Then I will see you in Wiltshire."

He strode towards the stables, and Frith called for horses for himself and the king, but Edward tugged on Teasel's sleeve. "Before I leave, I have a boon to ask of you."

She raised her eyebrows and waited.

"Will you take Athelstan with you? Fleyda loves him not, calling him a Mercian by-blow."

Teasel put her hands to her face. "Dear God, even now how deep the hatred lies. Is it only we two, half Mercian, half West Saxon, who can hold a hand in friendship?" She looked across to the minster door, where Fleyda stood watching. Waiting, it seemed, for Teasel to give her answer. Her arms were folded as they had been that day, years ago in the woods beyond Lord Wiltshire's house. Fleyda had made cow-eyes at Edward that day. The younger woman was chewing her bottom lip. This was not hatred; this was anxiety. *My God, she really loves him. It is not that she hates Athelstan, it is that she cannot bear for Edward to look upon him and mourn Gwen.* Teasel was overcome then with sadness for Fleyda. To love and be loved by Edward was no easy task. To love him with no chance of that love being returned...

So many of those whom Teasel had loved were either dead, or lost to her, or they had had their loving bliss torn asunder. Thank the sweet Lord for Ethelred, always loving, ever present. She stared at her brother, willing him to understand that when all else were dead, a good love was surely worth grasping tightly. She took his hand as she spoke. "Is this truly what you want? To send the child away? You love him."

"Ah, love. That is the thing. Love cannot come into it, do you not see? For my kingdom, I must turn my back on love. You are not a king. You cannot understand."

A very old pain jumped up and bit her inner throat. "Believe me, there is naught that I do not know about giving up love." If he wished to speak of duty, there was none who knew it better.

Dusk had long since given way to a deeper darkness when they reached Worcester. Ethelred had been urging more speed, but Teasel had made him slow down once the boy had fallen asleep. She held the lad in front of her and worried as much about controlling the horse as waking the sleeping child.

There was nothing odd about Alhelm's being there to welcome them home. But from the light of the brazier she could see that he was impatient for them to dismount, shifting his weight from foot to foot. He stepped forward, ascertained the identity of the slumbering boy and nodded. "We are all friends here, then. I will tell you, though it breaks my heart. Brihtsige has gone to fight alongside Thelwold. He left this morning, wounding one of my thegns as he went."

Ethelred knuckled his forehead and leaped down from

his mount. "As if my head did not hammer enough already. Are you ready to leave? Wait while I get my things."

He went inside and Teasel allowed Alhelm to lift Athelstan from her horse. He passed the boy to the door-thegn and held out his hands for Teasel, helping her to dismount by catching hold of her as she slid from the saddle. She caught his gaze as she came level with him, but said nothing. There were no words. Staring at his water-blue eyes, so pale that they shone almost transparent in the reflected firelight, she thought of Edward and how much easier it must be to send loved ones away, beyond the point where sight could cause hurt. Let him talk to her of hardship when he had lived within reach of those who were beloved but must remain untouched. Even when the passing years put distance between the wounded hearts, they remained damaged, so that it hurt all the more to know that the pain etched on Alhelm's face must be but a reflection of her own; both of them hurting for Ethelred and the resounding blow of Brihtsige's betrayal.

Ethelred emerged, his war saddle under his arm, shield over his shoulder. He walked towards Teasel to bid her farewell, but as he stepped forward his foot appeared to turn under, his knee folded and he fell to the ground. He dropped the saddle and the shield bounced and rolled away. He lay, right leg twisted under his body, arm limp at his side, eyes closed but mouth open, tongue lolling from a mouth drooping awkwardly to one side.

Always chasing, never catching. During nights of despair he had begun to think that he was, after all, a mere copy of his father. No, he was worse than that, for he had tried to rest his kingship on friendship alone. His father had, at least, tied his allies to him.

Edward had waited on the Mercian border for Ethelred, but he never came. He followed the heathens as they crossed the Thames but by the time he got to Braydon they had gone, leaving a smoking, ruined mess behind them. Perhaps they'd thought themselves safe as they vanished back to East Anglia. Perhaps they'd expected him to go home. Perhaps they did not know that Saxon women expected their men to return home with a kill, not leave the hunt before the quarry was even in sight. They certainly could not know that their foe was driven by demons of his own conjuring. Traversing Essex, Edward had built up a surfeit of angry energy. Like a charging boar, he had picked up too much speed merely to stop, turn and leave. So now he had them stuck behind their own defensive line, the dyke known as Miceldic rising up against the flat terrain, stretching northwest to meet the edge of the fenland. No doubt they thought themselves safe on the other side of the dyke ridge. He preferred the word *'trapped'*.

The late autumn easterly wind slapped at his face with shaving-blade sharpness and he turned his back to it. Frith came riding from the baggage train, his body crouched forward as he fought against the seemingly solid force of the blustering, squally air. He dismounted by Edward and the moment that he turned his face the wind caught his hair and glued it to the side of his head. Raising his voice against the gusting air that tried to snatch his words, he said, "I have sent men out to find some shelter." He pulled his horse around until the beast stood sideways on to the wind, then he cowered behind its flank.

Edward joined him. "I would be warm. We need to light a fire or two."

"Yes, my lord, as soon as the men come back I will oversee the laying out of a..."

Edward shook his head. The tents could wait. The camp could wait. "I was thinking of a much bigger fire."

"You meant the burhs and farms hereabouts? I will see to it." He clicked his tongue to move his horse about and began to walk away.

Edward tugged on his arm. "Will he come?"

Shouting once more against the squall, Frith said, "If he can. He would not leave you when he knows you are in need. Alhelm is not here either and they have sent no word. There must be something keeping them in Mercia."

Yes, but what? A death, and if so, whose? Edward shook his head. "I do not wish to brood over it for I will go mad. Keep my mind from it. Make this foul air blow black with cinders."

Now he was as bad as they, except that he had God on his side. Their farmsteads were burned, their crops destroyed and the ever-faithful Frith still had streaked hair weeks after they'd lit the first of the fires. The carts were full of reclaimed treasure, covers of hide tied tightly over piles of Church gold, chalices and crosses, and bags of coin. And not a hand had been raised against them. Why did the Vikings not come out of their hiding-hole? Perhaps he had made them understand that retribution would be swift if they left the confines of their stronghold again. "They will not come out and fight."

"If we bide a little longer?"

"Frith, my friend, your mouth does not speak of your heart's craving. It is nearly Christmas, I am cold, and I am wracked with worry over my sister. We will go home for a while."

Frith caught the attention of one of his thegns. "Gather the leaders and bring them to King Edward. We need to speak of withdrawal."

He and Edward bowed their heads against the wind and discussed their tactics as they walked to the tent to await the other divisional leaders. "We must keep steady along the lines. Not leave too swiftly or too loudly."

Inside the tent, Frith checked them off one by one as they arrived. "Wiltshire, Hampshire, Somerset."

No men from Dorset, of course, because Thelwold had taken most of them with him when he fled north. But the others were steadfast and true. Edward looked at them all, listening intently as Frith gave them their orders. He sat up and counted again. "Where is the Kentishman, Sigehelm? Who is here on behalf of the men of Kent?"

Frith turned and answered straight away. "I sent word to them. Someone will come soon."

He continued his briefing and Edward scratched his elbow. The itch spread and he slapped at his thigh. He reached up and jabbed his finger up and down his back, then he shoved his boot-top down to rake his calf. Sitting up, he said, "Enough. We need to leave. Kent?"

Frith patted the lord of Wiltshire on the shoulder. "Send word again, my lord. I leave you to see to it that the men of Kent withdraw with the rest."

In the great low flatlands of the east it was easy to turn round and see his troops spread out behind him and he did so, frequently, still waiting for the standard of Kent to show itself flapping in the devil's-breath wind that never ceased to blow. Even with his leather gloves on, Edward could not feel his fingers. Curled around the reins, they would surely snap like icicles if he tried to move them. At least he had his back to the wind, only facing it when he turned, again and again, to check that the yellow standard with the white horse of Kent had flocked to join the other proud symbols of Wessex, beating like bird-wings in the vicious air. But it was not there.

"How many now?"

Frith knew immediately what he meant, for he said, "I have sent word seven times, Lord. Either they do not hear, or they do not want to hear."

In the distance, a rider waved his free arm and shouted as his horse galloped towards them. "Lord Frith. Lord Frith!"

"It is the last man I sent out. Now we will know."

The messenger reined his horse in alongside them and pushed his words out with force from his gasping lungs. "The men of Kent, they did not follow. The heathens came after them…"

Edward clenched his back teeth with such force that what little was left of his tooth enamel ground uncomfortably. He hardly dared to ask, for the question would bring forth an answer. "Sigehelm?"

"Dead, my lord, along with his thegn, Edwold. It seems that they wished to bind themselves to the heathen horde but were misunderstood and the foe turned on them instead of welcoming them."

"Can the tide be turned?" Frith had his hand in the air, ready to motion to the troops to turn around.

"I think so, my lord," said the messenger. But we must go now."

The raven banner fluttered in the wind. The red cloth was shaped into points at its outer edge, the outline of the bird of doom painted in black. As Edward leaped from his horse at the edge of the battle site, he saw the raven drop to the ground. It was there only for a moment before resuming its flight, but its temporary dip gave him hope that they were not, after all, too late. The men of Kent, once defiant, now fought for England whilst they fought for their lives. The shield walls had broken and all over the battlefield men were fighting hand to hand, one on one. A burly Dane with a fur-covered helm lunged at Edward, sword slashing but connecting only with the king's shield. Jabbing with his own blade, Edward leaned against the inner edge of his shield, bending his left leg and steadying his balance with his right as he pushed forward against the man's bulk.

The Dane's mouth was open in a yellow-toothed snarl. "You will die, Englishman." He roared a pagan war cry and shoved hard against the linden board with his own shield. Edward overbalanced and slipped down on his knee, ducking his head to the side as the man's sword tip moved the air next to his exposed neck. Scrabbling to regain purchase with his back leg, Edward managed to get enough grip with his back foot to launch himself to his right and the Dane found himself suddenly pushing against nothing. Edward jumped up, whirled round and cut the flailing heathen's air off with a sideward slice across his windpipe.

Eager to get to the middle of the brawl, Edward ran forward, jumping over the prone figure of an English archer. His quiver lay, still full, by his side, the once-white feathers tinged pink where blood from his stomach oozed onto the ground. If Edward were still in line with the snipers he knew the main battle was being played out far beyond this point. But another Viking barred his way and Edward leaped at him with such force that their shields clashed and both men were wrong-footed by the impact. This new foe had a blood-red tunic and his breeches were short. He wore no leg bindings so that his calves were bare above his leather shoes. His beard was long and black and greasy, and it stank. He raised his sword and it sparked off Edward's, but before the brute could swing again, Edward, smaller, more lithe, had whirled around and thrust again

293

with his blade, sinking it into the soft flesh under the man's left ribs. He pushed him away with his foot, retrieved his blade, and ran forward. Around him, the battle noise diminished; fewer men were fighting now. To his left, a hulking Dane stood over an English thegn, taunting him with his banner. He had most of the cloth bunched up in his fist, but a yellow outline splayed out across the red sheet, enough of it on show to be recognisable as a runic symbol. But with banner in one hand, prodding, and axe in the other, the man had no shield and little defence when Edward came at him broadside, slashing down across his unprotected neck. The man fell on his front, grunting as the force of landing expelled the remaining breath from his body. Edward stooped to help the thegn, but the lad's face was pale. Edward looked down at the deep thigh-wound. There was so little blood left that it no longer pumped forth, but left only a trickle as it carried the last of his life's essence to the earth. Edward stood, panting, longing to take off his helm and wipe the sweat from his brow. As he looked about, he reckoned it worth the risk, for those Vikings still on their feet were walking away. He pulled the heavy metal dome from his head and rubbed the back of his hand along his forehead. The freezing air dried the sweat and cooled him instantly.

Frith came to stand beside him, blood leaking from a wound to his upper arm. Before Edward could enquire, he said, "'Tis naught, and it cost the man who did it his life. Come with me, my lord, for there is something over here that you should see."

Those Vikings who still lived walked casually from the battle as if they had won the day. Edward looked around and tried to assess the numbers of dead on each side.

Frith said, "They think that they have won. Here you will see why." He spread out his hand in gesture and Edward looked to the ground where he was pointing.

On their backs, arms crossed over their chests and swords laid along their bodies, ealdormen Sigehelm and

294

Sigewulf lay dead. Alongside them was thegn Edwold and the deaths of these three renowned men would be the cause for long months of mourning in Kent.

Edward sniffed and wrinkled his nose at the stench of blood that came with it. "The men of Kent held back, against my wishes. The men of Kent are dead. Little wonder that those scum," he nodded at the departing Vikings, "No wonder they think they have beaten us."

"Yes, my lord. But that was not what I wished to show you. Over here." Frith walked a few feet to the right, taking Edward to the outer edge of the central battlefield. It was trampled and dirty, but there was no mistaking that the dead man had red hair. He would be easy to identify, even though he lay face down in the East Anglian dirt, an English spear in his back. "Brihtsige," Frith said. "He was the son of Beornoth of Mercia, who was a great friend of Ethelred's."

Edward stared at his corpse. "They say that Judas had red hair." *And the last time I saw that red head, it was close in talks with Sigehelm of Kent. In my hall.*

"And over here, my lord King." Frith emphasised the last word.

Edward's gaze followed Frith's pointing finger until he saw why Frith was at pains to assert his kingship. In life, the man had been fidgety, gangly, his long limbs barely ever still. Now, they were at rest, but in death he had been caught in a parody of motion, his arms above his head and his legs sticking out at awkward angles. "Thelwold." Edward looked upon the body of the cousin with whom he had grown from boy to manhood and all he could think of was to wonder whether such a traitor deserved Christian burial. He knew that Frith would give the order, one way or another. "I will leave you to…"

At the same time, Frith said, "I will set men to digging for the burials."

Edward lifted the right side of his mouth into a half-smile. "They may write that I have lost the fight this day, at the Holme, but winning would not have felt sweeter."

He had no time for the seers who claimed that a man's sleep-thoughts held deep meaning for the future. And he needed no wise man to tell him the sense of last night's mind-wandering. In a storm-lashed land, he had stood on the edge of a cliff, the sea behind him, Thelwold, the Vikings and the men of Kent rushing up the hill towards him and Gwen standing firm between him and his foes. In the tiny moment before wakefulness, he had pushed her out of harm's way so that she stumbled, dropping the child in her arms. Where the boy landed, Edward did not know, for he sat up in bed and wiped the sweat from his chest with the edge of the blanket.

Now, he rode along the streets of Worcester, swallowing the bile that rose to his throat whenever another nightmare vision clouded his eyes. For weeks he had been picturing his sister's dead body, but at last a message had come from Mercia and it was fixed with Æthelflæd's seal. She lived. So, what, then? What had come to pass? Bad enough that it was the middle of December, but he could only curse the Vikings still on the prowl, who made life so much more difficult for English couriers to make and complete their journeys.

He turned the corner to ride into the enclosure in front of the great hall and tugged sharply on the reins. His son, Athelstan, was holding a wooden sword high above his blond head as he ran in his habitual circles, but his aunt seemed oblivious to his excess energy as she spoke to the bishop of Worcester. She also seemed to be ignoring the snivelling child who sat on the hall steps, banging a wooden toy on the floor.

Edward dismounted and stepped towards her, his breath coming in sharp, scared bursts and pushing little clouds of steam into the air. "You, you are, are you well?"

Teasel touched the bishop's arm by way of an apology for curtailing their conversation. "Yes. Why would I not be?" She stood up and brushed her hand across his brow and down to his ear. "Oh, love, it is good to see you. Athelstan, your father is here. Come and greet him."

Athelstan charged at his father, wrapping his arms round Edward's waist and thrusting his head against his belly. Athelstan stood up straight and Edward had to check his calculations, thinking that for a ten-year-old, the boy came up high against his father's chest. He embraced his son but looked across at his sister, the reason for his being alone at the Holme becoming all too clear. For if she lived...

Teasel said, "My lord Bishop, you will forgive us. I must take my brother to see the lord Ethelred."

Werferth nodded and moved off, murmuring something about tending to his bees.

Edward tried to interpret the look which passed between the holy man and Teasel, but it was too private to be readable. He said, "Ethelred is not, he is not dead?"

"No. But, well, come and see."

Inside the hall, Edward saw few faces that he recognised. Most of the old Mercian guard, stalwarts like his uncle, had passed away, to be replaced by younger men whose worth Edward did not know. They sat, variously sipping ale, gaming, or arguing points of law. In the corner, drawing Edward's gaze by naught more than his stillness, was the Welshman, Anarawd, all dark eyes and wayward hair. He smiled, apparently neither surprised nor cowed to see another king walking into the hall unannounced. In the middle of the room, ealdorman Alhelm was sitting at the high table, surrounded by piles of vellum charters. He held

297

one in his hand and used it occasionally to bat away the over-animated scribe who, because he knew what was written on the charters, would not give the layman the time to read the words thoroughly. Edward nodded at him, suppressing a smile, and followed his sister into the chamber at the back of the main hall.

Ethelred lay on the bed, propped up with pillows. His left leg was bent, giving extra support to his body, while his right leg lay straight, the foot turned out. He held a document in his left hand, but his right arm hung by his side, resting on a pillow. Edward looked at his brother-in-law's face, noting that his eye seemed to have slipped down towards his cheek. Below it, one half of his mouth had dropped nearer his jaw.

Edward realised that his own face must be expressing horror, for his sister had gripped his arm. "It looks worse than it is. There has been naught more to worry us since the first time he fell. And you can speak now, my love, can you not?"

Ethelred nodded, and pulled his mouth into what should have been a smile, but emerged as something more akin to a grotesque snarl. Edward touched his sister's elbow and gently turned her towards the door. "May I speak with you, outside?"

As they came back into the hall, Teasel and Alhelm exchanged glances. But no, Edward thought, this was not an exchange; this was a look, shared. Had he been wrong all those years ago, to dismiss as childish dream-lust his sister's feelings for this man?

He turned on her as soon as they reached the hearth. "I am deeply sorry for your loss, Sister, but I cannot leave Mercia without a leader. Not in these times."

She tilted her chin to look up at him and her eyes were free from tears. "How like you to come straight to business. But we have a leader. My lord lives."

"But he cannot fight."

It hardly needed saying, yet she seemed affronted. She

298

took a deep breath and crossed her arms. "He is of no use, so I should put him aside; is that it? Unlike some, that sort of thing would come hard to me." She glared at him. "But then I am blessed that I no longer live in a land where no whore must be acknowledged, but nor yet will a king's wife be named queen."

Edward dropped his gaze. "I will love Gwen until the day I die." He looked up. "But what else could I do? I have given up everything. The Vikings have shaped our whole lives, and even now they shadow us. You saw how our father fought and the toll it took. There must be no more on and off fighting; this must be the beginning of the end. I will drive them from our land. And they will not go if Mercia does not have a leader, a leader who will stand by Wessex." He touched a hand to her shoulder. "God lets me breathe only to watch over Wessex and to look after you."

"What do you mean?"

"Your husband is weak. What if other men take power?"

"What other men? Brihtsige is dead."

His mouth itched to say 'thanks to me', but he had no need, for he saw reflected in her eyes his own feelings of hurt and betrayal stirred up by Thelwold's treachery and knew that Brihtsige's rebellion had been as piercing to her own faith and flesh. Brother and sister bore the same wound.

"And there are no others here in Mercia who would wish to take the leadership. Or dare to. I cannot speak for Wessex."

If she was baiting him, he would not bite. He said, "Not by means of the sword. But through your bed? You have only a daughter for now, but if a son were to..."

Her eyes narrowed and her freckled nose seemed to become inflamed as her nostrils widened. "Let me warn you, Brother, that you speak too boldly to me. I will also tell you that I will never have another child. Nor another lover."

She turned to walk away and he felt a sense of shame,

that in deflecting a perceived barb, he had pricked her with his own sharp words. "Teasel, don't go." He skipped two steps to catch up with her, placed his hand on her shoulder and pulled her round. "You must understand. After all, half the blood that flows in you is West Saxon. You know what it would mean should this fellowship break."

She stared up at him and narrowed her hazel eyes. "And you are half Mercian, tied by your mother's blood to these proud folk who will be ruled only by their own. Do not stir things needlessly. We are all right as we are."

This time, he let her go, watching from the door as she walked through the gate and out into the fields beyond. Sensing company, he turned to see Alhelm moving to stand beside him. His anger needed a more deserving target and he said, "Do you love her?"

The Mercian stared at him. The pouches of middle-age had begun to puff up under them but his eyes were still the palest blue, pierced by tiny black pupils. He spoke with his usual soft tone. "Yes, I love her. We all do. And if, through her, we can hear my lord's thoughts and wishes, we will heed her every word."

As he stood facing his suddenly wary friend, Edward became aware of movement behind him. A backward glance confirmed that the other Mercian lords had stood up from their seats on the mead benches and had begun to edge towards him. Only Anarawd of Gwynedd remained seated, his black eyes flickering as he watched the men walk forward. His presence was a reminder that Wessex was not Mercia's only friend. Edward thought of a fox watching a henhouse. But was it Mercia that had the Welshman licking his lips, or the Mercian lady? In marking Alhelm, had Edward fixed his sight on the wrong man? The Mercian lords stepped slowly round him and then went to stand beside Alhelm. Edward gazed at each of them, noting their narrowed brows, their jutting chins, and said, "You are all as one on this?"

They responded in turn. "I, Eadric, stand by my lady."

"I, too." "I am Ordlaf and this is my brother, Ordgar. We will follow the lady." "I am Eadnoth, and I follow her unto death."

Edward barked out a laugh of disbelief. "All of you say that you would rather follow a woman than put your own names forward. Why?"

The old man who had given his name as Eadnoth stepped forward. "Let us be forthright. The lady was not welcome when first she came here, being a West Saxon."

The old man coughed and Edward wondered if he were about to spit after mentioning Alfred's race.

"But she showed fearlessness, steadfastness and is God-fearing. She has spoken up for Mercian rights and has stood by her lord in times of great woe. Our kings have always let us down; we do not crave another. And you and I both know how things truly are."

"If you mean that I would not let another man walk where Ethelred has trodden, then you are right." There must be no more Thelwolds, no more Brihtsiges, nor Sigehelms of Kent. His cousin's treachery had caused a wound that still felt raw and bloody, salted by the shame of not having foreseen the mutinous intent. He could not be distracted by having to stamp down another rebellion. He would not allow the Mercians to appoint another king and he would insist on all charters going out in his name as well as Teasel's and Ethelred's. Although he was standing in Mercia discussing Mercia's future, he had to be guided by his beliefs of what would ultimately be best for Wessex. But if these men would remain loyal to him as long as he left his sister as their figurehead, then perhaps he could also leave them their pride. And besides, his son was here. The Mercians loved Athelstan. He nodded at Eadnoth, but addressed Alhelm. "So be it. But it is only because she is my sister that I bow to you."

The sharp scything noise set his teeth on edge. Every Mercian in the room had his hand on his sword hilt, the blade hitched up to protrude from the scabbard. Alhelm stepped forward and fixed the piercing blue gaze on Edward once more. "No, my lord, it is only because she is your sister that we bow to you."

Edward withstood the intense gaze for as long as he could, but then he blinked and looked away. They must know that their words were only bluster, but he did not trust himself to challenge them. Was he so scared now of whispers in corners that it had impaired his judgement? Was he afraid to burst their puffed-up pride? *'Do not stir things needlessly.'* Gwen would have said the same. Damn Gwen. Forget Gwen. He had given up a good woman in exchange for a wife. These Mercians had grown to love Teasel and therefore were loyal to her. Perhaps, in time, his folk would have done the same because people would have loved Gwen. Had he been so blinded by his notion of destiny that he had given her up unnecessarily? His sister had managed to be both a good woman and a good wife and he was going to have to trust her. Her, and his own instincts. There was naught else left to him now.

He heard his brother-in-law leave. Lying on his bed, he listened to the sound of the hooves in the dust, and felt a tingling in his nostrils as tears began to work their way towards his eyes. Ethelred was feeling stronger but he knew he would never be as he was. He was not the first man to be thus afflicted after a fall and he knew what he could expect from his remaining years. He was forty-five years old and a cripple. And yet he had heard his men declare their willingness to allow him to rule on in name. The tears emerged, but he did not bother to lift a hand to wipe them away. The loyalty of his men was humbling enough, but his wife's unflinching response to Edward's assertions had been uttered with such force that it left him wondering if some of his physical strength had been taken by God and given to her. Her declaration of loyalty was a boon, yet he was still mindful that there was one man out there in the hall whose voice he had not heard. That man was his ally, lately a friend, but his Welsh bards sang not only of his battlefield prowess but his physical beauty. In Gwynedd, Ethelred had observed the women of Wales and had seen for himself that Anarawd's charms were as potent as elf-shot. He shifted on the bed, determined not to call for assistance, but instead cursing silently that he could only sit, ineffectual. His wife had overcome her resistance to the marriage, learned to put aside her youth-love and was now willing to lead a kingdom for him. If ever there was a time for him to overcome his reticence for long speeches and tell her how he felt about her, it was now. God obviously had a fondness for a joke.

She walked for miles, climbing higher and higher into the densely wooded hills, until her anger subsided and only then did she notice that she still had on her soft slippers. Feeling now every stone under her feet, she turned and sat down, looking out over the countryside below and blowing misty clouds of cold air out with each breath. She patted her arms in an effort to keep them warm. Curse Edward. He was always so sure of himself, so sure that his way of thinking was the only way. What did he know of the weeks of heartache they had all endured, waiting to see if Ethelred would recover even a little of his former strength? She threw out the silent accusation and almost immediately she heard her brother's response; that he had been busy fighting off a rebellion. So, they each had their own burdens to bear; each now had their own destiny to fulfil.

We are all right as we are'. But were they? Was she? Edward had not brought Frith with him and she needed his quiet strength and ability to see every job that needed doing. Alhelm, it was clear, could not cope with the administration and was happy only when seated in the saddle, sword in hand. Besides, she found it hard, even now, to speak to him when Ethelred was not there as a shield. The sun began to glow red in the afternoon sky and she stood up to make her way home before dark. Skirting a line of trees she detected the musty odour of rotting leaves, lying wet and undisturbed since the autumn fall. Turning away from it, she gazed across the valley, to a plume of smoke from a farmstead chimney, rising white against the purpling sky. What a peaceful scene, that changed only with the seasons. The leaves would decay, and help the spring growth. God grant her the strength to ensure that naught else came to change this landscape, so familiar to her, so beloved. '*I know this. I know here.*' They had been Ethelred's words, long ago, but now they were her thoughts too. She could help him. Many times before, she had been asked to do something for which she had no skills, no knowledge and somehow she had steered a straight course, and this time she had Ethelred to ask. Always before, she had stepped back, left the men to their business. Although she had learned long ago always to make the best of things, she had hated being Gunnhildr's custodian, being so close to the enemy with no real power. Thus was life for all women; but now her life could be different. And as she thought of how Ethelred needed her and how she could serve him, she put a hand to her heart as another thought struck her. *And truly does it strike me, for its truth is like a hammer blow.* If she did not stand firm against Edward, if she did not become Ethelred's stand-in, she was sure that Edward would take over the kingdom rather than allow another man to lead Mercia. Edward had always been ruthless; Gwen might have softened him but now that she had gone there would be no-one other than Teasel to counter his tendencies. As she stood on the hillside and looked out over her husband's beloved land, she knew that she was all that stood between Mercia and Wessex; she, the outsider, was Mercia's last hope of even nominal independence.

She hitched her skirt up, tucking the excess cloth into her belt and ran, ignoring the bumpy stones that pressed into her feet with each step. Side-sliding down the steeper terrain, she cared not for the mud splats kicking up onto her back. Heart thumping and breath too quickly snatched to stay long enough in her lungs, she arrived, gasping, at the hall. Alyth offered her daughter to her, but Elfwen was still whining and Teasel shook her head. Alhelm, back at his paperwork, looked up and pushed his brows together in an enquiring frown. She flapped her arms, but abandoned her explanation, shoving open the bedchamber door and rushing to Ethelred's bedside.

She stood for a moment, waiting for her breathing to calm, then she lay down beside him, on his good side. "Before you fell, you had begun to use me to ease your worries. Use me now. Tell me. Tell me how to do it."

From the left, his profile looked as it always had. His long nose remained perfectly straight, his jaw line was taut as ever and the tic that made his muscle twitch was still active from time to time. For a second she could believe that it had never happened. Now he turned to look at her and the lack of symmetry in his features was clear again. She knew he was struggling to form words and she waited, with patience newly learned.

In the darkened room, she could not be sure that she saw tears in his eyes.

Having moved his lips to the required shape, he tested the sound a couple of times and then simply offered her one word. "Build."

Part IV – Cwen (Queen)

AD 906

Edward rode into the courtyard, dismounted and handed the reins to a horse-thegn. The youth took the bay stallion to the stables and Edward brushed the dust of the road from his breeches before removing his leather gloves. He shouted after the young groom. "Take great care. I paid more gold than you will ever see for that beast's breeding."

Frith came from the hall and waved a hand in greeting. "My lord. What news from Wessex?"

"Naught that will not be made better by some answers from my sister," Edward said. He knew Frith was keen to hear more, for his head was cocked to one side as if waiting for an explanation, but Edward was in no mood to waste his anger on anyone other than the intended recipient.

Shouts and the thud of wooden swords diverted his attention to the paddock behind the hall. He turned the corner and walked past the long building to watch Athelstan working through his weapons practice. The boy, whose hair was still the palest blond, had grown even taller and now matched his father for height. Edward glanced at the array of shields propped up against the paddock fencing and noted that they were all full size. Athelstan was thirteen now, nearly fourteen, almost a grown man. Edward nodded with fatherly pride as he saw how agile the lad was, how quickly he dodged his master's sword thrusts, how swiftly he was able to regain his balance and offer a counter move.

"You must be a proud father indeed. He is a skilled

309

fighter already."

Edward turned at the sound of her voice and gave his sister only a perfunctory kiss, cross with himself for such petulance, but unable to suppress it. "He will need to be. Where is our great fellowship, the one that is meant to keep the Vikings from my door? I have had to buy them off, to keep the wolves from my flocks." *Like my father did.* "Where is Mercia; the leadership you told me would not falter?"

She listened without moving, her face devoid of expression. Even when he'd raised his voice and taken a step closer to spit out his last word, she had not flinched or stepped back.

"You did not ask for help."

Why did she have to be so reasonable? "I should not have needed to. Once, I *would* not have needed to."

"Well, things are not the same as they were. And we have our own worries to the north. Come, let us go and find Ethelred and on the way I will ask you to still your wrath. First," she put out her index finger and tapped it, "Two years ago, we were by your side in the witan when Frith asked for the renewal of a grant of land at Monks Risborough."

He sighed, his irritation growing. Her tone was that of the holy brothers who had sought to teach him his lettering when he was a boy.

She put out her second finger and tapped again. "Further, we put our names on the vellum when Frith also asked for the grant of land at Islington, once gifted to Beornoth, to be rewritten."

Edward opened his mouth but she put out a third finger.

"And another land-book that burned, Frith's own grant of twenty hides at Wrington? We were there when that was rewritten."

His jaw was tight, clamping his back teeth together. His words came out in a hiss. "Yes. My brain is not so addled that I have forgotten all that. But why speak of it now?"

"To remind you that Mercia is not asleep. My lord has been to many witanagemots and Frith is dealing well with land grants and gifts. Whenever we were freed from fighting, we have used the time to put right the disorder that arose when the churches were sacked and the land-books made into tinder."

Edward shrugged. He could have put Frith to much better use in Wessex, but at least he had implemented the restoration with more precision than Alhelm. But Edward needed an army, not an administration. Men like Frith and Alhelm were wasted with quills in their hands.

They rounded the corner of the hall and walked towards the steps. Alyth stepped forward with Elfwen, who had the knuckles of her free hand pressed to her eyes.

"She is whining again." Teasel stepped forward and sank to one knee to assess her child. "What ails her?"

"Naught, my lady. Like all children she takes her time waking from a nap. Do you wish to have her with you for what is left of the day?"

"My brother the king of Wessex is here. I shall be busy making him welcome."

Edward put a hand on her shoulder. "Go. I will see to it that my wrath is spent before I come into your hall. I am sorry that I shouted."

Teasel seemed less than keen to take the child, but she bowed her head and followed Alyth into the hall. Edward let out a loud breath and kicked idly at the dust in the courtyard.

"I am glad that you said sorry, for I would have asked you to, otherwise." Athelstan had followed them from the paddock and evidently had heard their conversation.

Edward looked up at his son. "I am sorry to have yelled, but not for what I said. Your aunt has let me down; broken her word."

Athelstan met his gaze, his bright blue eyes blinking in the sunshine. When he spoke, it was at a measured pace, slow and clear, the tone only occasionally breaking to betray

311

his awkward lodging between a child's body and a man's. "If you had come on any other day, you would have seen Aunt Teasel in there with me." He glanced back at the practice yard. "She has been learning almost every day how to wield a sword. And she and Lord Ethelred have not been idle. They have built a stronghold at Hereford and stocked it with men. Not fyrdsmen, who must go home after so many days. These men live there all the time, ready and waiting. So, my lord Father, you are wrong if you think we in Mercia have let you down."

'We in Mercia.' Edward stared at his firstborn as he let the words penetrate. His son considered himself Mercian, not West Saxon. He had given him away, only to lose him. Edward had his second family now, with the tireless but tiresome Fleyda, and he should be content. He sighed. He had long ago chosen the path of a king over the road of ordinary men and he must live with that choice. He swallowed hard and said, "How goes your learning?"

Athelstan shrugged. "Bishop Werferth tries his best with me, but I will never be a man of letters. He says he would have less of a trial trying to teach his bees to read. I am better with this." He swung the wooden practice sword around his head, the frantic circles of his childhood transformed into the whirling arcs of a weapon. "King Alfred wished me to learn to read. But I am first and last a weapon-man. I hope I do not shame him."

Edward ducked as Athelstan straightened his arm and the arc of the sword increased. "You do not. He, like I am, would be proud of you."

Inside the hall, the lord and lady of Mercia were sitting on their high chairs on the dais. Alhelm was by his lady's side, Frith was standing behind the lord's chair. A mother was holding a child in her lap, whose water-blue eyes put it beyond doubt that this woman and boy were Alhelm's wife and son. Alyth was sitting in the corner, trying without success to soothe the disgruntled Elfwen. She was a pretty child, who looked like her mother, with hazel eyes, high cheekbones and freckles, but her hair was darker, more like her father's. She paid rapt attention to Alyth and stayed calm whenever the woman dangled a colourful ribbon in front of her, or hid a small comb underneath an upturned bowl. But if Alyth turned away for a moment, the child's face reddened, her bottom lip protruded and the whining returned, quiet but insistent. Edward glanced at his sister and saw from the way her hands gripped the edge of the table that she was not immune to the child's distress. But she would not leave her husband's side, he who sat upright but leaning a little to the right. His clothes seemed a little too big for him, the shoulders sloping slightly, but he looked less unwell than when Edward had seen him last. He spoke to Frith and he seemed to have no trouble forming the words. Yet he was an old man now, in looks as well as age. It was almost as though the dark pigment had leached from his hair to that of his daughter, leaving him grey.

Edward sat down, swinging his legs onto the bench opposite and stretching out. He folded his arms across his chest and waited. She might be his elder sister but he was, after all, a king. He had said his piece; let her come to him now.

Teasel stood up. "My lord King," and then, more softly, "Brother. You have come to ask for our help; you say that you, like our father was wont to do, have had to buy peace. My lord has a thought on this."

Ethelred did not stand. He sat forward and Teasel swung her hand behind her, there for him to hold if he needed to. But he placed his palms in front of him on the table, using his stronger arm to lift the damaged hand onto the board-edge first. He took a moment to form his mouth into the right shape and said, "Buy land instead."

His brother-in-law's voice had lost some of its power, ringing out with less authority and lacking the momentum to reach the back of the hall. So, had Edward heard right? Was this the best that they had? Edward was ready to lose his temper all over again. He moved his legs from the bench to the floor, sat forward, and straightened his back. He could not keep the contempt from his voice, knew he was sneering when he repeated the words. "Buy land? From where and from whom?"

Teasel smiled. Her patient expression suggested that she thought she had something yet to tell him that would stir him. She used to smile at him like that when she had been given the key to the bake-house and knew that there were fresh loaves unattended.

She said, "You once told me that our father was a great friend of the earl of Bamburgh, high up in the north. The lords of Bamburgh have longed grieved for those parts of Northumbria stolen from them by the Vikings. We have sent word that we would like to renew that friendship, to form a fellowship that flanks the heathens to the north and the south."

Edward leaned forward and she said, "You see, Brother? You are listening now. We have not been idle; whilst you have been fighting in the south, we have been looking north. As I was saying, they share our belief that by granting land to thegns in the Viking areas we will have steadfast Englishmen in the heart of the heathen strongholds. Lord Alhelm has already bought lands in Derbyshire." She raised her hand and rubbed her fingertips together. "Eat into their lands, little by little."

She was waiting for his response. It was a good idea, but was it enough? It would certainly do no harm to have loyal men in the heart of the occupied territories and it was, after all, his avowed intention to drive the Vikings from all the kingdoms of England. With this strategy it would be possible to choose where to stage attacks and to remove Viking immunity from counterattack. Ethelred had lost his strength, both in body and voice, but not, it seemed, any of his cunning. His brown eyes, which like his hair, seemed to have faded, had shrunk back deeper into the sockets, but the lord of Mercia looked out on his world and Edward realised that those eyes missed naught. Edward opened his mouth but Teasel spoke again.

"And that is not all. I told you that we have our worries in the north. News has come to us that heathens have been slinking back into Chester. I am making ready to ride north and drive them out. My lord has already sent word to the Mercians there, telling them how best to make their stand against these Norsemen."

Edward felt the familiar jumping in his stomach, the excitement that preceded every fight. He leaped up, strode onto the dais, reached across the table and clasped his sister by the shoulders. "My lady, you have warmed my blood and lifted my soul. I was wrong to have doubted you."

She grinned. "I am not my father, but it is his blood that flows through me. And Ethelred's thoughts now come through my mouth. With that mighty brew, will I not be unbeatable?"

His smile stuck and his grip seemed to lock so that he could not let go of her. He had assumed it to be rhetoric, but it appeared that she actually meant to lead the men into battle. He smiled and nodded, but said no more. He let go, patting her once where his fingers had gripped and then stepped back, as if moving away from a mad animal that might leap at any moment.

'I am not my father.' She had said this by way of apology. Edward was not his father, either, but he saw this as no weakness. But in her case… *Oh Sister, you are, after all, but a woman. I need your men and I need you, but I wish my heart were as sure as yours that you can do this in Ethelred's stead; he who was unbeaten in the field.* Once, when he was a lad, he had watched the thatcher who sought to teach his son how to cover the roofs. The old man had to fold his arms and Edward saw how he clutched at his biceps, digging in with his fingers as he fought the urge to take over, knowing he would do the better job. The father had wanted the son to learn, but how hard it must have been for the old man, not to take the tools away to be certain that the roof would hold water.

She had dreamed of Vikings when she was a little girl. Always they had brought terror and death. Now she dreamed only of their defeat. Edward had spoken to her about how the Vikings had shaped their lives and it was true. Her childhood, swathed always in fear, her love for Alhelm, her wedding to her husband, her life in Mercia; all these had somehow come about because of the invasions. It might be womanly silliness, but she was sure that had the invaders not kept coming, had Ingimund not come from Ireland, making trouble on the way, her husband would still be whole. She looked at him now, lying on the bed, his once taut abdomen softened, tightening only when the cramping pains came. After her brave speech to Edward, he had said to her, '*So many words to say to you. Cannot say them now*' and she had wept. Before his illness, he had been learning to speak to her about his feelings, which, like hers, had taken some years to ignite but now burned to give constant, dependable warmth. Now, it was taking all his strength to learn again how to speak at all. In Teasel's mind, some foreign heathen was to blame for that, for the future stolen from her.

She lay down beside him on the bed and he put his strong arm around her. Laying her head on his chest she said, "Oh, my love. Can I really do this?"

There was the by now familiar pause, and then he said, "Yes, you can."

She wriggled round so that she could see his face. "But I might not have to, if the English folk who dwell in Chester have done what you said."

He shrugged.

"I did tell them what you said. Did I have it all right?" There was no fear of denigrating his efforts to talk; they both knew that even though it had taken him many hours, interspersed with frequent rests, to relay his ideas, the doubt lay in her interpretation of his strategy, not his words.

He motioned with his head, his signal for her to continue.

She said, "You meant that the English within the walls

must take the fight outside the gates. When they go out to fight, they must leave the gates open, and a throng of fighting-men hiding within. Then the strongest of those fighting outside should run as if beaten back inside, where the heathens will follow. Then those who are hiding will shut the gates, and set about slaughtering the foe."

He nodded and leaned in to kiss her forehead.

"But you still think we should go to Chester. You think there might be more fighting?"

He nodded.

She smiled. Many times had she heard it said that his brain was sharper than any when it came to battle tactics and even now he was planning, devising. What a cruel trick, that such a man should be struck down before his work was finished. Leaning over him, she stroked his hair away from his forehead and placed a kiss on his brow. "You are more of a king than any man that was ever given the name."

She stood up, swallowed the rising fear and fixed upon her face the regal smile that had ever been her disguise. Let her at least outwardly match his dignity; let the world see that she was worthy of this great man's love and capable of the task with which he had entrusted her.

Her horse had been saddled but there was little in the way of baggage carts. Ethelred had told her his views and it made sense that if they were to outfight and outrun the Vikings then they needed to travel as lightly as the invaders did. Alyth brought Elfwen to her and she bent down to look at the child. Seven years old. Seven years since she had cursed and screamed and thought that she would die whilst bringing her into the world. Seven years of crying and wailing. Worded thus, it sounded like a biblical plague. She was perhaps being too harsh. Alyth told her that some children were like this and that she would grow out of it. She bit her bottom lip. Somewhere within the city of Chester was the heathen who was responsible for this, too. Elfwen needed attention and her mother had none to spare.

317

Teasel kissed her daughter, once on each cheek, and stood up. Behind her, the rolling hills that bordered Ethelred's beloved valley rose up against a clear blue sky. Teasel shuddered as a little sob crept up on her and wobbled in her throat. For so many years she had prayed for a child, dreamed of walking in those hills with a loving, loved husband and a precious child. She looked down at the little girl. *My love, you came too late.*

They would gather more men along the way, but for now, she would ride off with these beloved few. Frith walked towards Alyth and placed a hand on each shoulder. He bent to kiss her, once, and then pulled her closer to him, wrapping his arms around her back. Breaking the hug, he held her at arm's length and nodded. The nod was a question, and she answered with a nod of her own, before putting a kiss on her fingers and placing it on his lips. She walked away and Teasel swallowed. Their love, undiminished after so many years, was once a source of discomfort and envy. No more. She was cared for in just the same way. And although Ethelred was not there on the steps to wave them off, he had given her a gift to carry with her. It was all the sweeter for never having come before, and now, when it might have seemed too late, it brought forth the notion that her future had perhaps not been stolen, that there might still be hope. When she took her leave of him, in the privacy of the bedchamber, he had managed to lift both hands to hold her face, and he had said the word, 'love'.

Frith mounted his horse, and brought it to stand in line with Alhelm's. If Alhelm had embraced his own wife and children then he had done it earlier, away from the gaze of others. With these two on her left, Teasel found courage and, turning to her right, she found another reason for hope, for a future. Not for her, on this venture, for she had none, save that she did not disgrace her husband's name, but hope for Mercia. Athelstan had tied his blond hair at the nape of his neck. He was wearing a fine blue riding-tunic and a childlike grin that displayed all that she needed to know about his thirst for a fight. Pride moved her mouth into a wide grin. But as they moved off, Elfwen broke from Alyth's grasp and ran.

"Mother, come back."

Teasel pulled on the reins and turned to Frith. "What must I do? I feel like there are live eels in my belly, but there is no other who can do this. Ingimund called Ethelred a king. If I do not go in his stead..." She could not finish her sentence without rudeness.

"If you send mere ealdormen, it will not frighten him so? Is that what you mean?"

She felt her cheeks reddening, even though his smile told her that he was not the least offended. She said, "You are a father. Tell me what to do."

He leaned across and put his hand over hers. "You are a wife. Does your husband send you to Chester?"

She nodded, all the while staring at the little girl below.

"Then you must go."

Yes, I must. Not to kill a foe, but to slay the fear. Teasel slid from the saddle and knelt down beside her daughter. "I have to go. Father wishes it. But I will come back. You have my oath."

A leader should not have stood to wave them off; he should have ridden with them. And a leader who could not even stand without leaning on a staff should not show his face at all. So before they left, he went and sat on his bed, picked up the cloth and moved it slowly and rhythmically up and down his sword blade, stopping now and again whenever he thought he saw a spot of tarnish. He listened to the sound of the hooves in the dust, the shouts of farewell and the inevitable keening of his daughter. The crying continued, but faded in volume and he knew that Alyth had taken the child off. What a good woman she was, when she had her own children to look after. He smiled, even though the movement was more inside his head than on his face. The muscles felt to him as though they were working, although he knew that they weren't. Still, the thought continued to amuse him that Alyth would originally have welcomed the novel prospect of tending to a girl-child, but might by now have come to think that noisy, wayward boys like her own were the easiest to raise. His daughter was in good hands and he had no need to worry. He hoped that the same was true of his wife. She rode out only as a figurehead, he knew, and she would be in no real danger, not with Frith and Alhelm by her side, for they would die a thousand deaths before they would let so much as a gnat dare to bite her. But she would be frightened. She had lived with fear all her life; this he knew. He also knew that by taking charge of a kingdom and riding out to meet the enemy, she believed that she would drive that fear away. The knowledge that she was prepared to undertake this feat, she who was never even comfortable in the saddle, brought on a battle within his body. Gratitude cowed him, rendering his body weak, willing to surrender to circumstance, whilst pride expanded his chest, pumped blood to his muscles, and proved the stronger of the two emotions. The pride was reinforced then by anger and he cursed all the wasted time and opportunities when he had stood back, waiting for her to recover from Alhelm instead of telling her how he felt. Now, that chance had gone and he could not woo her with words. But he could do something. He stood up, sheathed his sword, and reached for his staff. Calling for his hall-thegn, he began to make his way through the hall and out towards the practice yard. If his wife could learn to wield a sword when her husband was ill, then it was time that he did, too.

Ethelred stifled a yawn. He was beginning to understand why the day to day running of Mercia had overwhelmed Alhelm. Lying in bed after his fall, with only half his body still alive, he thought he had learned all there was to know about boredom. But here in the scriptorium he was being shown how many more facets there were to the condition.

The young monk made a tutting sound. "It is too damp."

Ethelred inclined his head and moved his face into what he hoped would appear to be an expression of interest. "Too damp?"

The monk nodded. "The vellum curls when the air is damp. Forgive me, my lord, but I must stoke the fire."

Ethelred waited until the brother had his back to him before he reached up to wipe the sweat from his brow. Dear God, if he made the room any hotter it would rival the very fires of hell. He reached out and stroked his finger against the pot of blood-red vermillion ink, then idly picked up the little scratching tool which the monk used to erase errors from the manuscripts. He twirled it around in the fingers of his good hand, then felt the edge of the blade with his thumb to ascertain its keenness.

The door creaked open a few inches and the light was immediately blocked out by a silhouetted figure.

Ethelred said, "Come."

Thegn Eadric stepped forward. "My lord, there is news."

Sending a silent prayer of thanks for his deliverance, Ethelred put his left arm out and beckoned the young man further into the room. He liked Eadric, even though the lad was so dark many at court accused him of being Celtic, and joked that he was one of Anarawd's men, sent to keep watch on Mercia. But there was such an innocent air about the boy that it made the joke even more amusing, for this lad's face was so wide and childlike that there was no room on it to hide even the smallest lie.

"What is it?" Ethelred said.

"A rider from Chester, my lord. His tidings are not good, I am sorry to say. The folk of Chester went out to fight, as you told them to, and many Norsemen were killed. But even after the slaughter, they are bent on taking the town and have made hurdles to hide under while they dig under the walls."

Ethelred let out a sigh, only now aware that he had been holding his breath. Teasel and Frith would come upon the heathen outside the walls and the Norse would be trapped between the townsfolk and the Mercian fyrd. "She will come behind them."

Eadric tugged jerkily at his tunic cuff and shuffled his feet. "I think not, my lord. The rider has taken a long time to get to us. And," he shifted his weight to his back leg, "We think that by now, the lady might be within Chester itself."

"Christ." Ethelred staggered towards the door, instinctively moving as if he would mount up and ride straight to her aid.

Eadric dashed forward and took hold of his shoulders, easing him back onto the chair. "My lord, be soothed. We do not know yet whether it is true, but we have had word that the Welsh have come from Gwynedd. King Anarawd might, even now, be with her."

The news was indeed soothing. Ethelred sighed and sat back, his fears for her safety allayed, but leaving room for another, ill-defined sense of unease.

AD907

Chester

It was like every dream she had ever had. She was unable to move, like ice on the river, her heart thumping freely like the fish beneath the frozen surface. Here it was again, the unseen foe that had haunted her every moment, waking and sleeping. She held her breath and heard the loud hammering of her pulse in her ears, matched in volume only by the scrabbling sound from the wall. A figure loomed into view, swinging a leg over the top of the palisade and only narrowly avoiding the sharpened ends of the fence poles. Arrows skimmed past his body and he kept his head tucked low. He swung his other leg over the top he began to lower himself to the ground. He was hanging with both arms fully extended when another arrow flew past and one hand slipped. In a heartbeat he was no more than a bent heap on the ground. Dead at her feet. Now the fear would depart, now she could breathe. It was over. But he moved, testing his limbs and shaking his head. He lifted up onto his elbows. On his knees now, he reached across with an injured arm and felt for his sword. He stared up at her. But even now she could not look upon the foe that plagued her.

Everywhere she looked she saw many faces but only one expression. Every Englishman and woman who had decided to come to the abandoned city of Chester and revive it as a thriving trading centre now wandered its rock-strewn streets, heads bowed, looking up only after they saw her decorated hem, holding her gaze with staring eyes that conveyed none of their earlier pioneering spirit now, only fear. Flaming arrows, rocks, and the occasional sheep carcass flew over the walls with enough regularity that the townsfolk walked with hunches, ever ready to deflect the missiles as they landed. For weeks, Teasel had been unable to offer any words of comfort, for she had thrust herself into a man's world, and she, a woman, had been as scared as the folk who huddled against the walls of buildings and wondered how long their meagre food rations would last. The chickens grew smaller with less to feed on, and they in turn made less of a meal, even for folk who were also growing thinner. No-one spoke of it, but everyone knew that, inevitably, sickness would follow starvation. Always present was the strange crunching sound as the enemy continued to tunnel under the walls. Day and night they sounded like an army of scratching mice. Like a toothache, it could be tolerated for so long but every now and then, it agitated the temper. Anger tightened her muscles; the sort of ire that bubbled up inexplicably when Elfwen hurt herself, when loving worry forced the eye to glance around for something, or someone, to blame. Teasel shouted out. "Oh stop it," and picked up a rock, hurling it towards the wall. It clacked against the wall and bounced off again. "Would that I were taller," she said. She walked away towards her hall, but almost as soon as the thought came to her, she called out to a burgher, standing by the shuttered tannery. "I have been told that there are loose rocks where the Norse are digging. Get some of my men and send them up on the walls; sling the rocks over the wall. See how they like it when it rains stones from above."

Inside the hall, Anarawd of Gwynedd was sitting by the fire, holding one hand across his chest and resting on his shoulder, the other supporting the elbow to keep it there. Athelstan was sitting with two of Alhelm's thegns, discussing the distribution of food.

Teasel said, "We shall not starve. They will be through the walls long before then." She flung her cloak across a chair and sat down with force.

Athelstan looked up, his young brow remaining crease-free even though he frowned. He waved the thegns to silence and said to his aunt, "You have lost hope?"

"Pay no heed. I am a bad-tempered old woman, that is all. She looked across at the Welshman. "But I think that when they come, they will break through more easily than you did."

Anarawd grinned and lifted his injured arm. "I bear this wound with pride. For, in falling, I got past their arrows and did not get skewered."

He probably thought that he had hidden it from her, but she saw his wince and went to stand over him. "Show me," she said.

He looked up at her with his dark eyes as he put out his arm, making her think of a hound with a thorn in its paw. She lifted the arm carefully, holding it as gently as she could at the elbow, turning it one way and then the other, listening for the moment when he caught his breath and she knew that it had begun to hurt. "The bone is not broken, but it might have shifted a little. You must rest."

"Then what use am I to you, Lady?"

"You have shown enough fearlessness merely in getting through to us. It lifts my heart to know that you are here and that your men are fighting for us beyond the walls. Every day that I have been here, I have been a weak, frightened woman trying to live in a man's world." She gave him back his arm, rolling his sleeve back down for him. But though she pushed gently, he would not move his arm back in towards his body, so that she was forced to prolong the touch. Eventually she had no choice but just to let go.

He cradled his wounded limb once more and said, "Right now, I am glad indeed that you are a woman, with a woman's soft touch." He looked up at her again and smiled, though his eyes remained wide open. "Even with this," he indicated his bad arm, "I am more whole than Ethelred. And yet I cannot help but envy him."

The heat from the fire was stronger than usual. Teasel felt her cheeks reddening and a flush began to heat her neck then spread down her body. She could not hold his intense gaze and she looked down at her hands. "I do what I can in his name. I am his woman." She had tried to emphasise the word of possession, but when she looked up she found that he was still staring at her.

He nodded slowly. "And what a woman."

Her mouth was dry. She turned away and scanned the room until she saw the ale jug on the table next to Athelstan's. Walking over to pour a drink, she coughed and said, "Yes, well, only a woman would have begun hurling stones at her foes."

Her nephew chuckled. "Not at all. We were getting through too many arrows. Good thinking, Aunt."

"Edward would not think so." She looked at the boy. She must stop thinking of him as such, for he was fifteen now, away fighting with the men. But she had always regarded him as her boy and it would be hard to let go. "Your father, my brother, sent…"

She paused, remembering another lady who had uttered that phrase. Burgred's queen had been given to Mercia as a bride and then been sent her brother's child to foster. *'You have been my as my own child and I have loved you dearly.'* She leaned forward. She had heard those words before, many years ago, when her aunt had spoken to her and they were true for her, too. She patted his hand. "We are both firstlings, you and I, sent to Mercia from Wessex, and both of us have learned to love it as our home. Little wonder then, that we are drawn to one another."

He grinned. "At least I might be of use to you here, for although we were both taught to read by Bishop Werferth, I think he found his task a little harder when it came to my turn. He said he always needed to spend time with his bees after teaching me, so that he could cool his wrath."

"Yes, well, you should not look as if you are proud of it." But there was no force behind the admonition. She remembered the peaceful little abbey garden in Worcester where Werferth kept his apiary. All the bees seemed to know him and it would fret him when they left the hives, leaving him unable to settle until they had all come home. She asked him once why he was never stung and he had answered that they would only sting those that wished to steal from them. She sat up straight and said, "Nephew, fetch Lord Frith."

Gloucester

Ethelred was beginning to understand. Despite growing stronger, he had fallen over on his way to the latrine and he had to admit that his balance was compromised because his eyesight was getting worse. He had shouted at the serving-girl yesterday because there was no wine cup laid on the table for him. She had picked it up and shown him it was there and he grumbled an inadequate apology, unable to acknowledge out loud that he could no longer see anything unless he was staring directly at it. After the last fall, he had been ordered by his Leech to rest. Ethelred had shouted at him, too, but had to concede that, come evening time, he was tired enough to follow orders and retire to his bed. But if he could not ride, or wield a sword, he could still see straight ahead.

Eadnoth, crunching an apple, was sitting beside him, ensuring that his quiver was full. The target, a sack stuffed with straw, lay plumply against the far end wall of the hall. Ethelred experimented again, unsure whether to use his weakest arm to hold the bow, or pull the string. At least with the target dead ahead and stationary, he could see it, even when closing one eye. But the bow was wobbling and the arrow flew wide of the mark. He was perspiring now from the effort, made worse by hobbling over to the sack to retrieve his blunted ammunition from the timber wall. He would not give up, though, and Eadnoth, too long a friend, sat on his stool and made no effort to help.

"Did you hear that Eardwulf's widow has died?" Eadnoth picked a piece of apple from his teeth and examined it. He looked up and said, "Loose. Oh, never mind. Go again, you are doing well."

Ethelred wished that he had breath to spare with which to fire a witticism. He planted his feet and positioned the next arrow, lifted the bow and pulled the string taut. He closed one eye and tried to still his body.

Eadnoth continued with his chatter. "The lady will be thrilled to see what you have learned while she has been away. Well done, you hit it. You know, this brings to mind the day when you and I and Wulf and Beornoth rode to Shrewsbury and drank their Welsh ale. You are swaying less than you were that night."

He sat back, silent while Ethelred bent down to pluck another missile from the quiver, but resisting the urge, if he had any, to lend a hand of support.

Ethelred balanced as best he could on his stronger leg and silently blessed his old friend. He was a true hearth-companion, who knew of a warrior's pride and would do naught to injure it.

The door opened, and the young thegn, Eadric, came in. He flashed a look of opprobrium at Eadnoth and stepped towards Ethelred. "Let me help you, my lord."

Ethelred waved him away, but the thegn stepped forward and placed his arm at Ethelred's elbow, lifting the quiver and holding it aloft with one hand, whilst placing the other at the small of Ethelred's back to hold him steady. But Ethelred put the bow down on the bench and sat down, shuffling his buttocks back into the seat of the chair and dragging his bad leg into a bent position. "Well?"

Eadric looked for a moment as if he had forgotten why he had come in. Ethelred said, "Is it not my brain which is the addled one?" and Eadnoth leaned forward to take the quiver from the young man's hand.

The young thegn slapped his forehead. "Oh, yes, my

lord. We have news, such as it is. This was not a rider sent by the lady, but word has come from a man who says he has heard it from another..."

Ethelred sighed. "Go on." Hearsay was better than nothing.

"This man says he heard that the Norse have given up on Chester. He was told that the lady ordered the townsfolk to hurl rocks upon them. Then she bade all the women to boil ale and pour it over the walls. Many below were badly burned, but they put hides over the hurdles and carried on digging. This, my lord, is the best bit. He was told that the lady unleashed many bees on them and they were stung all over. Thus hurt, they gave up their digging and went away."

Ethelred felt his chest rise and fall as he chuckled.

"I must say again, my lord, that we do not know the truth of it. The Welsh from Gwynedd were without the walls and likely it was they who saw an end to the heathen. It is a good tale, but..."

"Knowing my wife, I could easily believe it. She, at least, has a good eye and will think naught of hurling things when she is in a temper." He swallowed some excess saliva and said, "Is she coming home?"

Eadric scratched his head. "This is what makes me wont to think these tidings are false, my lord. The man said he had heard that my lady has gone to Wales."

"Rhuddlan? You have been there all this time? Why no word?"

"We were on our way home. It was not so far away and when we heard that Anarawd was there fighting the Norse..." She was still slightly out of breath from the journey, and there was little incentive to continue to push words out when his face held such a stern expression. She had been so miserable when Frith suggested that they overnight at Shrewsbury and she had insisted that they come away at first light. Still wearing her thick riding cloak, she had burst into Ethelred's bedroom to participate in a loving and enthusiastic reunion. But, even though she was accustomed now to his limitations, still she felt that he was not as thrilled to see her as she was to be home.

"You call him by his name? Not, 'the king of Gwynedd?'"

"We have become close." She lowered her gaze. She unfastened her cloak and folded it carefully into a chest, wondering why there were no servants to do such tasks and then suspecting that Ethelred had sent them away. Glancing up, she had no need to guess from his expression what his thoughts might be, for this was one book which did not need to be opened to reveal its content. She told him, "As two leaders might become close; that is all."

"You were there a long time."

Yes, she thought. *I was*. Anarawd had said the same.

'We have been together many long weeks now. You should go home, Cariad, for your husband will have need of you.'

And her reply had been immediate. *'But the burh is not fully built. You need my men, still, to make Rhuddlan safe.'* It was her excuse to stay, and the only one that she was prepared to acknowledge. Her reluctance to leave had to be justified, to the world and to herself.

'I will be forever grateful for your help, Lady. Gwynedd and Mercia will ever be friends. But I fear that Ethelred and Anarawd will not be friends if you and I bide here much longer.'

She smiled at her husband and said, "Yes, I was there for a good while. There was much that needed to be done. But there is now a strong burh with good walls so if the Norse think to head back to Wales it will not be so easy for them."

She sighed and sat down beside him on the bed. For months she had been away from home, making decisions in his stead, symbolically carrying the banner for Mercia and her husband seemed unimpressed. She picked up his hand and stroked it while she talked. "I thought you would be proud. I thought I was doing what you would have done."

He gave a lopsided smile, but he looked sad. "Is there

something between you?"

So, that was it. Again, her thoughts turned to her last conversation with Anarawd.

'If you and I bide here much longer…'

And she had said, *'There can be naught between us. I have a husband. I stand here in his stead as leader of Mercia.'*

'And you love him. As do I. Even so, Cariad, it is time you went. I, too, am a leader, but as a man I am weak as any other when it comes to comely women. Go, lovely lady, os gwelwch yn dda.'

She kissed Ethelred's hand and gave it back to him, patting his fingers as she tucked his arm close to his body to keep it warm, and gave him his answer. "Yes, we are friends. We worked well together. And now I must tell you something my love." She lay down next to him, close enough to warm him, but careful not to put her weight on him. "I liked it. I have lived my whole life watching men give their whole lives to fighting the heathens. Now it is my turn. I live only to carry on the life you cannot have." Lifting up on one elbow, she leaned over and kissed his cheek. "And there is room for naught else." She thought she saw the sadness lift, the deep creases across his brow soften slightly. He should have no worries, especially those without foundation. "From now on, you and Mercia are all I live for." She kissed him again, this time gently on the lips, and stood up. "I must go to see Elfwen." When she reached the door, she turned and said, "Oh, yes, I meant to ask you. What does 'os gwelwch yn dda' mean?"

The muscle in his cheek twitched. Probably, she thought, with the effort of trying to remember. He shook his head. "I do not know."

As she walked across the hall, glad to have eased his worries, she thought it was a pity that he did not know the translation. She felt sure that Anarawd's words contained yet another element of bardic poetry. The untamed Welshman, who always evaded her questions regarding his wife, had given her naught but beautiful words. She knew nothing of him, his thoughts, his loves. She only knew that he smelled of sweat and leather, the musk of a fighting man, yet he spoke like a scop. Alone now, she felt free to recall the rest of his words, with no eyes gazing upon her to reflect her feelings of disloyalty.

There can be naught between us. I have a husband.'

You say you are his woman and I say I am his friend. It is not strong rope that binds us to that, but a wisp of air. I could bid you follow me; you would set me on a straight path, or you would end your days wishing that our paths had never met. You are a swan, who mates for life and if I do not step back I will leap in and muddy the waters of your lake. I should not bruise a heart that is not broken.'

She had packed her belongings into her travel chests then, hearing the sense in his words, but musing that his vigorous defence of her virtue had felt somehow strangely like an insult. Safely home, she allowed herself to be a little sad not to have stayed. And then she left the thought alone, not willing to follow its thread to the end. For God knew that this was her home, and that her heart lived here.

Long after she had left, he lay staring at the shadows. They came in the same form every evening and, suffering his prescribed rest, he now knew each one. The long one with snaked-out fingers that bent across the floor towards the corner was caused by the lowering sun shining through the window and then through the back of the little chair in front of it. A larger, rounder shape came when the last of the rays hit the trees beyond the paddock outside, and covered the large wooden chest at the far end of the room like a black cloak, so much so that at first he wondered why, every night, his riding-cloak had been left out by the servants, even though he never used it now. Soon he would hear the noises from the hall; the servants laying the tables, the menfolk hanging up their weapons, the sound of the chatter. Some evenings he drifted off, only to wake thinking he could hear the sound of geese on the water, realising when fully awake that what he could hear was the conversation and laughter from the next room, reverberating through the wall and losing coherence on its journey. Tonight it would echo more loudly, for Teasel was back, along with Alhelm and Frith, and before those two made their way home to their own estates, there would be celebration. And where would his wife's thoughts wander; through here, where he lay helpless, or to Wales, where she had left her heart? All these months he had been waiting for news and none had come. Now she had told him breezily that their unconfirmed reports were true; she had been with Anarawd. She seemed to take no account of how much more slowly the time had passed for him, the hours of enforced bed-rest stretching out as he found naught better to think on than that his wife was with another man. Perhaps he should ask his two faithful deputies what, if anything, had passed between his wife and the Welshman, but dare he show his vulnerability by asking? Reason told him that they would already have informed him if they knew anything. Reason also told him that such self-torment was inadvisable, but he could do little else. He could shoot an arrow or two, but what was that when shown up against a man who could fight, as he could no longer do, and bewitch pretty women with his eloquent speech, as he had never been able to do? Swordsmanship and word-craft; these were powerful weapons that would beguile any woman, not least one who had witnessed neither in such a long time. He had lied when she had asked for the translation, for he had heard that Welsh phrase many times. Just what, exactly, had Anarawd been asking her that he needed to beg, 'Please'?

Ethelred sat up, putting his strong leg on the floor and lifting his weaker one down. With even pressure on each hand, he pushed himself to standing, putting his working arm out ready to lean against the wall if necessary. He stood for a moment until he could be sure he was steady, then made his way to the door. God would have to do without his amusement tonight; for the lord of Mercia was done with spending his evenings rotting in bed and was going to take his place with his wife in the mead hall.

AD909

"I will not. And you cannot make me." Elfwen folded her arms tightly across her chest.

At the far end of the yard, the reeve was barking out his orders to the men working on the maintenance of the town's defences, shouting above the noise of their hammering that when they had finished on the walls and fences, they could take their tools and fence the new drain on the church street and weed the walkway between the minster and the hall. Above it all, the yapping of the smith's dog came in bursts of five staccato yelps.

Alyth bent down and laid her hands on Elfwen's shoulders. "We can make you go, young lady. And furthermore, we will." She looked up at Teasel.

Teasel nodded. "That is right. The tooth is bad and will have to come out. We can drag you to the smithy if you will not go yourself." She glanced across at the reeve, hoping that Elfwen would shy from the suggested threat of being marched there by one of her mother's officials.

Her daughter looked up at her, hazel eyes blinking rapidly as if to keep the tears from spilling. *Good girl*, thought Teasel. *Do not let us see you weep.*

"I hate you."

Elfwen stamped her foot, sending a shower of mud over Teasel's hem, and ran off towards the forge without a backward glance. Alyth began to rub at her lady's dress, but

335

Teasel waved her away. "Did she mean it?"

Alyth brushed the fabric once more before straightening up. "What? Oh, that. No, my lady. Children say these things all the time. Pay it no heed. She will love you again right enough when the tooth is pulled and she needs a knee to sit upon."

Teasel shook her head. "I never, that is, did yours ever say that to you?"

They walked towards the bake-house. Alyth said, "My Athelstan was always a sweet thing, but Tuold had his evil days, as did Adric. Adric, may I say, was once so bad that Frith wondered if I had slept with the devil one night, nine months before he was born."

"Both our Athelstans are rightly named, then, for they are both even-headed, steady as stones."

At the bake-house the first batches of bread were already cooked and ready to go across to the main hall. Teasel tore a chunk from one loaf and kept it for Elfwen to suck on, for comfort and to help staunch the bleeding from her gum. But as the child walked back from the smithy, holding her cheek, she caught sight of her mother and quickly looked away, as if to pretend that she had not seen her. Teasel stepped forward but Alyth held her back.

"Let her go."

"No, I must... Elfwen, I have bread for you. Freshly baked."

The girl stopped, took a step forward, stopped again and turned to face her mother.

"I have only been hurt by the smith's tongs. Give it to my father. His needs are greater than mine. Or so you tell me." This last was muttered softly. She stalked off, head held high but hips shaking, a ten-year-old trying to walk like a grown-up and succeeding only in stepping with a very stiff back.

Alyth laid a hand on Teasel's arm. "She does not mean it."

Teasel shook her off, gently but firmly. "No, she is

right. Ethelred needs me, for I left him sitting in the sunshine and must go now to see if he craves aught." Elfwen was not the only one who could muster false dignity. After all, from whom had she learned to do it?

Leaving Alyth to rejoin the women in the bake-house, Teasel walked to the minster, stopping to talk with townsfolk on the way. Two women came back from the river with baskets of wet sheets. Teasel asked the older of the two if they had used wood ash for cleaning.

The woman bobbed her head. "No, my lady. We used the soapwort as you asked."

Teasel nodded, pleased; his bed linen would be the softer for it. "Good. I want only the best for my lord. Will you heat the smoothing stone and run it over Lord Ethelred's sheets? I thank you."

In the bishop's private garden, she found Ethelred where she had left him earlier that morning, sitting on a cushioned stool, leaning against the wall, his face turned up to catch the summer sun. Next to him, kneeling on the ground, was a young abbot, his face round and ruddy and his forehead shiny with perspiration. He was digging with a small trowel, carefully pulling weeds away from the brightly coloured cornflowers and cowslips that seemed to thrive, transplanted, in his artificial garden. He looked up when he saw the lady and he smiled, revealing a wide gap between his two front teeth.

"Abbot Ecgberht has been looking after me, my dear," said Ethelred. "He keeps me from loneliness and sings well."

The abbot's face grew even more red, but he acknowledged the compliment with grace and wit. "My lord is kind, but in the same way that too much honey makes you sick, so I might bore you yet if I do not stop for a while. I will come again and sing for you a little later, when you have had time to forget how dull it really was." He nodded, showing a tonsure which was equally red and shiny, and stood up, pushing one foot out whilst still resting on the other knee, tilting to put his hand on the ground and heaving himself upright.

Teasel spread out her dress and sat down on the ground beside Ethelred. She leaned her head against his thigh. "This good weather is making you better and better, my love," she said. "You spoke without stammering and when we walked here this morning you did not halt. I am hopeful that you will be fully well soon."

He reached down and stroked the top of her head. "It is my belief that your ministrations will make me fully better or hasten my end." He laughed, low and quiet. "And I do not mean the goat's milk that you tell them to feed me."

She could have told him again that it was easier for him to digest than cow's milk, but she forbore, and chuckled too, thinking back, as she knew he was, to earlier that morning. Until he had asked her once more to his bed, as wife rather than nurse, she had not thought about how much she missed his touch. The unhappiness made itself known only after it was banished. It came in the form of tears, briefly, then it left. Now, months later, she knew contentment. They had vanquished the forces that once had conspired to inhibit their love. It was meet that she could sit here with him and feel the summer sun bringing warmth and shedding benevolent light on and around them, and she was thankful that their dark days were behind them.

The sounds in the abbey garden differed so from the noise around the farmsteads. There, she knew whose cattle were lowing, whose sheep were gossiping. But the surprise was that here, in the cultivated garden, the sounds were more wild, declaring freedom from ownership, with one stripy exception. She closed her eyes, listening to the droning of Werferth's bees, the singing of the chaffinch, blackbird and song thrush, and then the bell, calling the monks to sexts. "Midday, my love," she said. "We should go."

The bell was nearby, and therefore loud, but she was sure she heard hoof beats outside the garden in the minster courtyard. She listened, her head to one side, but no-one came. Thinking she had been mistaken, she stood up to help Ethelred to his feet.

"Sister."

She turned round. "Edward. You made my heart leap. What are you doing here, is aught wrong? The children?"

Edward came forward and hugged her. He nodded at Ethelred and said, "No, naught is wrong. But there will be. I have come to borrow Mercian men, lots of them."

Teasel went back to stand by Ethelred, bending at the knee and offering her arm for him to lean on as he stood up. The three of them walked slowly back towards the great hall. "You may take as many men as you need, Brother. All I ask is that you tell me why you need them."

Edward stepped in little skips, keeping to their pace but obviously anxious to be moving faster. On the way, he gave her the names of loyal men who had been persuaded to buy land in the Danelaw and who were now ready to provide weapon-men from those territories and join in alliance with the English lords of Bamburgh. "But I need fyrdsmen as well. I am going to Northumbria," he said. "I am going to start a fight."

Athelstan walked across the hall and stumbled over a wooden bucket. He kicked out at it, hurt his foot and swore. "Satan's arse. Who left that there?" He walked away, still muttering dark threats to unknown addle-brained cooking-women.

Teasel, at the gaming board with Alhelm, looked up and smiled. "He will curse forever the day he took himself off fishing and missed Edward's call to go north."

"And you, my lady, do you yearn to fight again?"

She could not be sure, but she thought she heard him making soft buzzing noises as he studied the game on the table.

He moved one of his pieces and said, "That should put some *sting* into our little game." His hand hovered over the board.

She tapped it away and said, "Stop it. This is how tales grow in the telling until they are believed by all as truth." She could only laugh at his pretence at hurt pride. "Put your lip away, my lord. You do not need me to tell you that you are a better swordsman than you are a wordsmith."

He stared at her mournfully with his clear blue eyes, but was distracted by the procession of a group of priests through the hall. "Is this to do with your latest shrewdness?"

She smiled, making no attempt at false modesty. "Yes. They are here to oversee the burial of the Saint's bones in the new building."

Alhelm nodded, pulling his features into an expression of mock reverence. "This would be Saint Oswald of Northumbria."

She tried to keep the grin from lifting her mouth. "It would." God would forgive her, she was sure, for she had ordered the preservation of the saint's bones by removing them to the safety of Mercia and building a new priory to house them. And the God she knew would not mind if, at the same time, she was able to show to the world that Mercia would be Northumbria's ally, even saviour, against the heathen menace who now sat wedged between two Saxon kingdoms, while her brother stirred up a whirlwind in their gardens.

Alhelm said, "It is a Godly act indeed, my lady. You are a skilled builder."

She'd had the finest teacher. She lifted her hand. "I have many skills." She picked up one of her gaming pieces and held it just above the board, so that he could see her intention. The game was hers.

He held his hands up, conceding. His smile disappeared though and he groaned. "There is the lord. Must he be a witness?"

Teasel looked over her shoulder. "Ah, my love. Come and watch me make my last move and beat this bold-cheeked ealdorman. Again."

She reached her hand up by her shoulder and Ethelred clasped it in his own, standing beside her as she made her final move. "She has you trapped, friend."

Alhelm sat back and pushed his hands through his hair. "Bested by a lady. There is naught for it but to drown my shame in ale." He snapped his fingers and a little slave boy brought a fresh jug to their table, poured out three cups and ran back to his place, curled up by the hearth.

Ethelred sat down on the bench alongside his wife and she raised her cup. "Be hale," she said, and the others echoed the toast.

Teasel looked at Alhelm and smiled, wishing that the gesture could somehow convey all her thoughts. She felt compelled to display her wedded bliss, yet she knew that the impulse ironically meant that the love for Alhelm must still be there and she was embarrassed, apologetic that she should be content with her lord when it seemed a betrayal of her first, enduring love. Shutting a door to the past was to lock it, and she could not do that, always needing, no matter how satisfying her life with Ethelred, to leave the door ajar. She was like the weaver, presented with a brand new loom and pleased to have it, who, nevertheless could not quite bear to break up the old redundant loom to use for firewood.

Athelstan clattered back in through the doorway, having exchanged irritable heavy-footedness for an agitated lightness of movement. "Father is here."

Teasel stood. "I will fetch Alyth."

"No need, my lady. I am here." Alyth stood with a pile of folded sheets, her fingers squeezing and kneading one corner, pulling more and more of the cloth into the crease with each movement.

Teasel laid a steadying hand on hers. "He will be well. You'll see."

She had barely finished speaking before Frith appeared in the doorway, blood-streaked, mud-streaked, but whole.

Alyth rushed forward and Teasel had to sidestep the pile of linen dropped at her feet. She watched their heart-strong embrace, acknowledging that she, too, was relieved that Frith was home, unhurt. This was a man whom she had known since her youth, upon whom she had begun to depend, and a man whom she loved. Their bond was understood by all and, much as she wanted to throw her arms around him, it was not her place and she would never, with body or heart, step between him and Alyth. She cast a glance behind and saw Ethelred and Alhelm, standing shoulder to shoulder, both waiting for the news. And then she understood; Ethelred and Alhelm had ever thus stood together, leaned upon one another. Alhelm could never have stepped between his lord and his lord's wife. She directed her smile at the ealdorman, hoping that it conveyed simple, friendly affection and was rewarded to see his puzzled expression warm into something which more closely matched hers. She turned back to face the door. She would always love him, but perhaps now she could forgive him for not loving her.

Content, finally, to let him go, she glanced back one more time to send a warm smile of unequivocal friendship and caught him staring at her. His delicately pale blue eyes were so different from the deep dark brown of Ethelred's and yet the expression was unnervingly similar. Could it be that he really did, after all... She shook her head, refusing to make acquaintance with that thought after all these years, and shifted her gaze back towards the door.

Edward pushed his way into the hall. He, too, was filthy, his cornstalk hair transformed to dusty grey. His grin was triumphant, his embrace with Athelstan all hearty slaps and warrior grunts. Teasel felt a moment of sadness to think that his welcome home in Wessex would perhaps be less convivial. Fleyda was too queenly in her ways.

The slave boy scurried to and from the brew-house bringing more ale, and servants brought more benches for the men to sit on. Edward sprawled onto a bench, lifting his legs to rest on the table. Elfwen appeared from the back-chamber and Teasel beckoned her. "Come and say good day to your uncle Edward."

Elfwen ignored her. "Where is Alyth?"

"You must do without her today, my love. Frith is home."

Elfwen's lips crinkled and shrank, like plums drying in the sun. Her cheeks went red and she opened her mouth, looked round at the assembled nobility and kept her reply in her head. Folding her arms across her chest, she puffed all the air from her cheeks and went back to the chamber.

Teasel stared after her for a moment, and then shook her head, refusing to allow whatever thoughts had risen to take shape in her mind. "So, Brother, tell me your tidings." She watched his face, and held her breath. She imagined that they were at the top of a hill, about to roll down it without stopping.

Edward gulped his drink, setting the cup down empty. He let out a satisfied sigh, called for a refill and said, "There is not much to tell. We teamed up with Bamburgh and for five weeks we have been like Vikings, harrying, stealing and making banes of ourselves. We slaughtered their herds and we burned their crops. To tell it small, we showed them how we have lived these many years, by their hand. I think they will like it not."

A jump of excitement fluttered in her belly. "What next?"

"Now they will lie still, or they will come to me. Either way, let the end come."

343

AD910

Tettenhall, Near Wedensfield, Mercia

Sweat ran down his nose guard and he unbuckled his chin strap, took off his helm and wiped his face and eyes with the back of his hand. Putting the helmet back on, he rejoined the men, running until he caught the front of the pack, and relaxing into the steady jog as they pressed on to meet the Vikings as they came across the river. Having harried Mercia for most of the summer the pagans must have thought that they would return home to Northumbria unmolested. Edward felt the heat from the pack of bodies; his army was huge and he ran with a comfortable gait, confident that they had the advantage of numbers. Pray God his sister, busy building a burh further south, had been left with enough men for defensive purposes. Rejoining Frith at the centre of the front line, he fell into step beside him. The sun was nearly up and they had been on the march since daybreak; under his chain mail he was perspiring heavily, but for once they would have battle in the high summer, not the winter raiding that the Vikings had so often preferred. Five days after Lammas and he knew his men should be home helping with the harvest, but the Northumbrian dogs that he'd provoked last year had now broken their chains and come snarling. It would be rude not to let them bite the stick that had poked them.

Frith, loping alongside him, scanned the horizon and put his arm up. They slowed to a walk and waited. Frith said, "They are further on than we thought."

Below them, on the lower ground nearer the valley bottom, the Northumbrian raiders were fanned out in a long line stretching across the horizon. Their shields were up, in a colourful display. One was decorated with green stripes, emanating like spokes from the central boss, another was sectioned into thirds, the top portion painted with a symbolic representation of a winged creature. Further down the line one had double spokes painted red, another had three painted circles and one had a curious axe-head design, in bright yellow and black. Fearsome they looked, but Edward looked down his own flanks and saw a red shield with a green cross on it, another with a blue cross, and Frith's own shield, decorated with a beautiful cross with a ring at the intersection of the upright and crossbar, all the spaces around it filled in with intricate swirls and interconnected spirals. Fluttering just behind them was his own banner, white in essence with a red cross, and fringed with tabs of the same vivid red. Further along the line a pale blue banner with a simple cross flapped in the wind. The Northumbrian Danes might seek to intimidate with their mythical beasts and lurid paint hues, but there was no doubting on whose side God was fighting this day. Frith's hand was still in the air, signalling to those behind that the front lines had come to a halt. His checked cloak billowed in the breeze and his long hair fanned out behind his shoulders. Further along the shield wall were Alhelm and his north Mercians. Beyond them, the men of Kent stood with new, loyal leaders and a little further back, the men of Devon, Hampshire, Wiltshire and Somerset all waited for the signal to advance.

On the other side of the meadow the Vikings began to clash axe handles onto shields, a rhythmic percussion to accompany their cries, a uniform howl of a Scandinavian word which was hard to pick out on the other side of the field.

Edward raised his sword and began the retort, "God

Almighty! God Almighty!" shouting with a hoarse throat until he could be sure that the refrain had been picked up right through the ranks to the young archers beyond the main gathering. "God Almighty! Godemite! Godemite!" Turning, he satisfied himself that all the English swords and spears were jabbing up and down in time to the rhythm of the shout.

Frith nudged his arm and pointed to the loaded carts of booty, lined up by the Viking flank. "Shall we take that back?"

Edward sniffed. "Only after we have killed them. Every last one of them. They all know what we are about; there is no need to spare any to tell the tale." He swung his sword in a high arc above his head in two slow revolutions and then he pointed it forward and set off at a run down the slope and towards the enemy shields.

The falling ground level helped them to pick up pace and they smashed against the opposite wall, shoulders behind their shields, momentum carrying them onto the enemy shields and bringing them to a heavy halt as linden board smashed against linden board. The force of Edward's bodyweight hurtling forward was enough to knock his first opponent off his feet. As he fell backwards Edward lunged with his sword but could not get a clean jab before the shield wall closed up. Shoving against the wall, the English forces jabbed and stabbed, swords going high over the shields and low underneath them, slashing at legs, lashing out towards necks. The Englishmen knew to jerk quickly backwards, familiar with the change in pressure that gave them a narrow miss from a spear point jabbed from the enemy wall. Any foe who managed to break through were despatched by axe blades wielded by those at the rear and the wall quickly closed again. From behind Edward, those same axes came thrusting forward, sometimes sticking into the shields in front of them. In a tussle to retrieve an axe, the yielding shield went back and then suddenly forward, forcing Edward's own shield upwards and knocking it into his face. He tried to think how to remember to check all his teeth at the end of the day, but pushed the thought from his mind as he lifted his shield to deflect a Danish axe-blow. To his left, he spotted a shield devoid of its metal outer rim and, having detected its weakened state, he tried to lift his sword to bring it crashing down to slice another nick from the battered wood. His thrust was deflected by the shaft of a spear, and the jolt set the nerves in his arm humming. As he steadied himself before resuming the forward push, he glanced along the line to see how his own wall was holding. He thought he saw Alhelm go down on one knee, but could not be sure. Frith was still to his side, slicing and slashing, grunting with every exertion. The sun beat down callously, favouring neither side, and dust flew up from the dry ground beneath their feet. All around him the battle noise rang out; the cracks of wood as the shield walls broke away and came back to each other, the dull clang of the shield bosses suffering yet more dents competed with the singing swish of blade upon blade. Occasionally the distinctive smack of fist on jawbone told of a struggle becoming more personal. All the while Edward was sure that he was moving forward. It was not just the press of those behind him surging towards the enemy, eager to get a chance to slash at the enemy. Steadily, the Northumbrians were moving backwards, step by painful step, reluctantly giving ground. The archers had come round to the flank and arrows flew over the main ranks, catching those on the outer edges of the wall. With each casualty, another Viking came forward to patch the breach, but they came more slowly, until Edward could see that it was no longer a one for one replacement. Shoving hard against the man who breathed foul air in his face, Edward nearly toppled as there was nothing else to push against. The Viking shield wall had collapsed. Edward struggled to stay on his feet as those behind him surged forward, coming through the gap in the wall and beginning the fierce one on one combat.

A splinter of shield flew in the air and hit Edward's

cheek. It would be bleeding, he knew, but other than that, so far, he was whole. With his shield in his left hand, he shoved hard against an oncoming Northumbrian, butting him with the shield boss and off-balancing him. With his right arm, he swung his sword with a sideward cut, aiming at the unprotected neck of an adversary. All were packed so close that he could hear the other man's breath, feel it in his face as he attempted to sever his air supply. Each time Edward thrust his sword, the Northumbrian parried, blocking his blade. Then, he was gone, sinking to his knees, colour draining from his face. Edward glanced to his right, saw Frith nodding at him, and nodded back his thanks. Frith withdrew his sword blade from the man's ribs, and moved on for the next bout. Edward took a few jagged gasps of breath before he, too, lurched forward. His foot slipped and he looked down. A raven banner lay in the mud, already trampled. Edward had now added his boot print to it and the black outline of the bird, once so distinguishable against the carmine background, was fading fast, the mud blurring the black and red, all merging to brown.

A Viking was on the ground, blood pumping from a thigh wound. Edward put his foot on the man's lower torso, and ran his sword through the panting heathen's chest. He moved on, lunging across his body to the left with his sword, bringing his arm back and punching to the right. There was no time to look about him to assess the state of the battle; all he knew was that he was moving forward. He lifted his sword arm to deflect an axe-blow, feeling the sweat running from his armpit to his waist. His helm no longer sat tightly on his head, but swivelled a little with every movement, lubricated by perspiration. He became perversely aware of a chafing under his chin strap, which began to irritate him more than his fatigued muscles and aching face. He knew for certain that he had lost a tooth when the wall shield ricocheted into his face and the cut from the later splinter was stinging. But more and more, the feeling grew that all he wanted to do was rip his helm from his head and relieve his rubbed-sore neck.

A hefty Dane, well above six feet tall, came at him with a heavy axe, threatening permanently to solve the problem of his raw neck. Edward ducked low to avoid the chop, slashing behind the giant's knee before he stood up. The man sank to his knees and Edward was ready with a slicing side-blow, catching the man between shoulder and neck, cutting downwards into the shoulder. The man toppled and Edward readied himself to move on. A group of men came past him, one carrying the banner of the men of Somerset. Edward snatched a momentary glance behind and saw his entire army swarming forward. He looked ahead and realised that it was over. His men stood over the prone bodies of the heathens, kicking them for signs of life and despatching them with sword and spear thrusts where necessary. The only banners flying above the field belonged to Englishmen, the only shields still held aloft bore familiar markings; the yellow and black whirling segments of Frith's thegns, the red and white quadrants of Ordgar of Wiltshire. Edward, breath heaving, removed his helm and threw it to the ground. It fell upside down so that the decorative metal boar on its crown sank into the earth. Edward pressed his hand to his sore neck, but soon realised that no soothing relief would come from such a hot, sweaty hand. He ran his fingers through his matted hair and looked about him. Were there many stragglers, and were they worth pursuing? He looked for Frith, expecting him to be at his side immediately answering his unspoken question, telling him that riders had already been despatched to chase down the fleeing remnants. But Frith did not come.

Edward picked up his helm, removing it carefully from where it lay, skewered, in the ground. Saying a prayer of thanks that the boar remained intact, and thus that the supporting framework underneath still functioned, he also prayed that all who mattered to him had been as fortunate this day. He walked across the battle field, checking as many of the dead as he could, working his way slowly towards a small copse where he could see that many of the wounded men were sitting propped against the trees, resting while their wounds were tended. Edward looked across at each cluster of men, but could not see any with long, blond hair. His normal inclination was to walk quickly, but he tarried, unwilling to come upon the unpleasant truth any sooner than he had to. Where was he? Edward edged his way to the copse, more fearful now than at any time during the fighting. A young thegn was kneeling down, wrapping a makeshift bandage around another's ankle. Edward touched him on the shoulder. "The lord Frith?"

The thegn did not look up, but nodded his head in the direction of a large oak tree. "Over there my lord King."

The thegn's quick answer, devoid of emotion, gave Edward courage to hope as he looked in the indicated direction. He saw the blond hair, falling in damp straggles down Frith's back. So instant was the good news, so quick the relief, that Edward had to shake his head, convince himself that he had seen clearly. He jogged over to Frith, a hearty slap ready in his arm, a crude greeting on his lips. As he bounded up to him, Frith turned round and moved slightly to one side. Now Edward could see past Frith to the figure slumped against the oak trunk. *Dear God, why did you let me smile so soon?*

Alhelm was lying with one leg bent awkwardly behind him. His face was pale and around his mouth there were smudges of dried mud. He must have eaten the dirt when he fell. His breath came in shuddering, scratching snatches, the sound just like a child pushing a blunt blade up and down the edge of a table. His pale blue eyes stared straight ahead and his gaze did not shift, even when Edward knelt beside him and grabbed his hand.

Frith said, "He cannot see, my lord. It will not be long."

"No, no, no, no," Edward said, all the while shaking his head and stilling the urge to shout out that he was king and he would not suffer to see his friend die.

There was a change; in the air around him, or possibly the light. Or perhaps there was a shift in sensation, of pain and stiffness, ignored and now penetrating consciousness again. No, Edward realised what had altered. Alhelm's rasping breath had quietened. The watery eyes with their ink-black centres had closed. The ealdorman of northern Mercia was dead.

Bremesbyrig, Mercia

The tree-wrights were busier than usual this morning, anxious to finish the palisade and secure the gates. Felled trees came rolling in, pushed by the labourers and the young men of the town, keen to help out where they could. The carpenters then set to work, stripping and shaving the bark with their slicing tools and dressing the timber with t-blade axes. Teasel watched them with an aching grin stretched across her face. She breathed in the sweetness of the bare, new timber and rejoiced at the hammering, even though the noise had been a constant companion since they had arrived at this place. She loved to see the changes wrought, to see the quick rewards for endeavour as day by day, upright post by upright post, the town of Bremesbyrig disappeared from the outside world behind a solid wooden palisade. The decimated woodland behind the settlement would be carefully coppiced, so that in time the scars in the landscape would heal. Pray God that this new fortified burh, built to her father's model, would prevent further wounds being inflicted on the land by Viking marauders. Beside the tall fencing, the craftsmen worked to fashion the smaller supports needed to complete the platform which, when butted up against the inner wall of the palisade, would provide a raised level from which to defend the town walls. Two of the six watchtowers, built into the walls, were already permanently manned. Teasel had been in the one on the north side just yesterday, staring down at the pile of earth beyond the dug out trench, pleased at how little time it had taken to move the soil and make the trench. Now, in the morning drizzle, she knew it would be filling with water. Even better. She breathed in deeply, savouring the aroma of wood shavings and wet earth. If only her mother had been given such a distraction as this, instead of sitting at home wringing her hands and waiting for bad news. Word had come that Edward had caught up with the Northumbrians; Teasel was glad to be able to be busy. She strolled further round the inner wall, and found Athelstan and Thegn Eadric, shirts off despite the soft rain, taking turns with a saw. They must also have been sharing a crude joke, for the moment they saw her, they suppressed their laughter and contorted their faces as they tried to pull them straight.

"A wholesome riddle, was it?"

Athelstan grinned. "Not wholesome enough to be fit for the ears of a fine lady, Aunt."

She glanced down and giggled, for here was the real joke. "I have never looked less like a fine lady in my life." At first, with no women to attend her, she had made the best efforts to turn out each day in her finest silks and embroidered veils. But as the weather grew warmer and the days grew longer, she grew bored. And so, with a simple homespun kirtle and hem hitched clear of the mud, she had pushed back her sleeves and helped where she could, usually carrying bucket-loads of mud away from the trench site, to spread as new soil on the fallow fields.

"Aunt, you could wear a monk's cowl and still look lovely." Athelstan dropped the saw and bowed low, laughing all the while.

She laughed too, but somewhere inside there lurked the nagging suspicion that she was right and he was wrong. Her handsome nephew, just eighteen and Eadric, perhaps in his twenty-fifth year, were young men in the best of their youth. Despite the smiles and the light-hearted teasing, Teasel was a woman past the age of forty and had she been a grandmother by now as might have been expected, she would have realised that she was an old woman long before now. Ethelred had always been older than she, so she had always felt young. And with a daughter not yet twelve, Teasel had forgotten to begin counting the years. "For all that you are but callow yet, you are skilled enough to make an old woman feel flattered," she said, adding what she hoped was a gracious smile.

"And yet I am not strong enough to saw this thing by myself," Eadric said.

Athelstan took the hint and took back the saw, resuming the rhythmic push and pull up and down the groove in the tree trunk whilst Eadric took a break and a swig of ale.

Teasel turned to go, but was waylaid by a messenger.

"Letters, my lady. From the king."

Teasel had breathed in and now the small gasp of air was stuck in her chest. Her mind cleared all its thoughts, ready to fill with new worries. But she exhaled and refused to think, reaching for the leather bag containing the letters and holding out her other hand. "Athelstan." She beckoned him forward.

She scanned the first letter, mumbling the key words out loud. "Fight at Tettenhall, win, many dead, Northumbrians fled, day is ours."

She squeezed Athelstan's hand. "Your father has beaten them back to Northumbria. He thinks they will not dare to come back into our part of England. Ever."

Athelstan picked her up and span her round before dancing a jig with Eadric. Panting, he came back to her and said, "Does he say aught else?"

"No, but there is another vellum." With Edward's personal seal. Her mouth remained closed as she began to concentrate on the written words. Somehow though, these did not spring as quickly from the page to her eyes. She found she had to read and reread, for the letters, even when they rose up off the page, seemed to find their entry to her mind completely barred. Her head shook, for there was no way she could let these words come in. Once in her head, they would become truth and that must not happen.

Athelstan put his arm around her shoulder. "Aunt?"

Time then. Time to bid it come into her mind and let it be so. "Alhelm is dead."

Turning towards him, she sobbed against Athelstan's chest, while above her head his voice rang out, sharing the news, barking instructions. He said to her, "You must go home. For his burial. It might not be too late; if you leave now."

She stood up straight and wiped her face. "No. I am needed here, I will not go." She could not go. Not everything in life was sufferable, and this would be one thing that she could not bear. He was never hers in life, so she had no right to him now. She must grieve in private while she learned how to live without something that she had never actually had, how to mourn something she had never known. She walked away, convinced that she would stumble now with every step. While Alhelm lived, she had drawn comfort from knowing that she breathed the same air as he. Now, her breath came cold into her body. It was as though a distant hearth-fire, to which she had never been beckoned, had nevertheless thrown its light and some vestige of its warmth onto her path. Now, the fire was dowsed and her shivering only made worse the heavy, breaking pain in her chest.

AD911

Deerhurst, Mercia

He had come home. His smile, if still slightly diminished, opened up his face and lifted his cheeks and all the familiar creases around his eyes settled into their habitual lines. He tilted his face the better to catch the sun's warmth. In a moment, she knew, he would turn and catch her looking at him, but until then she was content to gaze upon him. On their wedding day, she had only dared to take a brief sideward glance at this man. Now, she knew every wrinkle, every scar, even the funny little muscle just above his jawbone, that twitched whenever he was tense and clenching his teeth.

The royal hall here was small, but the surroundings were charming. Deerhurst, the ancient heart of the Hwicce people of old Mercia, nestled in the vale of his beloved river, a small, unspoilt part of oldest England that she wished they had visited more often. But now that there was a promise of peace, there was less that pulled them towards Worcester, Gloucester, Shrewsbury. Ethelred had spent his life fighting; let him now have quiet. Edward had destroyed the Northumbrian host. Even if they managed to rally, it would take them years to gather strength and numbers. Her aunt would have been envious of the close working relationship now between Mercia and Wessex. He might not like it, but Edward knew, and accepted, that he needed her just as much as she needed him. They had all grown up together;

she, Edward, and Frith. Dear Alhelm had been older, Ethelred was older still, but they had known them both since they were young. Burgred and her father had been only allies, mere political brothers-in-law. Perhaps it was love that was needed, love that made the difference. Ethelred turned and smiled at her and she said, "Yes, love is what matters."

He reached for her hand and squeezed it. There was still strength in his grip. He would never again walk without a limp, but he was not helpless and for the most part, he was content. Could she ever be so stoical, she wondered? *Would I take what God had thrown at me and bite back all harsh words, swallow my wrath? This man, for whom fear held no sway, who lived only to fight, to win back the freedom for his folk, his land, now bows to a greater lord. That we should all be so saintly.*

"I am dying," he said.

She sat back as if a boulder had been thrown at her chest. "What? Do not..."

"Mother?" Elfwen was walking towards them, her hands on her hips and her bottom lip sticking out under a puckered top lip. "Alyth says I must help in the cook-house all day. She is unwell, she says, and cannot teach me my sewing."

Teasel answered her daughter, but could not move her gaze from Ethelred's face. Still trying to understand what he had told her, she said to Elfwen, "Then you must do as you are bidden."

"Well, could I not spend the day with you instead? Must I work every day? I am high-born, after all."

"We all work, Elfwen. There is no rest for any of us. And your father and I need to speak on things that are, well, that are between us." His head had tilted and he was smiling, but she could not interpret his expression. She heard Elfwen stamping her foot.

"You always have things to do." The child stomped away, a rhythmic scuffling announcing how she was kicking at the ground with every step.

Teasel began to speak to Ethelred. "I cannot believe, understand. What do you mean?"

But he put a finger to her lips. "I cannot tell you. It is a feeling, that is all. I thought that I should warn you. So that you had time." He looked over at the church. "I would pray, if you do not mind."

Mind? She did not mind. She would refuse him naught. Only if he wished to go alone, she might demur, for she would not be parted from him, not on this earth. And so she went with him to prayer, into the little church, passing underneath the carved, wide-eyed beast heads that guarded the outer door and under the carving of the Virgin above the inner door. In the cool of the inside, she sat while he knelt, and she stared up at the pretty double windows rising to their sharp points from a central column, side by side, as if holding hands.

She sat with him during the evening meal, and served him fish caught fresh from the river, refusing to pay heed to the small amounts he was eating. Keeping a jug by her on the table, she poured his drinks all night, noting that his cup was only half empty whenever she refilled it, but deciding that after a quiet day, he was just not thirsty.

She went to bed with him that night, and did not stay up at the gaming tables. She lay next to him, her naked skin touching his and she savoured the warmth. She concentrated on all the little contact points where their bodies met. Feet entwined, her toes cold, his not so. Hip against thigh, where she felt the mat of hairs tickling her smooth upper thigh. With her elbows lifted and her arms tucked in close to her own body, she could feel the yielding flesh where the back of her waist rested just above his hip. Her head lay in the dip between his chest and arm and she turned her face, putting her lips against his chest, feeling the muscle underneath, once so powerful, softened now since his sword had been hung up. Pressing her mouth softly into his skin, she breathed in his scent, felt the hairs on his chest tickle her nose, the bristles on his chin catching in her hair as he moved his head. He wanted her to lift her face, so she did, shifting upwards to bring her head level with his, pushing her lips onto his, strongly aware of the returning pressure, breathing in his sweet, ale-scented breath. Yes, every moment, every detail, sight sound and touch from the moment they entered the church to the moment they fell asleep, was captured in her mind more perfectly than any picture the scribes could draw for her. And she was glad, then, that he had given her that time, to catch and store it all, for it was her last chance. In the morning, he was cold.

She did not look, for she knew she would see the face all contorted, dropped to the side, fallen. She clung to the warmth she had gathered from the night before and left the bedchamber without a backward glance. She did not cry and she did not scream, knowing that no human could make a sound loud enough to express the pain.

Beyond the hall door, the world was waking up. Dairymaids strolled by, their pails swinging empty for now. The baker dipped his head as he ducked into the bake-house to light the first fires and begin the day's bread-making. Two thegns were already in the paddock, swiping at each other with blunted blades, their aim so wild and their faces so ale-grey that they had probably not yet been to bed. Laundry-women dragged large wooden buckets out into the yard, ready to mix dyes for the yarn that came from the carding sheds. All around her, Teasel saw the day unfolding and she was part of it, because she lived, she breathed. Behind her lay the body of her lover, her husband, her life. She was part of that too, but could not be with him. So she stood, between two worlds, without any idea what to do next.

A groom tumbled across the yard, straw in his hair and a worried expression on his face. In trouble with the stable master, no doubt, Teasel thought, wondering why she was now spotting such inconsequential details. The groom cast a look at her, scratched his head and went to talk to one of the thegns in the paddock. Within moments, Frith was standing in front of her.

"Lord Ethelred; has he had another bout?"

She nodded.

"He is dead." There was no question in his tone. The news must be readable to any who knew her face.

She lifted her head. His own face was stricken, his eyes wide as if he had been agonisingly winded. But he put his hands gently on her shoulders and peered into her eyes, nodding. And the look told her all that he would do for her. Leave all things with me, it said, for they are my burden. I will do all that needs doing and then I will hold you when you cry. I will not mourn, who loved him too, until you have no more need of me, when your tears are spent. I will put aside my own pain until yours subsides enough to let you sleep.

She knew it, knew the truth of it, knew she was not imagining it. He would do these things, for her, for Ethelred. And so she surrendered, laid her head against his shoulder, opened the door she had built across her heart, strong as any burh palisade, braced herself, and let the pain in.

Gloucester

She had not been to a service since Martinmas, nearly a fortnight ago. She knew that Ethelred had made his peace with God, but if she were honest, she still had one or two things that she was unhappy about. She would speak to God again one day, but for now, she had not forgiven him for taking her love. It was turning out to be an exceptionally cold November and the old hall at Gloucester was particularly draughty. There were floorboards in the main hall, but none in the bedchambers, and even the areas that were boarded rattled and allowed draughts and damp odours to rise up. Yet Gloucester was where her husband was buried and she did not yet have the strength to leave him. She pulled the fur cloak tighter around her shoulders and made a fresh attempt to read the book that Werferth had sent, her father's English translation of the psalms. This copy was written in the Mercian dialect and Werferth's message had included the hope that she might find comfort from its words, but after hours of struggling with it she thought that the most comfort to be derived from it would be the warmth generated after she threw it on the fire. Somewhere behind and above her, she heard Ethelred chuckling at her petulance. She looked up. "It's all right for you, my love, safe and warm up there in heaven." The only warmth she had felt lately was the hand of a Welshman, clasped firmly around hers as she showed him where the

361

burial had been after he arrived too late for the funeral. She threw her questions heavenward. "Did you know it was going to be such a cold winter? Is that why you left?"

"Who are you speaking to?" Edward strode into the hall, pulling off his gloves and throwing them on the nearest table.

Teasel stood up and blinked away irksome tears. "The man who keeps my heart, even now. But if I cannot have him, there is no-one I would rather look upon than you. How are you, Brother?" She clasped him to her and then withdrew, holding his hand and guiding him to the chair next to hers on the dais.

Edward sat down and waited for a drink before he answered. "Cold and tired." He took three long gulps and set his cup down. "We meet in sad times. I am sorry that I was not here."

She nodded, but attempted no speech, not convinced that the tears had quite gone away.

"I am sorry, too about Alhelm. If it helps you to know, I have shed a tear for every one that you have wept."

She doubted it. She would not have believed her body held so much water if she had not seen those tears fall. That was why it surprised her that more were on their way. She had thought herself drained now, completely. "Whence did you come here?"

"From Hertford. The burh is built. If they try to come at us from Bedford or Cambridge they will find the way blocked. No more sailing down the Lea for them."

She smiled. "That is good. But you did not come here to tell me that. Should I ask again? I will try *wherefore* did you come here?" She gripped the edge of the table.

"Ethelred is dead."

Did he think to surprise her? "I know that."

He would not meet her gaze, examining the back of his hand as he spoke. "We need to speak about the leadership of Mercia, now that he has gone."

She looked down and saw that her own fingers had

gone white. She released the pressure and brought them up onto the surface of the table. Her brother was talking to his sister. But the king of Wessex was addressing the lady of Mercia. "I would have my witan here with me, Brother, before we speak on."

Edward clicked his fingers and the boy who had served him wine was despatched to gather as many noblemen as he could find.

"While we wait, I must say that I am willing to let things lie as they are, for the most part."

She had to yield to the sudden urge to smile, for Edward had sat forward as he spoke, palms pressed together as if in supplication. He was so eager to forward his opening manoeuvre that his tone had come as close as it ever would to sounding conciliatory. When Ethelred fell ill, Edward had anticipated no resistance. Now, he was not so confident. He was expecting a fight, but in no hurry to find it.

He continued. "The houses of Burgred and Ceolwulf have died out. I have no worries that another thegn or lord will try to take over and rule through you, for I hear that you are chaste."

A king spoke to her, but she only heard the voice of her younger brother, and he had never been noted for his delicate word-craft. It jolted her from her amusement. "Chaste?" She turned from his scrutiny and looked out of the window. The November squall had eased and though the sky was black, the sun had managed to puncture a hole somewhere in it and for a few seconds the world was washed with a yellow winter light that brightened without warming. Chaste. Some words were so imbued with truth that their mere utterance was enough to inflict pain. At so many welcome moments, the Welsh hand had reached out in friendship, maybe more. But she had shaken it off, even though its warmth had stirred her. Her whole life, she had been well-behaved, had been 'good'. She looked again at her brother. "Chaste? I am shrivelled. An empty shell." She heard her voice rising, in level and pitch. She was shrill; the tremor in her tone was the prelude to yet more tears. "I have lost my love; you say you are willing to let things lie 'for the most part'. I tell you that even if you were not willing, you could not, you *will* not, take Mercia from me. From us."

"Us?"

"She means all of us." Athelstan was the first to come in, and he was followed by Eadric, Frith and the other younger thegns who now made up Teasel's council.

Frith stepped up onto the dais. He leaned across the table and spoke quietly to his boyhood friend. "All the men in this room would lay down their lives for the lady." He paused. "Wherever the threat came from." Standing back, he said, "You must also bear in mind, as I do, what Ethelred once said."

Edward frowned. It was clear that, expecting a fight, he had honeyed his words, but somehow he had still managed to upset his sister and was visibly puzzled. "What did he say?"

Teasel enlightened him. "He was wont to say that it was the kingdom that mattered, not the king."

Frith nodded. "When my lord died I asked the lady if she would now go home. She told me that this is her home." He leaned forward once more. "Edward, the Mercians will follow her. And my sword belongs to both of you, for ere so long as I have strength to wield it." He looked at Teasel and they waited.

Edward sniffed. "Show me who now leads the north in Alhelm's stead."

Frith pointed out the young man who had succeeded to the ealdordom.

"Name?"

"Alfred."

Edward glanced at the youth, barely into his twenties. He was clearly not impressed by what he saw. "He is not ready. All eyes will be on north Mercia and the young hart will need your help while his antlers grow. You cannot be everywhere, so let London and Oxford come back into Wessex. I have more men, and I can get there swiftly if need be."

Teasel inhaled deeply. This was the remainder, the exclusion from the 'most part' of which he had spoken. "London and Oxford are dear to us, Brother. Oxford has ever thrived, as a market town and even as a mint in our father's day. And London is our life's blood; without the river, without the ships bringing the goods…" She looked at Frith and he gave a small nod. She said, "I would speak with Lord Frith."

Edward swept out his arm in a gesture of agreement and Frith jumped down from the dais to walk with Teasel to the farthest corner of the hall.

She laid her hand on his arm. "What do you say, old friend?"

Frith patted her hand. "I say that, in fighting the boar, we have speared ourselves. Once, where ealdormen throughout the kingdom would have gone about their work…"

She nodded, for he was speaking her thoughts. In seeking to prove themselves to Edward, they had centralised too much of the administration, leaving too few vacancies for ambitious nobles. "And those who would once have been ealdormen now go to be king's thegns, to fight the heathen. We have the new men, Alfred and Ælfwold, but it is not enough."

"You are right, my lady. It is the kingdom that matters, but we have no kings left. Not enough men left."

Teasel felt the stinging of the tears once more. Too many kings had capitulated. And now, with Ethelred and Alhelm gone, there was none left who was prepared to stand. There was only Frith, and he was not a Mercian. She cast a glance over her shoulder at Edward, who sat playing with the hem of his sleeve.

"He came here thinking he would have to fight us. After last time."

365

Frith laughed but without genuine humour. "We are too tired, Lady. We are all too old and tired. Let him take Oxford and London, for, in truth, we cannot stop him."

She sniffed. "We do not have to tell him that, though."

She walked back across the room with her arm resting on Frith's, her chin up and her gaze level.

She waited until she could be sure that she was in control of her voice, for when she spoke, it must be as a queen. "So be it." She let out a long breath. "What now?"

He smacked his hands together. "Now, we build. And we push them out."

So he had agreed to let her rule Mercia, but he had taken prime Mercian land. It would not be to Ethelred's liking, but there was no other way. She would rule the lands that were left to her, and do so in his memory. When Ethelred died, she had wondered if she were up to the task, but after losing Alhelm and then her husband, she knew she would never face anything so mighty again. In the dark place where she had dwelled in bereavement, her words to her mother had come back to taunt her. *'While they live, there is hope.'* And they no longer lived, so there was no hope.

Yet now, here was Edward, promising to let things lie, encouraging her to continue with the burh-building. And she thought, irreverently, that she would make sure that all the new halls were built with floorboards throughout. Here too, still, were Athelstan, Eadric, and dear beloved Frith. New men, too; Alfred and Ælfwold, so keen to walk in the giant footprints left by those who went before. So it was true. *Mother, I was right. While they live, there is hope. Mother, can you hear? Mother?*

"Mother, are you listening?"

Elfwen was standing next to Frith in front of the dais. "Alyth says Uncle Edward has come to take you away. Is it true?"

Teasel looked down at her and smiled. "No, Uncle Edward has come to tell me that I can bide here, and things will go on as before."

"So you are not going away?"

Suddenly, it was difficult. "Well, I might have to leave for a short while, to oversee more building works."

Elfwen squinted and, as she did so, her brows came together and two vertical lines appeared above the bridge of her nose. "I thought that when Father died, you would have time for me at last." She turned round and walked slowly from the hall.

Edward let out a low whistle. "I give thanks to God that my children are either boys, or meek. What do you say, Frith? Are you not grateful that you have no girls at all?"

Frith acknowledged Edward's joke with a smile, but he put his hand on Teasel's arm. "She is only twelve. She mourns. Give her time."

She smiled her thanks, but she was used to Elfwen's outbursts and usually forgave her, not because she was her mother and was indulgent, but because Elfwen so often spoke the truth. This time, however, her own shortcomings as a mother were not the cause of her discomfort. It was what she had seen as Elfwen left the room that worried her; the provocative smile that Elfwen had aimed at Eadric as she'd strutted out of the hall.

AD915

Weardburh, Northern Mercia

The little man made her laugh. Ethelred's scop, like all the wordsmiths, poets and singers, had carried himself with dignity, striving always for perfection in his art, searching for just the right word, struggling with rhyme and form, all the while with a dramatic frown etched into his forehead. This dwarf-like creature seemed only to delight in riddles, the cruder the better, and he followed her around the town and sang of her beauty with a loud and frankly less than soothing voice. But he served a purpose; always unable to accept a compliment with good grace, she scoffed at his light-hearted but well-meant praise, and, in protesting, she remembered that her feet walked upon the same ground where churls and slaves also walked. She was achieving great things, yes, but she belonged with ordinary folk here on earth and was not yet heavenly. Like all folk who were not rich, he wore the same tunic every day, but it was woven from such strangely patterned cloth that he could be spotted coming into the burh from many fields away beyond the gates. He would impress her, he said, and she would keep him with her as her scop, and for all the time she had been supervising the building at Weardburh, he had risen to his own challenge. Now, his yellow, red and blue tunic, too loose over his tiny frame, wobbled around as he danced before her and made her guess the answers to his riddles.

"My lady, I wonder if you can tell me what it is that

prods and prods until the forbidden softness yields and shows itself?"

She bit her lip to prevent a grin from escaping. "I will not speak the words you wish me to speak, you can be sure of that."

"Why, my lady, whatever do you mean? The answer is plain; 'tis a sparrow cracking a snail from its shell."

She laughed, and walked on with him still prancing alongside her.

"Have I a place by your hearth, now, my lady?"

"We shall see. If you are still making me laugh when it is time to leave here, then I might let you come with me."

She left him bowing down, his large nose almost scraping the ground. On the corner of the new street leading to the great hall, she met Frith and they linked arms, walking together to the meeting.

The interior of the hall was bare and uninviting. The walls had been lime-washed, but there were no wall hangings yet and the tables were new and pale, the naked, freshly planed wood seeming unprepared somehow for the years of knocks and ale stains to come. Footfall echoed unpleasantly and it would be a while before this hall offered itself as a place for intimate conversation. Teasel took her seat between Athelstan and Frith. She smiled at Eadric, noting how he had put on his best tunic and tidied his hair, securing it with a braided leather headband. "We will do this first." she mouthed the words to him and he nodded his thanks.

Further along the high table, Elfwen was sitting with her hands folded in front of her. Her dark copper hair was tied in a long plait, but her head was uncovered. At sixteen she bestrode both the sweet world of childhood and the exciting place that would be her womanhood. Her delicately freckled cheeks were a little red. Teasel thought that she must be excited about attending her first witanagemot. The girl had looked brighter, less sour-faced, since Teasel had made the decision to bring her travelling. It comforted the mother to know that she had leached some of the child's bitterness towards her. Now, Teasel could spend time with her daughter, and Elfwen could learn to understand the demands on her time that had kept them so often apart. Beyond Elfwen, the new ealdorman of north Mercia, Alfred, sat with his back straight, his gaze on the scribes' table, looking like a man who dare not move for fear of making a mistake. But Teasel did not share his worries; he was strong and capable. Frith had approved the investiture and they knew Alfred would, even if only adequately, fill Alhelm's shoes. She was pleased to see Abbot Ecgberht with the ecclesiastical contingent. He had been so kind to Ethelred over the last few years and today he had brought some flowers for her. The little posy lay on the table in front of him, a small wash of colour in the otherwise sparse room. She signalled to him, with a hand motion that mimicked lips moving, that she would like to speak to him after the meeting, and he nodded, adding his own gesture that could only mean the lifting of an ale cup.

Everyone was settled, so she began. "We are here this day to witness that I give my leave to Eadric, beloved thegn, to buy from Wulflaf ten hides of land at Farnborough, in Warwickshire. We acknowledge that there was, at one time, a land-book, lost by fire, in which it was written that the land was given to Bynna, kinsman of Wulflaf, by the great King Offa. Therefore the land is rightly Wulflaf's to sell, and we give leave for Eadric to buy it."

There was little other business and, what there was, was swiftly concluded. After the meeting, Teasel stood to make her way over to the Abbot. A thegn bowed before her, blocking her way. "My lady, the would-be scop wishes to come in."

Frith said, "The Irishman? Tell him to be gone."

Teasel laid a hand on his arm. "No, not an Irishman. He's a little man who sings for me and would be my scop when we leave here."

Frith patted her hand, the gesture identical to the one

Alyth used when correcting the children's mistakes. "My lady, believe me, he is an Irish Celt. He does no harm, and is no lover of the Norse who have settled in his homeland, but he is a bane."

"Well, he makes me laugh." This, from a woman of her years. Was that the best retort she could issue to cover her embarrassment at not recognising the little man's accent? She lifted her chin. "Bid him come in."

The odd little fellow skipped up to the dais, bowing low so that his body looked like it had curled into a ball. He stood up and made his announcement. "My lady, I cannot, after all, come with you when you leave here."

"Oh?" She fought the smile that itched to display her amusement at his impudence.

"Queen Æthelflæd, it is my sworn oath that I will sail back to my homeland of Ireland..."

At the mention of his country, she cast a glance at Frith, who raised his eyebrows and gave her a knowing, smug smile.

"There to tell wondrous tales of the great deeds of the mighty English queen, before whom all evil men fall away, to die or mend their ways, to..."

"Enough. I am not a queen, little fellow. And I will not fill your head with tales of my 'mighty deeds'. You are here to make me laugh, not to swell my head with pride badly earned."

Athelstan span in a little circle, pivoting round one leg, and clapped his hands. "We will tell you," he said and grinned at Frith. He sat down, waved his arm to signal for more drinks, and made himself comfortable by the hearth, one leg hitched up and resting on the other.

"Yes," Frith said, laughing, "We will tell you all about our 'queen'." He was clearly enjoying the show. She would have words later. But for now she had no choice but to listen.

Athelstan began. "Since our lady became 'queen'..."

She wished they would stop using the word.

"She has been busy every day that the Lord has sent. First, she built burhs at Scergeat and at Bridgnorth, that fateful spot where the Northumbrians forded the Severn to meet their deaths at Tettenhall."

Now her embarrassment turned into real discomfort. Her thoughts led her back to Bridgnorth and the painful journey she had made from there to the battle site. She remembered the wandering search, vision misted by a blur of tears, as the tried to find the tree where Alhelm had lain and taken his final breath. She inhaled, shuddering, and realised that Athelstan was still speaking.

"Meanwhile, King Edward built at Witham and a second fort at Hertford."

Frith took up the story. "Then the heathens in eastern Mercia began harrying once more. They were put to flight and in the summer our lady built a strong burh at Tamworth, and then, before harvest, another at Stafford, all the while pushing against the edges of Danish Mercia."

Teasel fidgeted in her seat, picking at a loose piece of skin by her thumbnail. Why did they not tell him of others, braver by far than she? She glanced down at the letter on the table which told of the English Northumbrians of Bamburgh, the lords who had colluded in the land-buying tactic and who had now courageously tried to fight off the Norseman Ragnall and his forces. These men had risen up against this new threat and their tale needed to be told.

Her nephew was speaking again. He scowled to give dramatic flourish to his tale. "Then, last year, a host came from Brittany, harrying in Wales and the south and then came to the Severn and into Herefordshire." He threw his arms out wide. "But the fearless men at Hereford fought them back and killed their leader."

Athelstan paused to allow all those present to applaud the foresight that saw a manned garrison built at Hereford. Teasel smiled, but again her thoughts took her away to the past, to a darkened bedchamber where Ethelred, his mind sharp as ever, struggled to convey his ideas for the fort. She tried to swallow away a bitter taste. Until the moment he died, her husband had been possessed of the keenest wits. Her more impulsive nature almost seemed an insult to his memory. It was not fitting that it should be she who sat here now, being lauded. Even as her thoughts lurched back to the present, they took her only as far as the previous month, when she had stood at the burial of dear, devout, devoted Werferth. All her loved ones should still be here, sitting with her.

Athelstan finished his tale. "Fleeing, the foe met Edward's fyrd and ran back to their island at Steepholme, until, starving, they went to Ireland."

The little man's face creased into a scowl and he muttered softly. "They will find no welcome there. Not from my kin."

Frith took over. "Last Martinmas, King Edward built at Buckingham, and the Danes of Bedford and Northampton came to him, and swore to him as their lord. Queen Æthelflæd built at Eddisbury and at Warwick. And before we came here, she had burhs built at Chirbury and Runcorn, all the while strengthening our lands against attacks from the Wirral and from Danish Mercia. They will not dare to come at us now from the Mersey." He looked over at her and frowned. He stepped towards her and lowered his head and voice. "And you do too much. You look careworn. You must rest soon."

And then what? What was a grieving widow to do with her time, if not fight to realise her dead husband's vision? Ethelred would never have lain down while he could stand. And Edward would never forgive her. But she was indeed weary, and he could see it.

He said, "Enough now. Little man, go home and tell your tales. This great lady needs to rest." He took hold of her elbow and walked her towards the end of the hall. "And I need to further your burden and speak to you. About Elfwen."

She could not think why. Surely there was naught to be

said; the child was by her side, and so could have no complaint. And she was in no danger. As soon as she and Frith were beyond eavesdroppers, she said, "What of her?" But she was looking at the door; Abbot Ecgberht was leaving the hall and Teasel knew her opportunity to speak to him had passed.

All in a moment, Frith, her old friend, he who knew her so well that he had not hesitated to tease her without mercy, now looked to have a knot in his tongue. He poked it from cheek to cheek, and stared at the rafters, all the while shuffling his feet as if stamping on ants. "This is hard for me, my lady, but I must be the one to say it. She is being somewhat, that is to say she bestows too loosely her..." He coughed and began again. "She makes too freely with the young men."

She looked at him, waiting for him to continue, until the sense of his words came to her and she shook her head. "You are mistaken. She is," and now she understood the flush to Efwen's cheeks during the meeting, "Love-struck, yes, but for Eadric. I have seen the way she looks at him. Even when she was a small child, I saw that she had feelings for him."

He took her hand, covering it with both of his. "And she has them yet. But Eadric has told her that they will never be together, for he says you are his lady, he a mere thegn, and it would not be right."

"Well, that is true. But I do not see how..."

"She seeks to show him that he is wrong. She seeks to fire him up until his love for her overwhelms his oath to you."

By sleeping with every other thegn in the court? "I will speak to her. I will not have her shame our kin-name in this way."

The journey from the hall to Elfwen's bower had not been far enough to cool a temper. The breeze only lifted Teasel's skirts and served to irritate her further. Banging the door aside, she strode into her daughter's chamber and thumped her fists onto her hips.

"Daughter, I have been given tidings about you that have made me sad. Wroth, even."

Elfwen looked up, her needle poised above her sewing. She raised her eyebrows, and then a shadow passed across her eyes and they narrowed. She tucked the needle into the cloth, folded her arms across her chest and looked down at the floor. "I know naught of which you speak."

"That might be true. So tell me, have you lain with any of my thegns?"

Elfwen flushed from her forehead to her neck. She began to fiddle with her embroidery, pretending to pick at an unsatisfactory stitch. "No."

Her mother took two steps further into the room. "You tell me no, yet all I see when I look at you is that I have had the truth from others." She laid a hand on her daughter's shoulder.

Elfwen shoved her away as she stood up. "It is not me whom you should seek to yell at. He told me our love was wrong. How can it be wrong to love? What kind of man puts love aside to fulfil a hold-oath to his lord? Or lady?" She looked directly at her mother.

Teasel met her gaze. She knew of the yearning for things not possessed, of learning instead to love what was owned. Oh, she could tell her exactly what kind of man put duty before love. The memory of those water-blue eyes blotted all reasonable thoughts from Teasel's mind and she gave no hesitation before damning her daughter. "You have shamed me. And you have brought shame to your father's name."

Elfwen's chin tilted upwards. "I am old enough."

"You are but sixteen. You are still my daughter."

"I did not ask to be brought forth from your womb."

Teasel took an involuntary step back. "Nevertheless, that is how you came into the world and I…"

Elfwen took a step nearer. "I would that you were not my mother." She stood, chin jutting, but eyes squinting, as if she expected a blow.

Teasel would not hit her. It was so long since she had been allowed to show her true feelings, never mind act upon them. A regal smile would not help her here, so all she could try to muster was a mask of indifference. "That might well be true. However, mother or no, I am still your lady. You will sleep alone, or I will send you to a nunnery."

She turned to go, but Elfwen shouted after her.

"Then do it, for I shall not live like a nun otherwise. Why should I? To give up love without a fight; who would live that way?"

Teasel paused, but did not answer. *I do.*

AD916

Hereford, Mercia, June 18ᵗʰ

"We are pushing at their edges. Edward is shrinking their Essex day by day. Soon we will have a line of burhs from Runcorn to Benfleet. Where next, Lady Æthelflæd?"

She looked up at the sound of her name. But of course, Eadric had never known her family name. Who did, of those around her? Only dear Frith and he still refused to be so familiar. Æthelflæd she was, then. In truth, it felt as if Teasel had lived a lifetime ago. "I am going to push north. For too long, the Danes have held Mercian towns. They have five of our boroughs in the northeast of Mercia and I would like them back. I am going to take Derby."

Frith walked in and raised his eyebrows. "Were you going to ask me what I thought about this madness, my lady?"

"No."

"Well I will tell you what I think. I will let you do it, but only if you bide at the back when the fighting begins."

"You will 'let' me? How dare you?"

He grinned. "I am keen to begin. When do we leave?"

She grunted in mock frustration at his teasing.

He laughed and bowed before walking away. "Eadric, come, we have work to do."

On their way from the hall, they stood aside to allow a messenger through. Frith turned, as if wondering whether he were still required, but Æthelflæd knew that this was not a courier from Edward and she waved at him to leave. This man looked more like the emissary who only a few cruel months ago had come to tell her of Bishop Werferth's death. He wore the black robes of a monk's habit, but there was no tonsure on show when he bowed before her. Like many devout men his face was devoid of expression so he gave no visual hint about the nature of the news he bore. He straightened up and she ordered wine, beckoning the visitor to sit down He took a chair and moved it so that he could sit opposite her, then he folded his arms, slipping his hands inside his capacious sleeves. Since he was in no hurry, she unclenched her jaw and relaxed her grip on the table, beginning to believe that he was not, after all, the bringer of bad tidings.

"My lady, I am Higbald. I was a thegn in Wessex but when I grew too old to wield a sword I craved to live out my days under God's law in an abbey. I went one day to speak to Archbishop Plegmund, and, at that time, Bishop Werferth was a guest at Canterbury. With him was his friend, who became mine. I speak of Abbot Ecgberht."

Æthelflæd sat forward, clutching the table again as if she would fall if she did not hold on. "What has befallen him?"

"I will not clothe this in fine silk, my lady, but show it to you bare. Two days ago, the Abbot, on his way to St David's, was set upon and killed, along with many others who rode with him."

Her hands went to her face. "No, it cannot be." Æthelflæd thought back to the summer afternoon in Werferth's garden, and the little abbot busying himself with the flowers while he sang to Ethelred. She heard again the tolling of the bell, but now the memory was corrupt, the melodious peals being replaced by the discordant clash of steel as she imagined the innocent abbot being pulled from his horse and deprived of his life.

She shook her head. This was no time to wallow. "Fetch Lord Frith," she said, to whoever might hear. "And send word to King Anarawd in Gwynedd. "We take a fyrd to Wales and ask for his help in righting this unholy wrong."

Brycheiniog, Wales, June 19th

Her body, moving, remained warm. Her hands and face, making no contribution to the push forward, but propelled nevertheless, felt the sting of the wind. Her back ached as it tried to support her legs. They slipped out behind her, getting no purchase in the liquefying mud. At the bottom of the hill, it had seemed madness to get off the horses and walk them up; now she could see the sense of it. Further up the hillside the sheets of rain billowed across the landscape, flapping thick grey swaddling blankets of misery around them. Reaching the crest of the ridge, they turned into the maw of the wind. Tired from the climb, she still could not fill her lungs as the gusts blew into her mouth but perversely took her breath from her. On the other side of the ridge, bent down like so many old men, a line of trees marked out the edge of the lake. Æthelflæd waved her arm in an exaggerated gesture, signalling to those behind that they would head for such little shelter there was and rest there awhile. Sidestepping down the slope, she thought how each stride brought her nearer to the man who had killed her beloved abbot and then run back to his wife, this Welsh princess of Brecon. Did they think that Mercia, ruled by a woman, would meekly stand by, like sheep, and let a wolf run wild through its flock? She had missed the chance to speak to Ecgberht at Weardburh, and now they had taken him from her. No more opportunities to talk to him, one less link with Ethelred.

It took some time until all the men had descended.

Now they were indeed like sheep, huddled in the rain. Æthelflæd had stuffed her boots with extra wool, but it was no defence against this determined rain, and her feet were soaked and cold. Frith came to find her.

"We will soon have the fires lit, my lady."

She smiled. "So you say, but you look as if you do not believe it."

"You know that my oath spoken is my oath fulfilled, my lady. You will be warm soon."

She pressed her back against the tree trunk, keeping as far under its sparse leaves as possible in an attempt to escape the rain. The foliage provided little shelter, though, so she drew her knees up, pulled her cloak tight round them and prepared to endure. Over on the other side of the little copse, Frith greeted a rider, who spoke to him in a conversation punctuated with waving arms. The stranger began to walk towards Æthelflæd, but Frith grabbed his arm and yanked him back. There was another exchange of words, Frith leaning in closely to speak into the man's ear. The rider nodded and his shoulders dropped. Frith patted his arm and began to make his way back towards her. As he came, he brought his hair round in front of his shoulder, wringing it between his hands to expel the water. He stood beside her, leaning against the trunk, one leg bent with the foot resting flat behind him on the bark. He did not speak.

Æthelflæd tried to prolong the silence, preserving the world as she knew it for just a few more precious moments. If it were merely an intelligence report, he would have spoken immediately, and they would now be on the march, or on the run. God bless him for keeping his bad news to himself, and sparing her for just a little while. He would wait until she was ready to hear it and so she sat, wishing that her powers over Mercia extended to the preservation of life. Water dribbled down her nose, finding its way over her chin, down her neck and over her collar bone, sliding onto her chest and chilling her even more. What kind of a world sent such a day as this in the middle of June? In this godforsaken place there was little cheer, so it was as apt a time as any to hear what he had to say. "Tell me, then."

"Anarawd of Gwynedd has died."

Did hanged men feel thus; a tightening around the throat and a pain from a sob that could not break free? There had been no battle, or surely they would have heard ere now. So if he had died in his bed, then it was not unexpected, for they were all getting older. No, old. Perhaps he had closed his eyes and departed this earth from a body that was wrinkled, grey, tired. But to her he would always look out from the past with those deep brown eyes, his black hair curling in its peculiar up-lick and the dimpled dent in his chin moving as he spoke to her. He had seen her worth, and Ethelred's, where she had been blind to both. He had been an adversary, an ally, and then a friend. He had held her hand and called her 'Cariad' and cared for her enough to send her home to her husband. He had been a small comfort in her bereavement; could have been more to her, in her widowhood. He would have come, and helped her stamp down this little upstart of a Welsh kingdom. He would have come. Despite the burning in her throat, she coughed and blinked away the tears. "They are on the far side of this lake?"

Frith remained standing above her. If he was surprised at her response, he did not show it. "Beyond this meadow lies the mere. They use an old hill fort overlooking an island on the water and there is a bridge leading to that. Athelstan and his riders tell me that the Welsh are all on the island."

"So we must take the island. They will not think to find us here only three days after they killed the abbot, would not guess that I was so near when I heard of their evil deed. These Welsh think that a woman cannot wield a sword and that her only might lies in tears. Show them that they are wrong. And bring the Welshwoman to me. From what I hear, this is her land. I will show them how a woman leader should be."

The lake was large, widening out at one end more than the other. Edging their way along the shore, the English watched for signs of life from the hill fort and found none. At the far end of the lake, a causeway led to the island and, from their hideout just beyond the reed beds, they could hear laughter and shouting from within the fortification there. Frith left Athelstan's side, wriggled across to Æthelflæd and whispered to her. "There is only one way that I can see of doing this. We must storm over the bridge and catch them unaware. Once we are on there, there will be little room. I must beg you to bide here while we fight."

She knew, for she had heard, how men could channel their anger to put an extra sharp edge on their blades. She burned for vengeance but had not the skills to rein in her wrath during such a fight. "Yes," she said, "I am more than willing to let you do this without me." *This time, I am glad to leave the men to their business.*

The rain had stopped and the sun began to dry up its mess. The wooden causeway was steaming as the summer heat lifted the moisture. Nevertheless, it would be slippery and there was a temptation to cross slowly. She knew that Frith's plan depended on speed and surprise and as the men left their hiding-holes, she urged them on. "Go and fight well. For God is with us and He will give us this day."

Five thegns remained with their lady; their turn today to be her personal guard, ready to give their lives for hers. Helmstan, Ælfric, Wulfnoth, Eadwine and Wulfwine surrounded Æthelflæd, their swords up, shields protecting the royal body. Æthelflæd coiled her fingers around her own sword hilt, clasping and unclasping, hoping that she would not have to use the blade, hoping that she would wield it well if called upon.

It was a fight that could be told in sounds. The rapid clumping of the men's boots as they ran across the causeway. The yelps of surprise as the Welsh discovered the intrusion. The battle cries and warrior screams as the fighting began, accompanied by the high-pitched scraping of blade upon blade. Æthelflæd and her guards listened, as if from a great distance away, where all was calm and the wading birds still fed serenely on the water. The sun, high in the sky now, shone down on the reed beds and threw shimmering patterns across the surface of the water, catching each tiny wave of the birds' wake. Grunting, cursing, death-blows and death-cries; it would not be contained for long. And so it was that the fight spilled out beyond the confines of the enclosure. Battling pairs broke out of the encampment, combat extra close because of the restricted space. Now the invaded began to flee; some jumped into the water, one was stopped by an arrow to the throat, and more still ran along the causeway, there to be met by Æthelflæd and her men. They formed a six-strong shield wall across the end of the causeway and braced against the onslaught. And, although she was taken aback by the amount of strength needed to hold a shield wall, Æthelflæd tried to remember everything Ethelred and Athelstan had taught her in the practice yard. She shouldered her shield, and thrust with her sword, minding her neighbour and filling any temporary breaks in the wall with stabbing jabs. A Welshman ran towards them, carrying only a small hand-knife, his bid for flight so urgent that he had not stopped to arm himself properly. He paused when he saw that his escape was blocked, and then decided to rush them. He slammed into the shield wall, right at the point of perceived weakness, but a sword was still a sword, even when held by a woman, and Æthelflæd found herself marvelling at the odd sensation when her blade pierced the man's torso. She was surprised at the force pushing on her arm as he slumped to the ground and she had to hold hard to the hilt to prevent the blade from being pulled from her grip. She had imagined that a dead man might simply fall away from the blade and quickly learned that she must extract it herself, or lose it. She stared at her victim and felt no remorse. His hair was dark and dirty, a week's growth on his chin. He was a mother's son, a youngling, and he took his leave of the world with a puzzled expression on his grubby face, his brown eyes open and staring. She expected to feel, if not remorseful, then at least regretful at this sudden loss of a life, but she did not. Glancing up, she saw more stragglers coming towards them and then she paused to reflect, feeling weak in the legs and more than a little tearful. Now, having been given time to think, she felt fear. And, worse, because it put other lives in danger, doubt that she could do the same thing again. But now there were scores of men on the causeway as the English, having despatched most of those in the fort, came to pursue those who had escaped. Trapped, the Welsh laid down their arms and Æthelflæd's thegns stepped forward to gather up their weapons.

Æthelflæd sheathed her own sword, and walked away from the bridge, beyond the reed beds and back to their temporary encampment. All anger spent, she sat back down beneath the tree, hugged her knees to her chest and howled her anguish, rocking back and forth as she cried out, dry-eyed, for Ecgberht, and by association, Ethelred. For kind Bishop Werferth, and dangerous Anarawd, and for Alhelm. Somewhere, many miles away in southern England, Edward fought on. But they were so few now. So few. And now she had this distraction in Wales, as if there were not enough tough, sinewy meat already on her plate. She had killed a man, yes, and she was avenged, but she still had not come face to face with the enemy that had stalked her dreams her whole life. She sat up and rubbed her face, dragging her hands across her cheeks. She felt tears beginning to bite at her eyes, and blinked hard. No, this would not do. This was no time for tears, and her anger was not misplaced. She composed her royal features, and held the mask in place as she walked back to the edge of the lake.

The prisoners were lined up for her inspection. The men, nigh on thirty of them, were not dressed so differently from the Mercians, except that few of them wore leg bindings. One or two still clutched their dented helms, and when she looked at the pile of captured shields, she noted that most had intricate paintings on them, the interlinked chain patterns interconnected with mythical beast heads. The Celtic knot-work, so similar to English decoration, was painted in bright swirls of red, green and gold. But there were no crosses among the intricate designs. Perhaps it was true, then, that this man whom some called Tewdr and some called Trewyr, was indeed a pagan. She cared little. Warriors, even pagan ones, were not without the need to be reminded that men died soon enough without being cut down for no reason. Ecgberht's death had been avenged, but it was not forgotten, nor forgiven.

At the end of the line, the Welsh princess stood with her hands clasped in front of her, tied with a leather binding. She was dressed in a plain blue kirtle which fell straight to the floor with no belt around the middle. Her cloak was checked with two shades of red and fastened on her right shoulder with a gold, circular brooch. Her pale brown hair was braided, threaded through with a leather ribbon. Around her neck, she wore a gold torc. She stood with her head tilted a little to the right and her face was open, unreadable, neither scornful nor cowed.

Athelstan said, "What shall we do with them, my lady? Are we to bring them with us?"

Once, long ago, she had played reluctant hostess to a foreign woman. Well, what was power if not the permission to make one's own choices? "I have had my fill of heathen bitches darkening my hearth. Send them to Hereford until the gold is gathered to buy them back."

The Welshwoman lifted her chin. "I am a Christian."

Æthelflæd regarded her for a moment. "Then behave like one, lady."

She turned to walk away, but said over her shoulder, "And when her menfolk bring me that gold, every one of them, be they kings or other, will bend their knee to me and swear oaths to me as their lady."

Frith followed her and she was grateful, for after

stalking off, she had no idea where to go next. He accompanied her back to the line of weathered trees and she stopped, turned, and fell against his chest, spilling her tears all over him. "This is what I have become; harsh and hard. This is how men must be, it is how I must be, but it is not how a woman is for we are not born to such things. How long can I keep it up?"

He stroked her hair and wiped her cheeks, with a calloused hand but the softest of touches. "As long as you have to. And you are not alone; I am always by your side."

'While they live, there is hope.' But so many now were dead. She shook her head. "You will leave me too."

He cupped her cheek with his big hand and moved her head away gently so that she could see him. "I have a wife who will tell you that I breathe only to serve you. No, no, be still; Alyth understands that I love her, but that my life is yours. Lady, I have not left your side in all these years, nor will I."

She sniffed. "Is that your oath?"

He nodded, smiling.

"Then it is an oath fulfilled. Forgive me. I was feeling weak. I am stronger now, with your help."

He held her by the shoulders and guided her until her back was against a tree trunk. Releasing her, he said, "So, where now?"

She sniffed and inelegantly ran the back of her hand across her nose. "As I was saying, before these bold-cheeked Welsh sought to pull us from our path, we go north."

Outside the Walls of Derby, Occupied Mercia

Ducking under showers of flaming arrows, bucket-loads of offal and boiling water, Æthelflæd and Frith ran back to the safety of their encampment. Frith held the tent flap open and Æthelflæd stooped to go in. Frith followed her inside, wiping soot from his tunic. "They will not give in. This will be a long fight."

Æthelflæd tried to catch her breath. "We are too old for this, you and I. And do not go there again without your byrnie." She pointed to his mail coat, slung in a heap upon a chest. He had the grace to look sheepish. She said, "They will not give in, you say. Well neither must we. We owe it to Ethelred. How he would have loved to know that the part of Mercia that Ceolwulf gave away is back in English hands. And we owe it to Edward."

With her brother's name hanging in the air, she looked over to her small table and glanced at the letter lying there. Well before Easter, it had proclaimed, Edward had built a fortress at Towcester to block the southern advance of the Danes from Northampton. Enemy forces from Northampton and Leicester had attacked him just a few weeks ago, but he had repelled them, and he'd held off an attack at Bedford. He took an army and stormed the Danish fortress of Tempsford, and Æthelflæd smiled with satisfaction to recall the news that a Danish king, and an earl and his son, had all been killed there. But while Edward was holding off any southern advances from the five stolen boroughs, she needed to continue their two-pronged attack. They needed to take Derby.

The heat inside the tent had built up during the day. She pulled her veil from her head and used it as a fan. Frith made no comment; no doubt he had grown used to her breaches of etiquette after so long on battle sites. She said, "My father saw to it that half of all men were ready at any time to fight, so that he could swiftly gather a fyrd whenever he needed to. He learned the hard way what befell his kingdom when men went home from the fight to bring in the harvest. Nevertheless, I would be glad to be home ere the sheaves are in."

Frith smiled. "It is a hot summer, you are right. We will win out but it will take time. We are digging, we are burning, and soon they will be starving. Meanwhile we will keep rushing the gates. Athelstan is there right now and Eadric is gathering men about him for another bout this afternoon." He sat forward. "Now, will you go and rest a while? I will send news when we have it."

She, too, leaned forward and as she moved, the sweat trickled down her back. "Thank you. I think I will, at least until the evening draws on and it is a little cooler."

Frith stood up and poked his head outside the tent. "Wulfnoth, your lady is ready to take her rest. Go with her."

She walked with her escort through the camp. The weary soldiers, grimy and tired, attended to their weapons and the smithy was busy as always, honing blades, straightening dents and casting new spear tips and arrow points. The men waited in line, headless hafts ready to be refitted.

Æthelflæd said to Wulfnoth, "You are on your own today. Where are the rest of my watchmen?"

"They are going with Lord Eadric to storm the gates, my lady."

"Then I will pray for them," she said, knowing full well that he had already been doing so all the time they had been walking.

388

She slept, but only in short bursts. She would turn, and wake, remember that Wulfnoth stood guard outside her tent and she settled down, lying on her right side and drifting off for a while, only to wriggle onto her left and wake up again. The noise from the walls was ever present, like bird song. For weeks she had lived with the shouting, hammering, scraping and banging. Shouts to muster were commonplace, as were the yelled curses in the foreign tongue from within the walls. As with the dawn chorus, it would wake her once in a while, she would acknowledge it for what it was, and sleep on again through the disturbance. She had lain on top of the bed, too hot to sink under the covers, and now, having slept for a while, she woke up feeling chilly. Grabbing at a blanket, she settled down again, not yet refreshed enough to consider rising. She lay down and closed her eyes once more. Then it came to her. There was no battle noise, no sound of machinery. Trundling cart wheels, digging spades and thudding boulders; all had stopped moving.

She sat up, pulled on her boots and left the tent. Wulfnoth had disappeared. She was not concerned; he would not have left her unless he knew it was safe to do so. With a growing sense of hope, she walked through a camp which was now near deserted. Dear God, they must have breached the walls, or the gates, or both. Coming to the edge of the encampment she saw the gates of the town hanging open, one almost off its great hinges. Beyond the open gateway, the Danes, surrendered and surrounded, had been herded together. A Mercian banner fluttered from the watchtower. A thegn on the tower pointed his sword at her and began a victory chant. It was taken up by those below, who all joined in, shouting their triumph in the name of their lady. But Æthelflæd was looking at Frith, who walked towards her with his sword still in his hand, hanging low, dragging. He had blood on his face and his long hair was matted. He had his mail coat on and she gave thanks for his innate tendency to be sensible at such times. But he walked like a wounded man, though she could see that he was whole.

He bowed on one knee before her. "Lady, Derby is yours."

She put a hand on his shoulder. "Tell me. Who do we mourn?"

His blond brows came together to form a single line above his eyes. Beneath those blue-grey eyes, dark shadows of exhaustion robbed him of his beauty. Careworn, fatigued, speaking carefully through a cut lip, he could give her no more than a list of names. "Helmstan, Ælfric, Eadwine, Wulfwine."

The rest of her personal guard.

"Eadric."

She opened her mouth but stood, gaping. What did she think to say? No? You are wrong? I misheard you? Of course he was not wrong; he would not break his own heart with lies. He struggled to his feet and she squeezed his arm. Nodding towards the inner courtyard she said, "Do what needs to be done here. I will speak to Elfwen."

She found her daughter in her tent. She wished that she could be like Frith, and give Elfwen a moment more of the world when it was right, before she plunged her into a deep lake where there was no light, only despair. But she knew that her face told Elfwen all that she needed to know. "Daughter, the town is ours. But many men died in the taking of it. Among them was Eadric."

Elfwen gasped but shook her head, believing as her mother had not, that the news was false. "No, that cannot be." But as she spoke, the words, having hit her ears as lies, must have come into her mind as truth, and she fell face down onto her bed and wept.

Æthelflæd stood still and let her cry out the initial pain, knowing that there would be more, for days, weeks, mayhap even months to come.

When the first waves had left her body and the sobbing subsided, Elfwen sat up.

"How can you stand there like that? Do you not care?"

Æthelflæd flinched. *She thinks I do not care because I do not weep. Once, many years ago, I would have thought the same thing. Dear Lord, I have loved and lost so often that I have forgot what the first time feels like.* She took a step forward.

Elfwen put out her hand. "No. Do not come near me. You are heartless."

Æthelflæd lifted her chin and let her head fall back. Her mouth opened and a strange animal cry came forth from her. It rose from within her core, and shocked her with its force. She looked her daughter in the eye and said, "Oh God, if I had opened my heart upon every death and cut out the part that died with them, it would not have the strength left to carry on beating."

She left Elfwen alone with her tears. The girl would have to learn the hard way. There was no other.

AD918

He walked across the hall, stopping theatrically to admire her new wall hangings, one with red and white vertical stripes, the other with green chevrons coming together to form a diamond in the centre. He whistled to test whether the fabric deadened the echo of the new building. "It will look like a home soon enough," he said. He thumped his foot onto the solid floorboards and then joined her on the dais, slumping into a chair beside her.

"Look at you, Frith, all grey hair and creaking knees."

He smiled. "It is true; I am getting too old to stride over frosted ground. I will not fight another winter."

And if he had noticed that it was some time since he had seen her without her veil, then she knew that diplomacy would forbid his mentioning it. Her own grey hair would be kept out of sight every day from now on. She would not go out campaigning again. Besides, there might be little need. Leicester surrendered to her forces with barely a thimble full of blood spilled and Edward had regained Huntingdon and Colchester and all the Danes in East Anglia and Essex had submitted to him. She patted the piece of vellum lying on the table. This latest news, that Edward was at Stamford, gave her the greatest thrill of all, for after Derby and Leicester, Stamford became the third of the five stolen boroughs to come back into English hands.

"I am ready to see them now," she said.

392

Frith clicked his fingers. "Send in the men from York."

She sat and listened to what they had to say. The man they called Ragnall and his Norse Vikings had fought for a second time against the English Northumbrians. The folk of York, an odd integrated mix now of English and Dane, would rather submit to the great lady whom the Irish called 'queen' than be subdued by Ragnall. With Æthelflæd as a strong ally to their south they could defend themselves against renewed attacks from the north. She nodded and agreed, for how could she not? She was distracted by a pain in her arm and had to fight a strong wave of tiredness. Did they know that this great lady whose protection they sought was, in reality, naught but a weary old woman? Barely even a woman, for her monthly bleed, once such a bane, had ceased altogether in these last few years. They spoke of her success in Leicester and she smiled as they entreated the help of one strong hound snapping at their heels against another barking at their heads. "Yes," she said graciously, "And my brother is at Stamford. We have almost an unbroken line of burhs from the northwest to the southeast. How timely for you to come to me now with your plea for help." Her teasing was lost on them, but Frith twitched a smile.

She ate only a tiny amount that evening, inexplicably tired and seeking her bed. Alyth was sleeping and she did not want to disturb her, so she undressed herself, used to the task after so many years in the battle camps and on the road. She smiled. What a change had been wrought. Who would have imagined that the child who was so reluctant to leave the relative safety of Wessex should have come to such a place; a burh built in the ancient capital of Mercia, from where she ruled over a territory that even Burgred could only have dreamed of. She and Edward fought for different reasons but made common cause. In the end they, like Ethelred, had been run as ragged as Alfred before them, but it was worth it. She looked up at the ceiling, and spoke, as she did nightly, to Ethelred. "We've done it, my love. You told me to build and look what we've done."

She fancied that she heard his answer, telling her how proud he was of her. She sat down on the bed, swung her legs up onto it and eased herself down onto the pillow. The pain in her arm persisted, another sign of old age. It would be better tomorrow. "Goodnight, my love," she said, and closed her eyes, still smiling.

June 15th

Edward met Frith in the hall and the two men embraced. Edward's breathing was jagged, still labouring after his long ride from Stamford. Frith's was unsteady, robbed of its rhythm by grief.

Edward looked over Frith's shoulder and saw Athelstan standing by the door to Æthelflæd's private chamber. Frith must have felt Edward's movement, for he turned and said, "He has barely left her. He is bereft."

Edward looked around the room. Alyth, Frith, Athelstan, the thegns, the cooks, the slaves, bakers, all were distraught. "She was well-loved," he said, trying, but failing, to keep the tone of wonder from his voice. He was her brother, and had always loved her without question, but these folk seemed truly stricken.

Frith said, "She never once put her needs before those of others. She was a king's daughter, a leader's wife, a leader in her own right, and, in her eyes, a woman last. But not to those who knew her. To them, she was simply their lady."

Edward looked again at the assembled mourners. "Where is my niece?"

Frith swept out his arm in a gesture for Edward to step in that same direction. They passed by Athelstan's self-appointed sentry post, to the second room leading off the main hall. Frith opened the door and allowed Edward to enter ahead of him.

All carefully rehearsed words of comfort fell silent from his lips, pushed away by urgent fury that would not stop for sympathetic soothing. "What in the name of Christ's holy blood do you think you are doing?"

Elfwen was dancing around the room, with one of her mother's silk dresses pressed against her and Æthelflæd's golden circlet perched at an angle upon her head. She stopped in mid step and her cheeks reddened. She let the dress hang limply in her hand and looked down at the floor. "These belong to me, now."

Edward's hands curled into fists and his nails dug into his palms. "Put them down."

Elfwen stuck her chin in the air and looked down her nose at him. Her freckles were prominent even with the flush of her cheeks and her hazel eyes flickered with reflected sunlight from the window. She was so like her mother it pained him to look upon her. She clutched the dress to her chest and said, "You cannot tell me what to do. You are not my father."

"No, thank God. And you are not your mother." He pointed to the gold arc on her head. "Even were that a crown, you would not have a right to wear it. Her clothes may pass to you, but her lands will not."

Elfwen let the dress slip to the floor. "What? You cannot!"

Too many times he had ridden to Mercia and agreed to a compromise. He had trusted Ethelred, worked with him, respected him, respected the knowledge that Ethelred had passed to Teasel. But her daughter? That was stretching the link too far. Athelstan had come to stand behind Frith in the doorway. He stood aside as Edward stepped back into the hall and pulled Frith close to him. "What say you, old friend? In these last years you knew her better than any of us."

Frith said, "I saw Ethelred fight. And I saw my lady fight on. All they ever wanted was a free Mercia; a kingdom standing alone, proud. But I know that if this could not be, they would both rather that Mercia be ruled by Wessex than by a nineteen-year-old whom men would not follow, unless it be to her bed. I am old and weak and cannot guide her. She would have us eating Viking herring within a month."

Edward nodded. "Thank you for your forthrightness; I know that it was hard for you."

Athelstan stepped forward. "I am here. I could be the new leader of Mercia."

Frith smiled at the younger man before addressing Edward. "He has fought alongside your sister. He is half Mercian and the folk love him."

Edward looked at his son. He tried to guess at Athelstan's deeper thoughts, but the boy's face was unreadable. Edward said, "I cannot give you what you ask. I have a true-born son in Wessex who by law must have a kingdom before you do."

Athelstan lifted his chin and his blond curls fell away from his face. His eyes narrowed and he said quietly, "By Wessex laws." He coughed and raised his voice. "I understand. You must ever be seen to do what is right."

His words were delivered with such an even tone that Edward wondered whether to take them as heard. But when he looked again, he saw the shadow of Gwen's face pass across Athelstan's features and he knew the bitterness that dwelled there.

He went back into Elfwen's chamber. "I say again that you are not your mother. Mercia belongs not to you, but to me. You will come to Wessex where I can watch over you and find you a worthy husband."

Elfwen stamped her foot on the floor. "No. You cannot make me. You think I am dull-witted and do not understand? You would be king of all the English so that you can better your father's kingdom."

Edward turned and started to walk away. She screamed after him. "Well, you are not your father."

In the doorway, Athelstan, his first-born son, stepped back and gave him the smallest of nods. "And neither am

I," he said.

Edward took a step into the main hall and stopped, turning to look at his son. The echo of unspoken words behind Athelstan's declaration gave him pause to wonder what would happen when he, Edward, was gone. He was not afraid of death. God was waiting for him and against all the victories he had won in His name, Edward had only one sin to confess, but he knew that Gwen was biding there for him and would plead his case with the Almighty, for she had forgiven him a long time ago. What then, of his son? The boy whom he had dismissed moments before was staring at him now, twenty-six years old, a man. He, Edward of Wessex, Alfred's son, could declare himself king of this land, but who would the weapon-men of Mercia stand behind? *'We are all right as we are.'* His sister's words came back to him and he looked around the room. Frith, the only man remaining of the old guard, was by his own confession too old to wield influence. The rest were new men, untried, too young. But Athelstan was fixed in Mercia, and it was doubtful that his rallying call would ever go unheeded.

Edward met his unflinching stare and then he took a step closer to his son, wondering. "Would you fight me for it?"

"I could. I have fought many times in these last years. The men of Mercia would stand beside me. But when I fought, I fought alongside my aunt, and she taught me that beyond all else, the thing that mattered was that all the English stood as one against the heathen foe."

Edward felt a constriction in his throat and he coughed. "She was a mighty woman."

Athelstan lowered his gaze. "She was a mother to me."

There was naught to be said that would not bring forth fresh tears. In the hiatus, Edward stared briefly at the top of his son's bright blond head and then turned his attention to the sound of sobbing emanating from the bedchamber. Teasel had not been a good mother to Elfwen. The route of her life had been forced down roads built by Viking

398

invaders and she had looked always to the men in her life. There was a difference between lives wasted on the battlefield and the men and women who spent their whole lives trying to push the Vikings away and Edward understood now that their sacrifices were different but no less far-reaching. When he told her all those years ago to do as she was told, marry a man whom she did not love, who could have foreseen how much she would have to suffer and lose in order to follow her destiny? In securing her victories, and protecting her adopted kingdom, she had left behind a daughter unfit to rule, unable to recall a mother's love. Oh yes, Teasel had understood that England mattered above all else. He looked around this hall at Tamworth, a testament to all she had achieved, but the fire had gone cold and her daughter was crying. Mercia, indeed Wessex, and all of free England, should weep too.

All for naught. She had left a weak, wilful child and Edward was on his own again. When he had arrived at Tamworth, he had taken one look at the silly girl who would wear her mother's shoes, and, as her mother had been wont to say, he had gone straight to business. Never let it be said that he, Edward, did not learn from his mistakes. He could not, would not leave Mercia as master of its fate any more. If he was to be on his own in this fight, then he would be in control. And yet now, it was as if his sister were still there, touching his arm, gently persuading him to pause for thought, giving him time to look, to see. He was not on his own; he was never on his own. Standing before him was Athelstan, a gift from his sister, a reminder of how fiercely a person could fight for their adopted homeland. Teasel knew what she was doing; it was not all for naught, it was all about kin. Teasel could not put right the harm done to Elfwen, but she had not died devoid of hope and she had left behind an opportunity for Edward to right the wrongs of Athelstan's boyhood exile.

He brought his gaze back to rest upon his son's face. "I cannot give you a kingdom; I have already told you why.

However, it would still my worries to know that you speak for me and lead the Mercians in my name when I am in Wessex or elsewhere."

Edward had barely closed his mouth before Athelstan spoke. "Yes."

Edward needed to know that Athelstan understood what he was being offered. "You will mint no coin, and charters will go out in my name. Would that be enough for you; to wait? Would you not rather come home now? I daresay that Frith could name another."

Athelstan did not blink. "I thank you, but I am home already. And yes, I can wait."

~*~

Edward died six years later, still on campaign in the north. The Mercian council immediately crowned Athelstan at Tamworth. Within a month Edward's successor in Wessex, his eldest legitimate son, was dead. Athelstan was declared king of Wessex, uniting both kingdoms under one ruler. Such was the legacy of Edward and Æthelflæd that he was freed to pursue English interests in the north. In 937, at Brunanburh, Athelstan defeated a combined force of Scots and Irish Norse to become undisputed king of Britain.

Almost all of the characters in this story existed and I have used their names, or versions of them, wherever possible. The five thegns who made up Æthelflæd's personal guard were an invention of mine, but it is recorded that at Derby she lost "Four of her thegns who were dear to her." For those familiar with this period, it might be frustrating not to meet the characters with their historical names, but this portion of Anglo-Saxon history seems more littered than most with names beginning with the diphthong Æ (Old English Æsc), so for clarity I have adapted them, or given nick-names instead. The use of titles as names, as in Lord Somerset, was a much later, mediaeval practice, but it offered me another way of avoiding the Æsc. For interest, below is a list of those characters and their real names.

Burgred's wife, deposed	
queen of Mercia	Æthelswith
Wulf of the Gaini	Æthelwulf
Lord Somerset	Æthelnoth, Ealdorman of Somerset
Thelwold	Æthelwold
Lord Frith	Æthelfrith
Lord Wiltshire	Æthelhelm, Ealdorman of Wiltshire
Elfwen	Ælfwynn
Alyth, Frith's wife	Æthelgyth
Fleyda,	
Edward's 2nd wife	Ælfflaed
Gwen	Ecgwynn (not an 'Æ' but a difficult
name)	
Ewith,	
Alfred's wife	Ealhswith (ditto)
Alhelm	Ealhhelm (ditto)
{Athelred}	Alfred's elder brother was known as

Ethelred. I changed the spelling to avoid confusion with Ethelred of Mercia

Some historians say that Edward married Thelwold's niece, to reinforce his links with the royal house of Wessex and strengthen his claim against Thelwold. It is true that Æthelhelm of Wiltshire had a daughter, Ælfflaed (Fleyda), who married Edward. It is also true that Thelwold had a brother, Æthelhelm. I was unable to establish, categorically, that these Æthelhelms were one and the same person. I decided to leave Æthelhelm, Thelwold's brother, out of the story; although it was technically possible that he was old enough to have fathered a daughter who was, in turn, old enough to wed Edward in 899, it was only just plausible. The tale seemed neater without his presence. It is probable that there was still a link with royalty through the lord of Wiltshire.

Ethelred's origins are a mystery. There is no documentary evidence of his life before he emerges as leader of the Mercians, but it seems likely that he was strongly connected to the Hwicce tribe. Since he was obviously much older than Teasel, I invented his tragic back-story to explain why he was unmarried when he met her.

All the details of land grants have been taken from extant charters. The stories about the bees at Chester and the Irish proclaiming Teasel to be a queen are taken from primary sources, though not necessarily reliable ones. Similarly, the attempted kidnap is legend rather than fact, but it seemed a shame not to include it in her story. Teasel did avenge the murder of Abbot Ecgberht, but I had to imagine the circumstances of their earlier meetings. An internet search will reveal a digital reconstruction of the fort on Llangorse Lake in Brycheiniog. For those who might be interested, the carvings at Deerhurst Church can still be seen. Where modern place-names exist, I have used them, but the precise locations of towns such as Bremesbyrig and

Weardburh have yet to be ascertained.

Better documented than some other parts of the 'Dark Ages', this period nevertheless presents a less than perfect picture and I have had to use supposition and artistic licence occasionally to fill the gaps and make my story flow. I have, however, only once knowingly played with the chronology: the fortification of Rhuddlan was accomplished much later, in 921, but I wanted another opportunity for Teasel and Anarawd to meet. I have to confess that there is no evidence to suggest that they ever knew each other, but it is not impossible either.

CPSIA information can be obtained
at www.ICGtesting.com
Printed in the USA
BVOW03s2248041116

466712BV00001B/26/P

9 781784 071653